THE FALL

MARIE FORCE

The Fall
By: Marie Force
Published by HTJB, Inc.

Cover by Hang Le
E-book Layout by E-book Formatting Fairies
ISBN: 978-1958035184

AUTHOR'S NOTE

This book was inspired by a ride into Newport, Rhode Island, one busy summer evening in 2006. A man driving a black Mercedes convertible was in traffic next to me, and on his Massachusetts license plate were his initials plus MD. I wondered where the handsome doctor could be going. *The Fall* is my answer to that question. As I developed the character of Ted, a pediatric oncologist, I realized I needed some day-in-the-life details to make his character more authentic. During an Internet search, I discovered a blog by Dr. Samuel Blackman, at the time a pediatric oncologist at Children's Hospital Boston. The similarities between Sam's story and the back story I had already given Ted were startling, to say the least. Sam generously allowed me to borrow anecdotes from his blog that added so much to this story. For that as well as his friendship and support, I'm truly grateful.

Thank you Christina Camara, Julie Cupp, Paula Del Bonis-Platt and Lisa Ridder, who read the early drafts and provided invaluable feedback. To all the readers who have made my author journey so rewarding, I'm eternally indebted to you. Your friendship has been one of the great gifts in my life.

To Dan, Emily, Jake, Brandy, and Dad, I love you best of all.

xoxo

Marie

For all the families, like mine, that have been touched by cancer.

To whom much is given, much is expected.
Luke 12:48

CHAPTER 1

Dr. Ted Duffy moved through the busy halls of Children's Hospital Boston, keeping his eyes down to discourage anyone from stopping him to chat. He didn't want any delays. These things needed to be done quickly, the way you would pull off a Band-Aid. His heart had been heavy since he received Joey Gaither's test results. The last round of chemo hadn't worked, and there was nothing left to try, no magic potion that would save the twelve-year-old who had become so much more than a patient to Ted in the four years since they had discovered the tumor in Joey's fibula.

He had known, of course. Before the test results arrived via e-mail that morning, Ted had known he wasn't going to save Joey. But *God* how he had wanted to save this special kid who had so many plans, so many friends, so much to live for. They were all special, but a few managed to work their way past his determination to protect his heart from the never-ending catastrophe that surrounded him. Yes, there were a few he loved, and Joey was one of them.

Ted ran a weary hand through his thick blond hair and took a deep breath to steel himself for what he had to do.

John and Melinda Gaither were huddled together outside their son's room. Melinda wept into John's shirt, and he held his wife with tenderness that should have been used up by now. Ted had seen many a marriage self-destruct in the midst of a child's critical illness and was relieved to realize the Gaither's union wouldn't be one of them.

Melinda looked up and saw Ted approaching them. "Dr. Duff," she gasped. "Joey's so bad today. What's going on?"

"Let's go to the lounge," Ted said.

Melinda exchanged glances with her husband. They had been doing this too long to miss the signs.

Ted led them to the lounge, which was thankfully empty, and reached for Melinda's hand.

She dissolved into tears. "It's bad, isn't it?"

"I'm sorry."

John dropped his face into his hands.

"If there was anything else—"

"We know, Doc." John wiped his face and reached for his wife's hand. "We knew this last round of chemo was a long shot, but we were hoping for a miracle."

"So was I."

"How long do we have with him?" Melinda asked, her pretty face ravaged by grief and years of worry.

"His kidneys have failed, so not long." The chemo had been aggressive, but rather than arresting the cancer, it had damaged Joey's already weakened organs beyond repair.

Melinda sobbed quietly.

"Do you mind if I spend a few minutes with him?" Ted asked.

"Of course not," John said.

Ted stood up.

"Ted?" Melinda said. "Thank you for all you did."

"I just wish it could've been more."

JOEY'S ROOM was filled with signed photos of his heroes—the Boston Red Sox. The Make-A-Wish Foundation had granted the boy's fondest desire to meet the team's all-star catcher, who had made Joey a part of the Red Sox family, even going so far as to allow him in the dugout during a few games the summer before.

Yesterday, the halls of the hospital had buzzed with the news that the catcher, shortstop, and ace pitcher had been by to visit Joey.

The child was shrunken into the big hospital bed, his baldness concealed by a Red Sox hat.

Ted reached for Joey's hand. He had ordered oxygen and morphine the night before. All they could do now was make him comfortable for whatever time he had left. Ted found it hard to reconcile the tiny body in the bed with the bright, dark-haired child he had once been, before he'd lost a leg and his childhood to cancer. But the cancer hadn't infected his spirit. He had fought so hard and for so long that Ted knew he would always remember Joey's special brand of courage.

He stirred and turned to look at Ted with chocolate-brown eyes heavy with medication and knowledge.

"Hey, buddy. Does anything hurt?"

Joey shook his head and reached for the oxygen mask covering his mouth and nose.

Ted helped him move it aside.

"No good, huh?" Joey asked. He had once asked Ted to tell him only the truth, and Ted had done his best to comply.

"I'm sorry."

Joey's fragile shoulders rose in a shrug. "Win some, lose some."

"I really wanted to win this one."

"I know."

When he saw him struggling for air, Ted put the mask back over Joey's face.

Joey took several deep breaths before he reached for the mask again. "Do something for me?"

"Anything." Ted wanted to weep for all the things that would never be.

"Keep fighting. Someday you'll win them all."

"I promise," Ted said, blinking back tears.

Joey nodded with satisfaction and squeezed Ted's hand before he drifted back to sleep.

Ted kissed the child's forehead. "Godspeed, buddy."

John and Melinda waited in the hallway. Ted hugged them both. "Page me if you need anything."

John nodded.

Since there was nothing more he could do, Ted left them to say goodbye to their son.

~

TED WOVE his black Mercedes SL convertible through the heavy traffic leaving Boston on that Friday night in early July. He lived for his summer weekends in Newport, Rhode Island, where he shared a rental with his three best friends. A colleague who skied covered for Ted most summer weekends in exchange for the same courtesy during ski season.

The rare, humidity-free night made it comfortable to have the top down, and the rush of fresh air was a welcome relief from the stagnancy of the hospital. After eighty hours of tending to sick kids that week, he welcomed the normalcy of traffic, of people rushing to get where they were going, oblivious to the epic battles being waged by cancer-stricken children. It was just as well they didn't know. On days like this, it was almost more than he could bear.

He received word from a nurse on the ward that Joey died at six o'clock. After that, Ted had moved quickly to brief his colleague on the status of his other patients so he could get out of there for the weekend.

When he left Interstate 93 and merged onto Route 24, the traffic finally let up, and he let the powerful car loose. Only when he crossed the Sakonnet River Bridge to Aquidneck Island did he begin to relax. He loved the view from the old bridge and was sorry he had missed the best of the sunset. The deep pinks and purples that remained reflected off the flat-calm water.

He hit more traffic in Portsmouth and Middletown as he made his way south on Route 114. The island, a popular summer tourist destination, was home to one of the guys who rented with Ted. Smitty, now a stockbroker in New York, took every Friday off all summer to get to his hometown as early in the day as possible. He usually shared the ride with Chip, a dermatologist in the city, and Chip's longtime girlfriend, Elise. Rounding out the group was Parker, known in the media as "The Prince" because of his billionaire real estate developer father, James King. Despite his lineage, however, Parker was a hard-working divorce attorney in Boston who often rode to Newport with Ted. He had called earlier in the day to say he was taking a half-day and would meet Ted at the house.

The four men had been friends since their sophomore year at Princeton when they had shared adjoining dorm rooms. They had seen each other through failed relationships, professional ups and downs, the deaths of several parents, and Smitty's spectacular divorce, which Parker had handled with great delight. None of them had liked Smitty's wife, Cherie, and were thrilled to see her go—no one more so than Smitty. Of the three, Ted considered Smitty his best friend. While he was close to Chip and Parker, he talked to Smitty most often.

Ted was always the last to arrive in Newport, since cutting out early wasn't usually an option for him. Tearing himself away for two days a week all summer was something he had gotten better at in the five summers they had been renting the house. He often wondered if he would have stuck with pediatric oncology without these weekends to look forward to. Between medical school, his internship, residency, and fellowship, followed by the first few years at Children's, he had been on the verge of burn out when Smitty suggested they spend summer weekends together.

The traffic in downtown Newport was heavy and typical for a July Friday. As he inched along America's Cup Avenue, Ted received a few appreciative glances from women on the bustling sidewalk. He was never sure if they were checking out him or the car, but once they saw the empty passenger seat they inevitably took a second look at the driver. His mother often accused him of being married to his work, so she would love to see him fill that seat with any of the pretty girls who gave him the eye from the sidewalk.

At the light on the corner of America's Cup and Lower

Thames, he was approached by a group of girls out for a bachelorette party. They would have jumped into the car had he given them the slightest bit of encouragement. Instead, he said, "Not tonight, girls," and took a right onto Lower Thames. A few minutes later, he finally pulled up to the large house on Wellington Avenue, overlooking King Park and Newport Harbor.

Ted grabbed the bag he had packed that morning from the trunk of the car and used his key to let himself into the dark house. No doubt the others were out at one of the waterfront bars they frequented. Ted could have joined them and most Friday nights he would have. Tonight he was grateful for the silence. He flipped on a light to find the dining room table littered with beer cans, the remnants of a poker game, and an ashtray filled to overflowing with cigar stubs. Ted chuckled, knowing the house was cleaned after every weekend and marveling at how quickly his friends had brought disorder to the place.

Strict rules governed these weekends at the house. Any of them could bring a girlfriend whenever he wanted to. If they were unable to make it to Newport for a weekend, they could give their room away to a short list of mutual friends. No one wanted to arrive after a long workweek to a house full of people they didn't know.

Ted never brought anyone with him, if for no other reason than he couldn't be bothered entertaining a guest. Also, inviting a date on a weekend getaway usually gave her the impression he was interested in something serious, which he wasn't. He was thirty-seven years old, and his mother was right—he *was* married to his work. For now, that was fine with him. The kids at the hospital were his family, and they required all his energy.

He grabbed two beers from the fridge and headed upstairs to his room on the third floor. Ted laughed at the loud snoring coming from Smitty's room on the second floor. No doubt Smitty had been drinking since noon and was down for the count until morning. Despite his strapping size, he had a well-earned reputation as a lightweight when it came to alcohol.

Ted had won the best room in the house by default. His friends considered his job the most stressful and had given him the top-floor room so he could decompress in relative peace. Attached to his room was a sweeping deck overlooking Newport Harbor that everyone used, but they were mindful of Ted's privacy.

He left his bag in the corner of the big bedroom and took the beers onto the dark deck. The Newport Bridge was lit up in the distance, and the harbor sparkled with hundreds of lights from boats at anchor. As he drank the first beer and took in the tranquil scene, it sunk in that Joey was really gone. He hadn't allowed it in until that moment when he was finally alone in the place where he felt the most at ease. Here it was possible to grieve, to mourn for what had been, for what would never be, and for his inability to save the boy.

Dropping his head onto the arm he rested on the rail surrounding the deck, he gave into the tears that had threatened since he said goodbye to Joey earlier in the day. He let it all out and almost had a heart attack several minutes later when a hand landed on his shoulder.

CHAPTER 2

Startled, Ted straightened and fought to suppress a gasp at the first glimpse of her face. As if he had sustained a punch to the gut, all the air seemed to leave his lungs in one long exhale. Something new and unexpected twisted in his belly, making him feel like he had been asleep all his life and was now finally awake with each of his senses on full alert.

Her.

The one he hadn't even known he was searching for, gazing up at him with concern in what might have been blue or maybe green eyes. In the dark he couldn't tell. Pale, translucent skin, short blond hair and a mouth shaped like a bow. The one . . . And he didn't even know her name.

"Are you all right?" she asked, her brows furrowing with concern. Her hair formed a halo around her face in the moonlight.

As he realized he was staring at her, the cool breeze drifting against the wetness on his cheeks had him brushing at his face. "Um, yes. I'm fine."

"You don't look fine."

"Bad day."

"You're the other doctor, right? Duff?"

"I also answer to Ted, but I'm afraid you have me at a disadvantage," he said with a weak grin as he fought to hide his overwhelming reaction to her.

She extended her hand. "Caroline Stewart."

Oh no, no, no! Smitty's new girlfriend . . . No! Life couldn't be that unfair! He studied her outstretched hand for a long moment, knowing if he touched her he'd be lost.

A quizzical expression on her face, she tipped her head and started to withdraw her hand.

Ted quickly reached for it, and the hum of awareness that shot through him at the feel of her soft skin made him want to moan. *This could* not *be happening.* "Nice to finally meet you," he forced himself to say, choking on the double meaning.

"You, too." She stared up at him with an odd expression on her face, as if she could read his every thought. He certainly hoped she couldn't.

Ted took back his hand and reached for his beer, desperate for a distraction—anything to slow his racing heart and surging hormones. "Want one?" he asked, gesturing to the other bottle.

"Sure."

He opened it for her and made a point to not let his eyes meet hers as he handed it to her. "Were you, uh, here the whole time?"

She nodded. "Want to talk about it?"

Glancing out at the harbor, he shrugged. "I lost a patient today. A twelve-year-old boy."

"I'm sorry," she said, resting a comforting hand on his arm.

"Thanks." His eyes shifted down to her hand on his arm, dismayed when his eyes filled again. "I'm kind of a mess tonight."

"Do all of them get to you like this?"

He wanted to talk to her forever. With a clarity he couldn't begin to fathom just then, he knew he'd never run out of things to say to her. "A lot of them do, but this one was special. I'm not sure why some touch me at a deeper level than others, but it happens. Joey was extraordinary, so full of life and plans." Ted wiped his eyes.

"He was lucky to have a doctor so devoted to him."

"I couldn't save him, though. I did everything I could think of, but nothing worked."

"Perhaps it was just his time to go."

"I think he was ready. He'd been through an awful lot, and he was tired. I just wish I'd been ready to let him go."

"How long have you been a doctor?"

"Six years, plus five years of training in pediatric oncology after medical school."

"I don't know how you do it." She shook her head. "Seeing kids that sick every day must be so heartbreaking."

"It can be. On days like this, it is. But we save more than we lose, and that's what keeps me going. I always start out thinking each patient is going to be one of the lucky ones. But as Joey said today, you win some, you lose some."

"I'm sorry for your loss."

"Thanks for listening. I don't usually unload on pretty girls I find sitting on my deck." The comment slipped out before he could stop it, and Ted had to once again remind himself to be careful.

She smiled. "Do you unload on anyone?"

"Not really. I used to try to talk to my dad and my grandfather about it. I followed them into the family business, but they don't have a lot of empathy for me. They say I have so many more tools in my arsenal than they had in their day. They tell me I need to stay focused on the ones I'm saving and chalk up the ones I lose to fate. I wish I could be so detached."

"I'll bet they weren't as detached when they were doing it."

"You're right," he said impressed by her insight and wanting her more than he had ever wanted anything in his life. It took all the willpower he could muster not to lean in and kiss those bow-shaped lips. "They weren't. I remember my father coming home from the hospital and knowing from the look on his face when he had lost a patient."

Ted took a long swig from his beer and forced it past the huge lump that formed in his throat as the dazzling array of implications began to set in. Smitty's new girlfriend. His *best friend's* girlfriend. Could he really be that much of a cliché?

Clearing his throat, he said, "Anyway, enough about me. Smitty's been telling us about you for weeks. How did he finally convince you to come to Newport?"

"I've been working on a big project and just finished it, so I'm free and clear for a while."

"What do you do?" He wanted to know everything about her.

"I'm a freelance writer in New York City. I just did a promotional piece for the convention and visitor's bureau. The money was great, but by the time it was done, I was ready to tear my hair out." She paused, looking almost stricken. "I'm sorry."

Confused, Ted asked, "About what?"

"I can't believe I'm complaining about my work to you. It sounds so trivial next to yours."

"Don't say that. It's not trivial."

"Still . . . what you do is so important."

"I'm envious of your writing talent. I always wished I was better at it."

"Obviously you were better at other things. Where'd you go to school?"

"Princeton undergrad with all of these guys," he said, gesturing to the house, "and medical school at Duke. The other Drs. Duffy were not at all happy that I refused to even apply to Harvard Medical School, the family alma mater."

"A little show of independence?" she asked, her eyes twinkling with amusement.

"Exactly. Where did you go?"

"NYU undergrad, Columbia School of Journalism for graduate school."

"Did you ever work as a reporter?"

She nodded. "Six years at the *Times*."

"Wow. Not just any paper, but *the* paper."

"It was fun and exciting and utterly exhausting."

"Why did you leave?"

"I was getting married and knew the all-consuming life of a reporter wasn't conducive to the direction my personal life was taking, so I quit. Then my fiancé got cold feet, the wedding was canceled, and I've been freelancing ever since."

Ted winced, wishing harm on a man he'd never met for the pain he'd caused her. "I'm sorry."

"Wasn't meant to be, I guess," she said with a shrug.

"Smitty said he met you through Elise." *Why couldn't I have met her first? Why?*

"That's right. Her sister is my former roommate, and we all still run around together. I usually hate fix-ups, but this time I was glad I went. He makes me laugh harder than anyone ever has."

Ted chuckled when he wanted to cry. "That's Smitty. He hasn't changed one bit in the twenty years I've known him. He still conks out early when he drinks during the day."

She laughed. "Yes, he does. Well, I should get to bed. It was good talking to you. I'm sorry again about your patient."

Don't go! Not yet! Don't get into bed with another man. Please . . . "Thanks for letting me vent."

"It was my pleasure," she said on her way into his room to go downstairs. With a glance back over her shoulder, she said, "Good night, Ted."

"Night."

He watched her go and then moaned as he let his head drop to his chest. "Oh my *God*."

TED TOSSED and turned for most of the night before slipping into restless sleep around dawn. Groggy and disoriented when he awoke at ten, he dragged himself out of bed. All at once, he remembered meeting Caroline on the deck the night before. His stomach fluttered with nerves and anticipation. And fear.

Knowing she was downstairs, no doubt having breakfast with Smitty and the rest of their friends, Ted was filled with the kind of fear he had seldom experienced. How would he ever hide his immediate and overwhelming reaction to her from the people who knew him best?

But maybe what happened the night before was nothing more than the emotion of the day catching up to him. Losing

Joey had been a tough blow. Perhaps he'd mistaken his attraction to Caroline for something it wasn't. He had probably experienced a delayed reaction to the grief. She'd been nice to him. Nothing more to it than that. If he'd been in his usual state of mind, he wouldn't have felt the way he had.

Determined to test his theory, he dressed in running clothes, checked his cell phone for messages, and gave his pager a quick look to make sure the hospital wasn't trying to reach him before he forced himself down the stairs.

"Morning," he said.

He was greeted by grumbles from the table where Chip, Elise, Parker, and Caroline nursed mugs of coffee and apparently a few hangovers.

Chip's brown eyes were bloodshot, and his curly brown hair stood on end. Parker looked only slightly better—at least his dark hair had been combed and his blue eyes weren't quite as bloody as Chip's. Elise, as always, could have just stepped off the pages of a fashion magazine.

And Caroline . . . *Oh, Caroline.* She was even more gorgeous than she'd been in the moonlight. Her pale blond hair, which had seemed short in the dark, was actually long, and her eyes were a startling shade of green with flecks of gold.

As their eyes met and held, he knew that nothing he'd felt on the deck the night before had been a fluke. He'd somehow managed to fall hard for his best friend's girlfriend during a thirty-minute conversation. Hell, who was he kidding? He had fallen for her the very instant he first saw her. The discovery made him want to run, to flee the house full of friends who meant more to him than life itself.

"Hungry, Duff?" Smitty asked from the stove where he fried eggs and something unidentifiable.

Clearing his throat and taking a deep breath, Ted reached for the carton of orange juice and poured a glass. Then he leaned around the towering Smitty to peer into the frying pan. "What the hell is that?"

"Chourico," Smitty said with a big smile on his round face. He was six-foot-four with dark hair, dark eyes, a booming voice, and an even larger presence. "You've had it before. It's a local specialty—Portuguese sausage."

Ted turned up his nose. "There's *no way* you got me to eat that."

"He's the health nut," Smitty said to Caroline. "We only put up with him because he attracts girls like honey attracts bees."

Ted bopped his friend on the head. "Shut up."

"Did you meet my Caroline?" Smitty asked Ted.

Ted's heart hammered in his chest. "Last night." He made a supreme effort to keep his tone light and teasing. "While you were snoring your ass off she agreed to run away and marry me."

Smitty lunged for Ted, who deftly dodged him, but in the fracas an empty metal bowl clanged to the tile floor.

Chip groaned and dropped his head into his hands. "*Not so loud, you guys.*"

Elise got up to fill a bag with ice and put it on Chip's aching head.

He looked up at her with gratitude, and she leaned in to kiss him.

"Who's running today?" Ted asked.

Chip groaned.

"That's one 'no'," Ted said with a smile.

"Count me out," Parker said. "And don't let me go out with him again tonight." He nodded his head toward Chip. "I can't keep up with him."

"No one can," Elise said. "I don't know why we try."

"You should've followed my stellar example and gotten a good night's sleep," Smitty said to guffaws from the others.

"So then you're running?" Ted asked, raising an amused eyebrow at Smitty.

"Fuck no. Who'll feed these people if I leave?"

"Hey, Duff," Parker said. "How's Joey doing?"

Ted's smile faded as he shook his head. "We lost him yesterday."

"Oh, God," Parker said. "I'm sorry, man."

Elise got up to hug Ted. "Me, too."

"Thanks."

Smitty enveloped Ted in a one-armed bear hug, saying quietly, "You gave him years he wouldn't have had otherwise." In a gesture typical of Smitty, he kissed the top of Ted's head.

Their support overwhelmed him.

"Are you okay?" Chip asked.

With a glance at Caroline, Ted said, "Yeah, I will be. I keep telling myself I'm not going to get so involved, but then I always do."

"You wouldn't be you if you didn't," Parker said.

Ted nodded to Parker with appreciation. "So," he said, clearing the emotion from his throat, "am I running alone?"

"How far do you go?" Caroline asked.

Smitty laughed. "You don't want to go with him, sweetheart. He's a machine."

"Compared to you, my grandmother's a machine," Ted said, and the others howled with laughter, providing a welcome distraction as Ted tried to process the idea of taking a friendly run with Caroline. He didn't know what he wanted more—for her to come with him or for her not to.

Smitty faked offense and returned his attention to the stove.

"Three or four miles," Ted said in answer to Caroline's question.

"I'll go," she said.

"Traitor," Smitty mumbled.

"Elise? You gonna let me down?" Ted wanted to beg her to join them so he wouldn't be alone with Caroline.

"I'm afraid so, Duff. I don't have the juice this week. Caroline can take my place."

"I guess it's just us," Ted said to Caroline, swallowing hard.

"Give me ten minutes," she said on her way upstairs.

"What are we doing today?" Ted asked.

"The vote was for the beach," Parker said. "Do you want your surfboard? I'll throw it in Chip's truck for you."

"Sure. Thanks."

"My dad's leaving the boat for us if we want it tomorrow," Parker said.

"Nice," Smitty said. "Sign me up."

"If we leave early, we can sail out to Block Island for lunch," Parker added. "But I'll let you New Yorkers decide if you have time for that. You've got the longer ride home."

Smitty raised a hand in protest. "I *refuse* to talk about Sunday night on Saturday morning."

Chip grunted in agreement.

Since they were all accustomed to Smitty's weekend rules, Parker just smiled. "We can talk about it tomorrow."

CHAPTER 3

Ted was surprised to discover Caroline could more than keep up with him as they settled into a steady pace on Harrison Avenue. On the way into the state park at Fort Adams, Ted pointed out Hammersmith Farm, the summer White House during the Kennedy Administration. All the while, he tried to figure out why this woman—and not any of the hundreds, if not thousands, of others he had known in his life—had stolen his heart. Why did it have to be her? Why did it have to be someone his beloved friend, who had led a hard-luck life, was clearly taken with?

He mulled over these and many other questions while they jogged to the far end of the Revolutionary War-era fort and circled around to a well-worn path on the Narragansett Bay side of the tan brick fort that formed one side of the entrance to Newport Harbor. The bay was already filled with boaters enjoying the summer day.

"I'm impressed," Ted said.

"With?"

"I rarely run with anyone who can keep up with me."

She laughed. "A little full of yourself, aren't you?"

"I guess that did sound kind of arrogant, but I run every day, so I guess I've earned it. It's the one thing I make sure I do."

"Me, too. I keep trying to get Smitty to go with me, but he hates to run."

"He always has, but he kicks ass at football."

"I can picture that," she said. "Did you play sports in school?"

"Just club soccer and intramural baseball at Princeton, but I've always been a runner. I did cross country in high school. How about you?"

"Field hockey and lacrosse."

They moved in companionable silence for several minutes before Ted asked, "So what's your next project? You said you just finished something big, right?"

She nodded. "I'm going to take a break for a couple of months."

He wanted to stop her on the path, tell her how he felt, and beg her to run away with him. They'd go somewhere that no one knew them. He'd give up everything—his life, his friends, his work, his family—if only she'd agree to go with him. Startled by that realization and the knowledge that he'd do it in a second if it meant he could have her, he forced himself to refocus on the conversation. "Any special plans?"

She glanced over at him, hesitating. "Sort of. I haven't said too much about it to anyone in case it doesn't happen."

"Okay, now I'm dying of curiosity."

"And I'm dying to tell someone," she confessed.

Oh how he wanted to be the one she told all her secrets to. "Perfect," he said with a grin.

"Well, I'm thinking about . . ."

Ted saw her stumble before she fell and was unable to stop himself in time to grab her.

"*Oh*," she moaned, cradling the ankle that had twisted violently in a small grass-covered hole on the path. The knee on her other leg was bleeding.

Ted squatted down beside her. "Let me take a look."

Her face was pinched with pain and all the color had drained from her cheeks. "Hang on a sec," she said, trying to catch her breath. "Okay. Go ahead."

Ted put a comforting arm around her shoulders and untied her running shoe.

She winced when he eased the sock over her already swollen ankle. "Oh, that hurts!" she cried as he did a perfunctory exam.

"I can't tell if it's broken without an X-ray, but if it isn't, it's a bad sprain." He tucked the sock into her shoe and handed it to her before he lifted her into his arms.

She sucked in a deep breath when her cut knee bent around his arm. "What are you doing? You can't carry me."

"Sure I can." He tried not to notice how perfect she felt in his arms. "You're light as a feather."

Her smile was weak as her arms encircled his neck. "Whose big idea was it to leave the phones at home?"

Ted had to remind himself to breathe as her scent surrounded him. "I never run with a phone or a pager." He carried her back the way they had come. "It's the one hour of every day I'm completely unreachable. Keeps me sane."

"I hope we can borrow a phone when we get back to the parking lot," she said, biting her bottom lip.

"Don't worry about it. I'll figure something out."

Caroline rested her head on his shoulder, probably because it was easier than holding it up.

Her soft, fragrant hair brushed against his cheek. "How you doing?" he asked.

"Hurts," she whispered.

"I know."

"Are you okay? I'm too heavy for you to carry me this far."

"I just told you what a big jock I am," he joked. "You're insulting me."

"Will they know where to look if we don't come back?"

"Not really. I kind of mix it up every weekend. Elise usually runs with me, but I don't go this far with her."

"Sorry to mess up your run."

"I'm sorry you're hurt."

When they reached the parking lot, Ted eased her onto a bench. "Hang on for just a second while I find a phone, okay?"

She nodded as she stretched her aching ankle out in front of her.

Ted found a young family eating a picnic at one of the nearby tables, explained the situation, and asked if they had a cell phone he could borrow. The husband handed Ted his phone while the wife took a bag of ice over to Caroline to put on her ankle. As Ted dialed the house and then Smitty's cell phone, he watched Caroline nod with gratitude to the woman who had returned with a wet napkin for her cut knee.

"Did you reach your friends?" the man asked.

"No answer anywhere." Ted rubbed the stubble on his face as he tried to think of what to do next.

"Can I give you guys a lift somewhere?"

"Would you mind? Our house isn't far from here."

"Of course not." After telling his wife he would be right back, the man pointed Ted to his car.

Ted carried Caroline and the bag of ice to the backseat of the SUV and gave their new friend directions to the house.

She stretched her injured legs out in front of her and leaned back against Ted with a sigh.

"I haven't forgotten the secret you were about to tell me when this happened," he whispered, hoping to get her mind off the pain.

"I'll get back to you on that."

"I'll hold you to it." He told himself that reaching for her hand was a gesture of comfort and not capitulation to the overwhelming desire to touch her. Reminding himself yet again that she was *Smitty's girlfriend,* he reluctantly pulled back when her fragrant ponytail brushed against his face.

The car hit a bump, and she squeezed Ted's hand in a reflexive response to the pain.

"Almost there," he said.

At the house, they thanked the man who had driven them. Ted lifted her out of the SUV and deposited her in the passenger seat of his car.

"Where are we going?"

"To the E.R. You need to get that ankle checked."

Tears rolled down her cheeks. "I don't want to."

"Doctor's orders," he said with an empathetic smile as he fought the urge to brush the tears off her cheeks. "Let me just run inside and leave a note for the others. I'll be right back, okay?"

She wiped her eyes and nodded.

"Keep the ice on it."

Inside, he found a note from Smitty: "We went to the store to get stuff for lunch. Meet us at the beach."

Ted ran upstairs to grab his phone, keys, and a clean T-shirt.

"They're already at the beach, which is why I couldn't reach them," he told Caroline when he returned to the car. "There's no signal out there."

"Smitty didn't wait for me?" she asked with annoyance.

"He went to the store to get lunch and then to the beach. He knew you were in good hands." Ted felt a stab of guilt as he said the words. Maybe she wasn't in such good hands, but judging by her pained expression, she didn't care at the moment.

"Well, I guess that's okay then." She leaned back against the headrest with her eyes closed as Ted drove them to the emergency room at Newport Hospital. On the way, he left messages for his friends to let them know where they were.

"Do you think they'll get the message?"

"One of them will check in with me when we don't show up, so don't worry."

"I feel so bad," she groaned. "I'm totally screwing up your day. The last place you want to be is in a hospital."

"It's no problem. Let's get you fixed up and on something for the pain. Then we can party."

"Yeah, right." She grimaced when she tried to move her swollen ankle. "Thanks for being so great. I can see why your patients love you."

He looked over at her, wondering if he should read more into her statement, but found only friendship in her green eyes. He chastised himself for being so foolish. She wasn't interested in him. *She's Smitty's girlfriend*. The words echoed through his mind like a chant.

Ted carried her into the deserted emergency room where he introduced himself as a doctor to the nurse at the triage desk.

They took Caroline right away, and Ted pushed her wheelchair to the X-ray department. The films showed a fracture, so the E.R. doctor called in an orthopedic guy.

Ted sat with her while they waited for the specialist to arrive.

"I'm not usually such a crybaby." She wiped new tears off her face. "I just can't believe this happened right at the beginning of summer. What a drag."

Without a thought about the implications, Ted reached for her hand. "Lucky for you, you're dating the green giant, and he can carry you anywhere you need to go until you heal."

She laughed through her tears. "That's true."

When an hour had passed with no word from the specialist, the nurse gave Caroline something for the pain, and she drifted off to sleep.

Ted took advantage of the opportunity to study her, while wishing with all his heart that he had met her first. Her face had lost its lustrous color, but even pale from the shock of her injury she was gorgeous. She was petite but not tiny, athletic in an attractive way, and easy to talk to. His eyes wandered to the rise and fall of her chest, and he wondered if her full breasts were as spectacular as they appeared in the tank top she had worn to run in. *Jesus Christ, Ted. That's enough.* But he couldn't seem to look away.

He was jolted out of his thoughts when he heard Smitty's loud voice in the hallway.

"Where is she?"

Ted got up to lean out of the cubicle doorway. "Pipe down, will you? She's in here sleeping."

Smitty's eyes were big as he came into the room to find Caroline in the hospital bed. "What the hell happened?" he asked in what he considered a whisper.

"She stepped in a hole on the path at Fort Adams. Broke her ankle."

"Shit. Are they keeping her?"

"Just until the orthopod gets here. After the swelling goes

down, she'll probably be in a cast for six weeks, the first few on crutches."

Smitty groaned. "She'll hate that." He squeezed Ted's shoulder. "Thanks a lot for getting her here, buddy. You don't have to stay."

Ted glanced over at Caroline who was still sleeping. "I don't mind hanging out."

"No need," Smitty insisted. "Go salvage your day. Parker's got your board at the beach."

He wanted to wail. He wanted to tell Smitty there was nowhere else he'd rather be. "If you're sure . . ."

"I'm positive. You're off duty, Dr. Duffy."

"She's going to be in a lot of pain," Ted warned him.

"No worries. I'll take good care of her."

"Okay. I'll see you back at the house." Ted walked out of the emergency room with a heavy heart, wishing he could stay with her. He wondered why it was that when he finally found a woman who made his gut ache with desire she had to be dating his best friend.

CHAPTER 4

After a long afternoon at the beach and an even longer stint at a bar where Ted tried—unsuccessfully—to get drunk, he left Chip, Elise, Parker, and his car downtown and took a cab back to the house. He listened for Smitty and Caroline, but the house was quiet, so he went into the kitchen for a glass of water. Rooting around in one of the cabinets he found a bottle of painkillers and took two to address the headache he always got from drinking in the sun. He rested against the counter for a long time before he summoned the energy to go upstairs.

On the second floor, he noticed the door open and the light on in Smitty's room. Telling himself he should just keep going up the stairs, Ted went to the doorway. Caroline was asleep, her broken ankle propped up on several pillows and an ice bag draped over it. Two prescription bottles and an empty glass were on the bedside table. Smitty was curled up to her with an arm looped possessively around her.

Ted stared at the two of them for an endless moment, until he realized his jaw ached from clenching his teeth so hard. He flipped the light switch to darken the room.

Upstairs, the shower pounded the tension from his neck and shoulders. Tilting his head from side to side to loosen his muscles, he stood there for a long time staring at the wall before he turned off the water and wrapped a towel around his waist.

Tugging on a pair of boxer briefs, he fell onto his bed and turned so he could see the harbor lights in the distance. The beer he'd consumed earlier swished around, making his stomach surge with nausea. Thinking of Caroline and how pale she had been after her injury, his heart ached. When he imagined her wrapped up with Smitty in bed, he wanted to punch something. Or someone. This weekend would surely go down as two of the most disastrous days and nights of his life. What should have been such a joyous event—finally meeting the woman his grandmother had sworn for years was out there waiting for him—was instead a mess of epic proportions.

He must have dozed off because he awoke just after four and couldn't go back to sleep. He lay there wishing he had brought the glass of water with him until he decided to get up and get another one.

For the second time in as many nights he found Caroline sitting alone in the dark when he turned on the light in the kitchen.

She winced from the sudden blast of light, so Ted turned it off.

"Sorry. Are you feeling okay?"

"The pain pill wore off about thirty minutes ago, and I just took another one. I'm sitting here praying it'll kick in soon."

In the faint glow of a streetlight coming in through the window, he could see how pale she was. Pain made her eyes appear even bigger than usual.

"Can I do anything for you?"

She shook her head. "No, but thanks for your help earlier."

"It was no problem." Realizing all at once that he was wearing nothing more than form-fitting underwear, he reached for a glass, filled it with ice and water, and downed it in three long gulps.

"Thirsty?"

"Mmm." He refilled the glass. "Want some?"

"No, I'm good."

He eyed the boot on her foot. "How did you get down here?"

Flashing him a sheepish grin, she said, "Slid down the stairs on my bum because I had to eat something with the pill."

He chuckled. "So what's the plan for getting back up?"

"I was just pondering that very question when you showed up."

He finished the water and put down the glass. "Can I give you a lift? For old times sake?"

She giggled, which he took as a sign the meds were beginning to work. "Why not?" Taking his outstretched hand, she let him help her up.

With her hand wrapped around his, Ted was staggered by the glow of the streetlight illuminating her beautiful face. Powerless to resist the magnetic draw for another second, he ran a finger over her cheek.

She gasped as her hand landed on his bare chest.

They stared at each other, the silence charged with awareness.

He was thankful the lights were off so she couldn't see the effect her nearness had on him. Never in his life had he wanted so badly to kiss another human being. Before he could give in to the need pounding through him, he tore his eyes off her and lifted her into his arms to carry her upstairs. At the door to Smitty's room, he reluctantly eased her onto her good foot.

"Ted," she whispered.

He shook his head. "Don't. Don't say something that will change everything."

She stared at him for the longest time before she turned away. In that brief moment he saw in her the same sense of awe, wonder and fear that had overtaken him. That she seemed equally affected by him didn't do much to ease his guilt over feelings he had no right to.

Ted watched her hobble the short distance to the bed where his best friend slept. Panic stricken by the encounter with Caroline, Ted continued up the stairs. In his room, he fell face down on his bed and moaned into the pillow as desire continued to thrum through his heated body. *This is insanity,* he thought, even as he suspected it was probably something much, much worse.

~

IN THE MORNING Ted awoke full of guilt and regret. Smitty was the best friend he'd ever had. *This is so wrong. I can't think about her anymore. If it came down to her or Smitty, I'd choose him in a second. Of course I'd choose him. Wouldn't I?*

Tormented, Ted went downstairs to find Parker at the kitchen table with a cup of coffee and the morning paper.

"Where is everyone?" Ted asked.

"Chip and Elise went out to breakfast, and Smitty and Caroline are still sleeping. Elise drove your car home last night." Parker pointed to the keys on the counter.

"Oh, good. Want to grab something to eat?" Ted asked, anxious to get out of the house.

Parker looked up at him with surprise. "Not running today?"

"I'll run when I get home this afternoon."

"Sure. Let me grab my wallet."

"It's on me. Let's go."

In Ted's car, Parker turned to study him. "What's wrong?"

Startled, Ted glanced at his friend. "Nothing. Why?"

"You look funny."

"Define funny."

Parker laughed. "Let me try another word. Off. You look off."

Pole axed. That might be a better way to put it. "I'm fine. I'm not funny or off, but thanks for asking."

"Hmm, if you say so." Parker continued to size up Ted. "Are you hanging out today? We've got the boat if we want it." The "boat" was a ninety-foot, ocean-going sailing vessel with a crew of six to dote on their boss—or in this case, their boss's son and his friends.

"I'm going to head home," Ted said, even though he would normally love to spend the day being pampered on the boat. Today, however, he thought it best to leave before the situation got any worse. "I've got some stuff to take care of before tomorrow. I'm on call for forty-eight hours."

Parker shook his head. "I don't know how you can keep up that schedule."

"You get used to it," Ted said with a shrug. "Being on call will give me time to work on a grant proposal that's due this week. I need funding for some research I want to do into the genetics of this one type of brain tumor I've been seeing a lot of lately. It's exciting stuff."

"Sounds like it," Parker said dryly.

Ted laughed. "I know it's not *Kramer vs. Kramer*, but it's interesting to me."

"Hey, not all of us can be curing cancer, so we have to get our thrills where we can."

"Is your father still after you to move to the Big Apple and onto the family payroll?"

"*All the time*," Parker said. "He never gives up."

"And he never will. He knows you're a great lawyer, and he wants you looking out for him."

"What he really wants is to get me under his thumb where he can control my whole life. No thanks. Been there, done that."

They ate at one of their favorite diners and lingered over a second cup of coffee.

"So what happened to that girl you were seeing?" Ted asked. "What was her name? Julie?"

"Julia," Parker corrected.

"That's right." Ted had only met her once.

"No spark, you know what I mean?" Parker spun his spoon around in his coffee cup. Forty-eight hours earlier Ted would have said no, but now he knew exactly what Parker meant. "Yes, I think I do."

"Yeah, you had it with Marcy."

Startled by the reminder of his college girlfriend, Ted stared at Parker. In that moment, Ted realized what he'd felt for his girlfriend of three years was insignificant compared to what he already felt for Caroline. Despair, the likes of which he had never known before, settled over him.

"What's wrong with you, man?" Parker asked with concern. "You look like you just saw a ghost."

"Nothing," Ted said softly. "Nothing's wrong. I need to go."

"Back to the house?"

"No, I need to go home."

Ted appreciated that Parker didn't ask any questions as he followed him out of the restaurant.

CHAPTER 5

Ted's abrupt departure resulted in a flurry of phone calls from all three of his friends, who wanted to know if something was wrong. Ted told each of them the same thing: Everything's fine, something came up, and I'll see you in two weeks since he was on call the following weekend.

As he ran through the marina near his condo late that afternoon, he tried to put the emotionally draining weekend behind him by making a plan to get over his infatuation with Caroline. *What I need is a girlfriend of my own. That will set things straight.*

Contrary to the gossip in the hospital, he *was* aware of the appreciative looks he got from the women he worked with and the whispering that went on behind his back as they speculated on his personal life—or lack thereof.

He knew they wondered if he was gay or afflicted with some sort of social disorder that kept what they considered a highly eligible bachelor out of the hospital's dating frenzy. Since the doctors, nurses, residents, and fellows worked so many hours together, the inevitable romances developed, but Ted had never indulged. Maybe it was time he did. Maybe if he hadn't been living like a monk he wouldn't have had such a strong reaction to Caroline.

The majority of his love and attention went to the kids he cared for, but at the end of the day he was left with an empty home and an even emptier bed. Suddenly, the life he had been so content with just a few short days ago wasn't enough anymore. Meeting Caroline had shown him exactly what he had been missing, and now he yearned for more.

Determined to jump start his love life, Ted decided to pay closer attention to the women at work over the next week and to find one he could ask out to dinner by the following weekend. He needed to start somewhere. Having drawn up a plan for his love life the way he would compile a treatment plan for a patient, Ted jogged the last mile back to his condo with a newfound sense of relief, if not satisfaction.

The late-afternoon sun hung like a ball of fire over the busy marina. As he watched a boat come in under sail, he found that despite his good intentions his thoughts had already wandered back to Caroline. He wondered how her ankle was, if she was in pain, and if she too was thinking about him and the instantaneous connection they'd shared. She had felt it, too. He had no doubt about that.

Ted groaned, realizing that not thinking about her was going to be a project in and of itself. He needed to get a life, not to mention a sex life. He couldn't remember the last time he'd had sex. No wonder why she'd rocked his world. But even as he told himself it had been far too long since he'd been truly attracted to a woman, he had to acknowledge there had never been another attraction quite like the one he felt for her.

He used the key he kept under a flower pot on his front porch to let himself into his house. The sleek condo, like the Mercedes, had been a gift from his grandparents, who took such tremendous joy in doting on their only grandson that he had long ago given up on trying to put a stop to their boundless generosity. While Ted had used the trust fund they had set up for him to pay for his education, his younger sister Tish had blown through hers to fuel a ferocious addiction to heroin that had preoccupied the entire family for almost a decade. Only when she had run out of money and options had Tish entered rehab. Now, six years later, she was married to a nice guy and had a baby on the way. Her years of drug addiction seemed like a bad dream since she had gotten her life together, and no one was more proud of her than Ted.

He checked his messages and found one from Roger Newsome, the colleague who covered for him on summer weekends. "Hey, Ted. Pretty quiet weekend, so no need to check in with me before tomorrow. I admitted Matthew Janik because his fever hit 103, and he was dehydrated after the last round of chemo. I'll check on him tonight. Also, Hannah Ohrstrom's mother called. Hannah had a fever, too, but it broke after two doses of Tylenol. That's about it. Call me if you have any questions."

The next message was from his mother.

"Hello, darling," she said in that breathless, Main Line Philadelphia voice of hers. "Just a reminder about the party on the twenty-first. Do feel free to bring someone with you and remember it's formal. Also, remind the boys they're invited as well. We'd love to see you out here before then if you can tear yourself away from Newport one of these weekends. Hope you're not working too hard. Give me a call this week. Love you bunches."

Ted mimicked the kisses that Matilda "Mitzi" Dunbar Duffy predictably tacked on to the end of the message. The party she referred to was Ted's parents' fortieth anniversary and his grandparents' sixty-fifth anniversary, which would be held under a tent at his parents' summer home on Block Island. The two couples celebrated their common anniversary with a fancy soiree every five years.

Another weekend in Newport down the tubes, Ted sighed, as he thought of the social event of the season his mother and grandmother were no doubt planning. He had grown up attending their little parties for two hundred of their closest friends and knew exactly what to expect. But despite their love of all things social, his mother and grandmother were the two best women he knew: loving, faithful, protective, and fun. All his life, Ted had considered them the ideal, and the women he dated had the misfortune of being measured against them and often found lacking.

Mitzi, who'd had a stiff and difficult relationship with her own mother, had found the mother of her heart when she married Dr. Edward Theodore Duffy Jr. She and Lillian hit it off from their first meeting and had been fast friends ever since, bonding over their love of a good party, a rousing tennis match, a frozen margarita at the end of a long summer day, and the blessings and burdens that came with marriage to pediatric oncologists.

Their grandparents had been such a big part of their lives that Ted and Tish had grown up feeling like they had two mothers and two fathers. Even in their late eighties, Lillian and Theo kept up an active, busy life that still included at least eighteen holes of golf each week.

While Ted adored them all, the only fault they had was their ongoing meddling in his life. They were forever calling about a woman he just *had* to meet, a stock he just *had* to invest in, a party he just *had* to come to, or a tidbit of gossip from their various social circles he just *had* to hear. Sometimes when he received calls from the four of them in the same day, it was all he could do not to remind them of how busy he was and how trivial their news was compared to what he was doing. He never stopped being amazed at how easily his father and grandfather had slipped into retirement, seeming to forget about how challenging, heartbreaking, and overwhelming their work had once been—and still was for Ted.

The one thing he *had* succeeded in was getting them to drop the annoying nickname they had given him at birth, until he left for college and let them know he would no longer answer to "Third." He had told them on his way to Princeton that although his name Edward Theodore Duffy *the third*, he'd decided to go by Ted in college, and he had better not hear any more of that *other* ridiculous name. There must have been something in his tone or the expression on his face that told them he meant it because none of them had ever called him that again. Occasionally his grandfather still slipped up, but Ted had perfected an icy look that usually set him straight. The name change was one of very few major battles he'd ever won with the mighty foursome, and he was proud of it.

Ted picked up the phone in his home office and dialed a number he almost knew by heart after three years of caring for Hannah Ohrstrom. As he waited for someone to answer, he gazed out the window at the sun setting over the marina.

"Hi, Peg. It's Ted Duffy."

"Oh, hi, thanks for calling. Dr. Newsome said you were out of town."

"I was, but I'm back now."

"I hope you did something fun," she said wistfully.

Ted knew her life had been anything but fun since Hannah had been diagnosed with acute lymphocytic leukemia at the age of six. After two years of chemotherapy, Hannah had been in remission for a year, and Ted was optimistic about her long-term prognosis. "I was in Newport where I rent a summer place with some college friends, but I heard Hannah was down with a fever, so I wanted to check in. How's she doing?"

"A little better today than last night. She's still kind of listless, though."

"Any temp today?" He fired up his laptop to log into the hospital's scheduling system.

"It was 101 this morning, but it's normal now."

"Any other symptoms?"

"No, just the fever."

"Why don't you bring her by the clinic tomorrow? I can get her in at eleven if that works for you."

"Sure," she said haltingly. "I can do that." She paused. "It's not back, is it?"

"I know it's hard to believe after everything you've been through, but not all fevers are sinister. I just want to take a quick look and do a CBC to be safe, okay? I'm sure it's nothing to worry about."

"Okay, thanks. I appreciate you checking in. I've told so many people about how great you've been to us. No one can believe we have a doctor in this day and age who makes house calls and cares the way you do. Thank you so much."

"It's no problem at all," Ted said, touched by her effusive praise. People like Peg and her adorable, precocious daughter were what he loved best about his job. "Page me if you have any problems during the night."

"I will. Thank you again."

"See you tomorrow." Ted hung up feeling like he had finally done something positive with this miserable day.

THE NEXT MORNING passed in a blur. After signing the discharge paperwork on the re-hydrated Matthew Janik, Ted saw nine patients in the clinic—seven of them frequent fliers and two of them new kids who were just beginning their journey with cancer—before he got to Hannah an hour later than scheduled. Knowing how worried Peg was about a recurrence, he hated to keep her waiting, but he had taken the time to coach one of his residents through his first-ever "day one" chat in which parents are told their child has cancer and are given the planned course of treatment.

These all-important conversations were handled with the utmost delicacy and compassion. Since there was a right way—and a wrong way—to do it, Ted was pleased with the job his resident had done. He had hit on all the most important points and had used the word "cancer" several times so the devastated parents were left with no doubt as to what they were being told. The resident had included statistics about the cure rate and had given them the cold, hard facts about what to expect during treatment.

Ted had been part of hundreds of day one conversations, but it never got any easier to watch a family's plans and dreams be derailed by cancer. After he left the family in the capable hands of his resident, Ted took the time for a quick cup of coffee to decompress before he continued with his clinic.

He pushed the exam room door open to find Peg chewing on her thumbnail as anxiety all but coursed through her slim frame.

"Good morning," he said. "I'm so sorry to keep you waiting."

"It's no problem. You snuck us in."

"Didn't you bring Miss Hannah?" Ted looked around the room at everything but the girl sitting Indian-style on the exam table. He washed his hands and pulled on latex gloves.

"I'm getting far too old for that game, Dr. Duff," she said with a dramatic roll of her soft brown eyes. Her dark curls were corralled today in a high ponytail.

"Then I'll just have to take my game up a notch in the future." He sat on a stool and scooted to the exam table. "How's the fever?"

"Gone. I feel fine. I told my mom that, but she still called this weekend."

"That's exactly what she should have done." Ted did a quick but thorough exam. He was only slightly concerned by the pallor in her cheeks, but it was enough to confirm his decision to order a complete blood count.

"Are you going to stick me?" Hannah asked, sounding more like a frightened nine-year-old and less like a bored pre-teen.

"I'm afraid so, but we'll make it quick and painless. I promise."

"Will you do it yourself? It never hurts when you do it."

"Sure," he said, even though it would put him further behind schedule. "I'll be right back."

He went out to the desk to ask one of the nurses to set up the blood draw for him.

"I can take it from here," said Kelly Hopper, one of his favorite nurses. She was a pretty blond with bright blue eyes and an infectious smile. The kids loved her, and she was very devoted to them.

"Miss Hannah requested a Dr. Duff special," he said with a self-deprecating grimace.

Kelly grinned, and Ted noticed for the first time that she had dimples. Cute dimples.

"Jeez, you've even got the little ones falling at your feet, don't you?"

"Oh yeah, there's a regular line forming."

"Are you going to Joey's funeral?"

Sobered by the reminder of his recent loss, he nodded. "John called this morning and asked me to say a few words at the service. Are you going?"

"A few of us from the floor are going. You can ride with us if you'd like."

"That would be great, thanks. I wasn't thrilled about going alone."

Remembering his plan to find a girlfriend, he studied Kelly like he hadn't seen her almost every day for six years.

"What?"

Ted cleared his throat. "Oh, um, sorry. I was just thinking."

"About?"

"Would you like to have dinner some night?" he asked before he could chicken out.

Kelly's eyes widened into an expression of shock that probably wouldn't have been all that different if Ted had knocked her over the head with a baseball bat.

"Or, um, if you think it would be too weird, I mean because we work together . . ."

"No."

"Oh, okay." Ted felt like a bumbling fool. Clearly, this dating thing was going to take some practice. "I understand."

She held up her hand and shook her head. "I meant no, I don't think it would be weird. I'd love to have dinner with you."

"Really?"

She nodded.

"Great. How about Thursday?"

"Thursday's good."

"Think about where you want to go."

"I'll do that, and I'll get that stick ready for you."

"Oh, yeah. Right. Thanks."

Ted watched her walk away and wondered if she always did that thing with her hips or if she had done it for his benefit. Either way, it had his attention. "Nothing to it," he whispered as he wiped a bead of sweat from his forehead.

CHAPTER 6

On Tuesday morning, Ted met Kelly and two of the other pediatric oncology nurses in the staff parking lot to go to Joey's funeral. Three of Ted's residents and one of the fellows would join them at the church. Ted wore a dark navy suit, a white shirt, and a Red Sox tie in deference to Joey's love of the team.

"Great tie," Kelly said with a nod of approval. She had worn a black suit and heels that brought her almost to Ted's shoulder.

He held the car door for her. "I think Joey would approve."

They sat together in the back seat of the car while one of the other nurses drove.

During the hour-long ride west to Worcester, Ted reached into the inside pocket of his suit coat for the notes he had jotted down earlier in his office and looked them over one last time.

"I don't know if I could do it," Kelly said softly.

Ted glanced over at her. "Do what?"

"Speak at his funeral."

"I'm hoping I'll be able to get through it."

"Have you done it before?"

He shook his head. "This is the first time I've been asked."

"I'm sure you'll do a terrific job."

"I just hope I can do him justice."

"You will."

Her smile of reassurance helped, and Ted was glad he had asked her out. He was looking forward to their date.

Ted watched the miles fly by out the window. "Imagine how many times Joey and his parents must've made this drive."

"Hundreds."

"I never think about what people go through to get to us. As if the disease isn't hardship enough, they have to travel, too."

Ted's pager interrupted his thoughts. Before they arrived at the church, he handled two minor crises at the hospital. Since he was on call, he'd had to arrange for backup so he could attend the funeral. He turned off the pager and his cell phone and stashed them in his suit coat pocket.

They joined the streams of somber people going up the stone stairs to the large Catholic Church. At the top of the stairs, Ted shook hands with the Red Sox catcher, who had also been asked to speak. They were shown to seats close to the front of the church.

A large photo of Joey from before his illness sat on an easel amid a sea of flowers on the altar. Ted stared at the photo, remembering his first meeting with Joey, when he'd still had hope that he could save the boy. His eyes burned with tears so he looked away from the photo. He hadn't experienced a lot of failure in his life, but cancer managed to frequently remind him of his all-too-human limitations. The disease was a formidable foe, and Ted was overwhelmed with sadness at what it had taken from this family.

The service began when four pallbearers—Joey's uncles according to the program—carried the small casket into the church. A family friend, a cousin, and Joey's fifteen-year-old brother John gave tearful eulogies. Next, the Red Sox catcher walked up to the microphone.

"On behalf of the entire Red Sox organization, I extend my condolences to John, Melinda, and the Gaither family. It was such a pleasure for all of us to have the opportunity to know Joey and to be able to bring him into our family over the last couple of years. Because of what I'm lucky to do for a living, I receive mail from many, many kids who tell me I'm their hero.

Well, I want you to know that Joey's my hero. The Sox will dedicate the rest of our season to Joey's memory, and each of us will wear an armband with his name on it in tribute to a young life that ended far too soon. God bless you, Joey, and God bless everyone who mourns your loss."

Ted swallowed a lump in his throat as he approached the pulpit. He gave himself a moment to get his emotions in check before he looked out at the sea of faces that filled the church and spilled out the open doors onto the stone steps.

"I want to thank John and Melinda for inviting me to share in this celebration of Joey's life. I know I don't have to tell any of you how special Joey was or how courageous. Those of us at Children's Hospital Boston who had the honor of caring for him will never forget his enthusiasm, his laughter, his great big smile, and his generosity to other kids who were just beginning their treatment. He had a way of making it a little less scary for them." Ted paused and took a deep breath to compose himself. "I meet children and their families at the worst time in their lives. Yet I often find that crisis brings out the best in them, which was certainly the case here. John and Melinda, your dignity and grace were an inspiration to all of us and a source of great comfort to your son. Joey was much more than a patient to me. I loved him, and I'll miss him."

John and Melinda stood in the front row to hug Ted.

When he returned to his seat Kelly reached for his hand and squeezed it as he wiped his eyes with his other hand. Comforted by the gesture, Ted held on for the remainder of the service.

THEY ATTENDED the burial and the luncheon Joey's family held at the home of one of his aunts. Before he left to return to Boston with the others from the hospital, Joey's parents thanked Ted again for everything he had done for them over the last four years.

"Give me a call if you get to Boston." Ted didn't envy them the road they had ahead of them as they picked up the pieces of their shattered lives, attempted to reconnect with their other children, and dealt with the post-traumatic stress that parents who had seen their children through cancer often faced. "We can have dinner or something."

"We'd like that," John said.

Ted knew he might hear from them, and he might not. Often he also mourned the loss of the relationships he had formed with parents when a child either died or recovered to the point that he or she required only occasional visits with him. There were times, however infrequent, that he was glad to see the last of a parent. But he would miss John and Melinda.

Ted was back at the hospital by three, and the first thing he did was check his e-mail for the results of Hannah's blood work. He was relieved to find everything within normal range and picked up the phone to share the news with Peg.

She broke down at the sound of his voice.

"It's good news," he said quickly. "Everything's fine."

"Oh, thank you!" she cried. "Thank you, God."

"Are you all right, Peg?"

Her voice was small and sad when she said, "How long do you think it'll be before I don't freak out over every fever?"

"You probably always will. But remember, the longer her remission lasts the better her long-term prognosis becomes."

"I know. I keep telling myself that, but then she has a fever and I go bananas. She hates that."

"Someday she'll have kids of her own, and then she'll understand."

"Do you think so?" Peg asked softly. "Do you really think she'll grow up and have children?"

"Well, you know there's always a chance the chemo damaged her reproductive organs, but nothing in her report gives me anything to worry about today."

"Then I'll try not to worry, either. Thanks for rushing the results."

"No problem. I'll see you in a couple of months for her regular checkup. In the meantime, don't hesitate to call if you need me."

"Oh, you know I won't," she said, and they shared a laugh.

After Ted hung up, he sent an e-mail to remind his friends about the party on Block Island. The guys had been to a few of the anniversary parties by then, not to mention numerous other parties thrown by one or both of the Duffy women, and Ted knew they wouldn't miss it.

He was working on his grant application an hour later when Smitty wrote back. Ted noticed right away that his friend had copied Caroline on the reply.

"Looking forward to the party," Smitty wrote. "Let us know the details. Black tie, right? Wasn't the funeral today? How are you doing?"

Ted stared for a long time at Caroline's e-mail address, realizing he now had a way to contact her. Not that he would . . . But the e-mail address loomed on the screen, almost taunting him with how simple it would be to send her a message. But he didn't do it. Instead, he replied to all of them.

"Yes, black tie," Ted wrote. "My mom said we can have the guesthouse for the weekend, so let's go out to the island that Friday afternoon. The funeral was today, and they asked me to speak. My colleagues said I didn't embarrass myself. Tough day, but then I returned to good news about one of my other patients. Life goes on, right?" He stopped typing for several minutes before he added, "How's Caroline's ankle?" and pressed "send" before he could talk himself out of asking the perfectly innocent question. Since he had been with her when it happened, no one would wonder why he was asking. Plus he was dying to know the answer.

Ted would have deleted Smitty's message along with the tempting address for Caroline, but it would have been pointless since he had already committed it to memory.

He tried to go back to work on the grant application, but his concentration was blown, so he decided to go up to the inpatient ward to check on some of his patients. Two hours later, he returned to his office refreshed by the time he had spent with the kids. They had a way of making his worries seem trivial. Messages from Smitty and Caroline had arrived in his absence.

Ted's heart kicked into gear as he forced himself to read Smitty's first.

"They put her cast on yesterday, and she was in a lot of pain last night. She's staying at my place, and I'm doing my best to dote on her. She's on the sofa with her laptop, so you might hear from her. Don't pay any attention to her complaints about my cooking! We'll miss you this weekend. Hope you manage to get some sleep while you're on call."

Ted was more bothered than he wanted to be by the image of cozy domesticity Smitty had portrayed. Another emotion blazed through him that was new since he met Caroline: jealousy. He was bitterly jealous of his best friend and couldn't bear the idea of them spending the week together in Smitty's Upper East Side co-op. In light of what had transpired over the weekend, Ted had hoped Caroline would end it with Smitty before his friend got more involved with her. Apparently, that wasn't going to happen any time soon. If anything, it sounded like the two of them had grown closer after her injury.

Ted clicked on Caroline's message.

"Hi Ted, thanks for asking about my ankle. It's been really painful (and getting the cast on was awful), but today was better than yesterday. I felt so bad when you left on Sunday. I hope you didn't leave because of me . . . I know today was a difficult day for you, and I hope you're holding up okay. Take care, Caroline."

She knows why I left. Why did his heart have to skip a happy beat at that thought? He sat back and closed his eyes, feeling as if she had given him permission to relive the powerful emotions she'd stirred in him.

When thinking about her became painfully overwhelming, Ted pulled himself back to reality and replied to her message. "Caroline, I left because I had things to do at home, so no worries." Desperate to protect his friendship with Smitty, he fought the desire to confirm her suspicions that he had, indeed, left because of her and what she made him feel. "Hope you can come with Smitty to Block Island and that your ankle mends quickly." When he couldn't think of anything else to say, he signed his name, hit "send," and dropped his head to his desk.

A knock on his office door interrupted Ted's thoughts of Caroline.

"Come in."

Kelly walked in with a shy smile on her face. "Hi."

"Hey." Ted struggled to regain his equilibrium. "What's up?"

"I was just wondering if you're okay." She twisted her hands as if she were nervous. "After everything today . . ."

If she only knew the funeral was the least of my problems right now, he thought. "Joey would've been thrilled to see all the guys from the Sox there."

"It was so good of them to come."

Ted nodded in agreement.

"I liked what you said about crisis bringing out the best in people."

He shrugged. "It's true."

"Is there anything I can do for you, Ted?"

Her heart was in her smile, and Ted wondered why he had never noticed it before. Or maybe he had, and that was why he'd asked her out. Either way, an uncomfortable realization settled over him. She had a thing for him, and he had the power to hurt her. Badly.

He got up and went around the desk.

Her eyes widened when he reached for her hand and kissed the back of it.

"I need to be honest with you."

"Okay," she stammered, glancing down at their joined hands as the pulse in her throat fluttered.

"I'm not looking for anything serious."

Her blue eyes flickered up to his. "I understand."

"I don't want anyone to get hurt."

Kelly smoothed her hand over his now-loosened Red Sox tie. "I'm a big girl, Ted. I can take care of myself."

Ted saw the desire in her eyes and decided to find out if the reaction he'd had to Caroline was because he had gone without for so long. In one smooth move, he pushed the office door closed and leaned in to kiss Kelly.

She wrapped her arms around him and uttered a sigh as her

lips met his. Her fingers sank into his hair as her tongue flirted with his, her avid response telling Ted exactly what she wanted from him.

His pager went off, and he drew back from her to reach for it on his belt. "They need me upstairs." He brushed a thumb over her cheek.

She reached up to kiss him one last time. "I'll see you tomorrow."

He watched her walk away, filled with regret and dismay. Kelly was everything he should have wanted in a woman. She was beautiful, fun, sensitive, caring, and sexy—really, really sexy—not to mention available. But when he kissed her, he'd felt nothing at all.

CHAPTER 7

John Smith was a fraud. To the outside world he was fun-loving Smitty, a persona he had worked so hard to perfect over the years he almost believed it himself. Anything was better than the truth—that he had grown up in Newport all right, just not in the part of town they featured in the tourist brochures. Sometimes it was hard to believe how far he had come from the housing projects. The son of James King, the richest man in America, was one of Smitty's best friends. Apparently, he had managed to impress James, and when James turned over the management of his personal fortune to Smitty, he had single-handedly guaranteed Smitty's partnership at the brokerage house.

He made his first million by the time he was thirty-two, and thanks to James and his referrals, he was closing in on his sixth million at thirty-seven. Looking out at the lights of Manhattan from the bedroom of his gleaming twenty-second-floor co-op, he felt like a total failure. He never talked about his childhood in the ghetto with a cocaine-addicted mother and a revolving series of "uncles" who only kept their hands off Smitty because he was bigger than most of them. What they paid his mother for sex fed her addiction. One of them had fathered him, but she had no idea which one.

She hadn't even loved him enough to give him a decent

name. Instead he was stuck with the most boring, nondescript name in the world. People often didn't believe him when he told them his name was John Smith, thus the creation of Smitty. Even his three closest friends had no idea what his life had been like as he had scratched and clawed his way to an academic scholarship at Princeton.

For the last five summers, Smitty had returned weekly to his hometown where he assumed his mother still lived. But he never saw her, never called her, and never thought of her except when these fits of pensiveness struck, usually when things were going a little too well. He wondered if she ever thought about him. Would she be pleased to know what he had done with his life? What he had made of himself? Would she allow her son to improve her circumstances or would she snort whatever money he gave her up her nose?

What would happen to the life he had so carefully cultivated if the people in his world ever found out about where he came from? Would James still trust him to manage his vast portfolio? Would Parker, Chip, and Ted, all of them from prominent, respected families, still think of him as a brother if they knew he was the bastard son of a drug-addicted prostitute? The luckiest day of his life had occurred at the start of his sophomore year at Princeton when he had been assigned to live with Ted and found Chip and Parker next door. They thought his parents were dead. Years ago he had shown them a big pretty house in Newport and told them he had lived there as a kid. They had believed him. Why wouldn't they? What would his lies do to his nearly twenty-year friendship with the three men who meant more to him than anyone in the world?

Their families had become his family. In particular, Smitty loved Mitzi and Lillian Duffy with a passion, and when people asked about his family, he thought of them. On Mother's Day, it was Mitzi and Lillian who received two-dozen pink roses from him—not the cokehead hooker who had given birth to him.

An economics degree from Princeton, a Wharton MBA, and a few million in the bank had put some pedigree between him and his shameful past, but it hadn't been enough to keep his wife around. Cherie had left him when he told her the truth three years into their marriage. She couldn't live with someone who lied, she said on her way out the door, but not before he saw the revulsion on her face. His friends thought he had pulled the plug on the marriage, and Smitty let them think he'd been as glad to see her go as they were. John, on the other hand, had been devastated by the loss of his wife and had vowed to never again give anyone that kind of power over him.

And then along came Caroline and away went all his resolve to protect his heart. Would she leave him too if she knew? Smitty turned away from the window and went over to where she slept in his big bed, her injured ankle propped on a pile of pillows, her arm curled over her head. Pretty pink lips were slightly open as she breathed through her mouth. She had kicked off the sheet, and the T-shirt of his that she had worn to bed had ridden up to her waist, giving him an unobstructed view of her spectacular, toned legs.

His heart contracted. He loved her but knew she didn't love him—not the way he wanted her to, not yet anyway. *Time,* he told himself. *Give it some time.* They had only been together for a little over a month, and she thought he was too wounded from his failed marriage to commit to anyone else. That's what he wanted everyone to think. It was better they not know how much he yearned for a wife who loved him, a real home, and children he could shower with everything he'd never had. Every day he went to work, played the market, hedged his bets, and built a small fortune as a down payment on the future he so desperately wanted.

He leaned over to brush the hair back from Caroline's forehead. In every fantasy he'd had lately about that future, she played the starring role. Somehow he had to make her see that she belonged with him.

Her eyes fluttered open. "Can't sleep again?" she whispered in a sleepy voice, holding out her hand to bring him down next to her on the bed.

He kissed each of her fingers. "No."

"I don't know how you function on so little sleep."

He shrugged. Insomnia was nothing new. The worries and fears he managed to keep at arm's length during the day tended to come home to roost in the dark of night.

Caroline reached for him, and he sank into her embrace.

Her fingers worked the kinks from his neck and shoulders. "So carefree, yet so full of tension. Why is that?"

"It's because I'm trying to keep my hands off your injured bod," he joked, dodging the question that struck too close to the truth.

She studied him with knowing eyes, making him feel like she could almost see inside of him. Would she like what she saw if she discovered who he really was?

He kissed her forehead. "Go back to sleep."

CHAPTER 8

Parker King was restless. He paced from one end of his Beacon Hill townhouse to the other but couldn't seem to rid himself of the energy that was so essential to his hectic days. Lately he'd had trouble turning it off when he got home at night, usually after a fourteen-hour day spent brokering the end of one marriage after another.

At least he knew what was causing all this restless energy. He hadn't been entirely honest with Ted when they had their discussion about "the spark." Parker had felt it all right—a spark so bright and so hot it had nearly consumed him for the past couple of years. She was a client who had been through a nasty, messy divorce, and Parker was crazy in love with her.

Her name was Gina, and she had walked into his office almost two years earlier looking like a wounded fawn. After ten minutes with her, Parker had known she was everything he had ever wanted. In light of that startling revelation, he considered not taking her case, but when he had managed to regain control of his heart and his hormones he'd realized he didn't want anyone else representing her. He was the best divorce lawyer in Boston, and he had made sure she and her two young sons got everything they were due from her lying, cheating, bastard of a husband.

The divorce had been final for eleven and a half months—

eleven and a half long months of self-imposed torture. Parker had been around divorce long enough to know she needed time to recover from the emotional rollercoaster she had been on for the last few years. So once the divorce was final he had marked his calendar for one year and made a plan to woo her without even knowing if she shared his feelings. That was why, late at night, after long days on the marital battlefield, he was filled with restless energy while images of her with another man filled his mind. He hoped he hadn't been a fool to wait so long to contact her.

No one knew about her, and Parker was just superstitious enough to be afraid that if he told anyone it wouldn't work out. The closer he got to the one-year mark the more time seemed to slow to a crawl, and he wished he could talk to his friends about what he was going through. The next two weeks, the end of his waiting period, were going to be a pure, lonely agony.

Parker couldn't deny that her kids gave him pause. Despite his close relationship with his own father, Parker didn't think of himself as father material. And since he had intimate knowledge of how little involvement their own father had with the boys, he knew any man in Gina's life would have to be willing to step up for her children, too. Parker had never met the boys, but he'd had nightmares about two-headed monsters with fangs chasing him from their mother's life. He hoped with all his heart that they were kids he would like and maybe even grow to love. But first he had to find out how she felt. Not knowing was killing him.

Eleven and a half months had also given him ample time to hatch a plan to convince her he was the man for her. He had already arranged for two-dozen yellow roses to arrive at her home on the one-year anniversary of her divorce. About sixty drafts later, he had finally settled on what he hoped was the right note to send with them:

"I missed seeing you this year. Call me. Parker."

He had enclosed his business card with his office, cell, and home phone numbers in case she had forgotten how to reach him. Over and over he had mulled whether putting the ball in her court was the right strategy, but in the end, he had decided he would make the first move and wait to see how she responded.

He had also spent an enormous amount of time wondering if she had any idea who he was—or rather, who his father was. Parker had learned to be extremely discerning about the people he allowed into his life. For the most part he'd been lucky, but he had been burned a few times in his younger years by gold diggers—male and female—who were more interested in what his father could do for them than they were in *him*. These days he had a solid reputation of his own, but still he was careful.

His gut told him he didn't need to worry about that with Gina. During her divorce negotiations, he'd had to push her to demand what she deserved, so Parker knew money wasn't the first thing on her mind. It was her sweetness that had first attracted him, not to mention her incredible eyes and her chestnut curls. He couldn't wait to bury his face in those curls and kiss her senseless. Just the thought of being able to touch her made him weak with desire.

She was someone he could curl up with on a cold afternoon, walk hand-in-hand with through the rain, and sleep with every night of his life without ever growing tired of her.

Parker groaned. *I'm never going to survive another two weeks of this. And what if, at the end of all this torture, she isn't even interested in me? Well, if that happens, I'll do whatever it takes to change her mind.*

TED ARRIVED at Kelly's apartment in the city right at seven. He'd had to scramble to get there on time after one of his bone marrow transplant patients developed an infection that threw his afternoon off schedule. The good thing about dating one of the nurses he worked with was he wouldn't have to explain such things to her.

He wanted to be more excited about the date. He wished he had thought about it during the day, counted the hours until it was time to pick her up, and obsessed about the details in an effort to please her. In reality, it felt more like dinner with a good friend than a date.

Reminding himself of his plan and determined to give Kelly a chance, he rang the bell.

All the excitement he lacked was reflected in the smile Kelly greeted him with. "Hi, Ted. Come on in."

"You look great," he said, admiring her short black cocktail dress.

"Thanks, so do you."

He had changed at the hospital into a blue blazer, a light blue silk shirt, and tan dress pants.

"I love your place."

"It's small, but it's home. Can I get you a beer or some wine?"

"No, thanks. I'm good." He strolled over to check out her view of the Boston Commons.

She brought her glass of wine with her when she joined him at the window. "This isn't going to happen, is it, Ted?"

Surprised, he turned to her. "What isn't?"

"I've hooked kids up to chemo who look less stricken than you did walking in here."

"Stricken?" he stammered. "I don't get it."

"Neither do I." She took a sip of her wine. "Why did you ask me out?"

He shrugged. "Because I like you."

"After six years of working together you suddenly want to date me?"

"If it's so strange, why did you say yes?"

"Because I've had a crush on you for years," she confessed.

He hung his head. "I'm sorry."

"What's going on, Ted?"

His jaw clenched with tension as he glanced at her and found a friend looking at him, her expression fraught with concern. "I'm afraid it might be possible...

"What?"

"I seem to have fallen for my best friend's girlfriend," he said quietly.

Her eyes widened with surprise. “So what was I then? A diversion?”

“No, not really.” His tone was less than convincing, even to him. “I never meant to hurt you. I just . . .” He was mortified when his throat closed.

“Oh, Ted.” She took his hand and led him to the sofa.

“I’m sorry. I shouldn’t have asked you out, but I had a big plan to get a life so I could get past this craziness. I guess I’ve always sort of sensed you’d be receptive, but I was wrong to involve you in this . . . this mess.”

“Tell me about it,” she said, continuing to hold his hand.

Relieved to have someone he could share it with, Ted told her about meeting Caroline the previous weekend and the immediate, overwhelming feelings he’d had for her. “I don’t know what to do,” he concluded, his voice full of despair.

Kelly shook her head with dismay. “There’s nothing you *can* do. He’s too important to you, and you’d never forgive yourself for hurting him.”

He dropped his head into his hands. “I know.”

She held out her arms to him, and he welcomed the comfort of her embrace.

“It isn’t fair for me to be dumping this on you,” he said when he pulled back from her.

“You needed a friend more than anything tonight.”

“Thank you.”

“I’m not going to lie to you—I’m kind of disappointed, but I’m not entirely surprised. I couldn’t figure out what had suddenly changed that would make you want to go out with me.”

“I was terribly unfair to you, and I’m sorry.” He squeezed her hand. “Do you forgive me?”

“Of course I do. I just wish there was something I could do for you.”

“There is one thing you can do.”

“What’s that?”

“Let me take you to dinner. You look beautiful, and we have reservations. What do you say?”

“Sure,” she said with a smile. “Let’s go to dinner.”

TED DROVE HOME after a delightful evening with Kelly. They'd done a lot of laughing, which had helped to cheer him up. He was grateful to have found such a good friend in her, especially since she had every right to be furious with him. Instead, she had offered only support and compassion, which was what he needed. How he wished he had fallen for her, rather than a girl he couldn't have.

The more he thought about it, the more he realized what a terrible situation he was in. How was he going to spend time with his friends without revealing his feelings for Caroline? How would he ever be able to stand being around her, knowing he could never have her? They were spending next weekend together on Block Island. How was he supposed to get through that?

Well, I've got eight days to get it together and stop thinking about her, he thought. *I'm a grown man—a doctor for God's sakes. I need to stop acting like a teenager in love.*

His brain had a firm grasp on the situation. Now, if he could only get his heart onboard he'd be all set.

CHAPTER 9

Ted rested the garment bag containing his tuxedo on top of Parker's and slammed the trunk of the Mercedes closed.

Parker locked his Porsche and got into Ted's car. "Top up or down?"

"Down," Ted said.

"What time is the ferry again?" Parker asked as he flipped a switch to take the top down.

"Eleven forty-five."

"I talked to Chip an hour ago. They're on their way."

"I need coffee." Ted was grumpy after pulling an all-nighter at the hospital so he could leave for the weekend.

"Did you get any sleep last night?"

"About three hours, in fits and spurts."

"Want me to drive?"

"Nah, I'm kind of keyed up."

After they had stopped for coffee, they headed south on I-93 on their way to I-95. "What a fucking week from hell this has been," Ted said once he had consumed half of his coffee.

"What happened?"

"It would probably be easier to tell you what *didn't* happen. First of all, we lost a six-year-old with a brain tumor who should've died three months ago. Those poor parents have been through it. Then we broke our single-week record for new diagnoses. And the highlight of this suck-ass week would have to be my seventeen-year-old bone marrow transplant patient, Pilar, who's done exceptionally well for six months." He glanced over at Parker. "Keeping them healthy for the first year is critical, so we put them in lock down at home to minimize the risk of viral infection. She was six months away from being able to rejoin society when she snuck out of the house to meet her boyfriend."

"You can kind of understand that, though, can't you?"

"Of course I can, but unfortunately for her the boyfriend's younger brother came down with the chicken pox two days later."

"What does that have to do with her?"

"The varicella virus, which causes chicken pox, can be lethal for transplant patients. And she'd never had the chicken pox."

"Oh," Parker winced.

"Exactly. So she's back in the ICU fighting for her life. Thus my night without sleep."

"God, what a bummer. She did what any kid would do, and that's what she gets for it."

"She's not *any* kid, though, and she *knew* that." Ted banged his hand on the steering wheel in frustration. "Her family has already been through so much and now this. The boyfriend was sobbing his head off in the hallway last night."

"Poor guy. Is she going to make it?"

"I don't know," Ted said, dejected. "I shouldn't even be going this weekend, and if it was any other occasion, I would've stayed in Boston. But I've got good backup, and if I didn't get the hell out of there, I might've killed someone."

Parker chuckled. "And of course murder kind of flies in the face of hospital policy, doesn't it?"

Ted laughed. "Just a bit. Sorry to unload like that. It's just so damned frustrating sometimes. We're already fighting a big enough battle without patients doing stupid shit that gives their disease the advantage."

"Does it happen often?"

"Fortunately, no. Most of them are so terrified of a recurrence they follow our orders to the letter. But it's harder with kids, especially teenagers. It's in their nature to be rebellious. It's so much harder on their parents than it is on the parents of the little ones. Bigger kids, bigger issues. Then toss cancer in on top of it, and well, you get the picture."

The only good thing about the week from hell was it had left Ted with almost no time to stew about Caroline. Unfortunately, he hadn't had much time to prepare himself to see her again, either.

"These stories are enough to keep me from ever having kids," Parker said.

"That's me, a regular dose of birth control."

Parker laughed.

"The good news is we're talking about a very, very small percentage. Most kids are robustly healthy."

"Do you ever see yourself with kids?"

Ted glanced over at him. "Not really, but then again I feel like I have a hundred kids at any given time. What about you?"

Parker shrugged. "I think about it sometimes. I can't believe we're all pushing forty with none of us married and no kids. We won't be having fortieth anniversary parties at this rate."

"We'll be in nursing homes by our twenty-fifth anniversaries."

"Still, sometimes I wonder if we aren't missing out on something the rest of the world seems to take for granted."

"I think we've had a lot of fun, and if the right girls come along and we decide to get married we'll do it with no regrets—unlike all the poor slobs who get married too young and wind up sorry."

"That's true."

"Why so pensive today? Are the divorce wars getting you down?"

Parker shrugged. "I've just been thinking about it lately. That's all."

"Any particular reason?"

Parker hesitated, as if there was something he wanted to say.

"No. Not really. But between my marriages on the rocks and your sick kids, it's no wonder we're both still single."

Ted wasn't fooled by Parker's attempt to change the tone of the conversation. "Are you sure everything's okay?"

"Yeah."

Ted decided not to push. "Got any good divorce stories?"

"The best one recently is the battle over a one-hundred fifty thousand dollar show poodle."

"You're kidding me, right?"

"Oh, how I wish I was," Parker sighed. "I've seen people give less consideration to their kids than this stupid dog is getting. Gertrude Givens Allister Von Hinkle is derailing the whole settlement."

Ted laughed. "I'm sorry. I don't mean to laugh."

"Feel free. Believe me, we've laughed our asses off at the pictures of the puff ball in question."

"What are the people like?"

"Just what you'd imagine the owners of a show poodle to be like. They say people start to look like their dogs after a while, and I can definitely confirm it's true."

"Which one's your client?"

"Mummy."

"*Mummy?*"

"That's what she calls herself when she refers to the dog. I'm not making this up."

Ted laughed so hard he had tears in his eyes. "For this you suffered through law school."

"No shit."

"So what did I miss last weekend?" Ted told himself he was *not* fishing for information about Caroline. "Anything fun?"

"It was kind of quiet, actually. Just me, Chip, and Elise."

"Smitty wasn't there?" Ted asked, shocked.

"No, he stayed in New York because Caroline didn't feel like going. The ankle was giving her a bad time, I guess."

Ted's stomach churned. "I can't believe Smitty missed a weekend in Newport."

"I know. Chip was saying he's never seen him this gone over

a girl. She's really nice, though. Nothing like Cherie, thank God."

"Yeah," Ted said softly. "Nothing like Cherie."

"You liked Caroline, didn't you?"

Startled, Ted looked over at him. "Of course I did. Why?"

"No reason. I just wondered."

"I liked her," Ted said, uttering what had to be the understatement of the century.

Chip, Elise, Smitty, and Caroline were waiting for them when Ted and Parker arrived at the ferry dock in the fishing port of Point Judith on Rhode Island's southern coast. Throngs of people, cars, bicycles, and dogs on leashes waited in line to board the ferry for the fifty-five minute trip to Block Island.

"Hey," Chip said. "We thought you guys were going to miss it."

"We hit traffic in Providence," Parker said.

"How's the ankle?" Ted asked Caroline, making a supreme effort to hide the burst of emotion that assailed him the moment he saw her.

"Better. The worst part is the itching inside the cast. It's making me nuts."

Parker and Ted added their stuff to the stack of bags in the back of Chip's Land Rover, which they were taking on the ferry.

Smitty held up the tickets he had bought for everyone. "We'll meet you up top," he said to Chip and Elise, who were waiting to drive the car onto the ferry.

Ted watched what seemed to be a well-practiced maneuver as Smitty tucked Caroline's crutches under his arm and bent to pick her up for a piggyback ride.

"Want me to take the crutches?" Ted asked.

"I've got 'em," Smitty said. "We've got this down to a science. Right, babe?"

"That's right." She looked at Ted as she said it.

Smitty and Parker were talking as they walked onto the ferry and didn't notice that Ted couldn't take his eyes off her.

CHAPTER 10

They went upstairs to the ferry's top deck to one of the long rows of benches. Smitty led them to a corner away from the crowd that had gathered in the middle. By the time Chip and Elise joined them, Ted was sprawled out on one of the benches with his Red Sox ball cap pulled down over his eyes.

He heard Parker tell their friends that he'd had less than three hours of sleep the night before. They were used to the catnaps Ted often took after hectic nights at the hospital and loved to tease him about the wide array of conditions under which he could sleep.

Ted let them think he was sleeping, but what he really needed was a breather to get his emotions under control after seeing Caroline again. He now knew for certain that she was always going to have the same effect on him, and somehow he had to find a way to deal with the fact that he was in love with her but couldn't have her.

He dozed but kept half an ear on the conversation. Smitty suggested they go down to the bar for Bloody Marys, and offered to bring one back for Caroline. Ted was aware the others had gone, and he was alone with her.

A few minutes later, his cell phone vibrated in the cargo

pocket of his khaki shorts, and he reached for it without sitting up.

"Duffy," he said.

"Ted, it's Kelly." He could hear tears in her voice. "I thought you'd want to know we lost Pilar."

Resting his forearm over the hat covering his eyes, he asked, "When?"

"Thirty minutes ago."

Ted ached when he thought of Pilar's parents and the terrible ordeal they had been through only to lose their daughter to the chicken pox.

After a long moment of silence, Kelly said, "Ted? Are you all right?"

"Yeah."

"I know you're upset, but try to have a good weekend. There was nothing you could've done."

Ted appreciated that she knew exactly what he was thinking. "Thanks, Kel."

"How are things going with your situation there?"

"Same as before. Thanks a lot for calling."

She must have sensed he couldn't talk about it because all she said was, "Okay. Take care."

Ted flipped the phone closed and held it to his chest as he absorbed yet another blow in what was shaping up to be his single worst month as a doctor.

"Is everything all right?" Caroline asked.

Ted took a deep breath and sat up, pushing his cap back so he could see her. "Lost another patient."

"I'm sorry."

"I'm starting to sound like a cliché, but this has been one hell of a month."

She slid her hand across the expanse of blue bench between them.

He glanced up at her green eyes and couldn't stop himself from taking the comfort she offered.

Her fingers wrapped around his, sending a jolt of desire shooting through Ted. They held hands and gazed into each other's eyes for what felt like an eternity. Everything and everyone disappeared.

"You've got me all tied up in knots, Caroline," he said softly.

"I wondered if it was just me."

"It's not just you."

"I almost didn't come this weekend, but when I tried to bail out—of everything, not just the trip—Smitty got so upset. He's been so looking forward to the party, and I didn't want to ruin it for him. I'm going to talk to him after the weekend."

Ted tugged his hand free and stood up to lean over the railing as the ferry steamed past the bluffs on Block Island's north end. When he had gotten a hold of himself, he turned to her. "I love him. Not like a friend, like a brother. He's family to me. He doesn't have anyone but us."

"He loves you, too. All of you, but you in particular and your family."

"And that's exactly why nothing can ever happen between you and me. He would never get over that kind of betrayal."

"I know," she said, the agony of the situation apparent on her face. "I really do, but I've just been wondering, what if this is it? What if you're the one for me? The one I've been waiting for?"

Ted winced as a burst of pain slashed through him. "*Caroline . . .*"

They heard Smitty before they saw him.

"See, I told you he'd be up by the time we got back," Smitty said to Chip as they carried Bloody Marys for Ted and Caroline.

Ted took the drink from Smitty. "Thanks."

Smitty lifted his drink in a toast. "Here's to good friends, good times, and good liquor."

Ted raised his plastic cup in salute to Smitty's toast and took a drink, catching Caroline's eye over the top of his cup. The shimmer of tears in her eyes told him she hurt every bit as much as he did. But rather than making him feel better, it only made the whole thing worse.

THEY WORKED their way down the three flights to the freight deck and piled into the Land Rover to drive off the ferry into the bustle of Old Harbor. Ted was squeezed into the back seat between Parker and Smitty, who had Caroline on his lap. *This is a nightmare,* Ted thought, as he glanced over to find Smitty's hand curled around her shapely rear end.

Chip navigated around bicycles, pedestrians, baby strollers, and motorcycles as he drove them to Ted's parents' Corn Neck Road home, which sat high on a hill. The back of house overlooked the Great Salt Pond where hundreds of boats were anchored. Crescent Beach was across the street from the front of the three-story Victorian main house. To the left of the house, a huge white tent with plastic panel windows stood ready for the party on Saturday evening. The two-story guesthouse sat to the right of the main house.

Mitzi Duffy came running out the front door of the main house as the car traveled up a crushed-shell driveway lined with pink cabbage roses. Mitzi was tall and athletic with shoulder-length ash blond hair and the same blue eyes as her son. She wore a white tennis dress that showed off her deep tan.

Smitty lifted her off the ground and planted a loud kiss on her cheek.

"Put me down, you oaf." She giggled as she usually did at Smitty's antics.

"Mrs. Matilda Mitzi Duffy, this is my girlfriend, Caroline Stewart." Smitty presented Caroline with a flourish. "Caroline, this is my adopted mother, Mitzi."

Mitzi kissed Caroline's cheek. "So happy to meet you, Caroline. Welcome to Sea Swept."

"Thank you, Mrs. Duffy."

"Oh, please, call me Mitzi," she said as she hugged and kissed Chip, Elise, and Parker.

"Got any love left for me, Mom?" Ted asked with a teasing grin.

She reached up to hug her son. "Maybe just a little."

The scent of her Chanel No. 5 reminded Ted, as it always did, of home. "Good to see you."

"You, too, darling, but you look like hell." She clucked with disapproval as she held his chin and studied his face. "Have you been getting *any* sleep?"

"Of course not." When he looked up and saw his grandmother standing on the porch, Ted walked across the driveway and took the stairs two at a time.

"Hello, my love." Her gray-blue eyes crinkled with delight as she smiled at her grandson. "I've missed you."

"Me, too." He kissed her lined cheek, and when he hugged her, he caught a hint of her Emeraude, another scent of home. He hated that she seemed tinier and frailer than she had a month ago. "You look lovely, Grandy. Did you just have your hair done?"

She smoothed a hand over her snow-white hair. "This morning," she said. "Your mother's right. You look exhausted, sweetheart."

"I'm fine." He offered her an arm down the stairs so she could greet his friends. "Are Tish and Steven here yet?"

"They're on the three thirty boat," Lillian replied. "Who's that big hulk of handsome man you brought with you, Ted?"

Smitty grinned as he folded the elderly woman into a gentle hug. "Hello, love of my life," he said before he introduced her to Caroline.

"Pleasure to meet you, dear." Lillian shook hands with Caroline. "You've got your hands full with this one."

"Nah, he's easy," Caroline said with a smile and was rewarded by snorts of laughter from Smitty's friends as they unloaded the Land Rover.

"What did you do to your leg, honey?" Mitzi asked.

Caroline accepted her crutches from Smitty. "I broke my ankle a couple of weeks ago when I was running with Ted in Newport."

"Oh, too bad," Mitzi said. "Well, at least you were with the right person when it happened."

"He was awesome," Caroline agreed with a glance at Ted.

He acknowledged the compliment with a small smile, and

when he looked up, he found his grandmother watching him with interest.

~

LIKE THE MAIN HOUSE, every bedroom in the guesthouse overlooked either the pond or Crescent Beach. Ted insisted Smitty and Caroline take the master bedroom on the first floor so she wouldn't have to contend with the stairs. He showed Chip and Elise to the second-floor room they had used in the past and he took the room next door. Parker dropped his bags in the third bedroom upstairs.

"What do you guys want to do?" Ted asked when they gathered in the living room. The house was decorated in bright colors, comfortable furniture, and beach- and boat-themed artwork. Big pots of petunias, impatiens, and geraniums sat on the back deck and filled the house with their fragrance. "Beach? Pool? Boat? What's your pleasure?" His father had a small sailboat anchored in the pond that Ted often used when he visited the island.

"It would probably be easier for Caroline to hang by the pool," Elise said.

The others nodded in agreement.

"Don't worry about me," Caroline protested. "Do whatever you want this weekend, and I'll do what I can. Besides, I'd hardly feel trapped if I had to stay here alone. This place is beautiful, Ted."

"Thanks. We've always enjoyed it. Anyway, the pool works for me. I don't have much gas today."

"Sounds good to me," Parker agreed.

"My mother said there's stuff in the fridge for lunch, so everyone help yourself."

They took lunch out to the pool deck, where they whiled away the afternoon watching the boats in the pond, listening to music, reading, sleeping, and relaxing. Smitty rolled out the cooler full of beer he had brought, but he paced himself so he wouldn't be asleep before dinner.

Ted slept for an hour on one of the lounge chairs and awoke to find Caroline curled up asleep on one of the other chairs across the pool deck. Someone had tossed a beach towel over her to protect her fair skin from the hot sun. The others had wandered to the back porch of the main house where Mitzi and Lillian were serving frozen margaritas.

He noticed his father and grandfather had returned from fishing and Tish and her husband had joined the party. But rather than get up to see them, Ted took advantage of the opportunity to watch Caroline sleep. Her questions from earlier echoed through his mind: *What if this is it? What if you're the one for me?*

He wanted to weep for what could never be because, unlike her, he had no doubt at all that she was the one. He knew it with every fiber of his being. She was the woman he wanted, and there would never, ever be anyone else for him. Knowing how she felt about him, Ted hoped she would end her relationship with Smitty before he got any more involved with her. He'd had enough heartache in his life, and Ted hated the idea of him having any more.

Maybe if she broke up with Smitty soon, Ted could "run into her" somewhere in a year or two and see her without harming his friendship with Smitty. *I can't believe I'm sitting here wanting my best friend's girlfriend to dump him,* Ted thought with disgust. This whole situation was turning him into someone he didn't like very much.

Caroline woke up and caught him watching her. For a long time neither of them moved as they took advantage of the opportunity to feast their eyes on what they both wanted but couldn't have.

CHAPTER 11

Dinner was a boisterous affair full of laughter, old stories, and tasty seafood prepared by Adeline, the cook who had worked for Ted's parents for twenty-five years. After dessert, they lingered over after-dinner drinks. Ted sat next to his sister Tish and her husband Steven at dinner, but he kept one eye on Caroline across the table between Smitty and Parker.

Realizing he might never see her again after this weekend, Ted committed everything he observed to memory. Earlier he had noticed the little hiccup she got in the back of her throat when she yawned. Before she'd gotten up from her nap on the lounge, he'd also discovered that stretching was a full-body affair for her, like a lion awaking from a long slumber.

Now, as she talked with Smitty and Parker, he saw that she ran her tongue over her bottom lip when she was listening, and that laughter could explode from her chest or roll softly from her as if she was surprised to be amused. Smitty kept an attentive arm around her and whispered in her ear to bring her into the loop whenever a person or event from the past was mentioned.

When Ted couldn't stand to watch their intimate back and forth any longer, he got busy fiddling with his spoon while the lively conversation continued all around him. As the night without sleep caught up to him, he was suddenly tired down to his bones. He was thinking about excusing himself to go to bed when he heard his name and looked up to find all eyes on him.

"Are we boring you, son?" his father asked with laughter dancing in his hazel eyes.

"What?" Ted asked, flustered. "No, of course not."

"You were a million miles away," Mitzi said.

"I was just thinking about going to bed, actually."

"So early?" his sister said with a pout.

"I was up all night with a patient. I'm cooked."

"Good outcome?" his grandfather asked.

Ted shook his head and hurt when he thought of Pilar, who had wanted nothing more than to be a typical teenager.

"I'm sorry to hear that, son," Theo Duffy said solemnly.

"We were going to hit Nick's and the Kittens," Smitty said, referring to two of the island's more popular bars. Ted could tell that his friend was trying to cajole him out of his funk the way he always did.

"Count me out," Ted said. Ten years ago he could've gone two nights without sleep but not anymore.

As everyone began to get up from the table, Adeline came in to clear the last of the dishes. Ted kissed her cheek. "Thanks for a great meal, Addie."

"My pleasure, honey. You look like you need some sleep."

"That's where I'm heading." Ted kissed his grandmother goodnight.

"You're working too hard and not taking care of yourself," Addie said.

"I said the same thing, Addie," Mitzi chimed in as she linked her arm through her son's. "Come on, darling, I'll walk you over."

"Hey, Duff," Chip called from the back porch where everyone else had gathered. "Maybe Mommy will read you a bedtime story if you ask real nice."

Mitzi turned to him. "You're not too big to be spanked, Charles."

"Oh, Mitzi, I *love it* when you talk dirty to me."

Elise smacked him as everyone else howled with laughter.

Mitzi chuckled as she walked with Ted down the stairs to the gravel path that led to the guesthouse. After they had strolled in silence for several minutes, she said, "I'm worried about you, Ted. You're not yourself today."

"It's been a hideous month at work. The worst ever."

"I'm sorry."

"So am I."

"I was hoping you might bring someone with you this weekend."

"I brought five people with me," Ted said in a teasing tone.

"You know what I mean."

"There's no one to bring, Mom."

"Your grandmother wants to see you settled down and married before she goes," Mitzi said, using a line Ted had heard a hundred times before.

Ted raised an amused eyebrow. "My grandmother does, does she?"

"Ted," she said with an exasperated sigh. "We worry about you."

"You don't need to. I'm fine. I just need some sleep."

She kissed him goodnight at the steps to the guesthouse. "Sleep late in the morning."

"I'll try."

"Love you, honey."

"Love you, too, Mom."

Caroline encouraged the others to go out without her. She used her ankle as an excuse, but more than anything she wanted some time to herself to absorb the storm of feelings swirling around in her. *Overwhelmed would be putting it mildly,* she thought, as she lay in bed in the large master bedroom. How had she ever ended up in such a situation? A love triangle, of all things! It was right out of a bad soap opera, for heaven's sakes. Unfortunately, it was all too real, and she was smack in the middle of two decent guys whose friendship meant more to them than almost anything in their lives.

She adored Smitty. He had been exactly what she needed as she waded back into the dating pool after her disastrous engagement. Brad had broken her heart when he called off their wedding a month before the big day—and after she had quit her job at *The Times* to focus on their relationship! She'd been left with no marriage, no job, and no hope. Fortunately, she had invested her money wisely and had the time to weigh her career options while she recovered from the horrible disappointment and embarrassment. Her career had rebounded as one freelance job led to another. Her love life, on the other hand, had remained on hold.

After a year had passed, her friends began pressuring her to get out and meet new people, which is how she had ended up in a Greenwich Village restaurant with Chip, Elise, Elise's sister, her boyfriend, and Smitty. They were part of a large crowd of educated, accomplished young New Yorkers, and while Caroline usually hated fix-ups, she trusted their judgment and agreed to meet Smitty. Besides, by then she was getting tired of her own company and was ready to rejoin the land of the living.

Caroline had liked him right away. He was fun, and he made her laugh harder than she had in ages. When he called the next day to ask her out, she hadn't hesitated to say yes. From the very beginning, she had enjoyed the contrasts she found in him. He knew the wine list at "21" inside out but could tell the raunchiest jokes she'd ever heard. As comfortable in a three-thousand-dollar suit as he was in fifteen-year-old Levis, he cared for his friends like they were family but had no family of his own. And he too had been hurt by a past relationship and was wary of commitment. In that way, he was the ideal man for her just then.

He often called to tell her he had tickets to a Knicks game, a Stones concert, or a gallery opening in SoHo. She teased him that she never knew what adventure she would be on before the day ended. Life with Smitty was all about the pursuit of fun, which was fine with her since she was in no rush to embark on another serious relationship.

They'd had three dates before he kissed her—a chaste peck on the lips at her front door after they'd been to dinner with Chip and Elise. The next night had ended in a more heated make-out session on her sofa. He had finally coaxed her into bed the week before he took her to Newport for the first time—the week before she met Ted and found the man of her dreams in her boyfriend's best friend. How she wished now that she had waited a little longer to go to bed with Smitty. But how could she have known then that her whole life would change just a few days later?

You're not thinking about Ted right now. Focus on Smitty. You have to figure out what you're going to do about him.

Sex with Smitty, like everything else, was fun and uncomplicated, and with neither of them looking for anything lasting, it was hard for Caroline to be disappointed by the lack of a real connection between them. Because that connection was missing, she had assumed their relationship would end when one of them either met someone else or wanted something more substantial.

Then she began to suspect he had fallen for her. He hadn't said the words, but the signs were hard to miss: a look, a touch, a word uttered in an intimate moment, the way he gazed at her when he thought she wasn't aware, the tender way he had cared for her after she broke her ankle. In a way she felt betrayed by his feelings for her. They had gone into this to have fun, not to fall in love. But she couldn't be mad at Smitty. How could she be mad at him? Especially when he had rearranged his life around her after her accident.

And then there was Ted with whom she'd had the kind of immediate, spontaneous, overwhelming connection people search for their whole lives and often never find. Now that she knew he was out there somewhere, how was she supposed to just go on like she had never met him? Was she to pretend her whole world hadn't been permanently altered during one momentous weekend? With a deep, pained sigh, she realized that was exactly what she had to do unless she wanted to be responsible for the end of a long and important friendship between two exceptional men, neither of whom would ever be happy if being with her caused their friend pain.

She had replayed that first weekend with Ted over and over again until she thought she would go crazy. Everything about him appealed to her on the deepest possible level. His compassion toward the kids he cared for, the grief he experienced when he lost one of them, and the close bond he shared with his friends and family were just a few of the things she admired about him. Of course she was also attracted to the more basic things like his muscular physique, his thick blond hair, those amazing blue eyes . . .

He was upstairs asleep right now, and knowing he was so close but out of reach was excruciating. *No one would ever know if I went up there just to watch him sleep, would they?*

She moaned. *God help me, but I want him so much—more than I've ever wanted anyone. I have to talk to Smitty as soon as this weekend is over. No matter what, I can't go on with him any longer—not feeling the way I do about his friend.* The hopelessness of the situation left her feeling despondent. For a long time, she lay there imagining Ted sleeping until she could no longer resist the temptation.

Almost as if she were watching someone else, she got out of bed and hobbled through the dark house wearing only a white cotton nightgown that fell to mid-thigh. At the bottom of the stairs, she looked up. Even though what she was doing went against everything she believed in, she was still unable to stop herself from taking the first step and then the second. In the upstairs hallway, she paused, hoping to slow her pounding heart before she ventured to the one door that was closed. Laying her hand on the doorknob, she rested her forehead against the wood door and tried to summon the courage to take the next step.

She turned the doorknob slowly and quietly. The last thing she wanted was disturb him when it had been so obvious to everyone how tired he was earlier. All she wanted was a glimpse of him, and the light from the hallway was just enough for her to make out his shape in the bed. He lay sprawled out on his stomach, and the sheet had shifted down over his hips. Her mouth went dry when she realized he slept nude.

Her heart pounded with desire and adrenaline as she crept closer to the bed. The half of his handsome face that she could see was slack with sleep, his breathing a soft whisper in the quiet. She wanted so badly to run her hand over the smooth plane of his back, but instead she used her index finger to brush a lock of blond hair off his forehead.

His hand shot out and grabbed her wrist.

Caroline yelped with shock.

"Did I mention I'm a light sleeper?" he mumbled without opening his eyes. "What are you doing?"

"I just, I, um . . ." She sighed. "I have no idea what I'm doing."

He released her arm. "You shouldn't be up here, Caroline."

"Believe me, I know. I feel like I'm going to be sick." She rested her hand on her stomach. "I've never been in a situation like this. I have no idea what to do."

"You have to go back downstairs before someone comes home and catches you up here. That's the last thing we need."

"I'm sorry I disturbed you."

He stared at her, his eyes hot and intense. "I'm not."

"Ted—"

They froze when they heard a thump downstairs.

"Shit," Ted whispered. "Say you heard a noise and came up to check. Go. Hurry."

With one last desperate look back at him, she moved as fast as she could on her broken ankle to get out of his room before whoever was downstairs found her. If her heart had been pounding earlier, it was about to come out of her chest now. She got to the stairs and hobbled her way down to find Parker drinking a beer in the living room.

"Caroline?" he said with a quizzical expression. "What's wrong?"

"Oh, Parker." Realizing the thin white gown revealed more than she wished to show Parker, she crossed her arms over her breasts. "You scared me. I thought you were out."

"Those bars are too crazy for me, so I walked home. What were you doing up there?"

"I heard something banging and went up to fix it before it woke up Ted."

"Did you figure out what it was?"

"The blinds in Chip and Elise's room were flapping in the breeze." She cursed herself for not thinking of something better and wouldn't blame him if he didn't believe her.

"And you could hear that from down here?"

"Uh huh. Well, I'll see you in the morning."

"Are you sure everything's all right? Your face is all red like you've been crying or something."

"I was sound asleep and woke up to the banging."

"Yes, the blinds." He took a long sip of his beer as he studied her.

"Good night, Parker." She escaped to the master bedroom before she could dig a deeper hole for herself. Closing the door, she leaned back against it. *I should've never gone up there. Ugh.* When she got in bed, the cool pillow soothed her heated cheek. She couldn't stop thinking about the hungry way Ted had stared at her.

Tears of despair pooled in her eyes when she realized she had found *him*. The one she had waited for forever. Her last thought before she finally drifted into a restless sleep was how would she ever live without him now that she had found him?

TED STOOD at the doorway to listen to Caroline and Parker talking at the bottom of the stairs. *Shit, that was close!* His heart galloped in his chest as he quietly closed the door and got back in bed. Running his hand through his hair, he took a deep breath in an attempt to get his heart and his emotions under control.

He held his breath when he heard Parker coming up the stairs. Grabbing the sheet to cover himself, Ted turned over and closed his eyes as Parker came to a stop outside his room. The door opened.

~

"DUFF?" Parker whispered.

When Ted didn't stir, Parker closed the door and leaned against it. Caroline was acting so strange, almost like she had been caught doing something wrong. *But what?* Parker didn't know her very well, but she had never struck him as the flighty type before. Ted was apparently out cold, so Parker couldn't ask him if he knew what was going on.

He went next door to Chip and Elise's room, and the hair on the back of his neck tingled when he turned on the light to find the windows covered only by sheer curtains that billowed softly in the breeze.

CHAPTER 12

Smitty let himself into the dark house. In the bedroom he dropped his wallet and the car keys on the dresser. Leaning over the bed, he kissed Caroline's forehead and smoothed his hand over her sleek blond hair, relieved as always to see her after being away from her.

He'd had to acknowledge some time ago that he had broken his cardinal rule when he allowed her into his heart. Around the same time he had begun preparing himself to lose her. She would leave one day. They always did. But for now she was his, and he was holding on with everything he had.

He left her to sleep and went into the kitchen for a beer. Twisting the top off on his way outside, he stepped onto the back deck where Parker sat in one of the rocking chairs.

"How's it going?"

Startled, Parker looked up at him. "Oh, hi. I didn't hear you come in."

Smitty gazed out over the placid pond and then up at a sky littered with stars. "Peaceful out here, isn't it?"

"Sure is."

Smitty took a long swig of his beer and slid into one of the other rockers. "Something wrong, Parker?"

After a long pause Parker said, "Nope. Did Chip and Elise come back, too?"

"She ran into a college friend at Nick's, so Chip's stuck having girl talk with them."

Parker chuckled.

"Was that place always such a meat market? It was unreal tonight. They were even trying to pick *me* up."

"Desperate times . . ."

"Hey," Smitty said with mock indignation. "What I lack in movie star looks, I more than make up for in portfolio power."

"Too bad you couldn't have had that line put on a T-shirt when you were working the singles scene."

Smitty howled. "Can you *imagine?*"

Parker shook his head with amusement.

"Well, those days are over now that I've got Caroline."

"Yes, I suppose they are."

"You *suppose?*"

"They *are,*" Parker clarified.

"What about you? Any good prospects?"

"I've got my eye on someone," Parker said, seeming to surprise himself with the confession.

Smitty pounced. "Really? *Who?* Do we know her?"

Parker grinned as he put up his hand to deflect the onslaught. "No. No one you know."

"How'd you meet her?"

"Through work."

"You're not going to give me anything else, are you?"

"Not now but soon I hope."

Smitty studied Parker for a quiet moment. "Then in the meantime, I'm going to hope that my very good friend gets whatever it is he wants from this woman he has his eye on."

"Thank you." Parker saluted Smitty with his empty beer bottle.

"I'm going to turn in," Smitty said with a big yawn and a stretch.

"Me, too."

They walked inside together to put the empty bottles in the kitchen trash.

"Night," Smitty said, turning toward the master bedroom.

"Smitty."

Smitty turned back. "Yeah?"

Parker chewed on the inside of his cheek as he glanced past Smitty to the closed door to the master bedroom. "Nothing. Never mind. I'll see you in the morning."

"Okay."

Smitty went into the room thinking that something was up with Parker. First, he had come home early, and then he had acted so odd, almost from the moment Smitty had stepped onto the deck. *Maybe it's the woman he's got on his mind,* Smitty thought, as he shed his clothes into a pile on the floor. It wasn't like Parker to be secretive or serious about women, so that was odd in and of itself. *I'll have to ask Duff what he knows about it.*

He got in bed next to Caroline, who was turned away from him. Smitty snuggled up to her and ran his hand down her back until he encountered smooth leg. Just the feel of her skin and the scent of her hair was enough to turn him on.

"Caroline," he whispered as he nibbled on her ear.

"Hmm."

"I want you." He reached under her nightgown to fondle her breast.

She rolled onto her back and seemed to come awake all at once. "Smitty?" She pushed his hand away. "What are you doing?"

He captured her hand and pressed it against his erection. "A good boner is a terrible thing to waste," he joked, using a line that had made her laugh in the past. But not tonight.

She tugged her hand free. "Don't."

He took his tongue on a journey along her neck. "Why not?"

She pushed him away and got out of bed.

Smitty lifted himself up on one elbow. "Sweetheart, what's the matter?"

"I just don't want to, okay?" Before he could answer she fled into the bathroom and slammed the door behind her.

What the hell? Smitty wondered as he flopped onto his back.

Ten minutes later she got back in bed but stayed as far away from him as she could get and still be in the same bed.

"I'm sorry, sweetheart." He rolled over to put his arm around her and found her rigid with tension. "Are you crying?"

She didn't answer.

"Caroline?" A jolt of fear went through him. "What is it?"

"I'm just really tired, okay?" she said softly.

"Sure it is. I shouldn't have bothered you."

She grasped the hand he had rested on her hip. "Sorry."

"No, *I'm* sorry." He raised himself up and kissed her cheek. "Go back to sleep." She relaxed against him, and soon the cadence of her breathing told him she was asleep. Smitty lay awake next to her for a long time trying to figure out why everyone was acting so weird.

TED AROSE EARLY the next morning to run before anyone else was up. He didn't want to be around to watch Smitty and Caroline emerge from the room they were sharing. Imagining the two of them in bed together had been enough to keep him awake half the night as it was. Full of pent up energy and anxiety, he pushed himself harder than usual on the run during which all his thoughts were of Caroline.

No matter how he looked at the situation, all he saw was the end of his friendship with Smitty, and most likely Parker and Chip, too. *Am I seriously considering that kind of sacrifice? Does it really have to be such a terrible choice?* He couldn't imagine his life without the three of them, but since he met her, he couldn't imagine life without her, either.

More conflicted than ever after an hour's run, Ted returned to the house where Parker sat on the front steps with a cup of coffee.

Ted's stomach dropped when he realized Parker was waiting for him.

"Hey," Ted panted as he bent in half to catch his breath and stretch out his aching muscles.

"Good run?"

"Yeah."

Ted stood upright, stretched some more, and wiped the sweat off his face with the bottom of his T-shirt. "Where is everyone?" He glanced into the house, hoping for a glimpse of Caroline.

"On the back deck." Parker put down his mug and got up. "Take a walk with me."

"What's going on?" Ted hoped his friend hadn't noticed that he had trouble getting the words out.

"I'm not really sure."

They walked to the end of the crushed shell driveway where Parker turned to him and told him about the odd encounter he'd had with Caroline the night before.

Ted fought to keep his distress from showing.

"Why do you think she would lie to me like that? It was so bizarre."

"I don't know. Did you talk to Smitty about it?" His heart all but stopped while he waited for Parker to answer.

"No, but I wanted to. I'd hate to start something over nothing, and I don't want Caroline to think I'm a big-mouthed jerk."

"Probably a good call," Ted said, relieved. The lawyer in Parker was having a hard time letting this go, which made Ted extremely nervous.

"So you didn't hear anything? I mean you were the only two in the house."

"No," Ted said, looking his friend in the eye. "I didn't hear a thing."

PARKER WENT BACK to the guesthouse while Ted walked his heavy heart over to see his parents and grandparents. This whole thing became a bigger nightmare with every passing day. He couldn't recall ever lying so blatantly to anyone before, let alone to one of his closest friends.

The main house bustled with activity as caterers, florists, and other workers set up for the party.

"Morning," Ted said when he came upon his parents and

grandparents enjoying a quiet breakfast in the kitchen, oblivious to the chaos.

"Good morning," Mitzi said, jumping up to kiss his cheek and pour him a cup of coffee. Today she wore a yellow sundress that made her look closer to forty than sixty. "Now, Ted, honey, why do you still look so tired?"

"Stop harping on the boy, Mitzi," his grandfather said with a wink for Ted. "He's on vacation."

"He's running himself ragged," Lillian said, disapproval written all over her still-pretty face.

"Just like we used to," Ted's father, Ed, said. "It's good for him. It keeps him out of trouble."

"*Hello.*" Ted waved his hand to get their attention—not that he needed any more of their attention. "I'm in the room, people."

Lillian giggled. "So no one told us Smitty has a new girlfriend. She's lovely."

"Uh huh," Ted agreed, accepting a cup of coffee from his mother.

"Do you think he's serious about her?" Mitzi asked.

Ted wanted to groan, but all he did was shrug. "Hard telling."

"Smitty doesn't know the meaning of the word serious," Ed said. "She'll be history in no time, just like all the others."

"I wouldn't be so sure about that," Mitzi said as she sat next to her husband. "I saw the way he looked at her last night. Maybe this one will stick."

"What do you think, Third?" his grandfather asked.

Lillian shot a pointed look at her husband.

"Oh, I mean Ted. Sorry."

"I really have no idea," Ted said, already wishing he had just stayed in bed today. Once again he noticed his grandmother's wise old eyes trained on him, and for the briefest of instants he felt like she saw everything he was trying so hard to hide. Desperate to shed the feeling and change the subject, he said, "So what can I do to help for the party?"

"Not a thing, darling," Mitzi said with a breezy wave of her hand. "We've got everything under control. Why don't you and the kids hit the beach today?"

"I'll see what they want to do."

AFTER SPENDING another half hour with his parents and grandparents, Ted walked back to the guesthouse like a condemned man heading for the gallows. He couldn't bear the idea of having to hide all he felt for Caroline, even for two short days. For the first time in his career, he wished for an emergency at the hospital that would demand his immediate attention. Anything to get him out of here. But that wasn't going to happen. He was signed out for the weekend, and Roger wouldn't think of calling him back to work. Besides it would take him hours to get there anyway, and he wouldn't do that to his parents and grandparents on their big day.

Marooned.

The word took on a whole new meaning as he trudged up the back stairs of the guesthouse where Elise and Caroline sat at the dining room table doing their nails.

Caroline looked up at him, and he was instantly held captive by her green-gold eyes. In that one endless, silent second she managed to use those magnificent eyes to remind him of the magnitude of the emotions ricocheting back and forth between them. Then he remembered they weren't alone.

"How's it going?" he asked. His voice sounded all wrong to him, and he wondered if they would notice.

But Elise just held up her hand to show off her manicure. "What do you think?"

Ted tried to act like he cared. "Looks good."

"Smitty left some breakfast for you," Caroline said. "It's in the oven."

"Thanks," Ted said. "Where are they?"

"They went into town." Elise blew on her nails. "They said they'd be back in an hour."

Absorbing a stab of guilt that was almost painful, Ted retrieved the plate of omelet and bacon Smitty had made for him. As he stood in the kitchen and took the first bite of crispy bacon, he was swamped with an overwhelming sense of foreboding and couldn't get anything past the huge lump that formed in his throat. Tipping the plate over the sink, he dumped the food into the garbage disposal. He watched his breakfast go down the drain and wondered if his friendship with Smitty would end up there too.

"Ted?"

He straightened his hunched shoulders and turned to Caroline. "Where's Elise?"

"Outside. Did you eat?"

"Couldn't. Couldn't eat. Couldn't sleep."

She gazed up at him with those potent eyes. "Me either."

They startled when the whack of the screen door warned them that Elise was coming back inside.

"We *have* to go to the beach today," Elise said, oblivious to the tension in the room. "It's a perfect day for it. I'm going to start getting ready so we can go when the guys get back."

"I'll help you," Caroline said.

"I'm going to grab a quick shower," Ted said, anxious to get out of there so he could be alone with his thoughts and away from temptation.

AFTER A LONG AND tedious afternoon at the beach that included the torture of Caroline's bikini, Ted stood under his second shower of the day. This time he also ran a razor over his face in preparation for the party. He stayed under the beating pulse of the water for much longer than necessary as he thought about the conversation he'd had with Chip at the beach.

Chip had told him about a patient of his who had been coming to him for acne treatment for years. "Then, the other day, she says, 'Dr. Taggert, can you look at this mole on my shoulder?' So she pulls her shirt down and shows me a melanoma. I didn't have to even biopsy it to know what I was looking at. She's sixteen years old!" Chip had shaken his head with dismay. "Don't get me wrong, I see my share of melanoma, but it's usually on people who've been sun worshipers for years. This was my first kid. All I could think about was you and how you deal with that and so much worse every day. I just can't imagine how you stand it."

Ted had shrugged. "I hate to say it because it sounds so callous, but you do get used to it after a while. The first year was the worst. I can still remember that feeling of being totally numb, but after a while you start to build up some defenses."

"Still, it has to do a number on you."

"I guess it does. That's why I keep up my gig in the pediatrics clinic once a month, just so I can see kids with hair to remind myself they're not all sick."

"I admire you so much, Duff. We're both doctors, but what you do is so much more important."

I wonder if he would still admire me if he knew I had fallen for Smitty's girlfriend, Ted thought, as he stepped out of the shower. He used his towel to wipe the steam off the mirror and studied his reflection. *She's not going to be Smitty's girlfriend for much longer. Even so, you can't start something with her the minute they break up. But what if no one knew? What if we kept it quiet for a few months?*

"Duff!" Elise hollered as she knocked on the bathroom door. "What's taking so long?"

Ted gave his weary face one last long look before he wrapped the towel around his waist and pulled open the door. "Sorry. I had to shave."

"You know I count on you to be quick," she said as she brushed past him into the bathroom. "Chip and Parker are the metrosexuals. I expect better from you."

Ted chuckled. "It isn't easy being the only girl in this group, is it?"

"You have *no* idea," she said as she closed the door in his face.

Ted loved Elise. She was perfect for his friend because she let Chip be Chip, even if at times he drove her nuts. The top photographer at *New York Style* magazine, Elise was tall and leggy with long dark hair and big gray eyes. Ted had no doubt she could have been on the other side of the camera if she'd had that urge. But she loved taking the pictures, and her work had won her wide acclaim in the fashion industry.

She had met Chip six years earlier, and from the very beginning, she had fit in effortlessly with their gang of four confirmed bachelors.

Ted shrugged into his tuxedo jacket and thanked the heavens for the ocean breeze that was keeping the humidity to a minimum. Without it, the jacket wouldn't have lasted long. He took one last look in the mirror to make sure his bow tie was straight, dabbed on a hint of cologne, and headed for the stairs.

He was halfway down when he spotted Caroline on the back porch. She wore a floor-length red halter dress that left her back and arms bare. A half-dozen glittering clips had captured her long blond hair into a casual, sexy style that stopped his heart.

As if she sensed him, she turned and their eyes met. The front of her dress hugged her full breasts, and the hand she rested over her heart told him what she thought of him in a tuxedo.

Smitty broke the spell when he burst out of the master bedroom. "Sweetheart, can you help me with these cufflinks?"

Caroline cleared her throat. "Out here."

"Looking good, Duff," Smitty said as Ted reached the bottom of the stairs. "Are you going over now?"

"Yeah."

"We're right behind you."

CHAPTER 13

Ted went in the back door of the main house where Tish was helping Lillian put on the pearls Theo had given her on their wedding day. Lillian wore a lilac chiffon dress with sheer sleeves and satin cuffs.

"Hey, baby." Ted kissed her cheek. "Wanna run away with me?"

She rested her hands on his lapels, her eyes twinkling with mirth. "What time do we leave?"

"Are you trying to steal my woman?" Theo boomed as he came into the room, looking jaunty in his tuxedo. What was left of his white hair had been tamed for the occasion.

"She's coming willingly. Told me she couldn't wait to be free of the old guy."

Theo hooked an arm around his grandson's neck. "I'll fight you for her."

Tish giggled. "That I'd like to see."

"I'll make you a deal," Ted said. "If you let me dance with her, you can take her home."

Theo's eyes narrowed as he appeared to give Ted's offer some serious thought. "I can live with that."

"Shucks," Lillian said with a pout. "He ruins all my fun."

"Do yourself a favor, son, and don't marry a shameless flirt," Theo said. "You can't let your guard down for a minute."

Ted smiled. "I'll try to remember that, Grampa." How he loved the two of them, and how he hurt when he thought of all the years he would have to get by without them. Would they live to see him married with children of his own? He thought of Caroline. Maybe.

"How was the beach?" Tish asked, jolting Ted from his reverie.

"Good. You should've come."

"I had to nap." She patted her rounded belly. "Or I wouldn't have gotten through tonight."

"Mom said you've been really tired."

"That's what I get for being a pregnant old lady," she joked. She was thirty-five and had their father's hazel eyes and light brown hair that she wore in a cute pageboy.

Ted ran a hand over her baby belly, covered tonight in a black maternity gown. "Don't shoot me for asking, but . . ."

"Yes, I'm bigger than I should be for seven months," she said with a sigh. "Steven's mother waits until I'm already pregnant to tell me he was a twelve-pound baby. Can I sue her for withholding that information?"

Ted laughed. "I would think so. Check with Parker. He can give you some advice on that."

"You take your time having that big baby, Tish," Theo said. "The words 'great-grandfather' make me sound so old."

"You *are* old, Theo," Lillian chimed in as she linked her arm with his. "But I still think you're cute."

"Cute," he muttered.

Hand-in-hand, Ted's parents came into the room. Mitzi was gorgeous in a navy gown, and her blue eyes danced with excitement. "Look at what your father gave me!" She held out her hand to show off a diamond anniversary band.

"That's beautiful, Mom!" Tish said.

"Very nice," Ted added. "Good job, Dad."

Edward handed a box to his mother. "Something for the other bride."

"Honey!" Lillian said. "You shouldn't have."

"You're making me look bad, son," Theo grumbled.

Lillian's gift was a diamond pin in the shape of a dolphin, her favorite animal. "Oh, it's lovely," she said with a kiss for her son. "Thank you."

Mitzi helped Lillian put the pin on her dress and kissed her mother-in-law's cheek. "You look beautiful, Lil. The dress is perfect."

"I have you to thank for that, honey."

"Well, look at this handsome family," Smitty said as he came in with Caroline, Parker, Chip, and Elise, who had brought her camera.

"How about a family portrait?" Elise asked.

"That would be wonderful," Mitzi said. "Let's go out on the deck."

Elise arranged the family so the sunset was in the background.

"Where's Steven?" Mitzi asked, looking for her son-in-law.

"I'll get him," Parker offered. He returned a few minutes later with a sheepish-looking Steven, who tugged on his tuxedo jacket as he joined them on the deck.

"Sorry. I was watching the end of the Sox game."

"Did they win?" Ted asked.

"Sure did," Steven said, putting his arm around Tish for the photo.

Caroline leaned against the porch rail, and Ted wanted to yell, "Wait! Stop! There's someone missing." But he swallowed the urge and smiled on command.

"How about one with all the boys?" Mitzi asked.

Parker and Chip stood on one side of the four Duffys while Smitty and Ted took the other side.

Ted's parents and grandparents stepped out of the next photo. As he felt Parker's hand on one shoulder and Smitty's on the other, Ted thought of the many photos of the four of them that had been taken over the years. *Would this be the last one?*

Judging by Caroline's pained expression, she wondered the same thing.

Elise took another shot of Ted and Tish with their parents and then one with their grandparents before they moved to the tent to greet the first of their guests.

Mitzi and Lillian had gone with a Polynesian theme in the tent, which was decorated with palm trees and tiki torches.

"Wow," Ted heard Caroline say as they were greeted by the scent of lush flowers that adorned the top of every table.

A lone musician in a festive Hawaiian shirt strummed a ukulele as guests began to filter into the tent. Waitresses wearing grass skirts circulated with hot hors d'oeuvres—or pupu as they were called in Hawaii. The large panels on the side of the tent facing the pond had been rolled up to maximize the view of the sunset and to allow in the warm summer breeze.

"I think Mitzi and Lillian have finally topped themselves," Smitty said, awestruck.

"It's beautiful," Elise agreed as she took more photos.

Ted was directed to a table in the front of the room to dine with his family. He scanned the crowd in search of his friends and almost stopped breathing as he watched Smitty pluck a red hibiscus bloom from the arrangement on their table and tuck it into Caroline's hair. She smiled at him, and he leaned in to kiss her.

"Son of a bitch," Ted whispered, his gut clenching with impotent, jealous rage.

"Sweetheart?" Lillian rested her hand on his arm and glanced up at him with concern. "What is it?" She followed his eyes to where Smitty sat with his arm around Caroline.

"Nothing." Ted shook it off and forced a smile for his grandmother. "Are you having a good time, Grandy?"

"How long have you been in love with her?" Lillian asked.

Ted blanched. "*What?* In love with who?"

"Take a stroll with your old granny." She tugged at his arm to lead him to the open side of the tent.

"Not now, Grandy," Ted said with a hint of desperation in his voice. "You can't leave your guests."

"Your mother has everything under control, and dinner won't be served for another half hour."

Realizing she wasn't going to take no for an answer, Ted escorted her from the tent. Mindful of her long skirt, he walked her slowly along the dirt path that led to shore.

"Talk to me, honey," she said when they were a good distance from the tent. The air was filled with the distant sounds of laughter, the tinkle of crystal glasses, and the ukulele music. "What's going on?"

"I don't know what you want me to say, Grandy." Ted worked at keeping his tone light and amused. "I'm not in love with anyone."

Her eyes narrowed. "You're in love with Caroline."

Shocked, he stopped and turned to her. "But how, I mean . . . How do you know?"

"It's all over your face when you think no one's watching. But don't panic, I don't think anyone else has figured it out—at least not yet."

Ted's jaw clenched with tension as he fixed his eyes on the pond.

"Oh, honey." She put her arms around him and rested her head on his chest. "What are you going to do?"

"I don't know," Ted whispered.

"How does she feel?"

"The same way I do, apparently," he said with a touch of awe over the still-new reality of it.

Lillian gasped. "Then what's she doing with Smitty?"

"She's going to end it with him after this weekend."

"Poor Smitty," Lillian sighed. "I think your mother was right this morning when she said he has a bad case for her."

"I keep hoping I'll find some clean way out where I can have her and still be friends with him, but so far I haven't had any luck with that."

"I've waited so long to see you fall in love with the right girl and settle down. I'm so sorry it had to happen this way."

"I am, too. You have no idea *how* sorry. But I'm not sorry I love her. I just . . . I never had any idea it could be like this."

Lillian took his hands. "I'm going to tell you something about me that only your grandfather knows. Even your parents have never heard this." She took a deep breath and squeezed his hands as if to give both of them courage. "I was supposed to marry someone else."

"Who?" Ted asked, astounded.

"He was a family friend, someone I grew up with. We were very good friends, and I was perfectly content with the idea of marrying him until I met Theo at a dance at the university. After two hours with him, I knew there was no way I could marry anyone else."

Flabbergasted, Ted tried to imagine his grandmother as a young woman caught between two men. "What did you do?"

"Well, at first I was afraid to say anything. The last thing I wanted was to disappoint my parents or cause them embarrassment with his parents who were their good friends. I was so sad about the pain I was going to cause a very nice young man who didn't deserve it. But the more time I spent with Theo, the more madly in love I was. Finally, I reached a point where I just couldn't hide how I felt any longer."

"You told your parents?"

She nodded, and Ted could tell by her expression that she had traveled back in time to that fateful moment. "Your grandfather came to the house, and we told them together. They were furious. My father screamed and yelled and told me I had made promises that I was going to keep. My mother, as I expected, was mostly worried about what everyone would think. Times were different then. Good girls didn't go around dumping lifelong friends for a man they met at a dance, even if he was a handsome medical school student."

"Yet here we are celebrating your sixty-fifth anniversary. Clearly you made the right decision."

"But at a terrible cost." She looked up at him with sadness in her eyes. "My parents never accepted Theo as a member of our family, and they hardly knew our boys. I made the right choice, but it *was* a choice, Ted. I chose Theo over my parents. I missed them every day for the rest of their lives, but I've never regretted for one minute that I chose him. He filled all the empty spaces."

"That's such an amazing story. I knew from my dad that your parents were never really a part of his life, but I had no idea why."

"Neither did he. Maybe now you can see why we were always such *involved* grandparents," she said with the twinkle returning to her eye.

Ted chuckled. "Involved. Yes, that's a good way of putting it."

"You understand why I told you this, don't you, sweetheart?"

"Yes, I think I do." He kissed her cheek. "Thank you, Grandy."

She reached for his face. "You're a kind and decent man, Ted Duffy. You have a difficult road ahead of you, but don't you think for one minute that loving this woman makes you a bad person or a bad friend. You've been a wonderful friend to Smitty for so many years, and eventually he'll understand that you never would've hurt him like this on purpose. He may be angry at first, but in his heart he'll have to know it wasn't intentional."

"Our family is his family, Grandy. If he loses me, he loses all of you, too," Ted said, expressing a thought that had been weighing heavily on his mind.

"Your mother and I have made him a part of our family, and that'll never change. I love him like one of my own, but I love you more, and I'll support you no matter what you choose to do. Don't you ever question that. You saved me after I lost my Tommy," she said, referring to her younger son who died in Vietnam. "When you were born you gave me a reason to live again, and I love you as much as it's possible to love anyone."

Ted had heard that his whole life and had never doubted it was true, but hearing her say it always put a lump in his throat.

"If she's the one for you, and she feels the same way about you, find a way to be with her. The rest will work itself out as it's meant to."

"Even if it means I lose the three of them?"

"She'll fill the empty spaces."

He hugged her. "I love you, Grandy."

"And I adore you. If you need someone to talk to, you know where I am, right?"

"Always." He offered her his arm. "Shall we rejoin your party?"

She tucked her hand into his elbow. "Lead the way."

CHAPTER 14

"Oh, there you two are," Mitzi said when Ted and Lillian returned to the tent. "We were just starting to worry."

"We took a walk to watch the sunset," Lillian said with a private smile for Ted as he helped her into a chair at their table.

"I heard my wife was seen leaving the tent with a young blond stud," Theo said, sliding into the seat next to Lillian. "I'm glad it was only you, Ted."

Ted surprised his grandfather when he leaned over to kiss his cheek. "She's all yours, Grampa. I wouldn't dream of interfering with a match made in heaven." His grandmother winked at him as he took the seat on the other side of her.

They dined on traditional Hawaiian luau fare that included avocado salad, teriyaki beef and shrimp, rice, kalua pork, pineapple broiled in ginger, and vegetable kabobs.

"This is outrageously good, Grandy," Ted said. "Who did you get to do it?"

"An outfit out of Boston. We thought it would be fun."

"It's fabulous." Ted watched his father get up to greet a late-arriving couple—his old friend and Ted's boss Martin Nickerson and his wife Jenny. Ed Duffy had been Martin's boss and mentor. When Ed retired, Martin became the chief of pediatric oncology and later hired Ted. He stood to shake Martin's hand.

"So sorry we're late," Martin said. "The ferry was running behind."

Mitzi squeezed Martin and Jenny into their table between Ted and Lillian and had dinner served to them.

"It was good of you to come, Marty," Ted said.

"We wouldn't miss a Mitzi and Lillian production. They've outdone themselves tonight."

"I couldn't agree more."

"I don't mean to talk shop, but I've been trying to get down to see you all week. You've been having a tough run of it lately."

Ted's gut clenched at the reminder of the recent string of losses. "It hasn't been my best month."

"You've been around this long enough by now to know we all go through these rough patches."

"That doesn't make them any easier. Losing Joey was a particularly tough blow."

"I'm sure you're taking good care of your people through it all," Martin said, sipping from his vodka martini.

"I'm doing my best, but some of them are taking it hard."

"To be expected. Listen, there's a three-day conference coming up at Sloan Kettering I'd like to send you to. It's personal development stuff about physicians dealing with loss and grief. I know you hate that crap, but in light of what's been going on—"

Sloan Kettering was in New York City, and so was Caroline. "I'll go," Ted said.

Surprised, Martin studied him. "That was far too easy. I was prepared for all your arguments."

Ted shrugged. "I could use a change of scenery."

"All right then. I'll set it up."

"When is it?"

"In two weeks."

"Marty, let Ted enjoy the party, will you?" his wife said, rolling her eyes at Ted.

"Don't worry, dear. We're done."

~

The toasting began right after dinner. Because he knew his mother expected it of him, Ted got up to take the microphone offered by the leader of the band that had been hired for dancing.

When he had the attention of the guests, Ted said, "On behalf of all the Duffys, I want to thank you for joining us tonight for this very special occasion. Many of you were with us five years ago, but for those of you who weren't, I want to tell you a little about the two couples who raised my sister and me, and about two marriages that, in my opinion, set the gold standard for how marriage should be done.

"Theo and Lillian met at a dance at Harvard University in the spring of 1941. Their wedding plans were interrupted on December 7, 1941 when the Japanese bombed Pearl Harbor." Ted recited the story he knew well but was still amazed to realize there had been so much more to it than he—or his father—had ever known.

"They were married on December 9, and Theo joined the medical corps later that month. He was shipped off to the European theater, and Lillian didn't see him for three long years, during which time she worked as a volunteer for the Red Cross. Their son Edward Theodore Junior was born almost ten months to the day after Theo returned home from the war, and a second son, Thomas, was born three years later. Second Lieutenant Thomas Duffy was killed in Vietnam in 1968. After World War II, Theo completed his medical training and went on to a long and prestigious career as a pediatric oncologist in several Boston-area hospitals. Lillian is well known in Boston for her philanthropic work, especially on behalf of the Dana-Farber Cancer Institute's Jimmy Fund Clinic, a cause that, as you all know, is near and dear to the Duffy family. Theo and Lillian retired in 1985 and now spend their time playing golf, traveling, and doting on their two grandchildren. And when I say doting, I mean *doting*," Ted said to laughter. "Soon they'll have a great-grandchild to ruin—I mean spoil."

Theo shot him a scowl, but his eyes were full of amusement and sentiment.

"Please join me in congratulating my grandparents, Theo and Lillian Duffy, on the occasion of their sixty-fifth anniversary." Ted led the thunderous applause that filled the tent.

Theo stood and offered his wife an arm to escort her to the dance floor as the band launched into "The White Cliffs of Dover." Ted watched his elderly grandparents move slowly but smoothly around the dance floor and thought about what she had told him earlier. She had no regrets about the choices she had made, and Ted could only hope he would feel the same way when he looked back on his life.

In that moment, he acknowledged that he was standing at a crossroads. The choices he made in the next few weeks and months were going to set the course for the rest of his life. He tuned back into the party when the guests applauded at the end of the song.

Wearing big smiles, Theo and Lillian returned to their table.

Ted stood to hug and kiss them both before he picked up the microphone again. "Our other guests of honor, my parents Ed and Mitzi Duffy, met in Washington, D.C., during a protest to end the war that later took his brother's life. Like his father before him, Ed was beginning his studies at Harvard Medical School. Mitzi was a junior at Bryn Mawr, and both were active in the student demonstrations that were a hallmark of the sixties. They were married in 1966 and settled in Boston where Ed followed his father into the family business. He retired as head of the pediatric oncology department at Children's Hospital Boston just a few years before he would have had to decide whether or not to hire yours truly." Ted paused when the guests laughed at his joke. "Like her mother-in-law, Mitzi devoted herself to her children and continues to be a tireless advocate on behalf of Dana-Farber and several other charitable causes in the Boston area. Ed and Mitzi will welcome their first grandchild in September. Please join Tish and me in congratulating our parents, Ed and Mitzi Duffy, as they celebrate their fortieth anniversary."

As Ed and Mitzi danced to "When a Man Loves a Woman,"

Ted noticed his grandmother dabbing at tears and reached for her hand.

"Their wedding day seems like five minutes ago," Lillian whispered in Ted's ear.

He smiled and squeezed her hand.

The microphone was passed around to friends and relatives who added their congratulations.

"Whenever I hear someone say all families are dysfunctional, I think of the Duffys who epitomize the word functional," Smitty said when the microphone reached their table. "I thank the four of you for making me a part of your functional family, and I love you all."

Ted was touched when Smitty's voice broke at the end.

"I spend my days brokering the end of marriages, and it would be so easy for me to become a cynical disbeliever," Parker said. "I think the only reason that hasn't happened is because of my long friendship with the Duffys. These two marriages have gone the distance and have done it with so much style. I also thank you for including me as a member of your family, and I'll be here in five years for the forty-five-seventy party."

Lillian rolled her eyes and groaned, which made everyone laugh.

Chip took the microphone from Parker and stood up. "I, too, have had the great honor to be included as a member of the Duffy family, and let's face it, we all want what they have. In keeping with this great celebration of marriage, I asked Mitzi and Lillian if they would mind if I hijacked five minutes of their party to do something I should've done a long time ago. I'm lucky that my beautiful girlfriend Elise has stuck with me for almost six years, and I'm hoping someday she and I will be celebrating an occasion like this with our family and friends."

Elise looked up at Chip with wary, expectant expression.

"Elise, I love you. Will you marry me?" Chip asked as he produced a ring from his pocket.

She gasped and then burst into tears as the other guests applauded.

Astounded, Smitty and Parker whooped and hollered when

Chip gathered Elise into his arms and kissed her before he slid the ring onto her finger.

Ted stood up to get a better view and saw Caroline wipe tears from her cheeks. "You two have been holding out on me," he said to his mother and grandmother.

Both shrugged with delighted innocence.

"You didn't have any idea?" Mitzi asked.

"Not a clue. I think Chip managed to pull off a total surprise. Elise looks floored."

"Go on back there with them," Lillian said. "You've done your duty up here."

"You did a wonderful job, darling," Mitzi added.

"I'll be back to collect that dance you owe me," Ted said to his grandmother before he made his way through the tent to his friends' table in the back. He hugged Chip and kissed Elise, who was still crying and gazing at the ring on her finger.

"Well done, buddy," Ted said to Chip. "You surprised us all."

"I was *dying* to tell you today at the beach," Chip said with a euphoric grin. "I didn't think I was going to make it."

"Did she say yes?" Ted teased. "I never heard a yes."

"Of course I did," Elise said.

"It's the end of an era," Smitty lamented with mock seriousness.

"Nah," Parker said. "Nothing's going to change."

Ted glanced at Caroline, filled with the sudden awareness that *everything* was about to change.

CHAPTER 15

Ted was dancing with his grandmother when he saw Caroline slip out of the tent and head in the direction of the guesthouse. Smitty, Parker, and Chip were enjoying cigars on the lawn, and Ted couldn't see Elise but assumed she was with them.

When the song ended, Ted escorted Lillian back to her seat and was on his way to a clean escape when his mother stopped him.

"Oh, Ted, darling, do you remember Madeline and John Harrington?"

They had been summer friends of his parents' for as long as they had been coming to the island. "Of course." Ted shook hands with both of them. "I ran into Jack in Newport a month or so ago," he said, referring to their son. "He was pushing a big stroller."

Madeline laughed. "His twin boys are two years old."

"Doesn't he have older children, too?" Mitzi asked.

"Yes, four of them. The oldest is in college. He had the twins with his second wife."

The small talk was killing Ted. "Would you all excuse me, please? It was great to see you again."

"You, too, Ted," John said.

He left them talking to his mother and followed the gravel path through the pitch black night to the guesthouse where the creak of a rocking chair told him Caroline was sitting on the back deck.

"I saw you leave. Are you all right?"

She didn't answer.

"Caroline?" His heart knocked against his ribs. "What is it? Are you all right?"

"I really wanted to . . ."

"What?" he asked, his heart pounding.

"Cut in on you and your grandmother, broken ankle and all."

He jammed his hands into his pockets to resist the overwhelming need to touch her. "This has been the *longest* day of my life," he whispered.

"Mine, too. I loved hearing about how your parents and grandparents met."

"My grandmother has us figured out."

Caroline gasped. "Oh, no! Oh, *God,* Ted, what she must think of me!"

"She thinks you're lovely."

"Does she think we're awful?"

"No, she thinks we're lucky. My boss is sending me to New York for a conference in two weeks."

"Really?"

"Uh huh, and I want to see you while I'm there."

"I want to see you, too. I don't know how I'll ever stand to wait two weeks."

"I want you to wear that dress again—just for me this time."

"Anything," she said, sounding breathless. "Anything for you."

SMITTY CRUSHED out his cigar and wandered back into the tent to look for Caroline. Elise was returning from the restroom where she had repaired the damage the flood of tears had done to her makeup.

"Have you seen Caroline?" Smitty asked, scanning the crowd. The red dress was nowhere in sight.

"Not in the last fifteen minutes or so."

"Maybe she went back to the house to get a pain pill."

"I thought she wasn't taking them anymore."

"She's been on the ankle a lot today. She might've needed one."

"Do you want me to go check on her?"

"That's all right. I'll do it." He kissed her forehead. "Go find your fiancé."

"Fiancé," Elise giggled. "That's going to take some getting used to."

"I still can't believe Chip pulled one over on all of us."

"He's just full of surprises."

"I'll be back in a minute." Smitty took the scenic route from the tent across the lawn behind the main house. The moonless sky was polluted with stars. Stopping for a moment, he gazed up at them, taking advantage of the rare opportunity to study them without any light to hinder the view. He picked out the Big Dipper before he continued along to the guesthouse.

He had almost reached the back deck when a sound stopped him. A whisper. Someone was whispering.

"I want you to wear that dress again—just for me this time."

"Anything. Anything for you."

"Tomorrow, after you talk to him, will you call me?"

Duff? Why's he whispering, and who is he talking to?

"I don't have your number."

Caroline? What the fuck?

Smitty heard the rustle of clothing and swallowed a growing tidal wave of panic and rage and disbelief. More than anything else, there was disbelief.

"Here's my card. Call my cell. I'll be waiting."

"I will."

"No matter what happens, remember we're in this together, and we'll figure it out. Somehow, we'll find a way to be together."

Smitty backed away before they could discover him, his heart in his throat as he cut between the two houses on his way to the driveway. Once he felt the crunch of shells beneath his feet, he began to run.

CHAPTER 16

People were beginning to leave by the time Ted returned to the tent with his heart still racing from the conversation with Caroline. Chip, Elise, and Parker were seated at their table enjoying another round of champagne.

"Hey," Parker said. "Where'd you disappear to?"

"My mother asked me to walk a couple of old ladies to their car since it's so dark." The lies were coming easier all the time.

"Pimped out by your own mother," Chip commented with a wry grin. "It's a sad day for mankind."

Ted laughed despite the tension coiled within him that threatened to burst at any second. "Where's Smitty?"

"He left a few minutes ago to find Caroline," Elise said, adding with a wink, "I'll bet we won't see them again tonight."

While Chip and Parker snickered, Ted fought to stay calm.

"I can't believe how well things are working out between them," Elise said. "He's so happy with her."

"I wonder if they'll be the next ones to get engaged," Chip said, kissing the ring on Elise's finger.

"What do you think, Duff?" Elise asked.

All eyes fell on him. "Who knows?" Ted's shrug did nothing to give away the sick feeling he had inside.

SMITTY RAN until his lungs burned and his legs were in jeopardy of giving out under him. The night was so dark that only the sound of surf hitting the shore to his right indicated that he had run to the island's northern point. He made out the hulking shadow of a large boulder by the side of the road and lowered himself onto it. Gasping for air and sweating profusely, he dropped his head into his hands and tried to absorb what he had overheard.

How the hell had this happened? They're involved? Since when? As far as Smitty knew, this was only the second time they'd ever even been together. *No one falls for someone that fast. Maybe I heard them wrong. No. No, I didn't. No way.*

As Smitty reviewed every minute he and Caroline had spent with Ted, he shed the tuxedo jacket and bow tie so he could unbutton the shirt that had tightened like a noose around his neck. That first morning, after they met while he was asleep, Ted had joked about running away and marrying her. The joke took on new meaning now.

Later that day, Smitty recalled Ted's reluctance to leave the emergency room after Caroline broke her ankle. *Had he already fallen for her then?* Smitty figured at the time that Ted hadn't wanted to abandon them in a medical situation. *Had there been more to it even then?* That week, Ted asked in an e-mail about how Caroline was doing with the ankle. Again, Smitty hadn't thought a thing of that question from his friend the doctor who had been with her when the accident happened. In fact, Smitty even encouraged Caroline to respond to the message herself. Other than the day she and Ted ran together and she broke her ankle, when had they even spent any time alone?

Smitty was certain he hadn't missed the signs because there hadn't been any to miss.

Another thought suddenly occurred to him. *Last night. Parker and Caroline were acting so strange. Did Parker walk in on something when he went home early? Ted and Caroline were alone together in the house for hours. Oh, Christ! Parker caught them! But wouldn't he have told me? There was something he had wanted to say to me, but then he thought better of it. If the shoe were on the other foot, would I have told him? I don't know . . . God. Does Parker know something? Caroline hadn't wanted to make love. Was it because she had already been with Ted?* The thought made Smitty sick.

Ted Duffy. My closest friend in the world. Tears of disappointment and bitter betrayal burned in Smitty's eyes. *If you had asked me thirty minutes ago who I trusted more than anyone, I would've said Ted Duffy.* As he absorbed the almost secondary blow—that his relationship with Caroline was over—a different sort of disappointment set in. Even though he had only known her six weeks, he'd had so many hopes tied up in her and now they had been dashed because apparently she fancied herself infatuated with Ted—someone she had seen just *twice.*

All at once, the whole thing struck Smitty as funny. He laughed so hard he almost fell off the rock. Then the pain came back in a staggering, agonizing torrent, and it wasn't funny anymore because he knew Ted Duffy, really knew him. And the Ted Duffy he knew wouldn't do something like this, wouldn't risk a friendship like theirs unless he honestly believed he was in love with her.

Somehow that hurt more than anything else—that Ted would endanger their twenty-year friendship for a woman he'd seen only twice in his life.

For all his success, for all his money, for all his so-called good friends, Smitty realized in that moment that his life was as much a house of cards now as it had been the day he left the projects. As he listened to the roar of the waves crashing onto the rocks far below where he sat, he gave significant thought to hurling himself over the edge. *Who the fuck would care anyway? Ted would probably be relieved to have me out of the way.* But the part of Smitty that was deeply, seriously pissed didn't want to let his *friend* off that easily.

So then what's the plan? He puzzled it over from every angle and decided preserving his friendship with Chip and Parker was his top priority. He couldn't lose them all. That just couldn't happen. Losing Ted would leave a big enough hole in his life and his heart. *And Ted's family,* he thought as a new wave of sadness rolled over him.

Smitty ran a shaking hand through his hair as he remembered years of Thanksgiving and Christmas holidays with the Duffys. They were the only family he had. Mitzi and Lillian called him every year on his birthday without fail. He never went on a long trip without letting them know where he would be so they wouldn't worry if they couldn't reach him. Sometimes he thought they were the only people in the world who truly cared about him. His friends loved hanging out with him, but Mitzi and Lillian worried about him. There was a difference.

Don't fool yourself, man. If it comes down to a choice they'll side with him because blood's always thicker than water. You may think of them as family, but he is *family to them—the golden boy wonder who's made them so proud his entire life. I wonder if they would be quite as proud if they knew what I know about him.*

After he had stewed over it for a long time, Smitty stood up slowly and with a roar of fury, he heaved his tuxedo jacket over the edge of the cliff. He began the walk back to the house on tired, trembling legs. *I know what I need to do. I just hope I can pull it off.*

THE SQUEAK of Nikes on wooden stairs alerted Smitty that Ted was on his way downstairs the next morning.

Ted came to an abrupt stop on the second to last step when he found Smitty asleep on the sofa still wearing what was left of his tuxedo.

Smitty kept his eyes closed and his breathing steady, aware of Ted studying him for what must have been a full minute before he continued on his way out the door to run.

After he was gone, Smitty exhaled a long deep breath he hadn't known he was holding. The events of the previous evening came rushing back to him, and his eyes pooled with tears. His head pounded from the half bottle of Smirnoff he had consumed in the abandoned tent after he returned to the Duffy's compound.

He wanted to get something for his aching head but couldn't

make himself move off the sofa. The longer he stayed where he was, the longer he could put off dealing with whatever this day had in store for him.

Ted had been gone for about thirty minutes when the master bedroom door opened. Caroline came out wearing the pink silk robe Smitty had bought for her after the first night they spent together. The memory made his heart hurt.

She too stopped short when she found him on the sofa in the clothes he'd had on the night before.

Unlike Ted, though, Caroline came over to the sofa and crouched down next to him.

"Smitty?" she whispered.

When he didn't stir, she brushed a hand over his face, and it was all he could do not to smack it away. He didn't want her anywhere near him. But he just continued to feign sleep.

She got up and went into the kitchen. A few minutes later, Smitty smelled coffee and opened his eyes just enough to watch Caroline take her mug outside to the back deck.

The others began to filter downstairs, each repeating the same routine when they discovered Smitty on the sofa. He could hear them whispering as they tried to figure out why he had slept there and why he was still in his tux.

Chip confronted Caroline on the deck. Their voices drifted in to Smitty through the open window.

"What's up with Smitty?" Chip asked.

"I don't know. I went to bed, so I didn't hear him come in."

"We thought he was with you," Elise said.

"No," Caroline said. "He wasn't."

"Where was he then?" Parker asked.

"I don't know, Parker," Caroline said with a testy edge to her voice that said she didn't appreciate his accusatory tone.

Yes, Smitty thought. *Parker knows something or he wouldn't be so sharp with her.*

Ted returned from running and stopped for another long look at Smitty on the sofa before he joined the party on the deck. "What's going on with Smitty?" he asked.

"We're wondering the same thing," Parker said.

Smitty could just imagine the look Parker had tossed at Caroline. He was in what they called his cross-examination mode.

Sure enough, she said, "I told them I have no idea. I was asleep."

Smitty didn't want to imagine what passed between Caroline and Ted. He listened to their speculation for a few more minutes before he pulled himself up and off the sofa with great reluctance. *Just get through this day, one hour at a time until you can be alone.* With a silent prayer for strength to a God he didn't much believe in, he pasted a grimace on his face and went outside.

All eyes turned to him.

"Morning," he said, rubbing his aching head and doing his best to avoid eye contact with Ted and Caroline. The blinding sun made his eyes water anyway.

"Hey," Chip said. "What the hell happened to you? You look like shit."

"Then I look as good as I feel." Smitty flopped into a rocker with a dramatic groan. *Don't overdo it, man.*

"Where'd you go last night?" Parker asked.

"I was totally smashed, so I took a little walk, got disoriented in the dark, and by the time I got back here you guys were all in bed. I didn't want to bother Caroline, so I crashed on the sofa." He had rehearsed it in his mind so many times the night before he almost believed it himself. *Spot on delivery, if I do say so myself.* Of course he couldn't add that he would've slept on a bed of nails before he got into a bed with Caroline.

"You didn't seem smashed," Parker said with a suspicious lift of an eyebrow.

"Snuck up on me all of a sudden after that last glass of champagne," Smitty said, counting on his well-known reputation as a lightweight to sell his story.

"Oh, well, okay," Chip said. "Want some aspirin?"

"I'd love some. Ten or twelve should do it."

"Three is more than enough," Chip said as he went inside to get the pills. Elise trailed behind him.

"I'll make breakfast," Parker offered.

He went inside, leaving Smitty alone with Ted and Caroline. *Fabulous!*

"I'm going to take a shower and help Parker," Ted said, beating a hasty retreat.

Smitty closed his eyes as he rested his head against the rocker, which moved gently back and forth.

"Are you sure you're all right?" Caroline asked.

"Couldn't be better—other than the headache, that is."

Chip returned with the aspirin and a glass of water.

"Thanks." Smitty got up from the rocker. "I'm going to take a shower and crash for a bit until the aspirin kicks in."

After he went inside, Chip turned to Caroline. "Is he okay?"

"Seems to be."

Chip shrugged and went in to help Parker with breakfast.

CHAPTER 17

Smitty slept for more than an hour. He woke up when Caroline crept in to get her bathing suit. From the other room, he could hear talk about going to the pool until it was time to leave for the ferry.

Now that some of the initial shock had worn off, the anger began to set in. He couldn't remember being this pissed since the last time he saw his mother.

He watched Caroline come out of the bathroom in her bikini and tried to remember what he had once seen in her. Whatever it was, it was gone now. Even her sexy body, which had dominated his thoughts for weeks, was no longer a turn on.

Smitty steamed as he recalled making love to her—at least that's what it had been to him. She'd been so responsive. Had that been just an act? *I'll probably never know for sure.* He realized they hadn't made love since she met Ted. That thought did nothing to soothe his aching heart.

After she left the room, Smitty turned onto his side and hugged a pillow to his chest. Over the music they had on, he could hear his friends laughing and talking by the pool. Ted's family was out there, too.

Why am I hiding in here? I didn't do anything wrong.

An inspired thought occurred to him, and he sat up with a burst of energy. *I've got a few more hours with them both before we go our separate ways. Maybe it's time to make them squirm a little.* A big smile spread across his face. *Oh, yes. Let's get busy.*

~

TED WAS SWIMMING laps in the pool when Smitty came out wearing his bathing suit and an unbuttoned shirt. A fat cigar dangled between his fingers.

"Looks like you're feeling better," Chip said.

"I'm back and better than ever before." Smitty bent down to lay a long, wet kiss on Caroline. "Sorry to desert you all day, sweetheart."

Ted burned as he watched Caroline brush her hand over her mouth.

"That's okay," she said, clearly flustered.

Smitty lit the cigar and sat on the end of her lounge chair. "Did everyone have a good time last night?" he asked as he massaged the bottom of her good foot with his thumb.

Caroline's eyes were almost frantic when she subtly sought out Ted in the pool.

"It was a great party," Mitzi said. "Everything was just as we hoped it would be."

"Having all of you here made it perfect," Lillian added.

Ted noticed his grandmother watching as Smitty's hand caressed Caroline's leg. Pushing himself up and out of the pool, Ted sat on the deck with his back to the happy couple.

"How about one last round of margaritas before you all have to go?" Mitzi asked, sliding on her sandals.

"I'll help you, Mom," Ted said.

"That's all right, darling. Come over for a drink when you're ready to go."

"So did you miss me in that big bed last night, sweetheart?" Smitty asked, reclining back against Caroline.

"Cut it out, Smitty. Don't be crass."

"I'm sorry." He kissed her hand and leaned in to capture her lips.

"You'd think they were the ones who got engaged last night," Chip joked.

Elise giggled. "They're next."

Ted felt like an elephant was standing on his chest as he struggled to take a deep breath.

"You might be right, Elise." Smitty kissed each of Caroline's fingers. "I said I'd never get married again, but that was before I met the lovely Caroline."

She tugged her hand free, nudged Smitty off her chest, and got up. "I'm going to pack."

Smitty jumped up. "I'll help you," he said with a wink at Elise.

"I don't need any help," Caroline said.

"Oh, sweetheart, I insist." He slung his arm around her shoulders and escorted her from the pool area.

Ted watched them go, filled with helpless, jealous despair. He glanced over at his grandmother and saw the despair on her face as well.

CAROLINE STORMED through their bedroom tossing clothes into her duffel bag. She was moving around much better on her walking cast and had all but abandoned the crutches. "What was that all about?" she asked Smitty.

He reclined on the bed to watch her pack. "What was what all about?"

"You may as well have lifted your leg and peed on me to mark your territory."

"Now why in the world would I have to do that in this crowd?" he asked, full of innocence. "I was happy to see my best girl. What's wrong with that?"

She stopped what she was doing to look at him. "Nothing's wrong with it. I just don't go for all that PDA. You know that."

"We were among friends."

"That's not the point."

"What *is* the point?"

She held his eyes for a long moment during which he could tell that she was debating something. "Never mind."

He reached for her hand and pulled her down next to him on the bed. "Tell me."

"There's nothing to tell."

When exactly do you plan to tell me you've got a thing for my best friend? But instead of asking that burning question, he said, "All right then, kiss me." He moved quickly to wedge himself between her legs and kissed her hard and fast. His tongue took deep possession of her mouth while his hand slid under her skimpy bikini to cup her bottom.

He wanted to swear when his penis reacted to the feel of her pressed against him. *Traitor!*

She pushed at his chest in protest, but he ignored her as he thrust his tongue even deeper and sank two fingers into her.

"Stop it!" she cried as she twisted away from his kiss and the invading fingers. "*Stop!*"

"Why?" He dropped kisses on her neck as he unclipped the front clasp of her bikini top. When it fell away, he rolled his tongue over her nipple. "I want you, Caroline. Let me make love to you." He tugged on the tiny scrap of fabric that still covered her.

"Smitty, *please,*" she begged, now on the verge of tears. "*Stop*. I don't want this."

Realizing he was about to force himself on a woman for the first time in his life, he released her abruptly. "What *do* you want, Caroline?"

She got up, and with shaking hands she reattached her top. "Not this," she whispered as she went into the bathroom and closed the door.

CAROLINE SLID down the back of the bathroom door and dissolved into tears. *This is a nightmare,* she thought as she was choked with sobs. *I need you, Ted. Come get me, and take me away from here.*

SMITTY LAY on the rumpled bed, fighting to catch his breath and control his emotions. He had never done anything like that to a woman before, let alone to one he had thought he loved only yesterday. *Well, I guess this proves you're not all that different from your old lady after all. At least she'd approve of using sex as a weapon.*

TED CAME into the house and stopped to contemplate the closed door to the master bedroom. When he thought he heard Caroline cry out in distress, it took everything he had not to storm in there to get her. *Son of a bitch!*

PARKER WALKED out of the kitchen with a beer to find Ted staring at Smitty's bedroom door with fire in his eyes.

What the fuck?

"Duff?"

Ted looked up at him with unseeing eyes.

"What's wrong?"

"I thought I heard someone crying."

"She looked pissed at the pool," Parker said, nodding at the closed door.

"Yeah." Ted's jaw clenched and a tick of tension fluttered in his cheek. "I'm going to pack."

"Okay." Parker took a long swig from his beer as he watched his friend take the stairs two at a time.

What the fuck?

"CHIP," Elise whispered with a giggle, tearing herself away from him. "Save it until we get home. We have to pack."

He grabbed her waist with both hands and hauled her back

to him. "That's hours and hours from now. I can't wait that long."

She pushed her backside against his erection in a pretend attempt to escape from him. "You just had some this morning."

He groaned from the feel of her pressed against him. "That was hours and hours ago." Cupping her breasts from behind, he teased her nipples. "Come on. Just a quickie."

"What's with you today?" she asked with amusement as she turned to face him.

"Being engaged makes me horny."

Wrapping her arms around his neck, she laughed. "What's going to happen when we're married?"

He backed her up to the bed and tumbled down on top of her. "I think it might get worse."

She trembled with desire. "Oh, boy."

CHAPTER 18

With the notable exception of the still-euphoric Chip and Elise, a quiet group left the Duffy's home to catch the three thirty ferry leaving Block Island that Sunday afternoon. Other than a gracious goodbye and thank you to Ted's parents and grandparents, Caroline hadn't said a word to any of them before they left the house. This time she squeezed into the front seat with Elise rather than sit on Smitty's lap.

The tearful goodbye with his mother and grandmother had left Ted feeling sad. He didn't get to spend as much time with them as he would like to these days, but they would be back in Boston after Labor Day. *I need to make a point of seeing Grandy and Grampa at least once a week from now on. They're not going to live forever.*

He glanced over at Smitty who stared intently out the window on his side of the car. *He and Caroline must've had a fight. Good timing in light of what she's going to tell him when they get home. By the time this day is over, she'll be free, but he'll be heartbroken.*

Smitty's behavior at the pool had rattled Ted—not just because he had wanted to scream at the sight of another man's hands on the woman he now thought of as his. No, it was more than that. Smitty's demonstration had given Ted the chance to see for himself how deep Smitty's feelings for her were.

The thought of his friend being hurt bothered Ted, but not quite as much as the thought of her being in bed with Smitty had bothered him. He was dying to know what had transpired between them when they returned to the house from the pool, but he would have to wait to find out until she called him later.

On the ferry ride back to the mainland, Chip and Elise stood by the rail whispering and giggling. Caroline pretended to be engrossed in a book, Smitty went downstairs to the bar, Parker tipped his head back and went to sleep, and Ted took advantage of the opportunity to gaze at Caroline when no one was paying attention to him.

Ten minutes before the ferry landed, an announcement called the car owners down to the freight dock. The New York contingent stood up and gathered their belongings. With quick hugs for Ted and Parker and murmurs of "good time," "thanks for having us," and "see you next weekend," they were gone.

Four hours back to the city and an hour to talk to Smitty. Ted checked his watch. *I should hear from her by nine thirty, ten at the latest. Five hours.*

SMITTY OFFERED TO DRIVE, which is how Caroline ended up in the passenger seat listening to Chip and Elise whisper and kiss in the back seat. *This is going to be a* long *four hours.* Smitty had ignored her since the incident in the bedroom, which was fine with her. As she glanced over at him to find his face expressionless and his eyes fixed on the road, she couldn't believe what had happened earlier. He had been like someone she had never met before and bore no resemblance to the generous, thoughtful man she had come to know. She couldn't imagine what had gotten into him.

She rehearsed what she needed to say to him. *It's been a lot of fun. I'm so glad I met you, but this isn't working out. I hope we can still be friends.* Her stomach fluttered with nerves as she imagined his reaction to hearing that. And then she thought of Ted, and the knowledge they would be together again in two weeks was enough to sustain her through whatever might happen with Smitty.

That's what I need to do. I need to focus on Ted and my feelings for him. That will get me through this. He'll be there for me when it's done. I wish I were with him right now.

With a deep sigh, she eased her head back against the headrest and drifted off to sleep to pass the endless time in the car.

THE RIDE back to Boston was marked by quiet, as well. Ted's mind raced as he relived the events of the weekend. He was filled with anxiety as he thought about Caroline breaking up with Smitty. Ted wanted that part done for everyone's sake.

"What's going on, Duff?" Parker asked about thirty minutes after they left Point Judith.

"Nothing. Why?"

"I've known you a long time, man. Something's up."

"I could say the same thing to you. Smitty asked me yesterday if I know anything about a girl you're interested in. Something you said to him the other night has him wondering what's going on with you."

"How'd this get turned around on me? We were talking about you."

"Well, now we're talking about *you*."

"There's not much to tell. I'm interested in someone, but I don't really want to get into it just yet."

"Who is she?" Ted asked, relieved to have something else to think about besides his own situation.

"Someone I met through work."

"Does she like you, too?"

Parker shrugged. "I have no idea."

"Well, when are you going to find out?"

"In four days."

"What's in four days?"

"The one-year anniversary of her divorce."

"She's a *client?*"

"Ex-client."

"Tell me," Ted urged.

Parker glanced over at him and appeared to be debating whether he should say more. "I'm afraid to jinx myself."

"Well, cross your fingers or something. But you have to tell me."

Parker laughed. "What kind of stupid superstition is that?"

"Old Irish folklore."

Parker raised a hand, crossed his fingers, and told Ted about Gina.

When he was done, Ted took his eyes off the road long enough to stare at his friend. "You've been in love with this woman for *two years,* and you've never said *anything* to us?"

Parker shrugged. "There was no point in talking about it when there was nothing I could do about it. Her divorce was ugly—as bad as it gets. She needed time to get her life back on track before she could think about being with someone else."

"But you've dated other people in the last two years."

"Just to kill time. I didn't sleep with any of them."

"You're kidding me."

"Nope."

"Holy shit, you've got it bad! If I were you I wouldn't wait one more day to contact her."

"I've waited this long. Four more days won't matter."

"Parker, come on! This isn't the nineteenth century. Chivalry only goes so far. What if you've already waited too long?"

"Believe me, I've had a lot of sleepless nights over that very possibility, but something tells me that giving her the full year was the right thing to do. I'm in the home stretch now anyway."

Ted sighed. "I hope you know what you're doing."

"I have no idea what I'm doing. I just know what I feel when she's in the room, and it's something I want to feel every day for the rest of my life."

Ted knew exactly what Parker meant.

"It's like Chip said the other night, we all want what your parents and grandparents have had. Is that too much to ask for?"

"No," Ted said. "No one should settle for anything less than everything."

"Exactly. Now, are you going to tell me what's going on with you?"

Oh, how I wish I could. I'd love nothing more than to unload on you, but I won't put you in that position, Parker. "For the first time, I'm dreading going to work tomorrow," Ted said, voicing a thought that had been on his mind lately.

"Why?"

"Up until recently, I've been able to deal with all the highs and lows, but the lows have been hitting harder and lasting longer than they used to. I'm starting to wonder if I might be burned out or something."

"I'm surprised it's taken this long."

"Sometimes it's hard to have perspective when you're in the midst of it," Ted continued. "My boss is sending me to a conference on grief and loss for physicians in a couple of weeks at Sloan Kettering. You know you're in trouble when you think you could actually benefit from that bullshit."

"Well, at least you can get away for a couple of days and have some fun while you're in New York."

"Yeah."

"Listen, Duff. Just because your father and grandfather stuck with pediatric oncology for their entire careers doesn't mean you have to. I know you worry about letting them down, but this *your* life. You have to do what's best for you."

"You're right, their opinions do factor in even if I wish they didn't. I'm going to give it some thought over the next few months and see what develops. I don't want to give one patient too much credit or blame, but losing Joey was a blow. It was like something in me kind of shut down after that. And in my line of work, being emotionally removed isn't a luxury I can afford."

"You've had a bad month, and it's probably best not to do anything rash right now."

"I know. I need to ride it out for a while until things are more normal and I can think clearly."

"That's a good idea. You love that job, Duff. It's getting you down right now, but I think you'd regret it if you walked away without giving it careful consideration."

"I know I would."

"Well, I'm here if you need to vent."

"And I'm going to be dying to know what happens when Gina gets those flowers."

"Me, too," Parker said with a sigh. "Me, too."

SMITTY PULLED up to Caroline's building right at ten o'clock. Traffic in Connecticut and on the New England Thruway had added an hour to an already interminable ride. Chip and Elise got out of the backseat and helped Smitty and Caroline retrieve their bags.

Chip shook hands with Smitty. "See you Friday, if not before."

"Sounds good."

Caroline hugged Elise. "Congratulations again. I want to hear all about the wedding plans."

"Oh, you will. Don't worry."

Chip and Elise got back in the car and pulled into traffic, leaving Smitty and Caroline standing on the sidewalk.

She looked up at him. "I want to ask you to come in because we need to talk, but after what happened earlier I don't know if I want you in my house."

"I'm sorry about that. I was totally out of line, and I apologize."

She eyed him warily. "All right, then. Come on in."

Smitty carried their bags and her crutches up the stairs to the brownstone where she rented the first floor.

She unlocked the door and flipped on the lights.

He dropped his two bags next to the door. "Where do you want these?" he asked, holding her bags.

"Right there is fine, thanks. I'll take care of them later. Do you want something to drink?"

"No, I'm good."

After a moment of awkward silence she turned to him. "Smitty—"

"Caroline—"

"Go ahead." She twisted her hands. "You go first."

"I really am sorry about what happened before. There's no excuse for that kind of behavior. No excuse at all. I hope you'll forgive me." He looked down, and his foot nudged at the edge of the faded oriental carpet that covered the wood floor.

"I do forgive you."

He slanted his eyes back up to meet hers. "I think we both know this isn't working."

She stared at him in amazement. He *was breaking up with* her? *For real? After the way he'd acted earlier at the pool?*

"I've had a really great time with you, but I think it's run its course, don't you?"

Astounded, Caroline stared at him. "If that's how you feel," she sputtered, "what was with that whole alpha male act at the pool today?"

He shrugged. "I was just enjoying the time we had left on Block Island. I can't believe you're surprised. I haven't exactly been feeling the love from you the last week or two."

"See, that's the thing. I'd kind of been feeling it from you. The love that is."

He snorted. "Sweetheart, you're a great girl, and we've had some fun times, but that's all it was. Fun. I'm sorry if you read more into it than that."

Thrown, Caroline said, "No need to be sorry. It *was* fun, and I enjoyed being with you. Very much. I hope we can still be friends."

"Sure we can. I'm going to be out of the country for a month, maybe two. When I get back we can go for a drink or something."

"Where are you going?" she asked, confused. *What's going on here?*

"My partners asked me to go to Sydney to check out a company we want to acquire that's headquartered there. I didn't want to say anything about it until after the Duffys' party."

"You haven't told the guys?"

He shook his head. "You're the first to know. I'd been putting off going because it's summer and we've got the house in Newport. But they told me Thursday they want me there within the week. I didn't want to get everyone wound up about it this weekend."

Caroline was reeling. "Will you let me know you got there safely?"

"I can do that. So what did you want to say?

"Nothing." She took a step toward him. "It doesn't matter now."

He leaned in to kiss her cheek. "Take care."

"You, too."

He picked up his bags at the door and turned back to look at her one last time but didn't say anything more.

After the door had closed quietly behind him, Caroline dropped into the closest chair. *What the hell just happened here?*

CHAPTER 19

Smitty left Caroline's and went to the corner to hail a cab. The Upper East Side traffic was heavy for a Sunday night in July, and when he had waited fifteen minutes without getting a cab, he decided to walk the ten blocks home.

Tossing his duffel and garment bags over his shoulder, he trudged slowly north through the humid night. He had gone about three blocks when the numbness wore off and the pain caught up to him. He lowered himself to a stoop in front of another brownstone and dropped his head into his hands. After the longest twenty-four hours of his life, he was finally alone and no longer had to hide how devastated he was by the betrayal of two people he cared the most about. He was finally free to let it out.

The street was deserted otherwise the sight of the strapping man crying surely would have attracted the attention of passersby.

She knew I loved her. Smitty wiped his face with the back of his hand. *She knew, which means he probably knows, too. Are they having a laugh at my expense right at this moment? No, Ted wouldn't do that.*

Smitty laughed through his tears. *Yeah, well, you didn't think he'd steal your girlfriend, either.*

He sat in the dark thinking about the time he had spent with

Caroline, the years he'd considered Ted Duffy his best friend, and the awesome task he had ahead of him as he learned to live without them. What he had told her about the trip to Sydney was only partially true. His company hoped to buy a small investment firm there. That part was true as was what he had said about being asked to send someone to check it out. He'd even had the ideal employee in mind for the due diligence study that needed to be done before the purchase could go forward. He'd had no intention of going himself until he overheard Ted and Caroline the other night and realized that being halfway around the world for the next month or two would have its benefits.

No way was he going to stick around to watch the two of them together. No freaking way. Since he planned to maintain his friendship with Parker and Chip, he would have to see Ted occasionally. That would be hard to avoid. But he needed some time to get used to the idea of Ted and Caroline as a couple before he had to see it.

I wonder what he plans to tell Chip and Parker about her. It's not like he can just show up with her in Newport next weekend and act like it's no big deal, right? So what's your plan, Ted? Going to have to keep this under wraps for a while, aren't you? You'll be concerned about alienating Chip and Parker, too, so you won't tell them—at least until a respectable amount of time has passed. Let me ask you this, my friend, how much time is enough when you've stolen your best friend's girl? I'm sure I'll hear all *about it when he decides to go public with her, but I sure as hell ain't going to be around to see it.*

Smitty got up, grabbed his bags, and covered the last seven blocks quickly. All at once he just wanted to be home.

TED WAS PACING in the living room of his condo when Caroline finally called at eleven fifteen. His heart in his throat, he pounced on the cell phone. "Hey."

"Hi. Sorry it's so late."

"I was starting to seriously freak out. Are you all right?"

"I think so."

"Was it bad?"

"No, it was . . . um . . . odd."

"Odd how?"

"He broke up with me."

Ted was speechless.

"He said, 'I think we both know this has run its course. It's been fun, you're a great girl, but it's not going anywhere.'" When Ted didn't reply, she said, "Are you still there?"

"I'm here. I'm just stunned. I mean he was making me crazy acting so possessive at the pool today."

"I asked him why he had done that if he was planning to break up with me, and he said he was enjoying the time we had left on Block Island. He said he was sorry if I had read more into it than that."

"Everyone was so sure he was in love with you."

"He laughed when I said that."

"I can't figure this out."

"Me either. Get this, too. He's going to Sydney for at least a month for work."

Processing it all, Ted ran a hand through his hair. "When did that happen?"

"Apparently his partners told him Thursday they want him to go check out a company they want to buy. He didn't want to say anything about it until after the weekend."

"None of this makes any sense."

"I've been sitting here for thirty minutes trying to make sense of it myself."

"You don't think . . ."

"What?"

"No . . ."

"What were you going to say?"

"Do you think somehow he knows about us?"

"No way," she said. "He would've flipped out, don't you think?"

"I would think so. What if Parker told him what he came

home to Friday night and somehow Smitty put two and two together?"

"Did Parker talk to you about that?"

"He asked me if I'd heard anything, and I said no. I hated lying to him, but it wasn't like I could admit that you'd been upstairs talking to me while I was in bed. He said he didn't tell Smitty about it, and I got the impression he didn't plan to."

Her sigh was deep and pained. "This is a terrible way for us to start a relationship, Ted. All these lies and people getting hurt because of us."

"I know. I think I'm getting an ulcer from the stress of it." He realized she was crying. "Oh, Caroline, don't."

"I can't help it. This has been a *very* long day."

"What happened after you guys left the pool?" The desire to know had burned in him for hours.

"Nothing," she whispered.

"When I heard you crying in there I almost took down the door."

She was crying so hard now she couldn't speak.

Ted's jaw clenched with tension. "Caroline, honey, tell me."

"I can't."

"You're frightening me. *Please*. Tell me." He heard her sniffling as she tried to control her tears.

"He wanted to . . . you know . . . have sex."

Ted exhaled a long deep breath and waited for her to continue.

"I told him to stop a couple of times, but he wouldn't. He was really rough with me, and for a minute . . ."

"What, honey?" Ted whispered.

"I thought he was going to rape me."

"*No*," Ted gasped. "No. He wouldn't. He *couldn't*."

"He was going to. I know he was. But I yelled at him to stop, and all of sudden he finally heard me. It was almost like he went a little crazy or something."

"I'm coming there. Right now."

"No, Ted! You can't! It's too late, and you have to work tomorrow. I'm all right. He apologized."

"I don't *care* if he apologized! I can't believe he would do something like that. That's not the Smitty I know." Once again Ted's gut clenched at the thought that Smitty might've felt he had good reason to want to punish Caroline. "I'm leaving right now." He picked up the bag he hadn't yet unpacked from the weekend. Whatever else he needed he would buy in New York. "Just give me your address, and I'll be there in a few hours."

"You don't need to come," she insisted in a voice still hoarse with tears and emotion. "What about work?"

"I'm going to do something I haven't done in six years—call in sick. I need to be with you right now, Caroline. I can't wait two weeks. Not after all this."

"You're going to fall asleep at the wheel. I can't let you do this."

Cradling his cell phone in the crook of his neck, he tossed his bag into the trunk of the car. "After what you just told me, do you honestly think I could sleep without seeing for myself that you're all right?"

"Ted . . ."

"I'm on my way. I can't believe everything that has happened, but it seems that I find myself head over heels in love with you, and I'm going to be there as soon as I can. Now, are you going to tell me where you live?"

She laughed through her tears and gave him her address. "This is crazy. You're crazy."

"Crazy about you," he said softly as he pushed the Mercedes up to eighty-five on his way to I-93 South.

"I never imagined I could feel so good and so bad at the same time."

"It's going to get better. We just have to get through this rough patch, and then everything's going to be fine."

"Promise?"

"I promise. I can't believe I can talk to you whenever I want to now. You're going to get fed up with me calling you all the time."

"I don't think I'll ever run out of things I want to tell you."

"I hope you never do. In light of this new-found freedom of

ours, do you know what I've been dying to ask you for two weeks?"

"What?"

"Right before you fell when we were running you were going to tell me something you said was a secret. We never got around to finishing that conversation."

She chuckled. "No, we didn't, did we?"

"What was the big secret?"

"I'm going to write a book," she confessed. "I've actually already started it."

"*Really?* That's awesome! What's it about?"

"A dashing young doctor falls in love with his best friend's girlfriend," she teased.

He laughed. "I'm sure it'll be a best seller."

"I don't know about that," she said softly. "But it's going to be one hell of a romance."

"Oh, yes." The rush of emotion took his breath away. "Yes, it is."

CHAPTER 20

Ted lost twenty minutes when he was stopped for speeding outside Greenwich, Connecticut. He tossed the four-hundred-dollar ticket onto the passenger seat and hit the gas the minute the state trooper was out of sight.

He had convinced Caroline to try to get some sleep and told her he would call her when he got close. At one thirty he stopped for coffee and called the hospital. He told them he had strep throat and asked them to call in another attending physician to cover for him for the next two days. As he got closer to New York City, his heart began to pound with excitement and nerves and anticipation. Twelve hours hadn't passed since he had last seen her, but it had been too long.

The city that never sleeps was indeed wide-awake at a quarter to three that Monday morning. Ted wove between trucks and cabs as he made his way to the Upper East Side. When he reached the east Fifties, he called her, and the sound of her sleepy voice was enough to arouse him. "I'm five minutes away."

"I'll be waiting for you."

He flipped the phone closed and willed his pounding heart and jittery stomach to chill out. Even though he was accustomed to going without sleep, he wasn't used to middle-of-the-night road trips and was wired from the caffeine he had relied upon to stay awake.

In a stroke of good luck that he took as a sign of things to come, someone was pulling out of a parking space in front of Caroline's house, so he grabbed the spot and dashed across the street. She waited for him at the top of the stairs wearing a pale green silk robe over the same type of short nightgown that had dominated his fantasies since he first saw her in it on Friday night.

He took the stairs two at a time and had her in his arms so quickly neither of them had time to brace themselves for the onslaught of emotion. Her tears were warm against his neck as he held her tightly to him.

Several long minutes later he pulled back to brush the tears off her cheeks with his lips before he tipped her face up to receive his kiss. "Finally," he whispered against her lips.

Ted felt the punch of the hot, deep kiss everywhere. He lifted her to him, and she managed, even with her cast, to wrap her legs around his waist. Without breaking the kiss he moved through the open door and into her apartment. Kicking the door closed behind him, he lowered her onto the sofa and came down on top of her. Urgent need thrummed through him, but he forced himself to slow down and to remember what had brought him here in the middle of the night.

He kissed her eyelids, the end of her nose, both cheeks, and then her lips again, but this time he was gentle.

She moaned and tightened her arms around him.

"Did he hurt you?" Ted whispered. "Are you hurt anywhere?"

"No, it wasn't like that. I don't want you to think about it anymore."

"If he was anyone else I'd want to kill him for hurting you."

"He didn't hurt me so much as scare me."

Ted trembled at the feel of her fingers on his back. "I love you," he whispered against her neck. "I love you so much. No one's ever going to scare you like that again. Ever." He found her lips and fell into another soulful kiss.

"I love you, too," she said. "I can't believe it, but I do."

"Believe it." He realized just then that he wanted to kiss her like this every day for the rest of his life. He'd never experienced anything quite as intoxicating as kissing Caroline.

"Did you call work?" she asked when they finally resurfaced.

"Mmm," he said against her lips. "I took two days because I'm so sick."

"Two days," she said with a contented sigh. "What do I need to be afraid of catching?"

"Strep throat." He dipped his tongue to tangle with hers. "It's highly contagious."

She met his teasing tongue with playful nips of her teeth. "I don't think I've been adequately exposed."

He chuckled. "I can fix that."

She writhed beneath him, her hips arching against his erection, causing his breath to catch in his throat.

"Caroline, honey, wait."

"What's wrong?"

"I want you so much that sometimes I think I'll go mad from wanting you. But everything's moved so fast. Will you think I'm crazy if I just want to hold you for a while until I catch my breath? Now that we have all the time in the world I'd like to take my time. Does that make sense?"

She silenced him with a kiss. "I'm kind of relieved to hear that actually. This has been such a crazy, emotional couple of days. I think we both need some sleep more than anything. Before we sleep, though, how about a snack?"

He sat up and took her hand to help her up. "What do you have in mind?"

"I make a mean omelet."

The word made his stomach rumble. "That sounds great." When he stood to follow her, he finally looked around at her apartment. The walls were a dark taupe, the sofas were red, the artwork colorful, and the pillows plump. One whole wall was a bookshelf filled to overflowing. Later he would take the time to find out what she liked to read. He couldn't wait to know everything about her. The kitchen was small, but painted in a bright yellow that made it seem bigger. "I love your place."

"Thanks. Do you want some coffee?" she asked, gathering the ingredients for the omelet.

"Not if I have any plans to sleep in the next twelve hours. I've already had a ton."

She smiled as she chopped a red pepper and dropped a bagel into the toaster on the counter.

Ted sat at the tiny table and watched her move efficiently around the kitchen. When she had poured the egg, pepper, and cheese into the pan he got up to hug her from behind as she stood watch over the stove.

"Do you like to cook or is it just a necessity?" he asked.

She leaned her head against his shoulder. "I love to cook."

"Oh, lucky me. I love to eat."

She laughed, and the sound filled his heart.

While his tongue explored her neck, he took his hands on a slow journey from her belly to her breasts, and her breath hitched when he teased her nipples.

"You're going to make me burn the eggs if you keep that up," she said even as she pushed back against his erection.

The bagel popped out of the toaster, startling them.

Ted laughed. "Bagel's ready."

She turned to kiss him and nudge him back into the chair so she could finish the omelet. But before she could escape, he grabbed her hand and tugged her onto his lap.

"Ted!"

He captured her protesting mouth in a deep kiss and then released her as suddenly as he had taken her.

"You're very distracting," she said with mock exasperation.

"You love me."

She turned to look at him. "Yes, I do."

He held her gaze for a long moment until the sizzle in the pan forced her to look away.

She brought bright yellow Fiesta plates to the table and went back for silverware. Opening the fridge, she said, "I have OJ, water, and milk. What's your pleasure?"

"OJ would be great. Thanks."

She carried two tall glasses of juice to the table and sat across from him. "How is it?"

He groaned with appreciation. "Fabulous." He took a drink of his juice. "There's so much about you I don't know, such as the fact you can cook like a dream."

"That's nothing," she said of the omelet. "What else do you want to know?"

"You've met my whole family, but I don't even know if you have brothers or sisters."

"One of each. My sister, Courtney, is a trauma nurse in L.A. She's married to a film animator named Paul, and they have two sons, Jimmy and Justin. My brother, Cooper, is an executive with an insurance company in Chicago. He just got married in April. His wife's name is Ellen."

"Who's the oldest?"

"That'd be me. I'm two years older than Court and four years older than Coop."

Ted chuckled. "I don't even know how old you are."

"Thirty-three. And you're thirty-seven, right?"

He nodded. "Thirty-eight in September."

"What day?"

"The fourth."

"September fourth." She rested her chin on her hand as she gazed at him. "That day will never be the same now."

"When's your birthday?" he asked with a smile.

"January ninth."

"And that day will never be the same for me." He drained the last of his juice. "What about your parents?"

"They still live in upstate New York where we grew up."

"What town?"

"Saratoga Springs."

"I went to the horse races there with my grandparents when I was a kid," he said. "A few times, in fact."

"I wonder if I was there! We used to go all the time."

He reached for her hand across the table. "Maybe we met decades ago and were fated to find our way back to each other."

"Maybe so."

"Do you believe in such things?"

"I do now."

He kissed her hand. "What I want more than anything at this moment is to take you to bed and make love to you until you forget every other man you've ever known."

"I already have," she said breathlessly. "There's only you."

He kept her hand at his mouth. "But I want it to be perfect, and between driving all night and work and thinking about you and thinking about you being in bed with my friend, I haven't slept in what feels like a week. I'm so tired."

She stood up and gave his hand a gentle tug to bring him with her.

"We need to clean up in here," he said.

"Later."

He followed her into the living room. "Let me run out to the car and get my bag." He returned a few minutes later with a sheepish grin on his face. "I didn't even lock my car before."

"That's dangerous in this city. Especially a car like yours."

"I wasn't thinking clearly when I got here."

Her smile was coy. "And are you now?"

He shook his head. "I'm beginning to understand that I'll never think clearly again."

With her hands on his hips, she brought him close to her. "The honeymoon period will end one day, and you'll be able to think again. We both will."

"It's not going to end." He brought her close enough to kiss. "It's never going to end."

She led him into the hallway where she pointed out the bathroom and her office in the spare bedroom. Her bedroom walls were painted a pale lilac. A framed Georgia O'Keefe print in full, glorious red hung over an elaborate wrought iron gate that served as a headboard. The bed was rumpled from her earlier rest, so she straightened it and turned down the other side for him. More books were piled on the bedside table next to a framed photo of two blond boys who he assumed were her nephews.

Ted put his bag on the white whicker chair in the corner and dug out his toothbrush. "Save my place. I'll be right back." When he returned, she took her turn in the bathroom. Ted tugged his T-shirt over his head and kicked off his flip-flops. When she came back, he was looking out the window as the sun began to rise, casting pale light on the flowers in her tiny backyard. The rustle of silk told him she had taken off her robe.

She came up behind him, looped her arms around him, and rested her face against his back. "You feel so good."

He put his hands on top of hers. "I can't believe I'm here with you like this—in your room, getting ready to go to bed together like we've been doing it forever." He turned to her and ran his hands over her nightgown. "This little number has been playing a big part in my fantasies since I first saw it the other night."

She smiled. "I have a bunch of them."

"I want to see them one at a time, first on you and then in a heap on the floor."

She giggled. "That can be arranged. Come on. You need some sleep."

"I'm wondering if I'm going to be able to sleep with you next to me."

"You will."

He dropped his shorts, got in next to her, and reached for her. "Finally," he sighed. "Finally in bed with you." With a finger to her jaw he tipped up her face so he could see her eyes. "There's nowhere on earth I'd rather be, Caroline."

"I've waited so long for you. I thought I'd never find you."

"Now that you have, I'm never going to let you go." He kissed her, and for a moment she let him. Then she pulled away to close his eyes with her hand.

"Sleep," she whispered.

Keeping his eyes closed, he said, "I have more questions."

"Two more and then sleep."

"Who's your best friend?"

"Tiffany Bartlett Wallingbrook."

He opened one eye to see if she was serious. "Is she as prissy as her name?"

Caroline laughed. "She's the sweetest girl I've ever known,

and she's been my best friend since first grade. I have a picture of us in Brownies together."

"I'm going to need to see that."

"After you sleep."

"Where's Tiffany Bartlett Wallingbrook now?"

"She went to Emory College in Atlanta and married Brett Wallingbrook, son of the now ex-governor of Georgia. They live in Atlanta with their daughters Savannah and Augusta, and Brett's on his way to a career in politics, too."

"They named their daughters Savannah and Augusta?"

"Sure did. If they had a boy he was going to be Macon."

Ted laughed quietly as sleep closed in on him. "Augusta's lucky she was a girl," he said. "Can I ask my second question?"

"Well, technically it's your third, but only if you promise to sleep after."

"Mmm," he mumbled in agreement as his breathing became heavier. "What are you most afraid of?"

She didn't hesitate. "Losing you now that I've finally found you."

He wrapped his leg around her and pulled her tight against him to let her know he'd meant it when he said he would never let her go.

CHAPTER 21

Smitty knew he was being a masochist when he asked his driver to take him down Caroline's street on the way to the financial district in lower Manhattan on Monday morning. The car and driver were one of the perks of partnership that he took full advantage of since battling his way from one end of the congested city to the other used to be his least favorite part of the work day. He usually used the time in the car to make phone calls and check his e-mail as well as the Tokyo and London exchange numbers on his BlackBerry. But today he stared out the window without seeing much of anything.

The Lincoln Town Car turned onto Caroline's street, which was still quiet at six thirty. Smitty fixed his eyes on her front door and had he not looked away in pain over what had transpired there yesterday he might have missed the black Mercedes with the unmistakable Massachusetts plates: ETD3MD. Smitty had been there the Christmas morning two years earlier when Lillian had given each of the doctors Duffy the vanity plates: ETD1MD for Theo, ETD2MD for Ed, and ETD3MD for Ted. They had been embarrassed by the silly—and vain—gift, but they never would have said so to Lillian, who had been delighted by her clever idea.

Smitty had thought he was mad before, but what he felt now was just rage—pure white-hot rage. *That motherfucker didn't waste any time*. Was he on his way here when I was still with her? Are they in her bed right now making up for lost time? *Son of a bitch*.

He admitted to himself right then that he had hoped to somehow salvage his friendship with Ted, despite what had happened. He had hoped his longtime friend would manage to explain his actions in a way Smitty could live with so they could continue to be friends. But all those hopes evaporated the minute he spotted that car parked on her street.

"Mr. Smith?" the driver was saying. "Mr. Smith?"

Startled out of his thoughts, Smitty said, "Yes?"

"Have you seen what you needed to see here?"

"Yes. I've seen more than enough."

STILL REELING, Smitty rode the elevator to the thirty-sixth floor. His large office overlooked the footprint of what used to be the World Trade Center towers. Today, though, he didn't take the time to look out and remember. He dropped his briefcase on his cluttered desk and went straight to the senior partner's office.

Bill Kepler's assistant waved him in.

With a perfunctory knock, Smitty walked into Kepler's massive office with its panoramic view of Manhattan, the Hudson River, and New Jersey in the distance.

"Morning."

"Hey, Smitty, come on in. I was just talking about you. Were your ears ringing?"

Smitty didn't notice the joking smile on his boss's face nor did he care why Kepler had been talking about him, but he knew better than to be curt to the man who had been so good to him in the ten years since he had joined the firm. "No ringing ears. What's going on?"

"I just got off the phone with James King. He's thrilled with the latest report and was singing your praises."

"That's good to hear. I need to give him a call today to run a few new ideas by him, but that's not why I'm here."

Kepler sat back in his large chair and eyed Smitty with interest. "What's going on?"

"I've decided to see to the Australia project personally. I just wanted you to know I'm on a flight to L.A. tonight."

Kepler's surprise showed on his face. "I thought you were sending Peter."

"I thought about it this weekend, and it's something I'd like to take care of myself."

"Is something else going on? I mean, don't get me wrong, I'd love to have you handle it, but it never occurred to me that you'd want to."

Smitty shrugged. "It interests me. It's as simple as that."

Kepler brought his hands together in an A frame under his chin as he thought it over. "You'd be able to maintain your accounts from Sydney, I presume."

Smitty knew he meant James King's account in particular. "Of course."

Kepler leaned forward to dig a thick file out of a stack on his desk. "Here's the file on the Jergenson Investment Company. As I mentioned in the partner meeting the other day, Norman Jergenson died two months ago. His daughter, Marjorie, is seeking a buyer, which fits well with our plans to expand into the Australian market. She approached us first and isn't entertaining other offers until we make a decision. I got the sense when I talked to her last week that she's primarily concerned with her employees and wants to find a buyer who'll retain as many of them as possible."

"If everything checks out I'd envision a name change but not much else," Smitty said as he flipped through the file. "Is that what you have in mind?"

"Exactly. If you're not liking what you see with Jergenson, let me know, and we'll have you take a look at some of the other possibilities while you're there."

"I will."

"Marjorie mentioned they have an apartment in their office building that's available to whomever we send for the due diligence study."

"That makes it easy." Smitty stood up and shook Kepler's hand.

"Marjorie's, um, what's the word I'm looking for . . . She's prickly. Well, you'll see what I mean. I'm sure you can handle her."

Smitty nodded in agreement. "I'll keep you in the loop."

Kepler gave him another measuring look. "Have a safe trip."

Smitty returned to his own office and closed the door. Reaching for his cell phone, he dialed Chip at his midtown office. When he learned Dr. Taggert was with a patient, he left a message and called Parker.

"Hey, you just caught me," Parker said. "I'm due in court in fifteen minutes."

"I can call you later." Smitty's nerves were raw as he took the steps necessary to make a clean getaway.

"I've got a few minutes. What's up?"

"I wanted to let you know I'm going to be in Sydney for the next month or two."

"Huh? What's in Sydney?"

Smitty filled him in on the trip but not his reason for going.

"Wow, well, that's a bummer. You'll miss the rest of the summer in Newport."

"I know. You guys can decide if you want to bring in another roommate. I don't care about the money."

"It won't be the same without you."

"You definitely won't eat as well," Smitty joked.

Parker laughed. "That's a fact."

"There's, ah, one other thing I wanted to tell you."

"What's that?"

"Caroline and I broke up."

"You did?" Parker asked, shocked. "*Why?*"

"Well, it didn't seem fair to ask her to sit around while I'm gone for a month, especially when we both know it's not going the distance."

"That's not the impression you've been giving us."

"It's either there or it isn't." Smitty winced. "In this case, it wasn't."

"Jeez, Smitty, I don't know what to say. I'm sorry. I really thought you might've found the one for you."

So did I, Smitty thought. "The search continues. Any progress with your situation?"

"Not yet, but in a few days I hope to be able to say more about it."

"Well, good luck. Send me an e-mail, and let me know what happens."

"I will."

"Can you do me a favor and tell Duff what's going on? I've tried to call him a couple of times today, and all I get is his voicemail. I don't want to leave a three-minute message, so do you mind filling him in?"

"Sure, no problem. Keep in touch while you're down under, you hear?"

"Oh, you'll be hearing from me, don't worry."

"Take care of yourself, Smitty."

"Will do."

Smitty hung up and when Chip called twenty minutes later, he had almost the same conversation with him. Finally, he called Mitzi on Block Island.

"Hi, honey, this is a nice surprise," she said in that breathless voice of hers.

"Thanks for the fabulous weekend. You and Lillian really know how to throw a party."

"It was fun, wasn't it? It's so sweet of you to call."

"I also wanted to tell you I'm going to be in Australia for the next month or so for work."

"Oh, no! You'll miss all of August in Newport."

"I know, but it was a great opportunity to spend some time in another country, so I didn't want to pass it up."

"Caroline must be beside herself."

Actually she's beside your son in bed at the moment. "We broke up yesterday."

"*Oh, Smitty,*" Mitzi gasped. "What happened?"

"Just wasn't meant to be, I guess."

"I was so sure about her. We all liked her so much. I'm sorry."

"I am, too. Well, I need to get back to work so I can get to the airport on time this afternoon."

"I'm glad you called. Are you all right, honey?"

"I'm disappointed," he said, putting it mildly. "But I'll survive. I always do."

"I'm here if you need me. You know that, right?"

Touched by her support, he said, "I sure do."

"Send us a postcard from Australia."

"You got it. Give everyone my love, and thanks again for a great time this weekend."

"We love you, Smitty. You remember that."

"I will," he whispered, surprised when his eyes filled. "Thank you."

SMITTY LEFT Kennedy on a six o'clock flight that got him into Los Angeles at eight forty-five p.m. Pacific time. At LAX, he killed almost three hours in The Qantas Club before boarding an eleven fifty flight to Sydney. Fourteen hours and thirty-five minutes of first-class luxury later, he landed in Sydney where it was Wednesday morning. Somewhere over the Pacific he had lost Tuesday, but he didn't care. Tuesday would have been a shitty day anyway.

CHAPTER 22

Ted chased Caroline in the fog. Screeching gulls, pounding surf, and powdery sand beneath his feet at the beach. The soft breeze had captured her long blond hair and the skirt of her flowing white dress. Two blond children ran in circles around her legs, making her laugh with delight. Ted tried to catch up to them, but no matter how hard he ran, he couldn't reach them. When they began to fade from sight, he called out to them.

"Hey," Caroline whispered in his ear. "You're dreaming."

Ted came awake slowly and was disoriented for a brief moment. "I couldn't get to you." His voice was hoarse from sleep. "And then you began to disappear."

"I'm right here." She put her arm around him and rested her head on his chest. "I'm not going anywhere."

"There were two kids." He twirled a lock of her long hair around his finger. "Two blond kids." He leaned in to kiss her. "If our children have anything other than blond hair, you and the postman are going to be in a lot of trouble."

She smiled and looked up at him, her green eyes shimmering with emotion. "Our children," she sighed. "Did we have boys or girls?"

"I couldn't tell." He yawned and stretched. "What time is it?"

"Two thirty."

He turned to see if she was serious. "Get out. Really?"

She grinned and nodded.

"We slept for *nine and a half* hours?"

"*You* slept for nine and a half hours."

He winced. "How long have you been awake?"

"About two hours."

"Sorry."

"Why? I had the best time watching you sleep."

Not sure whether to be touched or embarrassed, Ted sat up and ran a hand through his hair, realizing the cloud of fatigue that had hung over him for days had finally lifted. He couldn't remember the last time he'd had such a concentrated dose of sleep. "I'll be right back," he said, getting up to go to the bathroom. He returned a minute later and got back into bed with her. "So you really watched me sleep for two hours?"

Propped up on one elbow, she looked down at him. "Uh huh."

"You didn't have anything better to do?"

She shook her head.

He reached up to tuck a lock of hair behind her ear. "Did I snore or drool or do anything else embarrassing?"

"No, you were very cute. Your phone rang a couple of times. I wasn't sure if I should wake you up to get it, but I decided you needed the sleep."

"Sleeping through a ringing phone goes against all my training, but whatever it is, I suppose it'll keep. I've got much better things to do now that I'm *very* well rested."

Her smile reached inside him and wrapped itself around his heart.

He wove his fingers into her hair and slid his lips over hers in a gentle, easy caress. Urging her down on top of him, he found the hem of her nightgown and pulled it up and over her head. Tossing it to the floor, he whispered, "I like it better down there."

Her laugh faded into a moan as his hands investigated every inch of the warm, soft skin he had uncovered. With a surge of passion he hadn't known he was capable of, he reversed their positions and devoured her mouth. He trembled when her hands clutched his shoulders and then made a slow journey down his back.

"I need to get a condom," he managed to say.

"I'm on the pill."

He pulled back to look at her and brushed the hair off her forehead. "We're tested twice a year at work. I'm safe."

"I am, too. I always insist on condoms."

"Not this time?" His heart pounded with anticipation and desire and love like he had never known.

"Not this time." She hooked her fingers inside the waistband of his boxer briefs to ease them down. Once they were gone, she stroked him until he was so painfully hard he thought he would explode.

"Caroline," he sighed, grasping her hand to stop her before he reached the point of no return. "I love you."

"And I love you. Make love to me, Ted."

He reclaimed her lips, telling himself to slow down, to take his time, to savor this first time with her. But the desire was so overwhelming. He thought he'd known desire before, but nothing could compare to this burning need. Her soft skin, her scent, her silky hair, her soft sighs, her fingers on his back, urging him on . . . Until this moment, love had been a mystery to him. He hadn't understood or experienced the great power it had to change lives and alter destinies. Now he finally got what had taken him nearly thirty-eight years to understand—that faced with a choice, he'd gladly give his life for her.

Her breasts filled his hands to overflowing. He dipped his head to taste her nipple, and she moaned. Encouraged, he sucked her deep into his mouth and dragged his tongue back and forth over the rosy peak.

Caroline wrapped her legs around his hips, begging him for more.

Ted gasped at the feel of her moist heat against his throbbing erection and shifted to deny her, at least for now. His lips coasted over her belly as he made his way down, using his shoulders to keep her legs apart.

"Ted, *please* . . ."

"What?" he asked softly. "What do you need?"

"Come up here."

"I'll be back in a minute." He dragged his tongue over her in a teasing, darting motion.

"Oh . . ."

Sliding his hands under her, he stroked her with his tongue for several long minutes before he focused on the place she wanted him most and sent her flying into an orgasm that shook them both. She was still in the throes of it when he entered her.

For a moment neither of them moved as they gazed into each other's eyes. Stunned by the wonder of it, Ted began to move and the wonder was quickly replaced by fire. Reaching under her with one hand, he pulled her tighter to him and had to grit his teeth to hold on to his control when she cried out again.

With an expression of utter amazement on her face, she looked up at him with tears in her eyes.

Ted felt his own eyes burn when he buried his face in her hair and let himself go in an explosive climax that left him bewildered and breathless. Still trying to calm his racing heart, he dropped soft kisses along her jaw and then found her lips again. "God, Caroline," he said with a sigh. "I'm going to need to do that again—very soon and very often."

She laughed and held him tight so he couldn't get away. Her phone rang, and she looked over at the caller ID. "It's Elise. I'd better get it."

Ted moved so Caroline could reach for the bedside phone.

"Caroline? Chip just told me you and Smitty broke up. I'm in shock. I'm going to come over. I'll be there as soon as I can."

"You don't need to. I'm fine."

Ted curled up to her back and put his arm around her. He could hear every word Elise was saying.

"What happened? I can't believe this!"

"Nothing really happened. We just talked about it last night and realized it was over. Plus he's going to Australia."

"He's already gone. He's flying to L.A. in an hour."

Caroline sat up. "He's already left?"

"Uh huh. Chip said he sounded weird."

"I didn't realize he was leaving so soon."

Startled to hear Smitty was already gone, Ted got up to retrieve his cell phone in the living room. On his way back to bed he scrolled through the list of missed calls: Parker twice, Chip, and his parents' Block Island number.

"No, you don't have to come, Elise," Caroline was saying. "I'm really fine. I'll call you later in the week. Thanks for checking on me."

Ted listened to the message from Parker.

"Hey, I just talked to Smitty. He said he tried to get you a couple of times this morning and wanted me to tell you he's going to Sydney tonight for work. He'll be gone at least a month. In other news, he broke up with Caroline last night. Give me a call when you can."

The next message was from Chip. "Something's up with Smitty. Call me."

Ted's mother said, "Hi, darling. Talked to Smitty. Did you hear about him and Caroline? The poor guy. Give me a call."

Ted exited out of his voicemail and checked the list of missed calls again. Smitty hadn't called. "He knows," Ted said.

"What do you mean?"

"Smitty knows about us."

Caroline gasped. "Why do you say that?"

"If everything's normal, there's no way he leaves the country for a month without calling me. No way. He called my mother, for Christ's sake, and not me? He told Parker he tried to get me a couple of times this morning, but there's no call from him."

"Maybe he called you at work."

Ted shook his head. "He knows my cell is the only sure way to always reach me." He pulled on his underwear and began to pace the small room. "How could he have figured this out so fast? I just don't get it."

After she had watched him stew and pace for several minutes, Caroline cleared her throat. "May I say something that might sound totally insensitive and maybe even a little inappropriate?"

Ted stopped to look at her. "Of course."

"I don't really care if he knows." Her eyes shone with emotion. "We just made love for the first time, and I don't want to talk about him. I want to talk about you. I want to talk about us. I want you to *be* with me. I know this is a hideous situation, and he's been your best friend for so many years—"

"No, you're right." Ted turned off his phone and tossed it into his bag. "I'm sorry." He got back in bed and brought her into his arms.

She rested her head on his chest. "Am I awful?"

"No, honey." He tilted her chin up so he could kiss her. "You're absolutely right. This time is for us. We'll have to deal with everything else soon enough but not today or even tomorrow."

"Thank you for understanding."

"Will you always do that?"

"Do what?"

"Tell me what you need, straight out like you just did?"

"You might not always want to hear it," she said with a laugh.

"I'd prefer it to guessing games. I hate that more than anything."

"What else do you hate?"

"Olives."

She cracked up. "That's it?"

He gave it significant thought. "Yeah, that's about it."

She shifted to lie on top of him. "In that case, you're going to be very easy to please."

"Mmm," he said as she kissed her way to his belly. "If you keep that up, I'll be pleased in no time at all."

~

"I NEED A SHOWER," Caroline said more than an hour later as she launched into one of her full body stretches.

Ted was face down in bed listening to the blare of a car alarm and the clutter of voices drifting in from the city street. The sheer curtain billowed in the late afternoon breeze. "I watched you do that on Block Island."

She turned to him. "What?"

"Stretch from your toes to the ends of your fingertips. I committed that and a hundred other things about you to memory in case I didn't get to see you again."

She ran her fingers through his hair. "You're so sweet."

"I was so afraid we'd never have this."

"I had a feeling we'd find a way. This was too big to ignore."

"You were so beautiful in the moonlight that first night on the deck when I told you about Joey."

"I just wish . . ." She bit her lip.

"What, honey?"

"That the thing we're not talking about wasn't a factor. I know you must be so sad about it."

"When I talked to my grandmother about you she said something I didn't really understand until today when we were free to be together." He hooked a hand around the curve of her neck to bring her close enough to kiss. "She said if things went bad with my friends, you'd fill the empty spaces."

Caroline's eyes went soft with emotion as she caressed his chest. "She's right. We'll have each other no matter what happens."

He struggled against the lump that suddenly filled his throat. "I'm going to try very hard not to need anything else. If they turn their backs on me because of this, I'll do my best to live with it."

"*We'll* live with it."

Clutching her hand, he nodded.

"How about a shower?" she asked with a playful smile. "I'll wash your back, and you'll forget all your worries."

He brightened as he turned over to sit up. "I can't say no to that."

The only color in the stark white bathroom was the small black tiles mixed in with the white ones on the floor. "I think I've gone color blind," he joked as she pulled out two thick white towels.

"Don't you know white's the new black?" she asked with a saucy grin. "Of course no one told me it would be such a bear to keep clean."

The claw-footed tub had a wraparound shower curtain. She leaned in to turn on the water.

While they waited for the water to warm up, he put his arms around her and pulled her close. "You've completely corrupted me."

She looked up at him. "How so?"

"I don't even feel guilty about calling in sick to work. That's *so* not me."

"Think of it as mental health time. You needed it."

"I needed *you*." He lifted her against his erection.

She giggled against his lips. "Don't get any big ideas, mister. We can't get my cast wet."

"And how exactly does that work?"

"Carefully."

"Wouldn't it be easier to take a bath? You could hook it over the side."

"Can I still wash your back?"

"Absolutely."

"Then you need to put me down so I can plug the drain."

"Do I have to?" He kissed her so thoroughly that she was breathless by the time he inched her slowly back down.

When the bath was ready, Ted got in first and held her steady while she balanced on one leg and propped her cast on the side of the tub. She leaned back against him and sighed with pleasure. "Now if this isn't good for your mental health, what is?"

"I can't imagine anything better," he said as he worked shampoo into her hair.

"*Ted*," she moaned when he massaged her scalp. "That feels sinfully good, but I'm supposed to be washing your back."

"You'll get your chance. So tell me, what's your book really about?"

"A single dad named Cameron Littlefield. He's tall, dark, and handsome, and he's lived in my head for at least three years now."

"Do I need to be jealous of this *Cameron Littlefield?* I didn't know you preferred tall, dark, and handsome. I'm in big trouble here." He tried not to think about how well the description fit Smitty.

She laughed and reached back to ruffle his blond hair. "You've got two out of three. I'm definitely infatuated with Cameron, but I'm completely in *love* with you. So you've got nothing to worry about."

He nuzzled her neck. "I'm never, ever going to get tired of hearing you say that."

She turned to him. "Any time you need to hear it, just let me know."

He cupped her face with one hand and kissed her. "So what's *Cameron Littlefield's* problem?"

"I don't think I care for your tone," she joked. "His ex-wife got busted selling crack cocaine out of their basement, and she's in jail for two years. The town is full of rumors that she was selling more than crack, if you know what I mean."

"Ah, yes, the *other* crack."

She elbowed him, and water sloshed over the top of the tub. "That's truly gross," she snickered. "So *anyway*, Cameron's little daughters, Stella and Avery, are being ridiculed at school, and he realizes he needs to get them out of town or the stigma will stick to them forever. Because he's in construction and can work anywhere, he allows the girls to pick the place they want to move to—anywhere in the United States."

"Where do they decide to go?"

"I'm not sure yet."

"You don't know what's going to happen?" he asked with surprise.

"I know enough to get me started. I'm hoping the rest will come to me as I go."

"I always figured people who wrote books had lengthy outlines they followed and they know how it's going to end before it even begins."

"From what I've read, everyone has a different process. I don't want to spend the time on an outline because then I'd feel like I had to follow it or all the time I'd spent on it would be wasted. What if I get halfway through it and want to go in a whole other direction?"

"That's a good point."

"Let's switch places."

He got up and stepped over her as she scooted back against the edge of the tub.

"How's the cast doing?"

"It's dry but itchy. I hate it."

"Does your ankle still hurt?"

"Not really. I hear it hurts like hell when the cast comes off and you have to start moving it again. And then there's physical therapy. I'm not looking forward to that."

"I'll hold your hand."

"All the way from Boston?" she asked, massaging his back.

He relaxed against her. "I've been thinking about that. Why don't you and *Cameron Littlefield* come home with me tomorrow?"

Caroline's hands went still on his back. "Seriously?"

"Why not?" When she didn't answer he turned over to face her, sending even more water to the floor. "I want you with me, Caroline. Pack up your laptop and your plants and come home with me."

She smiled. "How did you know I was thinking about my plants?"

"I have to go back to work on Wednesday. My patients need me, but I need *you*. We can come back to New York the week after next for the conference."

"And then what?"

He shrugged. "I don't have an outline written because if I did, I'd feel obligated to follow it." He kissed his way up her neck. "And I might miss out on something truly amazing along the way."

Amused, she said, "You think you're very clever, don't you, Ted Duffy?"

"Will you come home with me? Tell me I don't have to leave

you tomorrow." He pressed his lips to hers. "I'm not going to be ready to leave you tomorrow."

She put her arms around him and sank into his kiss. They slipped under the water without breaking the kiss. She resurfaced sputtering and coughing. "Okay," she gasped through her laughter. "I'll come."

CHAPTER 23

After their bath, Ted flipped through a photo album as Caroline snuggled with him on the sofa and introduced him to the people in her life.

"That's Tiffany. We were in high school then. And that's my sister. Turn the page. I think the picture of us in Brownies is next."

Ted laughed at the shot of the two girls in their brown and orange uniforms. "Oh, you were so adorable! I want a little girl who looks just like her." He pointed to the young Caroline in her brown knee socks and beanie.

She kissed him and the photo album slipped to the floor with a thud. Trailing her tongue along his bottom lip, she smiled when he groaned.

He tried to close the small distance between them, but she kept her hand on his bare chest and continued to tease him.

"Caroline . . ." His hand snaked up under the T-shirt of his that she wore.

"What?" she whispered, turning her attention to his ear.

"You're making me crazy."

"I like you that way."

"You're playing with fire."

"I'll take my chances." She slid her hand down to see if her efforts were having the desired effect.

When she reached her destination, Ted sucked in a sharp deep breath. "Satisfied?"

"Not yet, but getting there."

His laughter got stuck in his throat when she stroked him through his shorts. "Caroline," he sighed, closing his eyes and giving in to the pleasure.

"That didn't take much effort." She tugged on the button and unzipped him.

"You only have to be in the room. That was a real problem for me before yesterday."

"Really?" she asked with amazement as she freed him from his clothes.

Enraptured by the gentle movement of her hand, he could only say, "Mmm."

"Have you had lots of girlfriends?" she asked as she dragged her tongue over the head of his penis.

His eyes flew open. "A few," he choked out.

"I'll bet there were a *lot*." She closed her lips over him and took him deep.

"None of them were you," he whispered as his fingers spooled through her long hair. "So none of them mattered."

Slowly, she slid her lips back up and looked at him. "Surely *someone* has mattered before now."

He reached for the hand that stroked him. "You're going to have to stop that, honey, if you expect me to talk."

"I have a better idea."

"I'm almost afraid to ask . . ."

"How about I finish it and then you can talk to me?" With her eyes still on his, she took him in again, swirling her tongue over him.

Ted groaned and gripped a handful of her soft hair. "Caroline . . ."

"Hmm?"

"Oh *God* . . ."

The combination of her hand, her warm mouth, and enthusiastic tongue drove him up fast.

"Baby," he gasped. "Wait . . . That's enough."

But rather than stop, she sucked him hard, and the orgasm roared through him, leaving him completely depleted in its wake.

Caroline sighed with contentment and snuggled into his chest.

"That was amazing, honey," he said when he had recovered the ability to speak. "*You're* amazing."

"I've never done that before," she said, her cheeks blazing with embarrassment.

Charmed by her, he asked, "Done what?"

"Let someone, you know . . . come in my mouth like that."

Ted sighed with contentment and tightened his arms around her. "I don't know what I ever did to deserve you."

"Now will you tell me what you were going to before?"

Ted took a deep breath to calm the surge of emotions. "I went out with a girl named Marcy for three years when I was in college. I thought I loved her. But now that I know how it feels to really be in love, I realize I didn't love her. Not like I love you."

Her green eyes filled. "I wasn't fishing for that, but it's sure nice to hear."

"It's true. What about you? What about this guy you almost married?"

She winced and rested her cheek on his belly, her eyes tilted up so she could see him. "I guess I asked for that, didn't I? I wish I could say I've never felt like this before . . ."

"I don't expect you to. Our lives didn't begin the day we met." Although Ted wondered if his life had in fact begun the night he met her.

"I loved him, but he was nothing like you. Since we broke up I've come to see he was very selfish in a lot of ways. I let him get away with far too much."

"Like what?" he asked, feeling the passion of a few minutes ago drain away to be replaced by something far more tender. Imagining her unhappy stirred his protective instincts.

"Our relationship was all about him—his work, his family, his friends. I kind of lost myself after a while. I even quit my job —a job he hated and I loved—to devote more time to him.

Knowing what I know now, I'd never do that again and not just because he called off the wedding. I gave him too much power in our relationship, too much power over me."

"I hope I don't end up doing some of that same stuff. My job can be all-consuming at times, and I'm already asking you to come to Boston with me tomorrow. My work often messes up my plans and seeps into my personal life. There'll be days when it'll appear more important to me than you are." He kissed her hand. "But that'll never be the case."

"There'll be days when it *should* be more important, and that's all right. I know that going into this."

"Are you over him, Caroline?"

She paused for a long moment. "When someone hurts you like he hurt me, it leaves you in pieces. And over time you put the pieces back together, but the picture changes. You're never really quite the same. I don't know if that makes sense."

"I'm sorry you had to go through that."

She shrugged. "If I hadn't, I wouldn't be here now. But I hope I'm never in that place again. It was the low point of my life.

He squeezed her hand. "That's not going to happen to us."

"I hope not. So to answer your question, I'm over him, but I'm different now."

"Well, I'm in love with the Caroline who's right here with me. I didn't know that Caroline, but I like this one a whole lot."

"You know what? I do, too. She's a lot tougher than she used to be."

Ted laughed. "Just my luck."

"You'd better watch out," she said with a menacing scowl.

"If I start to pull the same shit he did, don't let me get away with it, okay?" He tugged her close enough to kiss.

"Mmm," she said against his lips. "I won't. Hey, you must want to run after lazing around all day."

"Nope," he said without breaking the kiss. "Not without you."

"I miss running," she said with a moan.

"You'll be back to fighting form in no time. I can't wait to run with you again."

"I can't either. We were good together."

"We *are* good together—in more ways than one," he said with a lascivious grin.

She giggled. "Are you hungry?"

"Getting there. Want to go out?"

She mulled that over for a moment. "What if, you know, someone sees us?"

Ted shrugged. "It's a big city. I think we'll be okay."

"Do you like Thai?"

"I love it." He got up and helped her up.

After they got changed, she followed him back to the living room. "There's a good place about two blocks from here. I can walk that far."

"But you don't have to. You've got me." He squatted down to offer her his back. "Hop on."

"You don't have to carry me."

"I want to."

"You won't be able to stand up straight tomorrow."

"Shut up and get on."

"All right." She climbed onto his back and wrapped her arms around his neck. "Don't say I didn't warn you."

"I've carried you before. Remember?"

"How could I forget? I think I fell in love with you on that long walk back to the parking lot."

"Did you? That soon?"

She pressed a kiss to his neck that sent a tremble through him as he carried her on the sidewalk. "You were so caring and competent. How could I not fall for that? When did it start for you?"

"That night on the deck when I first saw you. I very distinctly remember having the feeling I'd been asleep my whole life and was finally awake. It was an amazing moment—one I'll never forget."

"Ted," she whispered as she tightened her hold on him.

"I usually have a hard time talking about the losses, but that night I didn't because you were so easy to talk to. It just kind of poured out. That was definitely the start of it."

"I was awake all night after that," she confessed.

"Me, too."

She squeezed him from her perch on his back and pointed to the restaurant on the corner. They ate at a small table on the sidewalk and shared a bottle of wine. The street was busy, and the night air warm but not overly humid.

As Ted carried her back to the apartment after dinner, she nibbled on his ear.

"I'm going to drop you if you keep that up."

She moved from his ear to his neck.

"Oh, that's a big improvement."

She giggled and kept up the mischief.

When they reached her building, Ted took the front stairs two at a time and pulled her key out of his pocket. Once they were inside, he eased her down onto her good foot and turned to her. Pressing her against the wall, he captured her mouth in a long, deep kiss. "See what you started?" he whispered in her ear as he slid his hands under her shirt.

She unbuttoned his shorts. "And are you going to finish it?"

"What do you think?" He pushed up her skirt and tugged her panties out of the way. Lifting her against the wall, he propped her legs on his hips and sank two fingers into her heat.

Groaning, Caroline rested her head on his shoulder and clutched a handful of his hair.

After a few minutes, he nudged at her top. "Take it off," he said, his voice husky.

She fumbled with the buttons as his fingers slid in and out of her at an increasingly faster pace.

"Bra too," he whispered urgently.

The clothes dropped to their feet. Ted lifted her higher and feasted on her nipple.

She climaxed hard, clutching his fingers and crying out with completion.

He freed himself and was inside her so fast the last waves of her orgasm gripped him from within. She was so tight and so hot, it was all he could do not to explode into her.

She gasped as she struggled to accommodate him and tightened her arms around his neck.

His tongue plunged into her mouth, mimicking the movements of his hips. What had earlier been slow and sensual was now fast and frantic. And when it was over, Ted was left flattened by the knowledge that in the course of this one day she had become more essential to him than anything or anyone.

"I love you," she whispered.

Since he couldn't speak over the giant lump in his throat, he just held her tighter.

CHAPTER 24

Ted carried Caroline's bags and her box of plants out to his car and then went back for his own bag. "Do you have everything?"

"I'm just trying to think. I stopped my mail, cleaned out the fridge, and took out the trash." She chewed on her thumbnail as she looked around her apartment. "I feel like there's something I'm forgetting to do."

"We've got time, so why don't you come kiss me until you think of it."

"Because if I do that, I won't be able to think at all. You stay over there."

Ted flopped down on the sofa and pretended to pout as he watched her think. He was so glad she was coming with him, especially after spending the night wrapped around her and then waking up to her in the morning. There had never been anything quite like opening his eyes to a new day and finding her there next to him.

She leaned over her desk, giving Ted an excellent view of her backside in a fitted white skirt. He couldn't believe it was possible that he already wanted her again.

Caroline turned around and caught him checking her out. "What are you doing?"

"Just enjoying the view, which I have to say, is even better from the front." He made no attempt to hide that he was fixated now on the cleavage made prominent by her light blue halter.

She hobbled over to the sofa and sat on his lap. "You make me melt when you look at me like that."

He pulled her closer. "I want you all the time, even when I've just had you."

"You'd better get a handle on that, sailor. You've got to go back to work tomorrow."

"Don't remind me," he groaned. "I'll tell you right now I'm taking a vacation in August, and we're going somewhere fabulous where I can keep you naked for a whole week."

"Oh, I like the sound of that." She kissed him with abandon. "Wait!" She pulled back, leaving him panting for more. "I thought of it. I almost forgot to pay the bills. You've got me totally distracted."

"Just bring them with you. We should get out of here before rush hour." He reluctantly eased her off his lap and stood up. "Do you need your crutches?"

"Nah, leave them." She tossed the bills and her checkbook into the bag where she had earlier put her computer. "I don't need them anymore."

Ted took the bag from her and slung it over his shoulder.

She locked the deadbolt and followed him down the stairs.

He opened the car door for her and stashed her bag behind the seat.

"The last time I was in this car we were on the way to the emergency room."

"Hard to believe that was only a couple of weeks ago." He flipped the switch to take the top down. "I feel like I've lived a lifetime since then." At the stop sign at the end of her block he stopped the car and turned to her. "I know what you forgot!"

"What?" she asked, alarmed.

"*Cameron Littlefield!*"

Her face lit up with a huge grin. "Oh, I didn't forget him. He's *always* with me." She put a hand over her heart.

"I hate him."

She leaned over to kiss Ted's cheek. "He's not the one I spent most of last night—and this morning—making love with."

"That's right," Ted said smugly. "Eat your heart out, Cameron, old boy." He hooked his arm around her to keep her close to him as he drove them out of Manhattan. "I was thinking about how you said you're taking a break to write about *Cameron,* but did you have other work to do this week that I'm dragging you away from?"

She shook her head. "I'm giving myself three months to write the book, and then I have to go back to work. I used my commission from the Convention & Visitor's Bureau job to pay three months' rent, so that bought me some time."

He brushed his lips over her soft blond hair. "You know, if you lived with me at some point you could focus on your writing full time—if you wanted to, that is."

She raised her head off his shoulder to look at him. "You're very sweet, but that's not me. I'd need to contribute."

"But you wouldn't *have* to. Maybe you'll write a runaway best seller, and I'll end up living large off you."

"Now that's a scenario I could live with."

"What about, if . . ."

"What?"

"If we have kids someday—before the best seller, that is—would you want to be home with them?"

"I would. I'd want that very much, but I'd probably still do some freelancing, and of course, there's Cameron to consider."

"I'm not leaving you at home alone with him every day. No way."

"I never imagined you to be the jealous type."

He heard her deep sigh. "Hey, what's going on inside that pretty head of yours?"

"I can't believe we just talked about me being a stay-at-home mother to our kids."

"Am I getting ahead of myself on our second full day together?"

"No. It all feels possible today, doesn't it?"

"It *is* possible—all of it. I've never been so content to spend two days the way we just did. I could spend a month like that and never be bored, never run out of stuff to talk to you about, and never, ever, *ever* stop wanting you."

Caroline pressed her lips to his until he had to pull away from her to focus on driving. "Thank you for coming all that way the other night when I needed you."

"I thought I was going to go crazy trying to get to you."

She held up the speeding ticket. "Is that how you got this?"

He winced. "You weren't supposed to see that."

"Ouch! Four hundred bucks! I'm not exactly a cheap date, am I?"

"Luckily you didn't eat much last night."

She laughed. "I didn't realize I'd already cost you so much money, or I wouldn't have gotten the shrimp."

"For you, baby, sky's the limit."

"Ugh," she said. "This traffic is beastly. It's going to take us forever to get to Boston at this rate."

"Want to take a detour and spend the night in Newport?"

"Do you have time?"

"I'm on twelve to eight tomorrow, and the house is ours until Labor Day even though we only use it on the weekends."

"What if Chip or Parker showed up there out of the blue?"

"They never would."

"They'd probably say the same about you, though, right?"

He smiled. "Yes, they would. I need to return their calls from yesterday anyway, so I could do that and find out where they are. What do you say?"

"You're the one who has to work, so whatever you want is fine with me."

"Hey, just because you're not working right now doesn't mean you don't get a vote. I want to be careful not to treat you the way old what's his name did."

"You're incapable of treating me the way *Brad* did."

"*Brad*." Ted turned up his nose with distaste. "*Brad* and *Cameron*. I hate them both."

"It's okay, baby," she cooed. "You're the only one I want."

Pacified, Ted smiled. "In that case, I'll let you go long enough to return those calls, and then I want you back over here with me." He lifted his arm to release her and reached for his cell phone to call Parker.

"Hey, Duff," Parker said when he came on the line. "Where've you been hiding?"

Ted swallowed hard. "Just been one of those weeks. I got your message, but couldn't call you back before now. What's up?"

"Jeez, man, did you hear about Smitty? Broke up with Caroline and went to Australia for like a month or something. All of this since we saw him on Sunday!"

Ted glanced over at Caroline who was looking out the passenger window. "Yeah, I got the gist from your message."

"Did you talk to him?"

"No, we never connected."

"I'm sorry, but the whole thing is so bizarre. He was all over her this weekend, but when he told me they broke up he was so matter-of-fact about it, like it was no big deal."

"Did you talk to Chip?"

"Yeah, he thinks it's fucked up, too. But I guess we'll have to wait until Smitty gets back from Sydney to get the full story."

"I guess so. Did you call Gina?"

"Two more days. I'm holding out."

"You're a sadist."

"I'm beginning to think you're right."

"How's your week going?"

"Hideous. I was in depositions all day today, and I'm in court all day tomorrow. Are we riding together on Friday?"

"I don't know if I'm going. Roger's wife is pregnant and she's had some complications, so I hate to ask him to cover for me right now." Only part of that was true—Roger's wife *was* pregnant.

"Oh, man, that sucks. You've hardly gotten to use the house at all this summer, and now with Smitty gone, our gang is dwindling."

"I know."

"Well, I've got a meeting. Give me a call on Friday if you can go."

"I will. Let me know what happens with Gina and if you hear from Smitty."

"Will do. You do the same."

Ted flipped his phone closed. "Parker's in Boston tonight."

"Who's Gina?"

Ted filled her in on the woman Parker was interested in.

"So he's waited a *year* to contact her? That's so romantic."

"You think so? I told him he was nuts to wait that long."

"It was the right thing to do. She'll have had time to put the pieces back together."

"Not only is my lady very beautiful, but she's very wise, too."

She smiled. "What did he say about Smitty?"

"Just that the whole thing seems bizarre. Let me call Chip and see what he has to say about it."

"Fucking crazy," was Dr. Taggert's take. "He spent the whole weekend with us and never says a word about going to Sydney for a month? What's up with that?"

"I guess he didn't want to put a damper on the party." Ted wondered if Smitty already had the trip planned or if it came up after he figured out what was going on between Ted and Caroline. And *how* exactly he had figured that out was something that continued to gnaw at Ted.

"There's something about it that stinks if you ask me," Chip said. "Did you talk to him? What did he say to you?"

"No, we never hooked up before he left. I was in the clinic all day yesterday, so we missed each other." Ted gritted his teeth to withstand the bout of conscience. He glanced over at Caroline, and just the sight of her was enough to remind him that the lies were worth it. "So how are you? Did you guys set a date yet?"

"Tonight. Elise's parents are coming in from Massapequa for dinner."

"That's exciting. Let me know what you decide."

"You know you're in the wedding, right? I'm going to have to draw straws among the three of you for a best man, but you know you'll be right up there with me."

"Sure I do. Smitty and I would understand if you asked Parker. We know you go back further with him." The two of them had first met in prep school.

"That's kind of what I was thinking, too, but I don't want you guys to think—"

"Chip, we wouldn't think a thing of it. I promise."

His relief was audible. "Thanks, Duff. I'll call you when I have the date."

"Give the bride a kiss for me."

"I'd love to."

Ted laughed and hung up. "Unless Smitty didn't really go to Sydney, we're good to go in Newport," he said to Caroline.

"Is there some way you can find that out?"

Ted nodded and flipped open his phone again to call Smitty's office.

"I'm sorry, Mr. Smith is out of the country. He's checking his voice mail if you'd like to leave a message."

Ted started to say no but then changed his mind. "Yes, please."

She transferred him to Smitty's extension, and Ted's gut twisted at the sound of his friend's voice.

"This is John Smith. I'm currently out of the country. Leave a message, and I'll return your call as soon as I can. If you need immediate assistance, please contact Peter Nielson at extension 337."

At the tone, Ted said, "Hey, it's Duff. Everyone's worried about you. Give me a call when you get a chance." There was more he wanted to say, but Ted decided that was enough for now.

To Caroline, he said, "Smitty's really gone."

She reached for his hand. "Then let's go to Newport."

CHAPTER 25

Smitty cleared customs and was met at Sydney Airport by Marjorie Jergenson's personal assistant, Harvey Waddell. A nervous guy with bright red hair and freckles, Harvey was a shrimp next to Smitty.

"Ms. Jergenson was sorry she couldn't meet you herself," Harvey said in a thick Australian accent sprinkled with a stammer. He had to scurry along to keep up with Smitty as they left the international terminal. "She was called into an early meeting. She said she'll see you later this morning or this afternoon if you wish to sleep after your long journey."

"I slept on the plane, so this morning's fine."

Harvey led him to a dark sedan and popped the trunk.

Smitty was thrown off when he realized the steering wheel was on the passenger side of the car. "We're not in Kansas anymore, Toto," he muttered under his breath.

"Did you say something, Mr. Smith?"

"No."

"Ah, yes, very well then."

On the way into downtown, Smitty learned Sydney is the capital of New South Wales and was voted the world's friendliest city six years in a row. He also discovered he had left summer behind at home. According to Harvey, while July was not the coolest month of the year in Australia, the average temperature was only nine degrees Celsius or forty-eight degrees Fahrenheit.

Harvey took the scenic route into downtown along Sydney Harbour where Smitty got his first view of the world-famous Sydney Harbour Bridge and the Sydney Opera House.

"You can climb the bridge if you're so inclined," Harvey said, clearly trying to make conversation.

Watching the morning rush hour traffic whiz by on the wrong side of the road made Smitty nauseous. "I'm here to work. I doubt I'll have time."

Harvey kept quiet until he pulled into an underground parking garage beneath a black glass office building. "Your apartment is on the sixteenth floor." Harvey handed the key and a business card to Smitty. "If there's anything you need, you can contact me day or night. I'm at your disposal."

"Thank you. I'm sure I'll be fine." For the first time in several hours, he thought of Ted and Caroline, and the sickening surge of pain led him to wonder if he would ever be fine again. He willed himself to not think about it and to focus on the task at hand. He and his partners stood to make a lot of money from this deal, so he vowed to give the review his full attention.

Harvey helped him with his bags and led him to the elevator. "You'll need your key to access the sixteenth floor."

The elevator opened into a hallway between two doors, and Harvey went to the door on the left. He stepped aside to allow Smitty to open the door and go ahead of him into the luxurious apartment overlooking Sydney Harbour.

"The bedroom's right this way. There are two bathrooms, one here in the hallway and the other's in the bedroom. The kitchen has been stocked, but if there's anything you need, just let us know."

"Thank you very much, Harvey," Smitty said, anxious to be rid of the nervous little guy who was so eager to please. "I appreciate you getting up early to meet me."

"Oh, it was my pleasure, Mr. Smith. When you're ready to work, come down to the twelfth floor and ask for me. I'll show you to the office we've set aside for you."

"I'll be down in an hour or two after I check in with my New York office."

"Very good. I'll expect you then."

They shook hands, and after Harvey left, Smitty strolled over to look at the view through the full-length window. He stood there for a long time without seeing much of anything. The pain lurked just below the surface. He'd put half a world of distance between himself and the source of the pain but was dismayed to discover he hadn't outrun it. He felt like he was wading through quicksand as he made the supreme effort to put one foot in front of the other, to take the next breath, to simply function.

Thinking of them together just compounded the misery. *I want to go back to Saturday when I was still ignorant of what was going on right in front of me. I want to go back to before I knew my best friend was capable of hurting me this way.* With a shake of his head to clear it of unpleasant thoughts, he turned away from the window and went to retrieve his laptop.

Ninety minutes later, he had caught up on the e-mail that had accumulated during his trip, checked the latest exchange numbers, and sent several messages to his staff in New York, where it was seven o'clock Tuesday night. *This fourteen-hour time difference is going to take some getting used to,* he thought. Two of his employees replied to his e-mails right away, and he was pleased they were working late even when he was out of the country.

After he unpacked, showered, and shaved, Smitty dressed in a dark suit, gathered his briefcase containing the Jergenson files, and went out to the hallway to summon the elevator. On the twelfth floor, he opened the double glass doors to Jergenson Investment Company LLC, which apparently occupied the entire floor. At the reception desk, he asked for Harvey who had apparently been standing on the other side of the wall waiting for Smitty.

He led Smitty down a long hallway, past offices where people were either hard at work or putting on a good show for the potential new owner.

"Do they know why I'm here?"

"Yes, sir. Ms. Jergenson is very big on communicating with her employees. She's done an admirable job of putting aside her own grief over the loss of her father to focus on the company and the people who now work for her."

Smitty wondered if young Harvey wasn't just a little bit in love with the boss lady.

"Did the employees like her father?"

"Very much so." Harvey gestured for Smitty to proceed into an office at the end of the hallway. "You'll find there're more than a dozen employees who've been with the company since Mr. Jergenson founded it thirty years ago. I'm sure it goes without saying that people are worried about what to expect once the sale goes through."

Smitty nodded but said nothing to allay the young man's concerns. There would be time for that later *if* he and his partners decided to buy the company.

"I'll leave you to get settled, and I'll let Ms. Jergenson know you're here."

"Thanks, Harvey." Smitty raised the blinds that covered the windows behind his desk. Like his apartment, the office looked out on Sydney Harbour. He watched a freighter steam through the crisp blue water as two sailboats tacked to get out of its way.

"Hallo, John. I see you've arrived safely. I trust Harvey took good care of you."

Smitty turned around to find a young woman in a smart black suit standing in the doorway. The only feature that gave her away as an adult was her height—she was at least five feet, ten inches tall.

"Um, yes. Yes, he did."

"Marjorie Jergenson." She extended her hand with a welcoming smile that made the corners of her brown eyes crinkle. Her long auburn curls, which were corralled by a batik headband, seemed better suited to a sixth grader than a chief executive.

What is she, twelve years old? Smitty wondered.

He shook her hand. "*You're* Marjorie? I'm sorry. I was just expecting someone a little . . . well, older."

"I'm twenty-eight, and *I* wasn't expecting my father to die and leave me in charge of an international investment company that employs three hundred people—most of them at least a decade older than me. So I guess that makes us even."

"Is that why you're so anxious to sell?"

"It's one reason."

"I'm sorry about your father."

"So am I. He was a good man."

"What happened to him?"

"He had an aneurism burst at home. By the time they found him, he'd been gone for some time." Her tone was matter of fact, but her eyes gave away her pain.

"Did you work here before he died?"

"No, but I've spent the last two months learning everything I need to know to make a good sale. My chief concern is protecting the people who've devoted their lives to my father and his company. Anything else will be secondary to that."

He nodded. "Duly noted."

"Well, John," she said. His name came out as "Jawn" with her accent. "Shall I introduce you around?"

He started to correct her use of his first name but stopped himself. Smitty was dead. He would be John here. "Yes, please."

By early that evening, he had met most of the executive-level employees and was concluding the day in a meeting with Marjorie and David McAvoy, the company's chief financial officer.

"You'll see that my father and David began following U.S. generally accepted accounting principles seven years ago in anticipation of an eventual sale to an American company. David has copies of our last seven audit reports, all of them containing unqualified opinions from American auditors."

David, who was in his late fifties, beamed with pride as Marjorie spoke of accounting principles and audit reports. She had obviously worked hard to familiarize herself with the business in the two months since her father's death.

"I'll have some questions about the audit reports tomorrow," Smitty said.

"The staff has been instructed to make themselves available to you as needed," Marjorie said.

"Thank you."

"Whatever you need," David said, "just let me know." He stood to shake Smitty's hand. "I'll see you both in the morning."

After David left Marjorie's office, she turned to Smitty. "Are you interested in dinner, John?"

Smitty had to think about that. "Since I haven't eaten since breakfast on the plane, I probably should be hungry, but my body has no idea what time it is."

"It'll take a few days to acclimate." She got up and retrieved a menu from the credenza behind the big desk. "We can order from the restaurant downstairs, and they'll send it up to my apartment."

"You live in the building?"

"I'm staying in my father's apartment, across the hall from yours."

He studied the menu and decided on steak, which seemed like a safe choice, and went to his office to get his briefcase.

Marjorie appeared at his door ten minutes later. "Ready?"

Smitty flipped off the light and followed her down the long hallway.

She stopped to say goodnight to the few people who remained at their desks.

He noticed she said something personal to each of them about their kids, spouses, or pets. "You've done an admirable job of gaining the support of your employees," he said when they were in the elevator.

She shrugged. "They loved my father. I'm benefiting from that."

Smitty thought she was selling herself short, but he kept the opinion to himself.

On the sixteenth floor, she opened the door to the apartment across the hall from his. Boxes, packing tape, and bubble wrap littered the sprawling space. "Sorry about the mess. I've been packing up my father's things in my spare time."

"That can't be an easy job."

"It needs to be done, and there's no one else to do it." She gestured for him to make himself comfortable in the sitting area by the window overlooking the now-dark Sydney Harbour. "Do you mind if I change?"

"Of course not."

"Help yourself to a drink." She pointed to the bar. "I'll be right back."

Smitty took off his suit coat, tugged his tie loose, and opened the top button of his shirt. He poured two fingers of whiskey into a cocktail glass. The heat of the liquor was soothing after the long trip and busy day.

Marjorie returned wearing jeans and a loose-fitting tunic that made her look even younger than she had in the suit. She fixed herself a glass of white wine and joined him on the sofa. Putting her feet up on the coffee table, she sighed.

"Long day, huh?"

"It's been a long two months."

"Where were you living before your father died?"

"In Paris. I went to the Sorbonne to study art history and stayed there after school."

"That's a long way from home."

"I came home twice a year to see my father, and he visited me whenever he could."

The far-away look on her face told him she was remembering happier times. "Will you go back to Paris after you sell the company?"

She shrugged. "I'm not sure what I'm going to do. I was working in a gallery on the Left Bank, but I gave up the job when I realized I was going to be here a while. I'll have to go back at some point to deal with my apartment there. By the time the sale of the company is final I'll probably need to sit on a beach for six months."

Bill Kepler had described her as prickly, but Smitty wasn't

seeing that. To him, she seemed more overwhelmed than anything after being tossed into a situation she was ill prepared for and was doing her best to handle.

When their dinner arrived, she got up to answer the door.

"Good evening, Ms. Jergenson," the uniformed waiter said as he wheeled in a table set for two.

"Hallo, William."

William nodded to Smitty. With a flourish, he lit the candles and uncovered the two entrees. "Is everything to your liking, ma'am?"

"It looks wonderful, thank you." She pressed a bill into his hand.

"Have a nice evening, Ms. Jergenson," he said on his way out the door.

"John?" She invited Smitty to join her at the table.

He realized just how hungry he was when the mouthwatering aroma reached him.

They ate in companionable silence.

She took a sip of her wine. "What's America like? Is it as big and as loud as it seems in the movies?"

"You've never been?"

She shook her head. "I've been just about everywhere else but never to America. I'd love to go someday. Maybe when I get things settled here."

"New York City is as loud and as crazy as it looks on TV and in the movies. But there's much more to America than that. There are lots of quiet, peaceful places, too." He thought of Block Island and was irritated when the pain resurfaced with a relentless disregard for his iron will to put it behind him.

"Are you sad, John?"

Startled, he looked at her. "Sad? No. Why do you ask?"

She held her wine glass in both hands as she rested her elbows on the table and studied him with eyes that were wise beyond her years. "You looked very sad for a moment."

Unsettled by her observation, Smitty shook his head and got up to refill his glass of whiskey. "I'm not," he said when he returned to the table.

"I'm sad all the time lately," she confessed.

"That's only natural. It must've been a terrible shock to lose your father so suddenly."

"When David called . . ." Her eyes filled at the memory, and she shook her head. "I'm sorry."

"Don't be."

She dabbed at her eyes. "I just hope you'll find everything in order so the sale can go through. I need to get this settled. If you had ridden in here today on a white horse I wouldn't have been any happier to see you."

Charmed by her honesty and her accent, Smitty chuckled. "I would've packed my suit of armor had I known."

"You think I'm kidding."

"I know you're not. Isn't there anyone who can help you with the packing and with the business?"

"No, it's just me. My mother died when I was in high school, and I'm an only child. My father's family lives in New Zealand. Other than the funeral, I haven't seen them in years. His sisters attended the reading of his will, took the money, and ran. Fortunately, I have David and the others helping at the office. I don't know what I would've done without them."

Smitty had never met anyone else who was as alone in the world as he was. All at once he wanted to get this sale done for her as much as he wanted it for himself and his partners. The responsibility weighed heavily on her, and he couldn't help but wonder what she would be like once the burden was removed from her capable but fragile shoulders.

"Thank you for coming, John," she said softly.

"You have *no* idea how happy I am to be here."

CHAPTER 26

Ted opened the door to the Newport house, flipped on a light, and punched in the code to deactivate the alarm. "I'm surprised I remember the code. I'm never the first one here."

Caroline walked in behind him and paused in the entryway. When she turned to him, he noticed her green eyes were unsettled.

"What's the matter, hon?"

"It just feels strange to be here again. The only other time I was here was the weekend I met you."

"Do you not want to be here? We don't have to stay. It's only another hour to my place."

She shook her head. "No, I'm fine. It was just an odd feeling."

Ted put his arms around her. "I feel it, too. The place belongs to the four of us, but he's the one who makes it happen. I see him everywhere in this house."

She rested her head on his chest. "I hate to think of him mad and hurt and all alone on the other side of the world."

"I do, too. I'd try harder to track him down if I thought he'd want to hear from me right now."

"Yeah. I guess it's probably better to leave it alone for a while and hope maybe he'll be in a forgiving mood when he gets home."

Ted didn't expect Smitty to ever forgive him, but he didn't think she needed to hear that. "Want to go into town and get some dinner?"

"Sure."

He leaned in for a kiss. After several long, hot minutes, he sighed. "Oh, I needed that."

"Maybe we should order in."

He raised an eyebrow. "That's the best idea you've had all day." When he felt her fingers skimming through his chest hair, he realized she had unbuttoned his shirt. Capturing her wandering hand, he urged her up the stairs.

"Where are we going?"

She struggled to keep up with him, so he lifted her into his arms and carried her to the third floor. He put her down to grab the comforter and pillows from his bed and take them to the deck. Then he came back and held out his hand to her. "I want to make love to you in the place where I found you."

She curled her fingers around his and followed him outside.

A half moon hung over Newport Harbor, and a soft summer breeze blew in from the water.

Ted rested his hands on the small of her back and slid his lips gently over hers. "I remember everything about that day." He dropped hot, wet kisses on her neck as he reached up to untie her halter. She shuddered when he nudged her top aside and kissed his way down to her breasts. "After a terrible day, I drove here with no idea of what was about to happen to me." He drew her nipple into his mouth, and she moaned. "Everything was different the next morning. Everything had shifted."

Her fingers were buried in his hair as he ran his tongue over her belly. "*Ted.*" She urged him up and pushed his shirt off his shoulders. Then she focused on getting rid of his shorts.

When their clothes were in a pile on the deck, he eased her down to the comforter.

"I was over there on that lounge when I heard your car. And then when you came out on the deck, the night became so quiet, so still, like the whole world was holding its breath. I saw you were upset, and then I was next to you. I don't even remember getting up, just that I needed to go to you."

He covered her, filled her, possessed her.

She arched her back and took him in.

"Caroline," he sighed.

Without losing the connection, she urged him onto his back and rode him with abandon. Her eyes were closed, her head tilted back, and her breasts rose and fell with her hips. Ted was powerless to do anything but go along with her until he couldn't bear it for another second. Gripping her hips he held her down and cried out just ahead of her.

Still joined with him, she was breathing heavily when she slumped down on top of him.

Against his chest he could feel her heart beating in time with his. Just when he thought it couldn't get any better, it did. Just when he thought he couldn't love her any more, he discovered there was still so much more. "We're going to have to buy this place and put a little plaque on the deck."

"Here in this place Ted and Caroline discovered there *is* such a thing as love at first sight," she said with a lingering kiss.

"Here in this place Ted had the best sex of his life," he added with a grin.

Her smile was smug. "Here in this place Caroline turned the man of her dreams into a pile of mush."

He nodded in agreement and found her lips, startled to realize he was already aroused again. "And here in this place Ted asked Caroline to be his wife."

She froze.

His heart in his throat, he kept his arms tight around her as he found her eyes in the soft light coming from inside. "I love you. I'll never love anyone the way I love you, and since that's not going to change in six months or one year or fifty, there's no need to wait to get it right. I've already waited all my life for you. Will you marry me, Caroline?"

Her hot tears fell to his chest. "Yes, Ted. Yes, I'll marry you."

He gently turned them over and made love to her again. Afterward, there were tears on his face, too.

~

Out of habit, Ted woke up early the next morning and took advantage of the opportunity to watch Caroline sleep, her hair spread out on the pillow and one arm hooked over her head. Ted ran a finger lightly over her bottom lip.

"Mmm," she sighed and rolled over to snuggle closer to him.

The flutter of his heart at the feel of her next to him was followed by a surge of excitement when he remembered they were engaged. Even though he had known for days he would marry her eventually, he hadn't planned to ask her last night. The words had just tumbled out in the moment, and in the bright light of day he had no regrets.

Caroline's eyes remained closed as her hand began to move on his chest.

He kissed her cheek and then her eyelids. "We have to get up," he whispered.

"Not yet."

Brushing his lips over her hair, he said, "I have to go to work."

She whimpered and tightened her hold on him. "You still have strep. I can tell."

"And on what do you base this diagnosis, Dr. Stewart?"

She wrapped her hand around his erection. "Your swollen glands."

His laughter filled the room. "Good one."

She glanced up at him, and their eyes met. "You can take it back, you know."

"No way. I need to get a ring and do it right, but there's no way I'm taking it back. And you said yes, so you can't take it back, either."

"I never would. But don't do it again. You got it right the first time."

"I'm getting you a ring," he insisted.

"I don't need it."

"Since I only plan to do this once, my fiancée *will* have a ring."

"Fiancée," she sighed. "It's kind of crazy when you think about it. We've only known each other a little over two weeks."

"I knew in two seconds."

She hooked her hand around his neck so she could kiss him. "Do we really have to get up right now?" she asked, caressing his back.

He consulted his watch. "I guess we have a little time, but we'll have to be quick."

"I can do quick."

THEY ARRIVED at Ted's condo at eleven fifteen. He carried their bags and her plants inside and held the door for her. "There's a key under that flower pot if you venture out at all. I'll find you one of your own tonight. The alarm code is 0904—my birthday."

"Oh, Ted, this place is fabulous!" She turned to look at him. "Did you do this?"

He snorted. "Hell no. It's a Mitzi and Lillian production."

She ran her hand over the back of a dark leather sofa. "I love it. And the view! Look at all the boats!" Sliding open the door to the patio she stepped outside. "Cameron and I are going to spend a lot of time out here."

"Make sure you tell him you're engaged," Ted said with a menacing growl.

"I broke the news to him in the shower this morning. He was heartbroken."

Ted smiled as he kissed her. "I hate to say it, but I've got to get moving. I want to show you around and tell you where everything is, but if I don't leave in the next fifteen minutes, I'm going to be late."

"Go get ready." She gave him a gentle push. "I'll figure it out on my own—that is if you don't mind me poking around."

"What's mine is yours, honey. Make yourself completely at home." He took the stairs two at a time on his way to the loft that was his bedroom. Halfway up he stopped and turned to look at her. "I'm glad you're here." He continued up the stairs and disappeared into his bedroom.

Caroline went out to the patio to take another look at the marina. In the distance airplanes took off and landed at Logan Airport.

Ted came back ten minutes later wearing a yellow dress shirt, pressed khakis, and Nikes. He was knotting a blue tie as he joined her on the patio.

She reached for the ID card that hung from a lanyard around his neck. "Sponge Bob?" She raised an amused eyebrow at the strip of stickers tucked in behind his badge.

"The reigning king of kid TV."

"Ted Duffy, MD," she read from the ID. "Pediatric Oncology."

"That's me." He slid the tie into place and adjusted his collar. "I have no idea what's in the fridge, but there's a flyer in the kitchen for a grocery store in the neighborhood that delivers. I have an account there, so call them and order whatever you want."

"I'll be fine. Don't worry about me."

He raised her chin to bring her eyes up to his. "Listen to me, because this is important. Are you listening?"

She giggled at the intense expression on his face. "Yes, Dr. Duffy, you have my full attention."

"I don't want us to have to talk about this again."

She sobered. "About what?"

"The only two things of any value I have are my car and this condo, both of which I accepted reluctantly as gifts from my overindulgent grandparents. For the last six years I've worked ninety hours a week and have had almost no life outside that hospital. Do you know what happens when you work like that and don't have a life?"

She shook her head.

"The money tends to pile up a bit. So now we're going to live. You're going to call that grocery store and spend my money like money's going out of style, you got me?"

"All right," she said, touched by his speech.

"And anything else you want or need, for that matter. I don't want you worrying about money or spending my money. My money is your money."

"You're very sweet," she said when he wrapped his arms around her.

"We're a team now. After last night, there's no more you and me. There's only us."

She nodded.

"Now that we have that worked out, I'm going to make a promise of my own. The ninety hour work weeks are going to be a thing of the past—or as much as they can be."

"You do what you have to do. I'll be here whenever you get home."

"I'm off at eight tonight, and I'll call you if I'm going to be late."

"Call my cell phone. The number's on yours from when I called you Sunday night. That way I don't have to worry about answering your home phone."

He kissed her. "Okay." Leaning his forehead against hers, he said, "I can't seem to make myself go."

"I'll be right here waiting for you."

"Promise?"

"Promise."

"You're not going to change your mind about everything in the next eight or nine hours are you?"

"Not a chance."

He reached for her hands. "These last few days have been the best of my life. Even if we're married fifty years, I'll never forget them."

"I won't either. I love you. Go take care of your kids, and when you get home I'll take care of you."

He groaned and leaned in for a kiss that turned hot so fast he had to pull himself back or be lost in her. "Do you still have my card? If you need to reach me, call my cell first. If I don't answer, page me. Don't hesitate to do that, okay?"

With a nod, she turned him around, gave him another gentle push, and followed him through the house.

At the front door, he stopped for one more kiss. "Love you."

"Love you, too. Have a good day, dear."

He grinned and waved as he started down the stairs. At the bottom he turned right around and came back up. His hand cupped her cheek as he stole one last kiss.

"Go," she whispered against his lips.

"Can't."

"Have to." With her hands on his chest she eased him away from her.

"I should've gone with malaria or typhoid or something that wouldn't have cleared up in two short days," he muttered as he went down the stairs again.

Giggling, she said, "Next time." She watched him get into his car and blew him a kiss as he spun out of the parking lot.

CHAPTER 27

Caroline wandered through the condo. The living room and kitchen were one big open space with a high counter and bar stools dividing the two rooms. Everything in the kitchen looked shiny new and hardly used. Off the living room was an office done in light wood tones. Ted's laptop sat on the large desk, which had been positioned to maximize the marina view. On the wall were his degrees from Princeton and Duke Medical School. Another wall was covered with framed photos of family and friends. Caroline stopped to study one of the pictures: Ted, Tish, their parents, and grandparents when Ted was about ten.

"Oh, look at you." She ran a finger over the photo. "So cute. Even then." She moved on to group shots of what were probably his high school friends and several of him with Tish at various ages.

Caroline giggled at Ted's long hair in a picture with his parents at his Princeton graduation. By the time he graduated from Duke, though, his hair had been cut short. Mixed among the frames were multiple photos of Ted with his three best friends—in caps and gowns at their Princeton graduation, at the beach, on a sailboat, in tuxedos with unlit cigars dangling from their teeth. In every picture of the four of them, their affection for each other would have been obvious to anyone.

Her cell phone rang in the other room, and Caroline hobbled out of the office to find it. She laughed when she saw Ted's number on the caller ID. "Are you checking up on me already?"

"I miss you."

He sounded so forlorn that she couldn't help but smile. "I miss you, too. Where are you?"

"I just got to the hospital, and I'm walking in. My throat is feeling sore again. Maybe I'd better come home."

"Your kids are missing you after five days. They need you."

"That's playing dirty," he growled. "What're you doing right now?"

"I was just looking at the pictures in your office. You were such a cute little boy. And I loved your long hair in college."

"I'll grow it back for you, but my mother won't be happy. She hated it."

"I like it better the way it is now. There's just enough to run my fingers through."

"*Caroline . . .*"

She laughed. "Go to work, will you? You're bothering me."

"I'm going to bother you, all right. About two minutes after I get home—if it takes that long."

"Thanks for the warning."

"Have a good day."

"You, too. I love you."

"Love you, too. Bye."

"Bye," she said.

"Hang up."

"Not 'til you do."

He laughed and ended the call.

Caroline hugged the phone to her chest and was swamped with such joy that she would've danced around the room if it weren't for the damned cast. Suddenly, she was dying to tell someone about him. She reopened her phone and dialed her parents' number.

"Hi, honey," her mother said. "This is a nice surprise. How's your ankle?"

"It's much better. The cast is smelly and itchy, and I can't wait to shave my leg, but at least it doesn't hurt anymore."

"You must be hating that you can't run."

"I am. I feel all cooped up."

"How was the weekend on Block Island?"

Caroline chewed on the inside of her cheek as she tried to find the words to tell her mother everything that had happened. "It was great. The party was fabulous."

"Now tell me again who had the party. I can't remember what you said."

"Smitty's friend, Ted Duffy's parents and grandparents." Caroline's stomach fluttered as she said his name. "They've been married forty years and sixty-five years."

"You don't hear that every day, now do you?"

"No, it was quite a party." Caroline paused, inhaled a deep breath, and took the plunge. "Listen, Mom, there's some stuff I need to tell you—nothing bad—it's just—"

"What, honey? Are you all right?"

"I've had a crazy couple of weeks, and I want to tell you about it, but it's going to sound so nuts."

"Just tell me, Caroline. You're making me nervous."

"It's nothing to be nervous about. It's good news, the best news. I've fallen madly in love with the most amazing man. I can't wait for you to meet him."

"You mean Smitty, right? The man you've been seeing?"

"No, Mom. Not Smitty. Ted."

"Smitty's *friend?*"

"Yes," Caroline said in a whisper. "I know how it sounds, but you just can't believe what's happened." Caroline spilled out the whole story to her mother, culminating with the news that she and Ted were engaged. "Mom? Say something. Please."

"I don't know what to say, Caroline. You're telling me you're engaged to a man you've known for two weeks and you've come between him and his best friend. What am I supposed to say to that?"

Caroline wanted to weep at how seedy it sounded.

"After what you went through with Brad, I just can't believe you'd risk your heart like this again."

"I'm not risking my heart. When you meet Ted you'll see why I love him so much. It's so different than it was with Brad. I've never felt as cared for and as cherished as I do now. Being with him makes me feel like anything's possible."

Her mother sighed. "You're a grown woman, Caroline, so all I can do is tell you to be careful. I don't want to see you hurt again."

"He'd never hurt me. He's the most wonderful person I've ever met."

"What does he do?"

"He's a pediatric oncologist, and he cares so much about the kids he takes care of. He's just, well . . . He's perfect. I know you're going to love him."

"When do we get to meet this perfect doctor of yours?"

"Soon. We'll come home in the next few weeks when he can get away."

"Let me know, honey."

"I will. Be happy for me, Mom. I've never been happier in my life. I need you to be happy for me."

"I want what you want, Caroline. You know that. I just hope you're being careful."

"When you meet Ted, you'll see that you don't need to worry."

"I'll look forward to meeting him. How's your book coming?"

"I've got three chapters done. I'm feeling good about it so far."

"That's wonderful. I can't wait to read it. Can I tell the family you're engaged?"

"Sure," Caroline said, realizing that would make it official. "I'll give you a call when I find out what Ted's schedule looks like."

"Sounds good. I love you, Caroline. I'm glad to hear that happy sparkle in your voice again. It's been too long."

"Yes," Caroline agreed. "Yes, it has. I'll talk to you soon."

~

TED WALKED in just after nine to candlelight, soft music, and the smell of something mouthwatering cooking on the stove.

"Oh, you're home!" Caroline started down the stairs wearing a pale peach dress.

Ted tossed his keys on the counter and met her on the stairs. She was one step above him when he hooked his arm around her neck and kissed her with a day's worth of pent up passion.

He urged her back up the stairs.

"Are you hungry?"

He nodded but kept moving them toward his bedroom.

"I made linguine with clam sauce," she said against his lips.

"Mmm, I love that," he whispered as he lowered her onto the bed.

"So do you want to eat?"

"Eventually."

Her laughter was soft but shifted quickly to a moan when he turned his attention to her neck.

"I couldn't wait to get home to you."

"Have you been speeding again?"

Nodding, he unbuttoned her dress and eased it down. He nuzzled her breasts and kissed her everywhere but where she wanted him most. "What did you do today?"

"I can't talk when you're doing that," she panted.

"Tell me or I'll stop," he teased.

"I worked on the book." She arched her back. "Made dinner."

"What else?" He rubbed his lips lightly over her nipple.

She gasped. "*Ted . . .*"

"What else?"

"I, um, I told my mother we're engaged."

For that, she was rewarded.

"Do you want to eat now?"

"No, no," she sighed. "I want *you* now."

~

THEY MADE it downstairs to eat at ten thirty. Caroline wore a blue and white striped robe of Ted's, and he had pulled on shorts. The candles on the table were burned down almost to nubs by the time she brought the plates over from the stove.

He reached for her hand and kissed the palm. "I've never done this."

She sat down across from him. "Done what?"

"Come home to someone and had dinner here like this."

She smiled. "How do you like it so far?"

"I could get used to it very quickly."

"That'd be all right with me."

He tugged her chair closer to his. "You're too far away over there."

"How did everything go today?" she asked, taking a sip of the wine she had poured for them.

"It was hectic because of the two unplanned days off, but thankfully there were no disasters. I was relieved to hear we haven't lost anyone since Pilar on Friday, which is a good stretch in light of the month we've had. I missed her memorial service yesterday, so I'll have to give her parents a call this week."

Caroline squeezed his hand. "Maybe your string of bad luck has come to an end."

"God, I hope so. This clam sauce is amazing, by the way."

"I'm glad you like it."

He took a sip of his wine and found his thoughts drifting to something else that happened during the day.

"What're you thinking about?"

"I got a call today from a hospital in New Hampshire. They're looking for someone to head up their pediatrics department."

"Does that happen often?"

"About once a week. Sometimes more."

"You're in hot demand!"

He shrugged. "I never even return the calls." He poked at the food on his plate and looked up at her.

"What's on your mind, love?"

"Lately I've been toying with the idea of doing something different."

"Really?"

He nodded and told her about the conversation he'd had with Parker on the way home from Block Island.

"I agree with him. You can't let the expectations of your father and grandfather dictate how you run your career."

"I'm not looking to do anything right this minute, and it won't necessarily be the New Hampshire thing, but I might start returning some of the calls. Would you hate to live somewhere like New Hampshire?"

"Would you be there?"

He smiled. "Yeah."

"Then New Hampshire sounds perfect to me."

"Don't you prefer the city?"

She shrugged. "We can always visit. Are you really thinking about giving up oncology?"

"I think I am. The other day when I talked to Parker about it. . . That was the first time I've actually said it out loud. Don't get me wrong. I love it. I love the kids and most of the parents and the people I work with. When I first started, I used to think I just needed time to get some legs under me. I figured once I got used to it I could cut back on the hours. But it's been six years and nothing's changed. If anything, the commitment's gotten bigger as I've earned some rank and seniority."

"You're not doing this for me, are you, Ted? Because I don't expect that."

"I'd be lying if I said you didn't factor into it a little. But I'd been thinking about this even before I met you. So mostly I'd be doing it for me. I want to have more of a normal life. And now that I have you, I want so many other things—things I've never really wanted before. I want to be a father and coach T-ball and have tea parties with little girls who look just like their mother. I'll never have that kind of life in this job."

She laced her fingers through his. "Do you think you'd be challenged enough as a regular pediatrician?"

"That's my greatest fear. I imagine it'll be like going from a freeway to a dirt road."

"I'll bet the twists and turns you'll encounter along the dirt road will surprise you in ways you can't even imagine right now."

"Do you think so?"

She nodded.

"How'd you get so wise?"

"I'm not wise."

"I say you are." He leaned over to kiss her. "So is this engagement of ours going to be a long one or a short one?"

"Well, since it's been such a long relationship, I see no need to delay the wedding."

"Wise *and* funny," he said, laughing. "Do you want a big wedding?"

She shook her head. "I almost had that once before, and I have no interest in doing that again."

"You do know that this time it would actually happen, right?"

"Yes, but I'd rather have something small—just our immediate families and a few close friends. Could we do that?"

"Baby, we can do whatever you want. As long as when it's done you're Mrs. Duffy, I couldn't care less how it happens."

"You don't have *any* preference on how we do it?"

He held her hand against his lips. "Just one."

"What's that?"

"Soon. I want it to be soon."

"Soon is good." She gazed at him. "My mother wants to meet you."

"We could go to Saratoga Springs next weekend if you want. Since we can't exactly go to Newport this weekend, I told Roger I'd be on call. Next weekend I'll meet the parents."

She exhaled a long deep breath. "This is starting to feel real."

"It *is* real, and you're going to be my wife as soon as we can make it happen."

"Your wife," she sighed. "I like that. When are you going to tell the guys?"

His smile faded. "I'm trying to figure out the best way to do that. I talked to my mother today, and as much as I wanted to, I couldn't bring myself to tell her. I so was pissed off with myself about that. I love you so much, Caroline. I want everyone to know."

She got up and slid onto his lap.

He wrapped his arms around her.

"Remember the other day when I said I'd felt this way before?"

"Vaguely," he joked.

"I was wrong." She brushed her thumb over his cheek. "This is different. It's more."

"Caroline," he whispered as he buried his face in her hair.

"It's fire and passion, but it's also peaceful and easy and calm." Her lips found his in a light, undemanding kiss. "It's more than I've ever had before, and it's everything I've ever wanted. When the time is right for you to tell the people in your life, you'll know it. In the meantime, I'm not going anywhere."

"You stop my heart."

"And you fill mine. To overflowing."

He stood up and carried her back to bed.

CHAPTER 28

Parker stared into the mirror for a long time before he reached for a towel to wipe the last of the shaving cream off his face. He ran a comb through his dark hair and brushed his teeth like this was any other day, and not, potentially, the most important day of his life. Knowing he wouldn't be able to focus on work, he had decided to stay home and had given his assistant strict instructions to forward any personal calls to his cell phone. All he could do now was wait. And hope.

He got dressed and went downstairs to brew a pot of coffee. When Gina had been his client, she could never meet with him before nine thirty because she had to put her sons on the school bus. With any other client, that detail wouldn't have registered with Parker. With her, though, *every* detail had registered.

A check of his watch told him it was eight thirty. He pictured her walking two boys with backpacks to the corner—yes, he had driven by her house, but only once and just so he would know where she lived and be able to picture that much of her life. Then he remembered it was the middle of the summer, and he panicked. What if they were somewhere on vacation?

Forcing that unpleasant—and unimaginable—thought from his mind, he pictured her having a solitary cup of coffee in a bright, sunny kitchen. Or maybe she had popped in an exercise video or was sleeping in. One thing he was quite certain she didn't do—thanks to the settlement he had brokered with her slimy ex-husband—was work. Parker had seen to it that she didn't have to.

Her ex was a successful sales rep for a pharmaceutical company and made plenty of money. Parker smiled with satisfaction at how much of that money the bastard now had to fork over to her every month. *She had earned every dime of it,* Parker thought, remembering her humiliation over her ex-husband's many affairs. Any man who would cheat on her was a fool, and Mark Mancini was definitely a fool. Parker thanked God for that since Mark being a fool had led him to Gina.

When his cell phone rang Parker almost spilled his coffee in his haste to answer it.

"Hello?"

"Hey, boy-o, what's going on in Boston?" his father asked in his usual booming voice. "Too busy to call your old pop?"

"Hi, Dad. Can I give you a call later? I'm waiting for an important call."

"Sure thing. I just wanted to check in before I leave for Rio tonight."

"Going by yourself?"

"Of course not," James King scoffed.

"I should've known," Parker said. "Don't marry this one, okay?"

"No chance of that. You'll be glad to know I've finally learned my lesson on that front."

"And none too soon," Parker mumbled.

"I'll let you go, but don't be a stranger, huh?"

"Call me when you get back," Parker said as another thought occurred to him. "Hey, Dad, do you have a number for Smitty in Australia?"

"I'll have Janet e-mail it to you," James said, referring to his assistant.

"Thanks. I'll come down to see you when you get back from Rio."

"I'll look forward to it."

"Bye, Dad."

Parker had no sooner ended that call when his cell rang again. This time he checked the caller ID and saw it was Ted.

"Hi," Parker said.

"Hey, isn't today D Day?"

"Yep."

"What time are the flowers being delivered?"

"Nine."

"How are you holding up?"

"*Great*. Perfect, in fact."

Ted laughed. "Whatever you say. If I wasn't in clinic this morning I'd come hold your hand."

"If you weren't in clinic, I'd let you."

"Hang in there, man. She's going to call."

"I hope you're right."

"Hey, um, are you busy for lunch tomorrow?"

"No, I cleared the afternoon to go to Newport. I take it this means you aren't going?"

"No coverage."

"That sucks. So why are we having lunch? What's up?"

"I'll tell you tomorrow. Call me in the morning?"

"All right."

"Good luck with everything today, Parker. I'll keep my fingers crossed for you."

"Thanks."

CAROLINE SAT on the countertop in the bathroom and watched Ted shave.

He glanced at her out of the corner of his eye. "You're making me nervous."

"You're so rough with that razor. I can't believe you haven't cut yourself."

"Why aren't you sleeping in? If I didn't have to go to work, I know where I'd be right now."

"I'd rather watch you shave," she said, reaching for her birth control pills.

He dabbed some shaving cream on the end of her nose. "Why don't you quit taking those?"

"Now?"

"Why not? We're getting married soon, and let's face it, I'm not getting any younger."

"But," she sputtered. "Shouldn't we at least talk about it?"

"We *are* talking about it."

"You can't throw this at me before coffee."

"Okay, then I won't throw it at you." He cajoled the pill pack out of her hand and tossed it into the trash. "Two points."

"Ted . . ."

He kissed her. "Relax, honey. It's not going to happen overnight." He rinsed the last of the shaving cream off his face, acting as if they hadn't just had a life-altering conversation. "What are you going to do today? I feel bad you're trapped here while I'm at work."

She shrugged and tried to move on from what had just transpired. "I don't mind being trapped here. It's good for Cameron to have my undivided attention."

He scowled at her and combed his hair. "As long as he keeps his hands off you, he and I'll get along just fine."

"I want you to read what I've done so far."

"Really?"

She nodded.

"I'd love to. I'm dying to read it, but I didn't want to ask."

"You could've asked." She reached up to caress his smooth cheek. "Mmm, bring that over here."

He complied by rubbing his cheek against hers before he kissed her. "I've never enjoyed shaving quite this much before."

She followed him into the bedroom to keep him company while he got dressed. "So what have you got going today?"

"I have to check on a couple of patients on the in-patient floor first thing. Then I'm in the clinic all morning followed by rounds in the afternoon."

"I'm trying to picture you in your doctor mode," she said, buttoning his shirt.

"Why don't you come with me and see for yourself?"

She looked up at him. "I could do that?"

"Why not?"

"I'd love to!" She clapped her hands with delight. "I can be ready in ten minutes *with* a shower."

"That I'll need to see to believe."

Sure enough, as he downed a cup of coffee in the kitchen, she hobbled down the stairs ten minutes later wearing a pink top and matching skirt. He poured coffee into a to-go mug for her. "Why don't you bring your laptop so you can work in my office while I'm in the clinic."

"That's a good idea."

She retrieved her laptop and followed him out the door a minute later. "This is so exciting," she said when they were in the car. "Thanks for inviting me."

"I just hope . . ." He bit his lip and glanced over at her.

"What?"

"It can be upsetting the first time you see it."

She sobered and reached for his hand. "I know, but maybe if I see it I'll be able to understand it better and be more supportive."

"As long as you know it's okay if it upsets you. That's only natural."

She nodded. "So what did Parker say? How's he doing?"

"He's a total mess."

"I can't say I blame him. I hope she calls. Are you really going to tell him about us tomorrow?"

Ted nodded.

"What are you going to say?"

"I'm going to tell him the truth—exactly the way it happened and hope for the best."

She chewed on her thumbnail and stared out the window.

"What's going on over there?"

"I know we said we'd get through it together if it happens, but I don't know what I'm going to do if they desert you because of me."

"I've been thinking a lot about that, too, and I've decided it's not going to happen. We've been through so much together I can't imagine them turning their backs on me. I've tried to be the best possible friend to each of them. For instance, when Parker's mother was sick and dying, I got him in with specialists and found the answers to all his questions. I even went with him to the funeral home to pick out her casket. I could give you dozens of other examples like that with all three of them. There's been a lot more between us than fun and games. That's got to count for something, don't you think?"

"I hope so. I really do."

When they got to the hospital, they went first to Ted's office to drop off her computer and the bag he had carried to work.

"Glamorous, huh?" he asked, referring to the hole in the wall that served as his office. He donned a white coat with the name "Dr. Duff" embroidered on the left side, checked his pager to make sure it was on, and clipped it to his belt.

"It a nice office," she said. "Oh, look at this!" On the wall she had found the framed copy of a *Boston Globe* article from four years earlier with the headline "Childhood Cancer War Spans Three Generations for Boston Family." In the photo that accompanied the article, Theo and Ed stood behind Ted with their hands on his shoulders. "What a great story this is."

"We got a lot of attention when that came out."

"They look so proud. I'll read it while you're in your clinic."

He draped his stethoscope around his neck and ran his hands over her arms. "Are you sure you're up for this?"

"I'm sure."

"If it gets to be too much just give me a sign, and I'll get you out of there, okay?"

"Don't worry about me. I can handle it."

He dropped a light kiss on her lips and reached for her hand. "Okay then. Let's go."

They took the elevator to the in-patient floor and stepped into a world that was all about kids. There were brightly colored murals on the wall, cartoon character decals on the floor, and doctors and nurses wearing festive scrubs. The first person they encountered was Kelly at the nurse's station.

"Hey, Ted." She filled him in on the rough night one of his patients had had before she noticed he wasn't alone. "Oh, I'm sorry. I didn't realize you had a guest with you. I'm Kelly." She extended her hand.

"This is Caroline," Ted said, catching Kelly's eye as she realized this was *the* Caroline.

Caroline shook her hand. "Pleased to meet you, Kelly."

"Likewise."

Before the moment could turn awkward, Ted quickly got down to business with Kelly, who gave him status reports on several other patients. She used only first names to protect the patients' privacy.

"Let's go see who's hanging out in the lounge," he said to Caroline. They found several kids in the large, sunny room where a big-screen TV was tuned to Nickelodeon. Two pre-teen girls, both of them hooked to I.V. poles, came over to hug him. Neither had hair and both faces were marked by the sunken look reserved for only the sickest of children.

"Hello, ladies. This is my friend Caroline. Caroline this is Becky and Sarah. We call them the dynamic duo because you'll rarely see one without the other."

The girls shook hands with Caroline.

Only Ted noticed how hard she was trying to rein in her emotions as she got her first concentrated dose of cancer-stricken children.

Ted talked to the girls about how they were feeling while Caroline wandered over to look at the paintings they had been working on at a nearby table. "These are excellent," she said.

"Caroline's writing a book," Ted said proudly to the girls, who peppered her with questions.

A boy in a wheelchair rolled over to them.

"How's it going, Simon?" Ted asked.

"Pretty good, Dr. Duff. Who's the foxy babe?"

Ted chuckled. "Hands off, my man. She's taken." He checked his watch. "I need to see a couple of patients up here and then get to the clinic," he said to Caroline. "Want me to walk you back down?"

Caroline glanced around the room. "Would it be okay if I

stayed here and visited with these guys? I can find my way downstairs after a while."

"I'm sure they'd love the company. I'll ask Kelly to get you a volunteer badge so no one hassles you." He led her away from the prying eyes of the curious children. "Are you sure you want to do this?"

She nodded. "I really want to."

Everything they felt for each other passed between them as he kissed her cheek. "I should be done in the clinic by two. If you want to meet me downstairs we can grab a late lunch. Or if you get hungry before then, go on down to the cafeteria. Anyone up here can tell you where it is."

"I'll be fine."

BY THE TIME Gina finally called at ten, Parker had worn a path in his living room carpet. When he saw her name on the caller ID he had to remind himself to take a deep breath before he answered the phone. *This is it,* he thought. *Two years have come down to this moment. Don't blow it.*

"Hello," he said, doing his best to sound light and casual.

"Parker?"

"Hi, Gina. How are you?"

"I'm looking at the beautiful roses you sent. That was so thoughtful of you. Thank you."

"I'm glad you like them."

"I can't believe you remembered."

"Well, it was an important day for you." He wanted to shoot himself for sounding so dorky after rehearsing this in his head for a year.

"Yes, it was."

An awkward pause seemed to stretch on for hours before he said, "So how are you?"

"I'm doing well. We all are. The boys keep me busy."

"I'm glad to hear that." *You're just a regular conversationalist, aren't you, King? Come on! This is Gina! Take it up a notch!* "Listen, Gina—"

"Can I ask you—"

"I'm sorry," he said, kicking the sofa in frustration. He should have hired a high school boy to take care of this for him. No doubt the kid would've done a better job. "What were you going to say?"

"I was just going to ask you, I mean, do you send flowers to all your clients on the anniversary of their divorces?"

Parker chuckled softly. "No. You're the first."

"Oh." After a long pause, she added, "*Oh.*"

"Do you think maybe we could have dinner tonight?"

Another long pause ensued during which he died a thousand deaths waiting for her to say something.

"Are you, um, interested in me, Parker?"

He smiled. "That's one way of putting it."

Flustered, she said, "I don't understand. If that's the case, why haven't you called me before now?"

"Have dinner with me, and I'll explain."

She was quiet for so long he wondered if she was still there. "Oh, God, you waited," she said in a small, incredulous voice.

He realized she was crying. "Gina, don't. Please, don't."

"I can't help it," she sniffed. "That's about the sweetest thing anyone's ever done for me."

"It wasn't supposed to make you cry."

"I'm sorry, but this is just a bit overwhelming."

"I know, and I wish it wasn't. I really, really want to see you. My assistant will baby sit." He was prepared to offer his assistant a thousand dollars to change her plans for the evening if that's what it took.

Gina laughed through her tears. "That's not necessary. I can take them to my mother's."

"So is that a yes, then?" His heart galloped in his chest as he waited for her reply.

"Yes, Parker. That's a yes."

He wanted to whoop, but instead he calmly said, "I'll pick you up at seven."

"Do you know where I live?" she asked and then laughed. "Duh, of course you do. You sent the flowers."

"Can I ask you something?"

"Sure."

"Is there anyone else?"

"No."

He sat down on the sofa when all the oxygen seemed to leave his body in one long sigh of relief. "Good. That's good. I'll see you at seven."

"Okay."

When the soft click on the line told him she was gone, he dropped his head into his hands and fought the urge to weep at the painful surge of emotion that charged through him. She'd said yes. All the days and weeks and months of hoping had paid off. She'd said yes. "Now take a deep breath and play it cool," he said out loud. "You're going to freak her out if you let her see how bad you've got it for her. Don't be an idiot."

He got up and took his coffee cup into the kitchen. Leaning over the sink, he shook his head with wonder. "She said yes," he whispered. "I'm going to see her tonight. *Tonight!*"

TED LEFT Caroline in the lounge and went to find Kelly at the desk.

"So that's *her*, huh?" Kelly asked. "I guess things have changed since I talked to you last.

"Everything's changed."

"I'm happy for you, Ted." She reached across the desk to squeeze his hand. "Really."

"Thank you. Would I be a total ass if I asked you to scrounge up a volunteer badge for her?" he asked with a sheepish grin. "She wants to hang with the kids for a bit."

"Oh, sure, so she's nice, too," Kelly teased. "How's that fair?"

"Thank you, Kelly," he said in a sing-song voice.

"You owe me one, Ted Duffy."

Their friendly banter was a relief. They were going to be

okay after their dating debacle. He was in danger of losing enough friends without adding her to the list, too. "I owe you more than one, but I'm sure you won't let me forget it."

"Never."

At two thirty Ted returned to his office to find Caroline at work on her computer. He dropped a kiss on her forehead. "Were you waiting long?"

"I just came down half an hour ago."

"You were up there all this time?"

She nodded and when she looked up at him her eyes were glassy with emotion. "It was . . . life changing. There's no other way to put it. I thought I loved you before, but seeing you here and meeting your kids . . . Thank you for sharing it with me."

"Thank *you* for spending all that time with them."

"It was entirely my pleasure. I was thinking I might like to volunteer up there once in a while. Could I?"

"That could be arranged." He leaned back against the desk and reached for her hands to pull her up and into his arms. He held her for a long time before he said, "I thought I loved *you* before, but having you here, having you *get* it, just makes me love you more."

She kissed his jaw and then his lips.

He hooked an arm around her neck to kiss her properly.

A knock on the door startled them, but Ted didn't let her go. "Come in," he said.

Caroline inhaled sharply, causing Ted to turn toward the door. "Mom? What are you doing here?"

CHAPTER 29

Mitzi stared at them, her face rigid with shock.

Caroline tried to pull away from him, but Ted kept his arm firmly around her.

Mitzi looked from her son to Caroline and back to Ted. "I don't understand."

Ted released Caroline and went to draw his mother into the room, closing the door behind her. He kissed Mitzi's cheek. "What are you doing here, Mom? I thought you were on Block Island."

Her eyes lingering on Caroline, Mitzi said, "Grandy wasn't feeling well last night, so Dad wanted to bring her over to see her cardiologist. As long as Dad and Grandpa were with her, I decided to come to the auxiliary meeting here."

"Is she all right?" Ted asked.

"Dad just called to tell me they're admitting her to Mass General to run some tests." She glanced at Caroline again as if to confirm that her eyes were not deceiving her. "That's what I came to tell you."

"Cardiac tests?"

She tore her eyes off Caroline and nodded. "Dad said they're just being cautious, and she doesn't want everyone rushing over there. She said, and I quote, 'Tell Ted he can call me tonight, but there's no need for him to come over here.'"

"You're telling me the whole story, right?"

"Yes. They're probably only admitting her because it's summer and we're living on the island where there's no hospital. We'll be in town for at least a week until we know for sure that she's okay to go back."

Ted let out a deep breath. "I'll respect her wishes for exactly one day, and then I'm going to see her."

"I'll let her know." Mitzi cast frosty blue eyes at Caroline. "Are you two going to tell me what's going on here?"

Ted put his arm around Caroline again. "We're together now."

"What do you mean *together*? She's Smitty's girlfriend."

"Not anymore. She's my fiancée."

Mitzi gasped. "What in the world are you talking about? She was with him just last weekend. I saw that with my own eyes."

"Mrs. Duffy," Caroline said. "Mitzi . . . I know how this looks, or I can only imagine how it looks, but I love Ted."

"What about Smitty?" Mitzi sat down hard in the chair by the door. "Oh, God! This is why he left for Australia so suddenly! He knows! How could you do this to him, Ted? You know he has no one of his own. How could you do this?"

"Mom, listen, you don't understand—"

"You're right. I *don't* understand."

"Mrs. Duffy . . ."

"Please don't speak to me, Caroline. What kind of woman are you that you'd come between two men who've been closer than brothers?"

"Be careful, Mother. You're talking to my future wife, and you'll watch your tone with her."

Mitzi didn't try to hide her disgust. "Are you *serious*? What the hell's gotten into you, Ted Duffy? You're going to *marry* her? You don't even *know* her. And if she'll cheat on your friend, what'll stop her from cheating on you, too?"

Caroline gasped and took a step back.

Ted reached out to her. "That's enough!" he said to his mother. "I think you should go now. If you can't be civil to Caroline then we don't have anything to say to each other."

Mitzi stood up. "You've lost your mind."

"No, Mother, I've lost my heart."

"When were you planning on telling us?"

"When I was good and ready to. I've waited a long time for this, and I want you to be a part of it. I know it comes as a shock to you, but I'm asking you to be civil to the woman I love."

Mitzi's eyes held his in a fierce battle of wills.

"Do *not* force me to choose, Mom. Do you understand what I'm saying to you?"

"Yes, I believe I do." She grabbed her purse. "You've never done anything but make me proud. Until now." With that, she turned and walked out.

When Caroline's legs would have collapsed under her, Ted caught her against him and held her as she dissolved into tears.

"Shhh," he whispered. "It's okay. She'll come around."

Caroline was inconsolable.

Ted's pager went off, and he reached for it. "Crap. My residents are waiting for me upstairs to do rounds. Did you get to eat?"

"With the kids." Caroline was once again glassy eyed, but this time due to shock. "Go ahead and go."

"How can I leave you here like this?" He ran a hand through his hair in frustration. "I'm so sorry, honey. I can't believe the way she treated you. She was totally out of line."

"I guess I had it coming." Caroline wiped tears from her face. "Let's face it, I did cheat on him."

Ted put his arms around her. "Don't do that to yourself, Caroline. We both know the truth about how this happened. Nothing happened between us until it was over between the two of you. That's what matters." He wasn't sure if he was trying to convince her or himself. "We have to stay focused on what we know to be true."

She rested her head against his chest. "How is it that you're thinking so clearly? I'll bet your mother has never spoken to you quite like that before."

"I can think clearly because I'm totally committed to you and to us, and nothing's going to come between us. Not my mother, not my friends, not my job. Nothing."

His pager sounded again. "Well, my job's going to come between us for a couple of hours," he said with a wry smile as he clipped the pager back onto his belt. "You aren't going to run away on me while I'm gone, are you?"

"No. I'd be too afraid I might see your mother if I left this room."

Ted smiled and ran his thumbs over her jaw to tilt her face up to his. "I love you, Caroline. That's all that matters here, okay?"

She nodded, but he could tell she wasn't ready to move past the humiliating scene with his mother just yet.

"I'll be back as soon as I can."

"I'll be here."

"I'm counting on it."

With one last quick kiss he was gone.

CAROLINE SANK down into his chair and put her head back. Closing her eyes, she shuddered when she recalled Mitzi's cold disdain. "My future mother-in-law," she said with a sigh, "basically called me a whore. I'm coming between him and everyone in his life. How long will it take him to hate me for that?" A sob lodged in her throat, and she buried her face in her hands.

TED HAD COMPLETED his rounds and was typing orders into a computer terminal at the nurses' station when the father of one of his patients approached him.

"Dr. Duffy?"

Ted turned to him and shook his hand. "Hi, Mr. Hamilton."

"I missed you when you came by on rounds, and I wanted to talk to you about Jonathan having trouble eating since his last round of chemo. I was wondering . . .

I can't believe Mom talked to Caroline that way. I've never seen her so outraged. I expected her and Dad to be surprised and maybe a little bit shocked, but I never imagined she'd act like that. I know it's because she loves Smitty—and not just because he's my friend. She loves him for him. Hell, I do, too. Grandy understood the way I feel about Caroline. Why can't Mom? Grandy. I need to check on her. I hope she's all right.

"Dr. Duffy! Are you listening to me?"

"I'm sorry," Ted said, startled. "What did you say?"

Pete Hamilton stared at him, incredulous. "Am I *bothering* you with my concerns about my son?"

"No, of course not," Ted said, horrified that he had zoned out on a parent. "I apologize." He put his hand on Pete's shoulder. "Let's go talk to Jon and see what we can do about his appetite."

~

PARKER WORE a dark navy pinstripe suit but no tie. He had stressed out about that because he wanted her to think he had come right from work. She didn't need to know he had wasted the whole day killing time until seven o'clock. So he had decided the tie would be too formal. But as he pulled up in front of her two-story brick colonial in the Boston suburb of Stoughton, he wondered if he should have gone with the tie.

You're being an idiot, he thought, as he stepped out of the Porsche and walked up the sidewalk to the front door. Before he rang the doorbell he took a deep breath to calm his nerves. *Showtime.*

The door opened and all his logic flew out the window. *Oh, boy, there she is, and my memories of her haven't done her justice. Not at all.*

"Hi, Parker," she said with a smile, gesturing him inside.

"You look . . ." He shook his head when words failed him. "Amazing." It took every ounce of willpower he possessed not to reach out and twirl one of her long curls around his finger. She wore a dress that clung to all her curves, and he had to remind himself not to stare. "Your hair got long."

She reached up to touch it in a self-conscious gesture that tugged at his heart. "I needed a change."

"I like it." He was pleased to see the aura of sadness that used to be so much a part of her had lifted, leaving her eyes bright with what might have been excitement and maybe even anticipation.

"It's good to see you, Parker."

"Is it?" He hated that he sounded so needy.

She nodded. "I missed seeing you this year, too," she said, referring to the card he had sent with the flowers.

"I can't tell you how happy I am to hear that." *Easy,* he thought, as the urge to touch her became almost painful. *Go easy.*

"Would you like to come in?" She linked and unlinked her index fingers in a gesture that told him she was nervous, too.

"I'd love to." He followed her into the living room where his flowers were on the mantle. That they had been put where visitors were sure to see them pleased him. The room was cozy, but the baseball cards spread out on the coffee table and the light sabers propped in the corner were evidence that two young boys lived here.

"Thank you again for the roses."

"You're welcome." He pointed to framed photos on an end table. "Are those the boys?"

She nodded. "That's Anthony." She pointed to a dark-haired boy with no front teeth. "He's six."

The hint of mischief in the boy's brown eyes amused Parker.

"And that's Dom. He's nine."

The older boy was more serious. "He looks just like you." Neither of them appeared to be two-headed monsters.

"He *loves* hearing that."

Parker chuckled. "They're handsome boys."

"They've been through a lot, but it doesn't seem to have changed who they are. I'm thankful for that much."

"It's a testament to you and your devotion to them."

"That's a nice thing to say."

"I remember how hard you fought for them during the . . ." He didn't want to use the word divorce. "Proceedings."

"What else do you remember?"

"Everything." The word slipped out before he could remind himself he was trying to be cool.

She studied him for an endless moment. "My friends said I was bad cliché."

"Why's that?" he asked, intrigued.

"Because I had a terrible crush on my divorce attorney."

Parker's heart literally stopped for an instant. "You did?"

She bit her lip and nodded. "They said I should forget about you because everyone falls for their divorce attorney."

"And did you? Forget about me?"

"No."

"I don't know how many women fall for their divorce attorneys, but I can tell you I've only ever fallen for one client." He took a step toward her. The nerves were gone, the waiting was over, and standing before him was the woman he loved. "I fell for her about five minutes after she walked into my office, and I've been holding a torch for her ever since."

Her eyes filled. "That was two years ago," she whispered.

"Believe me. I know." He closed the remaining space between them and reached out to caress her face.

"Parker," she whispered, turning her face into the palm of his hand. "I can't believe you're really here."

"Neither can I."

"And I can't believe you gave me a year."

Filled with love for her, he brushed his lips lightly over hers. "You needed the time to heal. I'm just glad you didn't find someone else. I spent a lot of time worrying about that."

She was tentative when she rested her hands on his chest.

He kissed her cheek. "You can touch me, Gina. In fact, I really wish you would."

Empowered, she wrapped her arms around his waist under his suit coat and leaned her head against his chest.

Parker buried his face in her curls and fought through the riot of emotions that came with finally holding her. "I've dreamed about having you right here."

"I have to be honest. I'm a little frightened by this, Parker."

He tipped her chin up so he could look into her eyes. "We'll take it slow—as slow as you want. You'll set the pace, okay?"

She nodded.

"But I'm going to tell you right now—you have nothing to be afraid of. Not from me anyway. I'll never hurt you. *Never.*"

"I'm going to try very hard to believe you."

He kissed her and forced himself to keep it light. "Let me take you to dinner."

"In a minute," she whispered against his lips as her hand curved around the back of his neck.

Parker felt like he'd been struck by lightening when her tongue glided across his bottom lip. He wove a hand into her hair and plundered. Her tongue met his in a burst of pent-up passion that sent him spinning. "Whoa, sweetheart, wait," he said when he couldn't take any more. He leaned his forehead against hers in an effort to slow his racing heart. Wrapping his fingers around hers, he said, "Let's go before I forget I was planning to take you out."

Her cheeks flushed with embarrassment. "I didn't mean to be so forward."

Parker threw his head back and laughed. "Oh, honey, please be forward. Take full advantage of me. I'm all yours."

"You really like me that much?" she asked, the wonder of it written all over her face.

"Yeah." He kissed her hand. "I really do."

CHAPTER 30

"The boys would love this car," Gina said as Parker held the door for her.

"I'll take them for a ride any time they want." He closed the door and walked around to the driver's side.

"You wouldn't want them in here. They leave a mess wherever they go."

"That wouldn't bother me."

"You say that now, but when you're digging a peanut butter sandwich out of your stereo we'll see what you think then."

"That has *not* happened." He still wanted to pinch himself to make sure he wasn't imagining this. Gina was really in his car and not just in his dreams. "You're making that up."

She turned to him. "You know they come with the package, don't you, Parker?"

"Of course I do." He reached for her hand. "I know that."

"Will you forgive me if you don't actually see them for a while?"

He glanced over at her. "Don't you want me to meet them?"

"I do, but I'm not bringing anyone new into their lives until I know it's going to stick. They've been through enough without getting attached to someone who's not going to be around in a couple of months."

He wanted to protest. He wanted to tell her that wasn't going to happen. But what he said was, "I understand."

"Do you?"

"I'm trying to."

"It'll be complicated."

"It's already complicated—for me at least."

"I thought I remembered how handsome you were." She trailed a finger over his jaw. "But my memory failed me."

He captured her hand in his so he wouldn't drive off the road. "That's funny, because I thought the same thing about you when you answered the door." He glanced at her and then back at the road. "Do you know who my father is?"

"Yes, I do."

"Is that going to be a problem for you?"

"I can't see why it would be."

"You'd be surprised at the many ways it can be a problem for me."

She squeezed his hand. "I don't want you for what you have. You certainly know better than most people that I don't need it. You saw to that."

"Has he been honoring the agreement?"

"To the letter. The check arrives on the first without fail, and he sees the boys exactly two nights a month—and not for one minute longer than he has to."

"That must be hard for you. You never get a break."

"I'm lucky to have my family and a lot of good friends who help me. It's much easier now that the boys are older."

"I'm looking forward to meeting them—that is, after I prove to you that I'm going to stick."

Amused, she asked, "And how do you plan to do that?"

"You'll see."

TED KEPT an arm around Caroline as they walked to his car. "I'm sorry it's so late. I'm trying to pinpoint the exact moment when this day spun out of control."

"It's no problem. I knew you were busy."

"All I wanted was to get back to you. I had trouble keeping my mind on what I was doing. In fact, I even got taken to task by a parent, which doesn't happen very often."

"I'm sorry," she sighed. "I'm causing you all kinds of trouble. I hate that."

He leaned her against his car and hugged her. "You're causing me all kinds of happiness. That far outweighs the rest."

"If you say so."

"Honey, come on. Let's put this behind us and go have a nice dinner somewhere. What do you say?"

"I don't know if I could eat."

"You have to try. Besides, I'm starving. I never did get to have lunch."

"All right," she said as he held the door for her. "Did you get a chance to check on your grandmother?"

Ted nodded. "She's as feisty as ever and annoyed by the whole thing, which was a relief."

"That's good. Since she's the only one pulling for us, we need to keep her healthy."

He laughed. "That's true." He took her to one of his favorite restaurants in Boston where he managed to convince her to at least have a salad while he wolfed down a steak. By the time they had finished eating, Caroline was starting to come around. Her eyes, which had been dull and flat with shock after his mother's outburst, had brightened a little, and she'd even managed to smile a few times over dinner. He poured her another glass of wine and reached for her hand across the table. "Are you all right, baby?"

"I will be. How are you?"

"As long as you're here with me, I'm great."

"What are you going to do about your mother?"

"I'm sure I'll see her tomorrow when I visit my grandmother in the hospital. I'll talk to her then."

Caroline fiddled absently with his fingers.

"It's all going to be fine, hon. She just needs some time to absorb it. There's no way she'll let a rift form between us, not after what she went through with my sister."

"What happened to your sister?"

Ted told her about Tish's years of drug abuse and the terrible strain it had put on their entire family.

Caroline was amazed. "I'm trying to picture Tish as an addict. She seemed so together and so happy with Steven."

"She is now, but you should've seen her ten years ago. It was a total nightmare."

"I'm sorry. That must've been awful for you."

"It was." Ted almost choked on his wine as Parker walked past their table, hand-in-hand with a woman as they followed the maitre d'.

When Parker noticed Ted his face lit up with a smile, and he said something to the maitre d'.

Caroline gasped as Parker came toward them.

Parker stopped short when he saw who was holding Ted's hand.

For a long awkward moment no one said anything. Then Parker seemed to recover enough to remember his manners. "Gina, this is Ted and Caroline."

Ted stood and shook hands with Gina. "Pleased to meet you."

"You, too," Gina said.

Ted glanced at Parker, who made a concerted effort to avoid eye contact with him. "Parker . . ."

"We've got to go," Parker said. "They're holding our table."

"Let me explain," Ted said.

"Not now." Parker put his arm around Gina and led her away.

"Son of a bitch," Ted muttered as he sat back down to find Caroline's face once again devoid of color.

He signaled for the check.

"PARKER? WHAT'S THE MATTER?" Gina asked after they were seated.

Parker tried desperately to absorb what he had just seen. "He's one of my best friends."

Her expression was skeptical. "It didn't seem like that to me."

"I'm sure it didn't. I'm in a total state of shock right now."

She reached for his hand. "What's wrong? I don't understand."

Parker took a long sip of his water. "The woman he was with?"

Gina nodded.

"She was our friend Smitty's girlfriend until this past Sunday."

"Oh."

"Yeah." Everything suddenly made sense to Parker—finding Caroline on the stairs Friday night when she was alone in the house with Ted, his preoccupation with something—which he had blamed on work—and Smitty's abrupt departure for Australia. *Oh, Jesus. Smitty knows. That's why he left the way he did.* Parker's mind raced. *Ted lied to my face when I asked him about what happened Friday night. They both did. They were together, and I caught them when I came home early. Oh my God.*

"Parker? Are you all right?"

He forced himself to focus on Gina. "I'm so sorry, honey," he said, taking a deep breath and trying to shake off the shock.

"You don't have to be sorry. Why don't you tell me about it?"

"I don't want to bore you."

"Parker, you're obviously very upset. Talk to me."

Overwhelmed by the need to share it with her, he took another rattling deep breath and told her the whole story.

AFTER DINNER PARKER drove Gina past his house on Beacon Hill. "Now that you know where I live, you'll have to come visit me."

"I don't get into the city very often, but now that I have a good excuse . . ."

As he pulled up to her house just after eleven, he was amazed once again at how she had managed to salvage their evening by helping him through his shock at running into Ted with Caroline. "You can come over any time you want to. Or you can come by my office, or call me in the middle of the night, or call me in the middle of the day. Whatever you want."

She turned to him and smiled. "Thank you for dinner."

"Thank you for saying yes." Her face hovered inches from his in the tiny car, but he refrained from moving closer to her, reminding himself that she was setting the pace.

She put him out of his misery when she reached for him. With her hands on his face she pressed her lips to his. The kiss was sweet and gentle at first—until she sighed with pleasure, his heart skipped a beat, and he tipped his head to delve deeper. Her hand fell to his leg, and she tugged him closer as the kiss went on and on.

He finally pulled back and stared at her, amazed by the desire she stirred in him.

"Do you want to come in?"

"I don't think I should."

"I think you should."

"Gina . . ." he said with a grimace. "I'm trying to show some restraint here."

"Don't."

"I have to."

"Why?" She trailed her finger from his face to his throat and down to his chest.

He closed his eyes for a moment to absorb the overwhelming storm of emotions. "If I go in with you, I'll make love with you. And if that happens, I'll never be able to let you go, because I'm already desperately in love with you."

Tears sparkled in her eyes. "Come in with me."

"What about the boys?"

"They're staying at my mother's tonight and going to my sister's house to swim in her pool tomorrow."

He looked at her for a long time to make sure she knew what she was asking of him before he finally got out of the car and walked around to help her out.

Inside, she turned to him. "Do you want something to drink?"

"No, thanks."

She pushed his suit coat off his shoulders and hung it on the banister. Taking his hand, she led him upstairs to her room.

Unable to believe how the day he'd so looked forward to had unfolded, he held her close to him for a long time.

"I want you to know I never slept with him in this bed, Parker. After he left, I got rid of everything in here. I've never slept with anyone in this bed."

"I haven't slept with anyone since I met you."

Her fingers, which had been busy unbuttoning his shirt, fell still. "You aren't serious."

"I'm dead serious." He unzipped her dress and nudged it down. "How am I doing with proving to you that I'm going to stick?"

"Good," she stammered as he caressed her breasts through her lacy bra. "Really, really good."

He replaced his hands with his lips and urged her down to the bed. "Yes, it's going to be."

CHAPTER 31

Ted couldn't sleep. They had ridden home in silence, and for the first night all week, they hadn't made love. Their shock at running into Parker had made it impossible for them to celebrate that he had been with Gina and his plan seemed to have worked out just the way he had hoped it would.

Even though Caroline was right next to Ted she was out of reach as she tried to cope with what had happened. He knew she was blaming herself, which wasn't fair. They were in this together, and he'd be damned if he would let her pull away from him.

He turned over and put his arm around her. "Are you awake?" he whispered.

"Yeah. I thought you were sleeping."

"I can't." He drew her closer to him. "I need you, Caroline."

"I'm here."

"You're not. You've checked out on me, and I can't stand it. I've had this little taste of heaven with you this week, and it's just the beginning for us. Please don't take a step back because of what happened today. Step toward me, not away from me."

Her body shook with sobs.

"I love you so much," he whispered as he rolled on top of her. "Stay with me. Fight for us. You agreed to marry me, and I'm holding you to it." He kissed away her tears and trembled with relief when he felt her arms close around him. He made tender love to her, and by the time they quivered with aftershocks, he felt like they had reconnected. "We're going to get through this, baby. I promise you. Do you believe me?"

She nodded.

"Tell me. I need to hear you say it."

"I love you, Ted," she whispered. "I love you, and we're going to get through this."

"That's my girl." He kissed her and withdrew from her, keeping her tight against him.

They had finally dozed off when the phone rang. Used to middle-of-the-night phone calls, Ted was instantly awake and in doctor mode. "Duffy."

"Ted," his father said. "Grandy's had a heart attack. I think you'd better come."

TED FLEW OUT of bed and grabbed the first clothes he could find.

"He didn't say anything else?" Caroline asked.

"No."

"Do you want me to come with you?"

His eyes filled as he was overcome by the knowledge that he was probably going to lose his grandmother—and very soon. "I do," he said. "I want you with me."

She went into the bathroom and came out five minutes later dressed with her hair twisted into a clip. "Are you ready?"

He reached for her hand. "I'm sorry. I know I'm asking a lot after the way my mother treated you, but I really need you right now."

With her hand on his face, she said, "I'm right here, and I'll be wherever you need me to be. Okay?"

He nodded. "Let's go."

Ted got them to Mass General in fifteen minutes and did his best to slow his sprint into the hospital so Caroline could keep up with him. His parents and grandfather were in the ICU waiting room. Caroline hung back at the doorway when Ted went in to hug them.

"How is she?" he asked.

His father shook his head. "Not good. The heart attack was mild, but she's in congestive heart failure. They said it could be hours or days."

"Did you reach Tish?" Ted asked.

Mitzi nodded. "Steven is bringing her in."

Theo was weeping, and Ted was struck by how diminished his grandfather seemed in just the few days since he had last seen him. Ted folded the old man into his arms. "Grandpa, it's okay."

"She loves you, Third," Theo said through his tears. "You're her pride and joy."

"I know. I've always known that. Can I see her?"

Theo stood up and wiped the tears from his face. "Edward," he said to his son, "let's take the boy to see his grandmother."

The three of them went down the hallway together.

Mitzi turned to Caroline. "You have no place here."

Remembering how Ted had pleaded with her to fight for them, Caroline met Mitzi's frosty stare with one of her own. "My fiancé asked me to come, and because I love him, I wanted to be with him."

Mitzi rolled her eyes. "Your *fiancé*."

Caroline went out to the hallway to wait for Ted.

In Lillian's room, the doctor in Ted quickly assessed the situation. However, the beloved grandson wasn't quite so quick. Seeing her attached to tubes and monitors and oxygen was overwhelming. Only his father's reassuring hand on Ted's shoulder made it possible for him to move to her bedside.

"Grandy," he whispered, closing his fingers around hers. "Grandy, it's Ted. I'm here."

She gripped his fingers and opened her eyes. "Ted."

Tears flooded his eyes as he leaned over to kiss her. "Does anything hurt?"

"No," she said. "Don't be a doctor."

He laughed softly and wiped his face with the back of his hand. "I'll try not to be."

"My boy," she said. "My boy long before you were a doctor."

"That's right." Behind him he heard his father and grandfather sniffling.

"I need to talk to you. Tell those two to scram."

Ted turned to them, and they nodded to acknowledge that they had heard her. After they had walked out to the hallway, he turned back to his grandmother.

"We've always had something special, you and me," she said.

"Always."

"Your mother told me about what happened earlier. She's going to try to tell you it gave me a heart attack, but we know better, don't we?"

He smiled and nodded even as new tears filled his eyes.

She brought her hands together and tugged at the ring on her finger. When she had worked it free, she pressed it into his hand. "Give this to Caroline."

The two-carat diamond and sapphire ring had been a gift from Theo on their twenty-fifth anniversary.

"Grandy, I can't. You aren't done with it."

"I was always going to give it to you. Take it now so I know it's in good hands. Will you do that for me?"

Choked with sobs, Ted rested his head on her bed.

She ran her fingers through his hair. "Is she here? Did she come with you?"

"Yes."

Lillian chuckled weakly. "Good for her. She isn't easily intimidated. I like that. I want to see her. Will you get her?"

"I'll be right back." He wiped his face on his shirt and went to find Caroline in the hallway. He held out his hand to her. "She's asking for you."

Caroline took his hand. "Okay." Reaching up with her free

hand, she brushed the tears from his face and held him close for a moment before they walked down the corridor together.

"Caroline."

Ted kept a hand on Caroline's shoulder as she moved closer to the bed. "Yes, Mrs. Duffy. I'm here."

"I'm Grandy to you."

"Thank you."

"Do you love my grandson? Really love him?"

"More than anything in this world."

"So do I. He has something for you, something I hope you'll treasure as much as you treasure him."

Ted reached for Caroline's hand and slid the ring onto her finger. "It fits perfectly." He kissed her hand and wiped the tears from her face.

"I had a feeling it would," Lillian said.

Caroline leaned over to kiss Lillian's forehead. "Thank you. And thank you for understanding."

"I want you two to do something for me," Lillian said. "It's something big, and it's something I have no right to ask of you, but I'm dying, so I'm going to ask for it anyway."

"Anything, Grandy," Ted said. "Whatever you need."

"I want you to get married before I go. You can have a real wedding later, and I'll be with you in spirit. But I want to see it, and I don't have time to wait for the real thing. Will you do this for me?"

"Grandy," Ted sputtered. "We can't just . . ."

"Yes, we can." Caroline turned to Ted. "We can."

"Are you sure? Your parents won't be here . . ."

"I'm positive."

"Get a license in the morning, and ask Grandpa to call Judge Daugherty," Lillian said. As her burst of energy faded her eyes grew heavy. "Ted, I also want you to call Smitty. I need to see him. Tell him I'll wait for him."

Ted took a deep breath and wiped his face again. "Okay, Grandy."

~

AFTER THEY LEFT Lillian to sleep and went to the waiting room, it occurred to Ted that he had no idea how to reach Smitty in Sydney since his cell wouldn't work outside the country. He called Parker and when his voicemail picked up right away, Ted realized Parker's cell phone was turned off. "Hey, it's Ted. I need to speak to you right away—and not about what happened tonight. It's an emergency. Call me as soon as you can."

He left the same message for Chip, who didn't answer at home or on his cell.

Finally, he left a message on the voicemail of Smitty's assistant in New York.

"You'll hear from them in the morning," Caroline assured him.

"I hope so."

Tish and Steven came rushing off the elevator, and she fell into her brother's arms. "I'm not ready for this," she sobbed.

"I know," Ted said. "I'm not either." That his sister didn't seem surprised to see Caroline told Ted his mother had gotten to her, too.

"Come on, honey." Steven put his arm around his wife. "Let's go see her."

Ted took Caroline's hand and led her into the waiting room. After they had greeted Tish and Steven, Ted's parents came back into the room.

The four of them sat in uncomfortable silence for several long minutes before Mitzi gasped. "Where did you get that ring?"

"Grandy gave it to her, Mom. She wanted my wife to have it."

"This is outrageous!" Mitzi's face turned red and her eyes narrowed. "She's not well. She isn't thinking clearly. You need to give it back to her."

"Mitzi," Ed said. "She's thinking as clearly as ever. It's her ring to do with as she pleases."

Ted sent his father a grateful glance and then looked to Caroline for support before he said, "You may as well know that Grandy wants us to be married right away so she can be there to see it. We're going to do it tomorrow."

"No." Mitzi shook her head. "That's *not* going to happen."

"Yes, it is," Caroline said, tightening her grip on Ted's hand.

"Nothing happened between us until *after* Caroline and Smitty broke up," Ted said.

Shooting him a disgusted expression, Mitzi got up and left the room.

"Dad, you've got to help me out here."

"Your mother's upset, son, and justifiably so. You're going to have to give her some time to get her head around this."

"That's fine as long as she's civil to Caroline in the meantime. I'm not going to put up with her being rude to my wife. Grandy is asking us to do this, and there's nothing I wouldn't do for her. Mom needs to understand that."

"I'll talk to her, but your mother has a mind of her own, as you well know. You had to have known—both of you—that you weren't choosing an easy path with this."

"What was it you used to say? Nothing worth having comes easy?"

Ed's smile was tinged with sadness. "You always were too smart for your own good." He reached for Caroline's hand where she now wore his mother's ring. "It looks good on you, honey." He kissed her hand and then turned it back over to his son. "Be careful with it and everything that comes with it."

"I will," Caroline said.

MITZI STARED out at the darkness through the window at the end of the long corridor.

Ed wrapped his arms around her from behind and rested his head on her shoulder. "Talk to me."

"We can't let him do this. It's all wrong. They'll be divorced in a year."

"He's a grown man, Mitz. There's nothing we can do about it."

"Don't tell me you're condoning this! Your son is planning to marry a lying, cheating bitch—*tomorrow*!"

Ed turned her so she was facing him. "Our son has presented us with a fait accompli. It's a done deal, babe. We can either get on board and be part of it or be estranged from him and the family they may have together. Do we really want that?"

"She *cheated* on Smitty, Ed. What's to stop her from doing that to Ted?"

"That's not who she is, honey. She's not a bitch. You thought she was lovely last weekend, remember?"

"That was before I knew what she was capable of."

"Sometimes things just happen, and while it might not be how you'd choose it to happen, it happens just the same. Maybe we ought to give them the benefit of the doubt, no? We raised a good boy, Mitz. He knows what's he's doing. How about we have some faith in him? My mother does. Can you?"

"You know I hate this rational side of you."

He laughed and kissed her cheek. "And you know I adore your crazy, over-the-top side, but that's not going work here. You're walking a very fine line right now with that boy you love so much."

She leaned against him. "I'm scared for him. I've never seen him look at anyone the way he looks at her. What'll we do if she hurts him?"

"We'll do what we've always done: We'll surround him with love and get him through it. You don't have to like this, honey, but you *do* have to deal with it. He's asking you to support him. He's going to have a lot of trouble with his friends, so he's going to need us to be on his side right now."

"I'll try," she said in a small voice.

"That's all I'm asking for."

She wiped at the tears on her face. "I can't believe I'm losing my son and my best friend at the same time."

"Your son's not going anywhere—unless you drive him away—and your best friend will always be with you." His voice caught. "She'll always be with all of us."

Mitzi reached for him. "Yes, she will."

~

TED AND CAROLINE went home around four in the morning to get some sleep and to change. He called work to tell them he would be out indefinitely due to a family emergency, and he left a message for Martin Nickerson to let the department chief know he would have to send someone else to the conference in New York that week. Ted would either be at his grandmother's bedside or at her funeral over the next few days.

They were at Boston City Hall at ten o'clock to get a marriage license. From there they went to a jewelry store to buy wedding bands. As they were leaving the store, Ted checked his phone for the hundredth time since they had gotten up. "I wish Parker would call me back."

"Why don't you call his office?" Caroline suggested. "Maybe his assistant knows how to reach him."

"Good idea. I should've thought of that. You're going to need to do the thinking for both of us for a while, honey."

"I can do that."

Ted called Parker's office and learned he had called in earlier to let them know he was taking the day off, but they didn't have a number for him other than his cell.

"I'll bet he's somewhere with Gina."

"Try his cell again," Caroline said.

When Parker's voicemail picked up, Ted said, "Parker, my grandmother has had a heart attack, and she's dying. She's in the Mass General ICU, and she asked me to find Smitty to tell him she wants to see him. I need you to help me get in touch with him. I have no idea where he is in Sydney, and I figured that between you and your father, one of you has a number for him. I know you're upset about what you saw last night, but I need your help. I'll explain the rest as soon as I can."

"That ought to do it," Caroline said.

"I hope so. I can't imagine she's got a ton of time left, and we've lost a bunch of it playing bullshit phone tag games."

"I'm glad that things seemed to have worked out for Parker with Gina."

"I am, too. I hope I get a chance to tell him so."

"You will, Ted."

He pulled into a parking space at the hospital and leaned over to kiss her. "Thank you again for what you're doing for my grandmother. No one dreams of getting married this way."

"Are you kidding?" she asked with a smile. "Don't you know what a great story this'll give us to tell our children someday? 'Daddy and I were married three weeks to the day after we met.'"

He smiled. "Don't forget to tell them, 'It was okay for us but not for you.'"

"That goes without saying."

"Are your parents going to freak out when they hear about this?"

"Maybe a little, but I'll fix it with them. Don't worry about that. How are you feeling about your mother?"

He sighed. "I'm hoping she's going to be in the room when we get married. Beyond that, I don't know what to say."

With her hand on his face, she turned him to look at her. "I want you to know I'm not just doing this because your grandmother asked us to."

"No?"

She shook her head. "I can't wait to be your wife, and the last thing I want is for you to take these vows with me today and think I'm doing it for any other reason than I love you and want to spend my life with you."

"I love you, too, Caroline Ann," he said, teasing her with the middle name he had learned about at City Hall. "I don't know what I ever did to get so lucky."

"Let's go get married and give your grandmother some peace of mind."

CHAPTER 32

Smitty slept in on Saturday after having worked late into the night to catch up on all his regular client accounts. His assistant in New York had forwarded Ted's urgent message, but Smitty hadn't called him back. *Fuck him. I'm not ready to talk to him yet.*

After spending two full days examining the Jergenson files, he was pleased with what he had seen so far and had e-mailed Bill Kepler to let him know that from his initial impressions the purchase looked like a go. Smitty figured he would need two more weeks at the most to complete his review. Since he was in no rush to go home, he had decided to take his time.

He'd spent most of the last two days with Marjorie and had been impressed by her command of complicated business concepts as well as her devotion to her employees. From those who had known her since childhood, he had learned her nickname was Margo and she was a talented artist.

He was unsettled by the subtle interest in him that he had felt coming from her during their long days at work and over dinner each night when they discussed his lengthy list of questions. Since he couldn't be any less interested in pursuing romance with her or any woman, he had ignored the signals and focused on the work.

Under other circumstances he might have found her attractive. More than attractive, actually. All those curls and the sprinkling of freckles across her nose were really cute. She also had a way of sizing him up with her astute brown eyes that told him he wouldn't get away with much if he were to act on the signals she was sending. Normally, that kind of sassiness appealed to him, but since he wasn't interested, it didn't matter.

Smitty took his coffee with him when he went to look out at the sunny day in Sydney. He ran a hand over his bare chest and stretched out the kinks from the long, busy week. He found it hard to believe that just seven days ago he had been unaware of how dramatically his life was about to change.

A knock on the door interrupted his thoughts. He crossed the room and opened the door to Marjorie. She had tied her hair back in a high ponytail and wore jeans with a yellow T-shirt. Today she looked about eight years old, but her eyes skirted over his bare chest with a woman's appreciation.

"Come in." He stepped back from the door. "Want some coffee?"

"No, thanks. What are you doing?"

"I worked late last night, so I just got up. What about you?"

"I've been packing up my father's belongings all morning."

He couldn't deny that the sadness he saw in her every time she mentioned her father moved him. "How's that going?"

She shrugged. "He had a lot of stuff. Most of it will be sold at auction next month, so I'm putting aside the few things I want and packing up the rest."

"Why don't you pay someone to do that for you?"

"It doesn't seem right to have a stranger pawing through his things. I'd feel like I was violating his privacy."

"Is there anything I can do to help?" Despite his desire to stay detached, something about her touched him.

"Do you know what I really want?"

He had his suspicions but kept his expression vague as he refilled his coffee cup. "What's that?"

"I want to get out of here for a few hours. What do you say I show you around Sydney? You haven't been outside since you got here."

"I'm here to work not play tourist."

Her face sagged with disappointment.

"Oh, all right." He sounded more aggravated than he felt. "Let me grab a shower, and I'll come get you so you can show me Sydney."

Glee replaced disappointment as she clapped her hands. "Goodie," she said on her way to the door.

Smitty shook his head with amusement at her retreating back. He was *not* going to get sucked in by her too-adorable-for-words act. He had learned his lesson. Never again.

THEY BEGAN their tour in Sydney Harbour where she took him for an up-close view of the Harbour Bridge and Opera House. "Do you mind if we go to the zoo?" she asked as they strolled along the waterfront wearing jeans and sweaters.

"Whatever you want," he said, enjoying the fresh air and her company. "You're the tour guide."

They spent two hours wandering through Taronga Zoo where they saw red kangaroos, wombats, and the orangutan rainforest. "Oh, look at them!" Marjorie giggled at the faces the orangutans were making.

Smitty smiled at her childlike pleasure. "What about the koalas? I can't be in Australia and not see a koala."

"Right this way."

"You must've spent a lot of time here. You know this place really well."

"I used to come with my mother all the time. She loved the zoo."

Smitty thought of his own mother. She had certainly never taken him to a zoo or anywhere else for that matter.

"What are you thinking about?" Marjorie asked.

"Nothing special."

"You get this look about you every now and then that makes me think you have all kinds of deep, dark secrets."

"Maybe I do." He could tell she was showing restraint by not pursuing it further.

"I've always thought if you had only one day in Sydney, the thing you'd have to do is take the ferry to Manly."

Smitty hurt when he recalled his last ferry ride.

"There it is again." She glanced up at him. "More secrets."

Unnerved by her ability to read him so well, he glanced down at her. "What's the deal with this Manly place?"

"I've heard it said that Manly is 'seven miles from Sydney and a thousand miles from care.'"

"Hmm, a thousand miles from care." That might just be far enough. "How do we get there?"

THEY SPENT the rest of the day in Manly, wandering through the Corso—an outdoor pedestrian mall—before heading out to the far end of Manly Cove to visit Oceanworld with its underwater tunnel view of sharks and stingrays. As the sun began to set, they had a beer in a beachfront bar and then bought fish and chips to eat on the beach.

"This was a great day," Smitty said, reclining on the sand after they had eaten. "Thanks for talking me into it."

"Thank you for coming. I couldn't stand another minute locked up in that glass tower." She shivered and burrowed further into her white wool fisherman's sweater.

Against his better judgment, he reached for her.

Startled, she took his outstretched hand and scooted over to take shelter with her back against him.

Tentatively, he rested his hand on her hip. "Better?"

"Much."

As they watched the sunset in silence, Smitty was amazed to realize he hadn't thought of Ted, Caroline, or the mess he had left behind at home in hours. He glanced down at Marjorie and was grateful to her for getting his mind off his troubles, even temporarily.

They had snuggled together on the sand for at least half an hour when Marjorie put her hand on top of his.

Smitty told himself to get his hand out of there but couldn't quite work up the energy to make it happen. So he couldn't very well protest when she laced her fingers through his.

"Your hand is so warm, John."

"You know, you're the only one who calls me that—you and everyone here."

She looked up at him, but kept her firm hold on his hand. "What does everyone else call you?"

"Smitty."

"Smitty," she said, trying it on for size. "I like John better."

"I'm starting to think I do, too."

"Smitty's a boy's name. John's a man's name. It's a strong name."

"I've always thought it was kind of boring."

She shook her head. "No, it's not. Not like Marjorie." She made a face. "It was my grandmother's name, and it's better suited to an old lady."

"Do you like Margo better?"

"Uh huh. That's what my friends call me. You could call me that if you wanted to."

He could see she was offering more than friendship with the nickname and didn't want to encourage her. "We should get going back."

She kept her eyes trained on him for a long moment before she said, "Okay."

He helped her up, and they brushed the sand off their clothes, collected the trash from their picnic, and walked to the ferry. On the short ride back to Sydney, they stood together at the rail and watched the city lights come into view.

After they disembarked at the Circular Quay, they walked slowly back to the Jergenson building. Their hands bumped together, and Marjorie linked her index finger around his. As her signals became less subtle, his reaction to her confused him. She was so warm and easy to be with that remaining aloof from her was almost impossible.

They rode the elevator to the sixteenth floor, and Smitty was almost sorry to see their day come to an end. He hadn't realized how much he had needed the diversion, and the idea of being alone again with his own thoughts was unappealing after the relaxing day he had spent with her. "Do you want to come in for a drink?"

He could tell he had surprised her.

"That would be nice."

In his apartment, he opened a bottle of the wine he knew she liked and poured them each a glass. He handed one of them to her and raised his glass. "Cheers."

"To new friends."

He nodded and touched his glass to hers.

She kept her eyes trained on him while she sipped her wine.

"Marjorie . . ."

"I thought you were going to give Margo a try." Her teasing smile lit up her face.

"Margo," he said, trying to remain focused on what he needed to say to her. "You're a nice girl, a beautiful woman. You don't want to get mixed up with the likes of me."

"The likes of you?" she asked with a perplexed frown. "What does that mean?"

"You don't know me, and if you did you wouldn't want anything to do with me."

"Why in the world would you say that? I've spent long hours with you over the last few days, and all I've seen is a kind, generous man with a big heart and a sharp mind."

Smitty shook his head with scorn. "You don't know the half of it. And believe me, if you did, you'd run for your life."

She didn't let him look away from her and never wavered when she said, "Try me."

"You're mixing me up with the guy who's going to solve all your problems by buying your business."

Her eyes flashed with anger. "Don't treat me like a child, John. I'm fully capable of understanding the difference. You're just looking for a way around telling me why it is you think you're so unworthy of me." She put down her glass. "Thank you for a lovely day."

She had reached the door when he said, "Fine. You want to know who I am, I'll tell you. I'm a guy who never knew who his father was because his mother slept with so many men she had no idea which one fathered me. She forgot to feed me most nights because she was too busy banging men for money so she could buy her next fix."

Marjorie kept her back to him, but the stoop of her shoulders told him his words were having the desired effect.

"I haven't seen her since I left for college on a scholarship I would've sold my soul to the devil for, just so I could get away from her. My wife left me when I finally told her my sordid story three years after we were married. Oh, and just before I came here, my best friend of nearly twenty years made off with my girlfriend. I'm a multi-millionaire who has every imaginable possession, but I've got *nothing* that really matters. Is there anything else you want to know?"

Her face stained with tears, she turned, crossed the room, and launched herself into his arms.

Smitty took a step to keep from tumbling backward and closed his arms around her.

She rained kissed over his face and then found his lips.

As he realized she knew everything there was to know about him, all his dirty secrets, and didn't seem to care, he felt something inside him shift to accommodate the possibility that she might be the answer to every question. And then he kissed her as if there were no tomorrow, only right now.

She clung to him, and when he would have withdrawn from her, she didn't let him.

The phone rang, but they ignored it as he lowered her to the sofa. They were still there fifteen minutes later when the phone rang again. She whimpered when he pulled back from her.

"Let me get that," he said with a light kiss. "Only a few people have this number, so it might be important."

She released him, and he got up to answer the phone.

"Smitty?"

His lips tingled from Marjorie's passionate kisses. "Hey, Parker, how are you?"

"Man, I'm so sorry to do this to you, but Lillian's had a heart attack. It's not looking good."

"Oh, no," Smitty gasped. "*No.*"

"I know. It's awful. She's asking for you, buddy, and she told Duff to tell you she'll wait for you. He asked me to call you. Can you come?"

"I'll be on the first flight I can get."

"She's in the ICU at Mass General."

Smitty's eyes burned with tears. "I'll be there as soon as I can. Tell her I'm coming, Parker."

"Hurry."

Smitty hung up and a sob rattled through his big body.

Marjorie came up behind him and wrapped her arms around him. "What is it, John? What's wrong?"

"The woman who's been like a grandmother to me is dying." His voice caught. "I need to go home."

"Go pack. I'll call for a flight."

He squeezed her hand. "Thank you. I need to go to Boston."

She reached up to hug him and then sent him along to pack.

Twenty minutes later, she drove him to Sydney Airport for a twenty-six-hour trip that would somehow get him to Boston on Sunday morning. He would have to figure out how that would work when he was thinking clearly again.

"You have your passport?" she asked.

"Yeah."

"Will you be all right?"

"I just hope I get there in time." He wiped new tears from his face. "We were dancing at her anniversary party just a week ago. I can't believe how much has happened since then."

Marjorie reached for his hand. "I'm sorry."

Grateful for the comfort, he held her hand until they reached the airport.

She pulled up to the curb at the international terminal and got out to help him with his bag.

He embraced her in a tight hug.

"Call me when you can?"

He nodded.

"Will you come back, John?"

He studied her pretty face for a long moment. "Yes," he said, leaning in to leave her with one last thorough kiss. "I'll be back."

CHAPTER 33

Getting married turned out to be a bit more complicated than Ted and Caroline had expected. Lillian was groggy from some medication she had been given during the night. While they waited for that to wear off, Theo tried to track down his friend, the retired Superior Court judge, who was playing in a golf tournament on Cape Cod. When Theo finally reached him, Judge Daugherty promised to be at the hospital by seven that evening. So they spent the day taking turns visiting with Lillian and tending to Theo.

Parker came bursting into the ICU at six. "I just got your message an hour ago," he said, breathing hard from running. "I got here as soon as I could."

Ted noticed his friend was wearing the same clothes he'd had on the night before. "Did you call Smitty?"

Parker nodded. "He's coming. It'll be Sunday morning before he gets here, but he's on his way. Chip and Elise are, too."

"Good. Thank you."

Parker glanced at Caroline and then turned his attention back to Ted. "How's Lillian?"

"She's hanging in there. Come on, I'll take you in to see her."

Lillian was asleep, so they didn't disturb her.

Ted was touched when Parker wept at the sight of her in the big hospital bed. He reached for his friend and was relieved that

Parker let him offer comfort. Once Parker had collected himself, they walked out to the hallway.

"I was so happy to see you with Gina," Ted said.

"Yeah, it went a thousand times better than I ever imagined it would."

Ted grinned as he tugged on the lapel of Parker's suit coat. "Apparently."

Parker's smug, satisfied smile faded when he seemed to remember there were other things they needed to talk about. "What the hell's going on with you and Caroline, Duff?"

Ted checked his watch. "Well, in about an hour we're going to be married."

"What?"

Ted looked at his friend, and a thousand memories of joy and sadness and foolish fun passed through his mind. He hoped those memories would be enough of a down payment on what he was about to ask of him. "I want you to know how sorry I am that you found out the way you did. That wasn't how I wanted it to happen. You may not believe me, but I'd planned to tell you at lunch today." Parker started to say something, but Ted held up his hand to stop him. "There's a lot we need to talk about. But not today. All I'm going to say right now is I'm going to marry the woman I love in less than an hour because I was going to anyway, and my grandmother asked me to do it before she dies."

Parker's cheek twitched with tension, and he got busy studying his shoes.

"I'd like very much to have you there with me when I get married. I'm asking you to remember what we've been to each other for more than half our lives and to put everything else aside for the time being so you can stand up for me at the most important moment of my life." Ted's throat tightened with emotion as he tried to prepare for the possibility that his friend might say no. "Do you think you could do that for me, Parker?" He held up the rings he and Caroline had bought earlier.

After what seemed like an endless pause, Parker reached for the rings. "Yeah. I can do that."

"Thank you."

Parker nodded.

~

In the waiting room, Caroline found herself alone with Ted's sister while everyone else went to get something to eat.

"Um, Tish." Caroline waited until she had the other woman's attention. "I don't know what you think of all this . . ."

"I think it's very romantic," Tish said.

"Really?"

Tish nodded. "I've never seen my brother light up the way he does when you come into the room. I can see that he loves you. I only hope you love him just as much."

"I do."

"Then that's all I need to hear. My mother will put you through the paces at first, but you'll come to love her if you can be patient with her and give her a chance."

"I'll try my best to do both. I know we don't know each other that well, but I find myself in need of a matron of honor. Since my own sister can't be here, do you think . . ."

Tish reached out to her. "I'd love to."

"Thank you."

"Thank *you* for what you're doing for my grandmother."

Caroline smiled. "It's not really much of a sacrifice when you consider that at the end of the day Ted will be my husband."

"That's not such a bad deal."

"No, it really isn't."

~

Judge Daugherty arrived at seven fifteen full of apologies and complaining about the traffic between Cape Cod and Boston.

"Where're the bride and groom?"

"Right here," Ted said.

Mitzi stood off to the side with her husband and watched as Ted introduced the judge to Caroline.

"Well, you're all grown up since I saw you last, Ted."

"All grown up and practicing pediatric oncology," Theo said proudly.

"Ah, yes, the Duffy family business. Do you have a license?"

Ted reached for the inside pocket of his navy blue blazer. "Right here."

The judge propped glasses on the end of his nose and inspected the document. "Everything appears to be in order. Shall we?"

Theo led them to Lillian's room where she was propped up in bed wearing a scarlet bed jacket Mitzi had brought from home.

"Hello, Warren," Lillian said. Her voice was weaker than it had been the day before, but her eyes were still bright with life and, for the moment, excitement.

"Lillian, you're as lovely as ever." He leaned over to kiss her. "I'm sorry you had to wait all day for me."

"You're here now, so let's get the show on the road."

They all laughed at Lillian's feistiness.

The judge arranged Ted and Caroline so his grandmother had the best view.

Mitzi stood in the doorway.

"Do we have witnesses?"

Parker and Tish stepped forward.

"Very good." The judge gestured to Ted and Caroline. "Now, if you two would face each other."

Ted reached for Caroline's hands and smiled at her reassuring squeeze.

"Ted, repeat after me: I, Edward Theodore Duffy, the third, take you Caroline Ann Stewart as my lawful wife. To have and to hold from this day forward, to love, honor and cherish, forsaking all others, until death do us part."

Ted heard weeping in the background but had eyes only for Caroline as he said his vows in a voice heavy with emotion.

Tears running down her face, she followed suit.

"Do we have rings?"

Parker produced them.

After they had exchanged rings, the judge said, "By the power vested in me by the Commonwealth of Massachusetts, I now pronounce you husband and wife. Ted, you may kiss your bride."

Lillian clapped when Ted wrapped his arms around Caroline, kissed her, and then hugged her until he had gotten his emotions under control.

"I give you Dr. and Mrs. Ted Duffy," the judge said as the others applauded along with a group of doctors and nurses who were watching from the corridor.

"Theo, give them our gift," Lillian said.

Theo reached into his pocket and withdrew what looked like a credit card and handed it to Ted.

"What's this?" Ted asked.

"A key to the honeymoon suite at the Ritz," Lillian said with a gleam in her eye. "If you get going now, you'll still have most of the night. It's yours tomorrow night, too."

"I'm not going anywhere tonight, Grandy," Ted protested.

"You are *not* spending your wedding night in this hospital, Ted Duffy," she said, taking a deep wheezing breath.

Ed settled her back against the pillow. "Take it easy, Mother."

"I want you to go," she said to Ted. "I'll still be here tomorrow. I promise."

The others began to filter into the hallway, leaving Ted and Caroline alone with his grandparents.

"I don't want to leave you," Ted said.

"We've had thirty-eight wonderful years together, my love. Go be with your wife now. You've made me very happy today. Both of you."

Ted leaned over the bed to receive her hug.

In his ear, she whispered, "I've done my part. Now you do yours."

Ted pulled back to look at her and was taken aback by the calculating expression on her face.

Before he could ask her what she meant, Caroline nudged him aside so she could kiss and hug Lillian.

Theo hugged Ted. "I hope you'll be as happy with your wife as I've been with mine." He welled up when he looked over at Lillian, who was worn out from all the excitement.

After Caroline shared a tearful embrace with his grandfather, Ted took her hand and led her into a hallway, lined with people who wanted to wish them well, or who were at least pretending they did. Parker hugged them both, as did Ed, Judge Daugherty, Tish, and Steven.

Mitzi leaned against the wall on the other side of the hallway.

"Mom?" He could see the battle she waged on her face. She made no overture toward him. With a sinking feeling in his gut he reached for Caroline. "Ready to go?"

She nodded and took his hand.

They had made it to the ICU door when Mitzi called out to them. "Wait."

Ted kept his hold on Caroline's hand as he turned to his mother.

Mitzi reached up to frame her son's face. "I love you."

"I love you, too." He leaned down to kiss her. "Mom, I'd like you to meet my wife, Caroline."

Mitzi shook Caroline's hand. "Pleased to meet you."

"Likewise, Mrs. Duffy."

"Please call me Mitzi."

"I'd like that."

"Be good to my son," Mitzi said, her voice wavering. "I love him very much."

"I do, too. With all my heart."

Mitzi nodded.

Ed put his arm around Mitzi to watch their son and his wife walk hand-in-hand though the ICU door.

When they were out of sight, Mitzi collapsed against her husband and wept.

"Well done, honey," Ed whispered. "Very well done."

TED AND CAROLINE emerged from the hospital into the warm summer evening. When they got to his car, Ted stopped her.

"What is it?"

"I just need . . ."

"What, honey?"

He put his arms around her. "This." A deep sigh rattled through him. "Thank you for what you did with my mother. I wouldn't have blamed you if you'd told her to go to hell."

"I couldn't do that. She's my mother-in-law."

Ted smiled in amazement as the whirlwind finally slowed long enough for him to consider just how much had changed in the course of that day. "Yes, I guess she is." He held the car door for her.

After he got in, she said, "I'm glad I got to see her in a less stressful situation last weekend. Because of that I know there's another side to her than what I've seen in the last few days."

"She's usually so amazing."

"I was relieved for you that she took the first step just now."

"I was relieved for all of us. With my grandmother so sick, we don't need any more tension." He reached into his pocket and withdrew his cell phone. "What do you say we call *my* mother-in-law and fess up to what we've done?"

Caroline winced. "Do we have to?"

He smiled and nodded.

With great reluctance she took the phone and dialed the number.

"Hi, Dad." Caroline sent a fearful look Ted's way and tipped the phone so he could hear.

He reached for her free hand.

"Is Mom home? Can you ask her to pick up the other extension?" Caroline waited for her mother to come on the line and with a deep breath and another glance at Ted for reassurance she told them her news. After a long silence, she asked, "Are you guys still there?"

"We're here," her father said. "This is very surprising, Caroline."

"You did a nice thing for his grandmother, honey," her

mother said. "I'm sorry we weren't there to see it, but you did a good thing."

"That's how it feels to us, too, Mom. I promise you we're going to do it again very soon and have all of you there. Ted wants to talk to you guys, okay?"

She handed the phone to him.

"Hi, Mr. and Mrs. Stewart.

"Hello, Ted," she said.

"I'm sure you have a lot of questions and a lot of worries, but I want you to know I love Caroline very much, and I'm going to take very good care of her."

"That's good to know," her mother said. "We're looking forward to meeting you."

"Depending on what happens with my grandmother, we'll be up next weekend, if that's all right with you."

"Of course it is. We'll keep your family in our prayers."

"Thank you. Well, I'll give you back to Caroline."

She talked to them for a few more minutes while Ted drove them home to get what they needed to spend two nights at the Ritz.

After she ended the call, Caroline turned in her seat so she could see him. "Were you born with that or did you acquire it along the way?"

"Born with what?"

"The ability to charm the mothers, even over the phone, and even after you've just basically eloped with their daughters."

He rolled his eyes. "I don't know what you're talking about. Since I've never eloped before I don't have a whole lot of experience with how to talk to mothers-in-law."

"Well, you said exactly what she needed to hear."

"That's good. I was afraid we were going to be adding them to our list of problems by telling them after the fact."

"Why don't we put that list aside for tonight, okay?"

He squeezed her hand. "Absolutely."

ON THE WAY back into the city, Ted called the hospital and was relieved to learn there had been no change in his grandmother's condition.

"Your grandparents were so sweet to do this," Caroline said as they rode the elevator to their suite on the top floor of the Ritz Carlton.

"It's just like them to think of something like this. Their generosity has always been astounding and even overwhelming at times. I wanted to kill them when they bought me the Mercedes."

"Why?"

He shrugged. "It just seemed so excessive and embarrassing. But it's the *giving* that delights them, and because there was never a single string attached to any of it, I stopped saying no and learned to just say thank you."

"You're a good boy, Ted Duffy."

With the rakish lift of an eyebrow, he said, "I'm a good boy who's having some very naughty thoughts about his wife at the moment."

She smiled and stepped aside so he could open the door. "Oh," she sighed when she caught her first glimpse of the opulent suite.

"Wait." He lifted her into his arms and carried her across the threshold. "I don't want to forget anything I'm supposed to do tonight."

She looped her arms around his neck and kissed him senseless.

That's where the bellman found them when he arrived with their bags. Embarrassed to have been caught, Ted eased her down and went to tip the man.

"Will there be anything else, Dr. Duffy?"

"No, thank you."

"Have a nice evening."

Ted closed the door and leaned back against it to gaze at Caroline. "Oh, I plan to."

She giggled at his lascivious expression. "Shouldn't we eat at some point?"

"Probably." He crooked his finger at her.

She went to him.

Reaching for her hand, he said, "Let me see." He took a good first look at her two new rings. "I like the way they look on you." He sighed. "My wife."

"Let me see yours."

He gave her his left hand, and she kissed the ring on his finger. "My husband."

"It's still kind of hard to believe, isn't it?"

"Totally. A week ago tonight I couldn't imagine how we'd ever find a way to be together."

"And now we have the rest of our lives." Still leaning against the door, he buried his hands in her hair and fell into a deep, soulful kiss, the effects of which he felt everywhere. When he finally resurfaced, he peppered her face with kisses. "My grandmother said the strangest thing to me before we left."

"What was that?"

"'I've done my part,' she said. 'Now you do yours.' What do you suppose that means?"

"I don't know." She pressed against his erection. "But it seems to me you're doing your part at the moment."

Ted groaned and everything else was forgotten.

CHAPTER 34

"Then he asked me to stand up for him," Parker said.

"*Damn,* man, what did you do?" Chip asked, astounded.

Parker handed Chip another beer. "The way he asked me. . ." Parker shook his head. "You wouldn't have been able to say no, either."

"So then they just got married?" Elise asked, still stunned by the news. "Right there in the hospital?"

Parker nodded. "It was short, sweet, *and* legal."

"Do you think they're really in love?" Elise asked.

"Yeah," Parker said with amazement. "As crazy as it sounds, they really seem to be. This is exactly what he said—'I'm marrying the woman I love, and because I was going to anyway I'm doing it now because my grandmother asked me to do it before she dies.' I'll tell you one thing, though, Mitzi was steaming."

"When in the world did this happen?" Elise asked. "I mean she and Smitty just broke up on Sunday! I don't get it."

"I don't either," Parker said. "I was as surprised by it as you are."

"Did he say anything about Smitty?" Chip asked.

"Just that there was a lot he needed to tell me and he would eventually. It was pretty obvious he didn't want to get into it on his wedding day."

"Has anyone heard from Smitty?" Elise asked.

"He called me with his flight info before he left Sydney, but not since then," Parker said. "I sure do hope he gets here in time to see Lillian. She really seemed to fade tonight after the wedding. I don't know how much time she has left."

"He'll be a mess if he doesn't get to see her," Elise agreed sadly.

"Did Smitty say anything about Duff and Caroline?" Chip asked.

"No, we haven't talked about it."

"Jesus," Chip muttered. "What a fucking mess. There's no way Duff and Smitty are ever going to be the same after this. Nothing will be."

"I've been thinking a lot about that since I first saw them together last night," Parker said as he opened a bottle of wine for Elise.

"That must've been so shocking," she said, her eyes full of empathy for Parker.

"I felt like I'd been punched in the stomach or something. I just can't figure out how it happened. The not knowing is driving me nuts."

"Me, too," Elise said. "You know, I walked in on them in the kitchen last weekend when you guys were in town. I didn't think too much of it at the time, but now it occurs to me they were having a pretty intense conversation."

Parker told them about finding Caroline on the stairs when he went home early on Friday night and the lies she and Ted had told him about it.

"This whole thing is so fucked up," Chip said in a burst of anger. "He acted all surprised on the phone with me this week when we were talking about Smitty going to Sydney, and he knew *exactly* why Smitty went."

"How do you suppose Smitty found out about them?" Elise asked. "And *when*?"

"I can't imagine," Parker said. "None of us knew, so how did he?"

"Maybe she told him," Elise said.

Chip shook his head. "I doubt it, but somehow he figured it out. I'll tell you what: I just can't get over Duff doing this to him of all people. We all know how tough he's had it."

"Duff said something to me tonight that really hit me right here," Parker said with his hand over his heart. "He asked me to remember what we've meant to each other for more than half our lives. I hadn't looked at it that way before—the half our lives part—and now that's all I can think about. I'm trying to keep that in mind and not judge him solely on what's happened in the last week."

Elise got up from the barstool in Parker's kitchen and went around the counter to hug him. "You're very sweet to look at it that way."

"You're forgetting about Smitty," Chip reminded him. "You've known him for half your life, too, and he sure as hell didn't deserve this—from either of them, but him especially."

"This is *Ted*, Chip," Elise pointed out. "He hasn't forgotten about Smitty. He must be so torn up about doing this to him."

Chip's eyes flashed with passion. "This is a black and white issue, Elise. There's no gray area here. She was his *best friend's* girlfriend. Hands off."

"They fell in love, babe. Come on. Don't be so unforgiving." She kept her arm around Parker. "What would you have done if I'd been going out with Parker when you met me?"

Playing along, Parker wrapped his arms around her and kissed her cheek.

"Nothing!" Chip slapped his hand on the black granite countertop. "*I would've done nothing*! I wouldn't have done that to my best friend."

"You'd like to think so, but who knows what any of us would do," she said.

"You're being a romantic," Chip said. "We live in the real world where you don't do something like this to a friend. Am I right, Parker?"

Parker chewed on the inside of his cheek. "She does kind of have a point. We'd all like to think we know what we'd do in any given situation, but until you're in it . . ." He shrugged.

"See?" Elise said with a victorious smile. "That's all I'm saying." She kissed Parker full on the lips. "I'm leaving him for you, you sexy beast."

"While that's a very tempting offer, honey, I'm afraid I have to decline," Parker said with a grin. "I'm taken."

Elise inhaled dramatically. "*Do tell!*"

Parker told them about Gina.

"Oh," Elise said with her hand over her mouth. "Oh, *you're* the romantic! I never knew you had it in you. What an amazing story! Isn't it, Chip?"

"All these secrets." Chip shook his head in disbelief. "I thought I knew you guys as well as I know myself."

"I didn't tell anyone for two years, Chip. I finally told Duff about it Sunday on the way home from Block Island. He was the first person I'd told. So don't be offended."

"I'm not," Chip said, clearly working hard not to be. "I'm happy for you. You know that."

"Thanks."

"While we're talking about all this touchy-feely bullshit and since you've now had some experience with the job, I wondered if you'd be my best man—that is, if you can get your filthy hands off my woman."

"I'd love to." Parker laughed as he reached across the counter to give Chip a high five.

"Good. Thank you."

"Have you set a date?"

"Thanksgiving weekend," Elise said.

The doorbell rang, and Parker went to answer it.

"Hey, this is a nice surprise," he said with a delighted smile when he found Gina on his doorstep. "Come in."

"I'm sorry I didn't call first, but you sounded so down on the phone that I wanted to come see you."

"You don't have to call first." He hugged her. "I'm *so* happy to see you." He hoped his kiss told her just how much.

She caressed his face. "Did you get to sleep at all?"

"Nope. I ended up at a wedding. How about you?"

"A couple of hours."

"I'm sorry I kept you up all night," he said with a grin.

"I'm not. It was the most wonderful night of my life."

"Mine, too."

"I had no idea it could be like that."

"It's never been like that for me, either," he confessed. "Where are the boys?"

"Staying with my sister tonight. She's so thrilled about us that she's offered to take them whenever she can to give us some time alone."

"Remind me to send *her* some flowers," Parker said with another kiss.

"Who's out there, Parker?" Elise called from the kitchen.

Parker felt Gina's withdrawal even before she pulled free of his embrace. He reached out to bring her back. "Hey, she's my *friend*," he whispered. "Her fiancé is here, too, and he's one of my best friends."

Gina's cheeks colored with embarrassment. "I'm sorry."

"I'll be right there," Parker called to Chip and Elise. He took Gina's chin and urged her to look at him. "You don't *ever* have to worry about other women with me, Gina. I'm thirty-eight years old, and I've sown all my wild oats. I love you, I'll always love you, and after last night I can assure you I'll never be interested in making love with anyone but you."

Visibly touched, she said, "I have some rather significant issues with trust."

"That's understandable, but not all men are pigs. You can trust me."

"I'm sorry. You haven't done anything to deserve this."

"Don't be sorry. Just give me a chance to prove you can trust me."

She rested her hands on his chest and looked up at him with her heart in her eyes. "I love you, too, Parker," she said for the first time. "I've thought of nothing but you since you left this afternoon."

"Then we have that in common." He kissed the end of her nose. "Do you think maybe you could say that other thing one more time, just so I can be sure I heard it right?"

"What?" she asked with a teasing smile. "That I've thought of you constantly?"

"Not that. The other thing."

"That I'm sorry for not trusting you?"

Amused by this playful side of her, he said, "All these things are good, but they're not what I'm looking for."

"Hmmm," she said, pretending to give it significant thought. "*Oh!* I know." She tugged him down and pressed her lips to his. "I think what you're looking for," she said as she made him crazy with a devastating combination of lips and tongue, "is that I love you, Parker King. I love you, I love you, I love you."

"*Now* we're talking." He sank into the kiss until he remembered he had guests. "Come meet my friends."

TED HELD Caroline close to him in their enormous bed and listened to the soft music coming from the radio on the bedside table.

He sang along to "You and Me" by Lifehouse, about a guy who couldn't keep his eyes off the woman he loved.

"I love that song," Caroline said with a sigh of contentment.

"So do I. And now every time I hear it I'll think about being in bed with my gorgeous new wife at the Ritz."

"And when I hear it," she whispered in his ear, sending a shiver through him, "I'll think of my sexy new husband and how he drives me *wild* with that thing he does with his tongue."

"Wild, huh?"

"Mmmmm."

"Want me to do it again?"

She groaned. "Not yet. I can't take any more right now."

His smile faded.

She propped herself up on one elbow. "What's wrong?"

"I feel kind of guilty having all this fun when my grandmother's so sick."

"Oh, baby, she wanted us to have this night together. She arranged it for us. She wouldn't want you to feel guilty."

"I'm going to miss her."

"I know you are."

"It makes me so sad that she won't know our kids."

"You were lucky to have her this long. All my grandparents were gone by the time I was twenty-two."

"That's too bad. And you're right. I *am* lucky to have had them so long, but I'm afraid I'm less prepared for life without them than I should be."

"That's because they weren't your average grandparents," she reminded him.

"No," he said with a laugh. "They were never average."

"I don't think she'd want you to be sad. I don't know her very well, but I can picture her saying 'I've had eighty-eight wonderful years. I've got nothing to complain about, so quit your fussing, Ted Duffy.'"

Impressed, Ted turned on his side to face her. "That's definitely something she would say."

"Do you want to go soak in the Jacuzzi for a while to get your mind off it?"

"No." He got up suddenly. "There's something else I want to do."

"What's that?"

Ted went out to the parlor and returned with a hotel portfolio and pen.

"What are you up to?"

He got back into bed and reclined against the headboard. Pulling out a piece of Ritz Carlton stationary he put it on top of the portfolio. "Remember that list of worries we put aside for tonight?"

"Unfortunately, I remember it all too well."

"We need to make a different list."

"What kind?"

"Our plans. We need to make some plans."

Intrigued and amused, Caroline said, "Okay. What've you got in mind?"

He wrote their late July wedding date on the top of the page. "All right, number one, is meet Caroline's parents. That's a no-brainer."

"Number two has to be plan a real wedding or number one isn't going to go too well," she said.

"Now you're getting into the spirit of things. Number three is move Caroline from New York to Boston."

"Whew, that's a biggie."

"You want to, though, right?"

"I've already moved to Boston. The rest is just details."

He leaned over to kiss her. "I like your attitude. Number four is a honeymoon involving a significant amount of nudity."

She laughed. "Oh, God, I've married a nudist. I should've been warned about this."

"There was no time. That's what you get for rushing me into this marriage thing."

"Who rushed who?"

"Details, baby. Either way you're going to have to find out all my secrets as we go."

"So far, you won't hear me complaining. What's number five?"

He wrote, "Finish Caroline's book (See that Cameron? You've wormed your way into bed with us.)"

She dissolved into laughter and reached for the pen. "Number six," she wrote. "Figure out Ted's career and decide where we're going to live."

"Good one. Number seven," he said as he wrote, "have a baby."

She took the pen again. "Number eight, have another baby."

When he had retrieved the pen, he wrote, "Number nine, make sweet love every day."

She cracked up. "You're *dreaming*."

"If I am, don't wake me up, okay?"

"You say things that just go straight to my heart, Ted Duffy." She brushed her fingers through his hair and kissed him. "All right, I'll compromise." She reached for the pen and inserted the word "almost" in front of every day.

"I guess I can live with that," he said begrudgingly.

"I have one more as long as we're going for it," she said. "Number ten, live happily ever after."

"Perfect." He held up the page to admire their work. "We'll keep this on our fridge and check off each one as we get it done. It'll remind us of this amazing week and this amazing night. That way, whenever real life gets in the way of our plans, we'll remember how we felt on the day we began our life together."

"I won't need the reminder, but I love the idea."

"And I love you." He rolled over to kiss her, and the paper fluttered from his fingers onto the floor.

CHAPTER 35

They spent most of the next day at the hospital where Lillian was sleeping for longer stretches and was less lucid when awake.

After he and his father consulted with her doctor around noon, Ted said, "I don't know if Smitty's going to make it."

Caroline put her arms around him from behind. "She said she'd wait for him and she will."

Ted clutched her hands. "As much as I want him here because he belongs here, I'm worried about seeing him. He's going to freak when he hears we're married."

"He's had a week to get used to the idea of us as a couple."

"That's not long enough, baby. He's going to be shocked to hear we're married. Everyone is."

"I'll be very surprised if he says a word about it with your grandmother being as sick as she is. He's going to know this isn't the time or the place."

"Yeah, you're probably right."

Parker, Chip, and Elise came in late that afternoon, and after they had exchanged hugs with Ted's parents and sister, Ted took them in to see Lillian and Theo. Since the small room was getting crowded, Ted stepped into the hallway to wait for them.

Elise came out first, wiping away tears as she hugged Ted. "Are you doing all right?"

"I'm hanging in there."

"If there's anything I can do for you—any of you—I hope you won't hesitate to ask."

"Thanks, Elise."

"Um, congratulations. On the wedding and everything."

"Thank you," Ted said, touched by her support.

Parker and Chip came out of Lillian's room a minute later.

"Thanks for coming, you guys." Ted noticed Chip fixating on his new wedding ring.

"Do you need anything?" Parker asked.

"No, we're good," Ted said.

Chip put his arm around Elise. "Well, we're going to get going."

"Okay." Ted hid his disappointment at the brevity of their visit. "I know my grandfather appreciates you coming."

Chip nodded and escorted Elise down the long corridor. She looked back over her shoulder and blew Ted a kiss.

"He's pissed," Ted said to Parker.

"What did you expect?"

"I don't know. I've never been in a situation like this before, so I don't know what to expect."

"I think you know *exactly* what to expect."

"So you too, huh?"

Parker's shrug was weary. "I don't know what I am. I'm doing my best to keep an open mind, but I've got to be honest with you. It isn't easy."

"Parker . . ."

Parker held up his hand. "You've got enough on your plate right now. We'll talk about this later. Call me if there's anything I can do. I mean that."

"Thanks. Are you getting Smitty in the morning?"

"Yeah."

"Will you, I mean, can you . . ."

"Prepare him for what he's going to find here?"

Chagrinned, Ted nodded.

"Of course I will. Do you think I'd let him discover you've married his ex-girlfriend when he sees the ring on your finger?"

The shaft of pain surprised Ted and sent him reeling.

"I'll see you tomorrow," Parker said.

After he had walked away, Ted leaned back against the wall and hung his head, struggling to absorb the blow. When he looked up he found his grandfather watching him through the window. Ted managed a small smile for the old man.

Caroline came to find Ted a short time later.

"Did they leave?" Ted asked.

"A few minutes ago."

"Were they nice to you?"

"Elise was. Parker and Chip kept their distance."

"Same here. If everything were normal, they would've been here all day."

She put her arms around him. "I'm sorry, honey. Maybe with time . . ."

Ted pulled free of her embrace. "I need some air."

"Want me to come with you?"

"No," he said with an absent kiss to her forehead. "I need a minute, okay?"

"Sure."

His shoulders were stooped as Caroline watched him go.

"I take it his visit with the boys didn't go too well."

Caroline turned to find Theo behind her. "No, not so well."

"He's going to need you in the next few days, Caroline. Maybe more than he'll ever need you again."

"He's got me. I'm just afraid he's not going to let me in. After all, I'm the cause of this. I've come between him and his friends."

"You're his wife now. How that came to be is almost secondary at this point, wouldn't you say?"

Caroline thought about that for a minute. "Yes, I guess it is."

"My Lil knew what she was doing," Theo said with a proud smile. "Yes, she did."

"What do you mean?"

"She figured if you were married it would be a lot harder to walk away from each other when the going got tough. And it's going to get tough, Caroline. Really, really tough and maybe for quite some time. So Lil made sure you two got half a chance. The other half is going to be up to you and your husband."

Caroline smiled. "Crafty."

"Yes, she sure is. I've always loved that about her." His eyes filled when he glanced into Lillian's room.

She rested a hand on the old man's arm. "Are you all right?"

"Sixty-five years," he sighed. "How do you say goodbye after sixty-five years?"

"I don't know." Caroline brushed at the tears that suddenly wet her cheeks. "I can't imagine how you do that."

"It doesn't just happen, you know." He shifted his eyes back to Caroline. "Finding someone you love is only the start. The rest takes hard work. Every single day. Even the first day. Go find him. Make sure he knows he's not alone anymore."

Caroline hugged him. "I feel very lucky to have a grandfather-in-law who's so wise and a grandmother-in-law who's so crafty."

Theo grinned as he kissed her cheek. "We're happy to have you, honey. Now, go find your husband."

Caroline worked to compose herself in the elevator but couldn't seem to stop the flood of tears as the past few emotional days caught up to her all at once. Theo's grief had made her see how trivial her problems were in comparison, and she summoned the strength to support Ted. Theo was right. Her husband needed her.

She found him on a bench outside the hospital's main door. Bent over, leaning on his knees, he looked so sad and alone that Caroline ached for him. Sitting down next to him she laid her arm on his back.

He seemed almost startled to see her.

She eased him over to rest against her. "It's all right, baby," she whispered. "I've got you."

~

AFTER A SOMBER second night at the Ritz during which Ted didn't sleep at all, they packed their bags so they could get back to the hospital.

When she found him staring into space in the middle of the elegant parlor, Caroline put her arms around him. She was alarmed at the distance he had put between them since his friends had visited the hospital the day before. Reaching up to smooth the blond hair off his forehead, she couldn't miss the far-away look in his blue eyes. "Honey?"

He looked down at her, his distraction apparent.

"Hey." She gave him a little shake. "Are you with me?"

"Yeah."

"I know you're worried about seeing Smitty and about your grandmother, but no matter what this day brings, I'm right here with you, okay?"

He nodded.

"Do you remember what you said to me the other night about sticking together and fighting our way through this?"

"Yes."

"It's time to fight."

"Okay."

"I love you with my whole heart, Ted Duffy."

He clutched her hands and kissed her. "I love you, too."

"Stay focused on that today."

"I'll try."

They were in the hallway heading for the elevator when Caroline gasped. "Oh my God! We left our list in the room!"

He withdrew the key from his pocket and handed it to her.

She came back a minute later holding the piece of paper to her chest. "I would've been heartbroken if we had forgotten this."

"We could've made another one."

"It wouldn't have been the same," she said, adding with a teasing smile, "We never got to number nine last night."

"I'm sorry. I just wasn't in the mood."

"I know. I was only kidding." When she realized she wasn't

going to be able to cajole him out of his funk, she decided to stop trying.

~

PARKER MISSED Gina when he woke up without her after having her next to him the last two mornings. He was going to have to convince her to marry him so he could wake up with her every day. Before they could take the next step, though, he had to meet her sons. He hoped that could happen soon so they could get busy becoming a family. *A family*. Parker wondered why the idea didn't horrify him nearly as much as it should have. *You're a mess, man.*

He moved quietly through the house so he wouldn't disturb Chip and Elise, who were sleeping in one of his extra bedrooms. He had prepared another room for Smitty the night before. Parker downed a quick cup of coffee before he left for Logan Airport to meet Smitty's flight. His stomach clenched with nerves over what he had to tell his friend. *Lucky me. I really got stuck with the short straw in this situation. Thanks a lot, Duff.*

The traffic was light on that Sunday morning, and Parker made it to the airport in fifteen minutes, just before the red-eye from Los Angeles was due to arrive. He parked and walked into the terminal to wait. Smitty called twenty minutes later to let Parker know he was on his way down to baggage claim.

Parker honestly felt like he could puke as he waited for Smitty. If it hadn't been so early he would've called Gina for moral support. A few more minutes passed and desperation had him reaching for his phone to call her when he looked up and saw Smitty on the escalator. *Here goes nothing.*

With a two-day beard and bleary eyes Smitty greeted Parker with one of his signature bear hugs.

"You look like hell," Parker said.

"I feel like I've been on a plane for a month over the last week. How's Lillian? Please tell me she's still alive."

"She's holding her own."

A sigh of relief rattled through Smitty's big frame.

While they waited for his bag, Parker tried to work up the courage to tell Smitty what he needed to know before he went to the hospital.

"Spit it out, Parker. Whatever it is, just tell me."

Parker glanced up at him but couldn't get the words out.

Smitty kept his eyes on Parker. "Tell me."

"They got married."

Smitty's eyebrows knitted with confusion. "Who did?"

"Ahhh, Duff and Caroline. They're married."

"Married."

Parker nodded. "Smitty, listen—"

"I don't want to hear another word. Not one more word." He grabbed his bag off the carrousel. "Let's go. I need to see Lillian."

SMITTY AND PARKER came in through the ICU door thirty minutes later, and Smitty made a beeline for Mitzi without so much as a glance at Ted or Caroline.

Mitzi enveloped him in a tight hug. "Come on, darling," she said, leading him down the hallway.

At the door to Lillian's room, Mitzi stopped and turned to him. "I know this is going to be upsetting for you, but she's not in any pain, and she's saying she's ready. She'll be very happy to see you."

Smitty kept a tight grip on Mitzi's hand as tears tumbled from his raw eyes.

"Come here, honey." Mitzi reached for him and wiped the tears off his face. "Go ahead."

Smitty stepped into the room.

Theo got up to greet him with a hug. "Thank you so much for coming." He leaned over to gently nudge Lillian awake. "Sweetheart, Smitty's here to see you. He's come all the way from Australia."

"Smitty," Lillian whispered. "Theo help me sit up a little." After he had raised the bed she said, "Will you give us a few minutes, my love?"

Theo kissed her forehead. "Of course. I'll be right outside if you need me."

When they were alone, Lillian turned to Smitty. "You look exhausted, honey."

Smitty broke down. "I was so afraid I wouldn't get here in time."

"I told you I'd wait for you," she said weakly.

"I should've had more faith in you," he teased through his tears.

"That's right." She squeezed his hand as she studied him. "Your heart is heavy and not just because your favorite old girl is about to check out."

"I don't want to waste the time we have together talking about that."

"Honey, why do you think I asked you to come? I never would've put you through such an emotional journey if I didn't have something important I needed to say to you."

Smitty took a deep breath hoping to somehow manage the riot of emotions.

"I want you to do something for me, but mostly I want you to do it for yourself." She kept her eyes trained on him. "I want you to forgive him."

"I don't know if I can."

"If you don't, the bitterness will poison you. Your friendship may never be the same, but if you carry this around with you it'll eat away at you and keep you from finding happiness of your own."

"Lill—"

"You have to find a way."

"I only just found out they're married half an hour ago. I'm not feeling very forgiving at the moment."

"They got married because I asked them to. They were going to anyway. I just pushed things along a little." She paused to take a deep, wracking breath. "I know it was terribly selfish of me, but I wanted to see my Ted married before I left him. I wish I was going to live long enough to see the same thing for you."

"I don't think it's going to happen for me."

"It will. I know it will, but you have to make room for it. If your heart is going to be open to receiving love, it can't be full of anger and bitterness."

"I know you love him, Lillian, but he's done a terrible thing to me. You're asking a lot of me."

"I'm not saying you have to forgive him today. But eventually." Her face lit up with a coy smile. "I'm on my deathbed, so I could make you promise me . . ."

"You wouldn't do that to me."

"No, I wouldn't," she said with a fading twinkle in her eye. "You're a wonderful, kind, generous man, Smitty. You deserve a woman who has eyes only for you. Caroline wasn't that woman, and while I'm sorry you had to find that out the way you did, it's better now than later. There's someone out there just for you, and she'll see everything I see when I look at you."

He attempted a smile. "I met a woman in Sydney this week who seems to think I'm pretty cool."

"Then she must be a smart girl."

"She is."

"I'll be watching over you."

New tears coursed down his face as he kissed her hand. "Thank you for showing me what a real family is and for being *my* family. I love you."

"And I love you. Be good to yourself."

He leaned over the bedrail to hug her and dissolved into sobs.

Mitzi finally came in and eased him up. With her arms around him, she led him from the room and held him until he had collected himself.

He swiped impatiently at tears that refused to quit. "Will you understand if I can't stay here and wait with you?"

"Of course," Mitzi said.

"We're all at Parker's."

"I'll call you," she said. "It was very, very good of you to come. It seemed important to her that she see you."

"It was."

She escorted him back to where Parker waited for him.

Ted stood up and came to the door of the waiting room. "Smitty—"

"Are you ready to go, Parker?" Smitty asked.

"Sure." Parker kissed Mitzi's cheek. "Call us if there's anything you need."

"I will."

CHAPTER 36

Lillian died in Theo's arms at three thirty that afternoon. While Mitzi and Ed tended to his grandfather, Ted called the funeral home and Lillian's parish priest, who had been by earlier in the day to administer last rites.

As he was swept into the details that came with planning a funeral, Caroline watched Ted struggle to put his own troubles aside for the time being so he could focus on making sure his grandmother got the send off she deserved. Not that he seemed to notice, but Caroline was by his side every minute except for a couple of hours on Monday afternoon when Tish took her to buy something to wear to the wake and funeral.

Late on Tuesday afternoon, she watched from across their bedroom as he knotted his tie in front of the mirror. He had put a million miles between them since Smitty's snub on Sunday, and she had no idea how to reach him. She hoped that once they got past the funeral they could somehow get back on track.

"Ted?"

He turned to her.

"I was thinking, you know, about the wake and everything."

"What about it?"

"I know you're going to have to be in the receiving line with your family, and it might be better if I'm not with you, so you don't have to explain to hundreds of people that you've gotten married. It doesn't seem like the time or place for that."

He shrugged with nonchalance that hurt her. "If that's what you want."

"I want to keep the focus where it belongs—on your grandmother—and not have the whole place buzzing about us."

"That's fine."

Caroline wanted to scream. *Fine! Nothing is fine!* But this wasn't the time. There would be time for screaming—if it came to that—after they had gotten through the next few days.

The wake was mobbed with people wanting to pay their respects to a pillar of the community, a beloved friend, and a generous patron of the Dana-Farber Cancer Institute, among other local charities. The family photographs Elise had taken before the anniversary party sat on easels around the room.

Caroline found a seat in the back where she could see Ted but remain out of the way.

Chip, Elise, Parker, and Smitty came in about an hour after the wake began. Each of them hugged all the Duffys, including Ted, as they moved through the line and then stopped to pay their respects to Lillian. They were wiping at tears as they went past her open casket and merged into the crowded room.

"Caroline?"

Caroline looked up. "Oh, hi, Elise. The photos are beautiful."

"Thanks. Why are you hiding back here? Shouldn't you be up there with your husband?"

"I didn't want him to have to explain me to everyone. It didn't seem like the right time for that."

"How's he doing? Really?"

"He's having a hard time with a lot of things right now, but I'm sure he'll be fine." If he could use that word, so could she.

"How about you?" Elise asked with concern as she took the seat next to Caroline.

"I'm doing my best to support him. That's all I can do." She glanced up and unwittingly caught Smitty's eye. For a long moment, she couldn't make herself look away. Finally, he did. "How's Smitty, Elise?"

"I don't know. He won't talk to us about it. Parker and Chip have both tried, but he refuses to discuss it."

"That's not healthy. I'd rather hear he's ranting and raving than keeping it all inside. Do you think they're ever going to forgive Ted?"

Elise's grim expression answered for her. "Chip's really spun up about it, and Parker, being Parker, is trying very hard to be rational and see both sides, but he's upset, too. And Smitty, well, who knows what's going on inside his head?"

"If you think it'll matter, please tell them how sorry I am to have put them in this position. They mean the world to Ted, and I know he would do just about anything to make this right with them."

"I'll tell them if I get the chance. Can I ask you just one thing that's been driving me mad?"

"Of course."

"*When* did this happen?"

"The first night we met. Remember how Smitty crashed early and the rest of you went out?"

Elise nodded.

"I was on the deck upstairs when he arrived. He was a mess over losing his patient, Joey. We talked for a long time, and there was just this connection between us. And then the next day, when I broke my ankle, he was so awesome."

"But nothing happened between you then? Right?"

"No," Caroline said. "Not until Block Island when we acknowledged we had fallen in love that first weekend." She reached for Elise's hand. "Please try to understand. Neither of us would've *ever* wanted to hurt Smitty like this if we could've avoided it. But it was so big and so immediate and so overwhelming."

"Elise," Chip said. "We're going to go."

She looked up at him. "Okay." Hugging Caroline, she said, "I'll see you tomorrow."

~

After they got home from the wake, Ted spent the rest of the evening in his office working on what he was going to say at the funeral. Caroline wandered in to check on him before she went up to bed. Draping her arms over his shoulders, she pressed a kiss to his cheek. "Can I get you anything?"

"No, I'm fine."

Fine. Caroline was starting to hate that word. "You need to get some sleep, honey."

He shook her off. "When I finish this."

Stung, Caroline stepped back from him. "Okay." She went into the kitchen to get a glass of water and saw their list on the refrigerator. She ran a loving hand over the creamy paper. Their wedding night already seemed like a lifetime ago, and she wondered if they had any chance at all of getting to number ten.

The funeral was a blur of people and emotions. Theo asked Chip, Parker, and Smitty to serve as pallbearers along with Tish's husband Steven and two of Lillian's nephews. Caroline watched the three of them, handsome and somber in dark suits, as they went through the motions of ceremony in honor of a woman they had loved. Except for the ten minutes when he was at the microphone sharing eloquent and humorous memories of his grandmother, Ted kept a tight grip on Caroline's hand and on his emotions. Even though their shoulders were touching and their hands were intertwined, Caroline was aware of the gaping distance between them and found it hard to concentrate on anything else.

The long funeral procession to the cemetery shut down traffic between the cathedral in downtown Boston and Weston, the suburb twelve miles west of the city where the Duffys lived. After the burial, Ed and Mitzi invited everyone to their home for lunch. As the limousine from the funeral home delivered the family to the house, Caroline had to work at not being intimidated by the gated driveway, the rolling lawn, and the imposing two-story stone house where Ted had grown up.

He was a gracious host to his parents' guests and stayed close to Caroline. He introduced her as his wife and deftly answered the inevitable questions with his usual mix of charm and grace, which he turned off as soon as they were alone again.

"Do you want something to eat?" Ted asked as he sought out his friends, who were congregated on the other side of the huge living room.

"No, I'm not hungry. How about you?"

"I'm not either."

"Do you want to go talk to them? I'll stay here if it would make it easier."

"They don't want to talk to me."

"They're here, Ted. That counts for something, doesn't it?"

"They're here out of respect for my parents and grandparents. It has nothing to do with me."

"That's not true."

"Leave it alone, Caroline," he snapped.

Ted's boss, Martin Nickerson, and his wife, Jenny, approached them, oblivious to their tension.

"Ted, honey, you've been keeping secrets from us." Jenny kissed his cheek. "Are you going to introduce us to your lovely wife?"

"Yes, of course." The charm was back as he put his arm around Caroline.

She played the part of the doting wife even though she was dying inside as she accepted the very real possibility that she might have made a terrible mistake.

By four o'clock the house had begun to clear out, leaving only family and close friends sprinkled in groups throughout the rambling first floor.

"I suppose I should thank the guys for being pallbearers," Ted said, looking around for them.

Caroline pointed to closed double doors. "I saw them go in there a little while ago."

Ted opened the door to his father's study where Smitty was sprawled in a leather chair, Chip and Elise were on the love seat, and Parker stood at the window.

"You have to talk about this, Smitty," Chip was saying. "You can't act like nothing's happened and expect us to go along with that bullshit."

"Hey! It's the happy couple!" Smitty said with a big smile. His eyes were slightly glazed, probably due to the tall glass of whiskey he held in his hand. "Come in, come in. Join the party."

"Just remember where you are and why," Ted said in a low tone as he ushered Caroline into the room and closed the door.

"*Oh*, so, we're going to talk about decorum, are we?" Smitty asked with a chuckle.

"No, we're not," Ted said, pouring a glass of whiskey.

Caroline shook her head at his offer of a drink.

"Yeah, it *is* kind of late for decorum, isn't it?" Smitty said. "By the way, I haven't had a chance to congratulate you on your wedding." He made a big show of pulling himself out of the chair so he could kiss Caroline's cheek. "I'm sure you were a lovely bride."

"Thank you," Caroline said in barely more than whisper.

Returning to her side with his drink, Ted's closed his hand around hers as his jaw clenched with tension.

Smitty went to the bar to refill his glass, keeping his back to them. "There's one thing I want to know more than anything else, sweetheart. Were you doing him at the same time you were doing me?" He turned around. "Because, you know, that would be kind of unseemly, wouldn't you say? I mean with us being best friends and all that."

Shocked, Caroline stared at Smitty.

"That's enough," Ted said through gritted teeth.

Elise sobbed softly behind him.

"You're not going to speak to her like that," Ted said.

"Oh, *right*," Smitty said with a dramatic nod. "Right. I forgot. We're operating under rules of decorum. *Now*. I guess all bets were off a week ago."

"We never meant to hurt you—"

"Speaking of hurt," Smitty said. "I'll bet it hurt like the devil when you fell off that golden boy pedestal you'd been sitting on all your life."

"There was no pedestal," Ted said quietly.

Smitty laughed harshly. "Like hell." His eyes narrowed as he addressed Ted. "In my whole miserable, stinking, shithole of a life, there's only been one thing I always knew I could count on. *You.*" With a gesture to encompass the others, he added, "*This.* You have no idea what you've done to me."

"Nothing happened between us until you two were over," Ted said. "You can believe that or not, but it's the truth."

"The truth," Smitty said. "And I should believe you why exactly?"

"Smitty . . ." Caroline said.

His steely stare bore down on her. "I want to go back in time to before I knew that people I cared so much about were capable of this. I want to go back to that tent and my cigar on the lawn. I want to go back to when Elise was offering to go find you for me."

Caroline gasped and tried to take a step away from Ted, who tightened his grip on her hand.

"'Will you wear this dress again sometime, just for me? Anything for you, Ted,'" Smitty mocked. "I was so touched."

Caroline went pale as tears spilled down her face.

"So the next day, when you let her think you were going to rape her, who were you trying to punish?" Ted asked. "Her or me?"

A collective gasp went through the room.

If looks could kill, the one Smitty sent Caroline would have been the end of her.

"I'm sorry," Caroline cried, pulling herself free from Ted so she could face off with Smitty. "I'm sorry we hurt you because you're right, you didn't deserve it, and I would give *anything* to have been able to spare you that pain. But I'm not going to say I wish I'd never gone to Newport with you and never met Ted, because I can't say that. *I love him.*" She wiped at the tears on her face. "And he loves *you*—as much as he loves anyone in this world."

Smitty snorted. "He's got a strange way of showing it. I think I've heard enough—more than enough, in fact. I'm going back to Sydney. There's nothing here for me anymore." His glass landed on a table with a loud clunk.

"What about us?" Parker asked, throwing his hands into the air with dismay.

"You?" Smitty tilted his head to study his friend. "You knew something was going on between them, didn't you? That night when you went home early, you interrupted something."

"I only suspected," Parker said. "I didn't know for sure."

"And you didn't think I needed to know that?"

"I didn't know what to do. Put yourself in my shoes. What would you have done?"

Smitty shrugged. "I would hope I'd be a better friend to you than you were to me."

Astounded, Parker stared at him. "You can't seriously be saying that to me."

"Imagine my surprise when Mitzi mentioned who the best man was at this farce of a wedding," Smitty said. "You've made your position perfectly clear, Parker."

"No, I haven't!" Parker fumed. "I did that for Lillian more than anything."

"Oh, that's good to know," Ted said, shaking his head with disbelief. "Thanks a lot."

"What about me?" Chip demanded as he stood up to face Smitty. "I haven't done anything to you."

"Collateral damage," Smitty said with a small, sad smile for Chip before he opened the double doors and left the room.

"Great," Parker said with a furious glance at Ted as he followed Smitty. "This is just *great*. Thanks a lot, Duff. Really. I can't tell you how much I appreciate this."

"Ditto," Chip said with a stormy look at Ted as he led Elise from the room. "Nice job."

Caroline fell into the chair Smitty had vacated and sobbed. When she looked up a few minutes later Ted was gone.

CHAPTER 37

Ted's alarm woke Caroline at five o'clock the next morning. She raised herself up on one elbow as he got out of bed. They had exchanged few words since he had come back for her two hours after he left her crying in his father's study the day before. She had no idea where he had been for all that time. "What are you doing?" she asked, pushing the hair back from her face.

"Going to work."

"Why?"

"Um, because I have to. I've taken way too much time off lately."

"Ted, you just buried your grandmother yesterday and got married four days before that. I don't think anyone expects you to go to work today."

"Kids with cancer don't really care too much about those things," he said, opening his closet door.

"Does being crappy to me make you feel better? What happened to 'we're in this together' and 'we're going to get through this'? What happened to 'fight, Caroline' and 'step toward me, not away from me'?"

He came out of his closet, went into the bathroom, and shut the door.

Caroline fell back against the pillow and hurt when she

remembered sitting on the counter to watch him shave just a week ago. Was that all they were ever going to have? One beautiful, magical week?

He emerged from the bathroom showered, shaved, and dressed twenty minutes later.

"How long is this going to go on, Ted?"

He looped his hospital ID around his neck. "Well, let's see, I've lost my grandmother and my three best friends in the last few days. You'll have to excuse me if I don't have a timetable for how long it's going to take me to get over that."

Caroline winced. "I sure do wish I'd seen this side of you before I said 'I do.'"

"Too bad it's legal, huh?" he asked, tossing clothes into a duffel bag.

"Are you trying to hurt me? Is that your goal? Because if it is, it's working."

"No." He stopped moving all of a sudden, as if she had finally managed to penetrate the wall he had erected between them. "No, it's not."

She flew out of bed and went to him. "Ted, honey, *please*. Let's not self-destruct in the midst of all of this. *Please*. I want my husband back."

A look of utter despondency crossed his handsome face. "I have no idea where he is right now."

With her hands on his face she forced him to look at her. "He can have all the time he needs to get through this as long as he isn't shitty to me in the meantime. I put up with that once before, Ted, and I won't do it again. Not even for you."

His arms encircled her as he finally broke down.

She eased him onto the bed and held him close.

"I thought I'd be able to handle it. I really did," he said between gut-wrenching sobs. "I think I could've handled their anger and their disapproval, but I never imagined it would mess things up between the three of them, too. I never saw that coming."

"I didn't either."

"I don't know what to do, and I'm never in a situation where I don't know what to do."

"Do you want to know what I think?"

He nodded.

"It's going to take some time. It might be a month. It might be six months. It might be a year. But you guys *will* find your way back to each other."

Ted shook his head. "We've never had so much as an argument in all these years. I can't see us getting past this."

"Do you want me here, Ted? If it's too much for you to deal with a new marriage on top of everything else, I can go back to New York until you feel better. I'd rather do that than stay here and watch something so beautiful turn to shit."

"No, I don't want you to go." He combed his fingers through her hair. "I'm sorry for being such an asshole."

"I've been having the most awful feeling that I might've made a huge mistake here."

"You haven't, baby," he whispered as he kissed her. "You haven't."

Tears filled her eyes. "I love you so much. I can't stand all this distance between us."

"I love you, too." He kissed her again, more seriously this time, and the heat between them resurfaced with a new intensity. "I'm on duty tonight, so I'm going to stay at the hospital. When I get home tomorrow afternoon, we can go to New York to see your parents, okay?"

She wiped her face and nodded. "Call me tonight?"

"I will. Are you going to be okay here by yourself?"

"Of course. Besides, I need to give Cameron some attention," she said with a teasing smile.

He returned her smile with a weak one of his own.

"Are we going to be all right, Ted?"

"I'm going to try," he said. "I'm going to try as hard as I can to give you what you need."

"That's all I can ask."

~

AND HE TRIED. God bless him, he tried. He poured on the charm for her parents, who professed instant approval of Ted and Caroline's marriage and got busy planning a small Labor Day weekend wedding at their country club in Saratoga Springs.

When Ted and Caroline returned home to Boston, Ted worked at being the best possible husband he could be to Caroline. They laughed and talked and made love. Every night he read what she had written that day and made astute, insightful comments that made the book better than it would have been otherwise. They went shopping for a car for her and decided on an SUV. "One of us should have a backseat for when we get to number seven on the list," he had said with a smile that didn't quite reach his eyes the way it used to.

She got her cast off the second week in August, attended physical therapy, and slowly began to run again—at first by herself and then with him as she was able to increase her pace.

They didn't hear a word from Smitty, Parker, or Chip, and neither of them ever mentioned it.

As August faded into the first of September and they headed back to New York for their wedding, Caroline had to acknowledge that no matter how hard he tried, no matter how hard they *both* tried, the magic was gone and everyone was trying far too hard.

The night before the wedding, her parents had his family over to their home for dinner. Ted met Caroline's best friend Tiffany and her family as well as Caroline's brother and sister and their families. In town from California for the wedding, her towheaded nephews kept everyone laughing and helped to ease any remaining tension that might have existed between the two families.

After Ted's family had returned to their hotel for the night, Caroline found him sitting by himself on her parents' back deck. She slid onto his lap and put her arms around him. "Hi," she said with a light kiss.

He curved a hand around her hip. "Hi, there."

"What are you doing out here all by yourself?"

"Nothing special."

After they had watched the stars in silence for several minutes, she turned to him. "May I say something?"

He nodded and seemed surprised when she welled up with tears. "Hey, what's this? What's wrong, hon?"

"I want you to listen and not say anything until I'm done, okay?"

"Okay."

"We don't have to do this tomorrow." When he started to protest, she stopped him with a kiss. "You're listening, remember?" Once she had his attention again, she forced herself to continue. "I love you, Ted. I love everything about you. I love your smile." She traced his lips with her finger. "I love talking to you about everything and nothing. I love that you're the smartest person I've ever known. I love the way you feel and the way you look. I love making love with you, and I even love the way you've tried so hard to hide your pain from me." She brushed another kiss across his lips. "In fact, I love you enough to let you go if you just don't have it in you to do this tomorrow. I love you that much. So I'm giving you an out." She rested her hand over his heart. "If you're not feeling it anymore then let me go. I'd much prefer that to standing up there with you tomorrow and wondering if you're doing it just because you'd never put me through another cancelled wedding."

He rested his forehead against hers. "Am I allowed to talk now?"

She laughed through her tears and nodded.

"I never imagined I'd get so lucky to have someone who loves all those things about me. I love all the same things about you and so many others it would take me all night to list them for you. I appreciate what you're trying to do here, honey, but I don't want out. I want in. I want to be able to go home the day after tomorrow and check number two off our list. I know things have been off between us over the last month. I know that. And I'm working on it. I promise you I'm working on trying to get used to my life the way it is now."

"That you traded them for me, you mean."

"I don't see it that way."

"But that's what happened."

"I don't want to think about it that way."

"You must be thinking about it some. You're about to get married without them here with you. I can't imagine how that must feel. I know how I'd feel if Tiffany wasn't here."

"You asked me if I wanted out, and I'm telling you I don't. What I *do* want is for us to have this day tomorrow without any clouds hanging over it. I don't want anything to spoil it for you."

"What about you?"

"I'll be fine, baby. As long as I look up and see you coming toward me on the arm of your father, I promise you I'll be just fine."

While she believed him, she wished he had used a different word.

THEIR WEDDING WAS beautiful and elegant and sweet because of all the people who were there—and bittersweet because of all the people who weren't. Ted's brother-in-law served as his best man. Her sister Courtney and best friend Tiffany were Caroline's attendants. The bride and groom danced to the Lifehouse song, "You and Me," that they had listened to after their first wedding, cut their cake, and Caroline threw her bouquet.

After spending their second wedding night in a rustic Saratoga Springs inn, they went home to Boston and began making plans for a honeymoon in the Bahamas and to move Caroline out of her apartment in New York. They opened a joint checking account, legally changed her name, and got her a Massachusetts driver's license. In late September, they visited Tish and Steven in the hospital after their daughter, Lillian Elizabeth Spencer, was born weighing just over nine pounds.

They had four bright red check marks on their list by mid-October when they received an invitation to Chip and Elise's Thanksgiving weekend wedding in New York City. Elise had enclosed a note that said, "Please come. I know Chip wants you there even if he's too stubborn to say so. I love you both, and I miss you. Please come." The invitation sat on the counter untouched until the RSVP date approached and Caroline asked Ted what he wanted to do about it.

"Do you mind sending them something fabulous? I wouldn't have any idea what to get, but you would know."

"What do I say in the card?"

"That we wish them all the best?"

"Ted, why don't we go?" she pleaded. "He knows she invited us. Let's go."

He shook his head. "I can't."

"Would you go alone?"

"You're my wife, Caroline. I'm not going to a wedding without you. I don't care whose wedding it is."

"You're sweet to say that, but if it meant an opportunity for you to patch things up with them, my feelings wouldn't be hurt if you went without me."

"I'm not going to bring all that tension to Chip's wedding. He doesn't need that."

"Okay, but if you change your mind, remember it's fine with me if you go alone."

"I'm not going to change my mind."

Mitzi surprised them when she called the first week in November to invite them to Sunday dinner. While Ted wouldn't have used the word "estranged" to describe his recent relationship with his mother, it certainly wasn't what it used to be. So they were relieved when she reached out to them.

Over dinner Mitzi asked if they were going to Chip's wedding.

"No, we're not," Ted said.

"This whole thing is crazy, Ted," Mitzi said. "How long are you going to let it go on?"

"I don't want to talk about it, Mother."

"Do you even know about Smitty?"

Ted put down his fork. "What about him?"

"Mitzi," Ed warned. "Don't."

"Why not, Ed? He needs to know his actions have consequences." She turned back to Ted. "He married some girl he met in Sydney."

"What?" Ted whispered as if he hadn't heard her right the first time.

"He got married two weeks ago, and he's moving to Sydney to run her family's business. He's resigned his partnership at the brokerage."

Ted got up and left the room.

Caroline tossed her napkin onto the table and went after him. She found him in his father's study and couldn't help but remember the disaster that had occurred the last time they were in that room. Her stomach knotted with tension and a terrible sense of foreboding. With her hand on his shoulder, she said, "Ted?"

He turned to her, and with one look at his face she knew their marriage was over. There'd be no more fighting for it, no more trying. No more of anything. He wasn't going to be able to forgive himself. "Can we leave?" he asked. "Please."

"Yes. Of course."

During the long, silent ride home, Caroline tried to calm her queasy stomach and frantic nerves. She glanced over at him and found him staring at the road. If he blinked, she didn't see it.

He opened the door to the condo and held it for her so she could go in ahead of him.

"Ted, honey, let's talk about it. Come on."

"There's nothing to talk about." He took the stairs two at a time on his way to the loft.

She followed him.

In their bedroom, he pulled out a duffel bag and began to pack.

"Where are you going?"

"To the hospital tonight. Tomorrow I'm going to accept the job in New Hampshire. I'll be moving up there."

"By yourself?"

"Yes. I need some time, Caroline."

She swallowed hard. "How much time?"

"I don't know."

"It's not your fault. He's a grown man, Ted. He made his own decisions, and it has nothing to do with you."

"*Do you honestly believe that?* You don't know him at all, Caroline! You were with him for *six fucking weeks*. He was my best friend for *twenty years*! I'm telling you there's *no way* he's going to just get married. Not after what went down between him and Cherie. There's also *no way* he leaves New York and quits a partnership he spent the better part of a decade slaving for. So if you want to be naïve enough to think what we did to him has nothing to do with the choices he's making now, you're deluding yourself!"

"Why does it have to be the end for us?"

"Because it was one thing when our relationship was ruining friendships. That was bad enough. It's another thing altogether when it's ruining lives. I can't live with that, and every time I look at you that's all I'm going to see."

She took a step back from him, feeling as if he had hit her. "If you do this to me, Ted, if you leave me, I'll *never* be able to put the pieces back together. Never. Not this time."

He had tears in his eyes when he said, "We asked for too much."

"No," she sobbed. "*No*. We asked for just enough."

"Too many people got hurt, Caroline. How do we go forward knowing we hurt so many people?"

"How do we go forward alone after everything we've had together?"

"I can't stay here. I just can't be with you right now." He picked up his bag and left the room.

She followed him down the stairs. "Now or ever?"

"I don't know. I'll let you know where I am."

"Ted, please. Don't do anything tonight. Let's talk this out."

He dropped his bag by the door and reached for his keys. "You once called me a good boy. Do you remember that?"

"Of course I do! You're the best boy I've ever known."

"You're right. I am. Sometimes I wish I wasn't so good. Sometimes I wish I'd been born with the 'fuck it' gene. It certainly would've made my life a whole lot easier. But since the words 'fuck it' aren't in my vocabulary, I do what's expected of me, and I follow the right path. When my sister was strung out on drugs for ten years, I was finishing college and going to medical school. And now my mother can barely look at me. I took something that didn't belong to me, and people got hurt—people who mean the world to me. The 'good boy' can't live with that. I thought I could. I really thought I could. But tonight I discovered I can't. I'm sorry."

"What am I supposed to do?" she cried as he reached for his bag. "Where am I supposed to go while you're taking 'time'?"

"This place is all yours. You've got access to money. Use it for whatever you need."

"You made promises to me, Ted. Twice you promised to stand by me and to love me for the rest of your life."

His eyes were sad as he brushed his index finger over her cheek. "And I will, baby. I'll always love you. Love's never been the problem for us, has it?" He picked up his bag and was gone before she could think of what to say to stop him.

CHAPTER 38

Ted spent most of that long night composing a letter to his patients and their families. As he deleted one draft after another, he heard Joey Gaither's weak voice telling him to keep fighting, to not give up. "I'm sorry, buddy," Ted whispered to the empty room. "But I'm all out of fight."

By six o'clock the next morning, he had a letter he could live with and saved it onto his flash drive. After he spent a couple of hours catching up on a mountain of paperwork he'd let slide, he took the flash drive and another letter he had printed with him to the elevator.

Outside Martin Nickerson's office, Ted waited for Marty's assistant to get off the phone.

"Hi, Ted."

"Is he available?"

"He's in a meeting, but it's nothing you can't interrupt. Go on in."

"Thanks, Patty." Ted knocked and went into Marty's office.

"Hey, Ted, come in. Dr. Ted Duffy meet Dr. Aanandita Ramji. She's just agreed to join our team as an attending. She'll be taking some of the pressure off you and Roger."

Ted shook her hand.

"Call me Ana," she said with a warm smile. "Pleased to meet you, Dr. Duffy."

"Likewise," Ted said as he shook her hand.

"I've heard so much about you and your family's long history here."

Ted's gut twisted when he remembered why he was there. "I'm sorry to interrupt your meeting, but I need a minute when you have some time today, Marty."

"We were done." Ana stood up and shook hands with both of them. "I'll see you on the first, Dr. Nickerson." She nodded to Ted. "I look forward to working with you, Dr. Duffy."

"We'll see you soon," Martin said.

Ana left them and closed the door behind her.

Martin clapped his hands with glee. "Hot damn! We got lucky today, my friend. Yes, we did! She was trained at Johns Hopkins and had twelve other programs competing for her. It came down to M.D. Anderson and us."

"I'm sure it was your potent charm that won her over," Ted said with a weak smile. This man had been a part of his life for as long as Ted could remember, and suddenly the magnitude of what he was about to do sat like a weight on his chest.

"I'm glad you came by." Marty refilled his coffee cup. "I was going to bring her down to meet you."

Ted shook his head to decline the offer of coffee.

Marty sat down behind his large desk. "You look beat. Bad night on the floor?"

"No. For once it was quiet."

"What's on your mind?"

Ted handed Marty the second letter.

Marty perused it and looked up at Ted with shock. "I'm afraid I don't understand. You're resigning. Why?"

Ted's throat tightened. "The ten years I've spent here have been the most rewarding years of my life. But I can't spend my whole career here. I've suspected that for quite a while and have only recently come to realize it's time for a change."

"You had a bad go of it for a while there this summer. That's enough to make anyone take a second look. But to quit, I mean, Ted, come on. You know as well as I do that you're on your way to sitting in this chair someday. It's almost your birthright."

"I appreciate that you have that kind of faith in me, Marty, but it's not what I want. Not anymore. I couldn't have asked for a better boss and mentor than you've been to me. I know you've taken extra special care of me because my father did the same for you. You've invested a lot in me, and I'm sorry to let you down."

Marty sat back in his chair and released a deep sigh when he seemed to get that Ted was serious. "Have you told your father? And Theo?"

"Not yet. I wanted to tell you first."

"What are you going to do?"

"At eight o'clock this morning I accepted the job as head of the pediatrics department at Concord Hospital. They've been after me for some time. I went up there for a day about a month ago and liked what I saw, but I wasn't ready then to make a move."

"You're a talented oncologist, Ted. How in the world are you ever going to be satisfied with tonsils and croup?"

"I'm sure I'll find challenges along the way that I can't imagine right now," he said, aching as he used Caroline's words. He couldn't think of her. Not if he was going to get through this day. "I'm sorry to leave you without any notice, but they're desperate for someone up there."

Marty got up and came around the desk. "You're sure about this? Really sure?"

"I am, Marty."

"You know you can always come back if you get up there and are bored senseless, right?"

Ted smiled as he shook Marty's hand. "Thank you. For everything."

"You'll be impossible to replace, Dr. Duffy. Good luck and keep in touch."

"I will. Give me an hour to talk to my parents before you tell anyone?"

"Of course."

He left Marty's office and handed the flash drive to Patty. "I need a favor."

"Sure, Ted."

"Can you send the letter called 'families' to all my active patients and the parents of anyone I've lost in the last year?"

"Certainly."

"I need an hour before anyone in the hospital hears what the letter says, okay?"

She nodded. "I understand."

"Thank you, Patty."

As he drove to Weston, Ted tried to keep his mind from wandering. He had to stay focused on taking things a step at a time and just get through the day. Despite his best intentions, though, he thought of Caroline . . . and all their plans . . .

Four out of ten is not bad, he thought. *To say we had the deck stacked against us from the beginning, we got lucky to get to number four. Well, since we've figured out what I'm going to do about my career, I guess today counts as five. Halfway to happily ever after. That's more than some people ever get. It'll have to do.*

CAROLINE WAS RESTING on the sofa that afternoon when the doorbell rang. Her heart lifted at the thought that Ted might have come home. Then she remembered he wouldn't ring the doorbell. She glanced through the peephole and suppressed a groan. Quickly, she wiped her tear-stained face, ran her fingers through her untidy hair, tied her robe tighter around her, and opened the door to her mother-in-law.

"May I come in?" Mitzi asked.

Caroline took a step back to let her in.

Mitzi dropped her purse on the kitchen counter. "What's going on, Caroline?"

"I'm sure you already know or you wouldn't be here."

"He's quit his job. Do you know that?"

"He said he was going to."

"And you don't care at all about that?" Mitzi asked, incredulous. "Surely you know by now his position is not just a *job*. It's his legacy."

Caroline snorted. "Mrs. Duffy—Mitzi—my husband has left me. The husband I'd planned to spend my life with. The husband I'd planned to have children with. He's left me. So you'll have to pardon me if I'm not all that concerned today with the Duffy family legacy."

With some of her starch gone, Mitzi sat down in the living room. "You have to do something. You can't let him do this."

"I know you won't believe me, but he was thinking about making a career change long before you dropped your bomb on him last night. The bomb was just the final straw in several situations, but I'm sure you knew that when you dropped it. I'm sorry if you got more than you bargained for."

"I wasn't hoping he would leave you when I told him about Smitty."

"You'll have to forgive me if I don't believe you."

"Duffys don't get divorced, Caroline," Mitzi snapped. "That's not what I want for my son."

"And yet, here we are." Caroline smiled at the irony as she sat on the sofa. "He's done everything you've ever expected of him, Mitzi, and then some. The first time he veers off the approved path to pursue something *he* wants, he loses you and just about everyone else who matters to him. You raised a good and decent man who can't stand that he's disappointed you."

"So you're saying this is my fault?"

"No. If you're looking for someone to blame, I guess you don't need to look much further than me. I'm the one who came between best friends and ruined their lives."

"You left last night before I could tell you that Smitty sounded so happy when he called. Really happy, Caroline."

Caroline stared at her, incredulous. "As we'd say in the newspaper business, you buried the lead. Why would you let Ted think that he'd caused Smitty more unhappiness? Why would you do that?"

Mitzi looked almost ashamed. "I've been angry with Ted. And with you. I'm not about to deny that. I'd never begrudge him the happiness he deserves, but that so many people had to be hurt. *I* couldn't stand *that*. This whole thing was so out of character for him."

"Maybe that's what he needed, Mitzi! To shake things up a bit, to take a risk, to do something that *wasn't* expected of him! Do you know how he's suffered over what he did to Smitty? Do you have *any* idea?"

"No, I guess I don't." She stood up. "May I have a glass of water?"

"Of course. I'm sorry I didn't offer you anything."

"I'll get it," Mitzi said when Caroline started to get up.

Knowing Mitzi had outfitted the place, Caroline didn't bother to tell her where the glasses were.

Mitzi took her glass to the fridge to get ice. "What's this?"

"What?" Caroline turned and found Mitzi studying their list.

"Oh." Mitzi exhaled a long deep breath. "Oh God." Her hand came up to cover her mouth and her shoulders began to shake.

Caroline got up and went to her. "Mitzi . . ."

Mitzi turned to Caroline, her face a mask of devastation. "Oh, Caroline. It was the real thing, wasn't it?"

"Yes," Caroline whispered as her own eyes filled. "Very much so."

"What are you going to do? We can *we* do?"

"We have to wait. And hope. Unless he can find a way to forgive himself, there's nothing we can do."

Mitzi reached out to wipe the tears from Caroline's cheeks. "What are you going to do, honey?"

"I'm going to finish my book." She pointed to number five on the list. "And try to keep busy. Eventually I'll go back to work."

"Will you stay here?"

She nodded. "I live here now. Besides, if my husband should happen to change his mind, I'd like him to be able to find me."

"As long as you want to be busy, I know of some very worthy causes that could use the services of a talented writer," Mitzi said with a shy smile. "We're down one Duffy on the charity circuit, so I'd enjoy having you there."

"I'd like that, Mitzi." Caroline grasped her mother-in-law's hand. "I'd like that very much."

~

THE WORST PART about leaving Children's Hospital Boston was leaving the children. By the time he set out for Concord at ten o'clock that night, Ted was drained. He'd had tearful farewells with his coworkers, the kids on the in-patient ward, and with several of the parents he'd become close to. He still felt weepy as he crossed the New Hampshire border. But there was no sense looking back. Now was the time for moving forward.

An hour later, he arrived in the quaint city of Concord and checked into the first hotel he found. He'd have to go back to Boston at some point to get more clothes and a few other things he needed. To do that, though, he would have to see Caroline. Maybe he would just buy new clothes. That would be easier and less painful.

As he lay down on the hard bed in the nondescript hotel room, he wondered how she was doing. He wished he could call her and talk to her about how it had felt to leave his kids. She would understand, and she would know just what to say to make him feel better. But he couldn't call her. That wouldn't be fair.

Over the next two weeks, Ted settled into his new job. It was more administrative than he preferred, but it was a challenge, especially overseeing all the pediatricians at the hospital. Fortunately, he had been given a highly efficient executive assistant who handled the worst of the paperwork for him.

On the medical side, he became accustomed to seeing mostly healthy kids with minor illnesses and injuries and realized that once he had removed the word "cancer" from his daily vocabulary, he had also stopped constantly anticipating disaster.

He went to Weston for a somber Thanksgiving with his family—the first without Smitty in more years than he could remember, the first without his grandmother, and what should have been his first with Caroline—and returned to Concord the next day. Only the presence of his baby niece Lilly had saved the holiday from being a total disaster.

On Saturday, he spent most of the day on the sofa pretending to watch football, but all his thoughts were about Chip and Elise getting married in New York and how he was supposed to be in the wedding party. He hoped that Parker, at the very least, was with Chip.

Unfortunately, Ted knew all too well what it was like to get married without his closest friends by his side. He hurt to think of Chip going through the same thing. He hurt to think of them all, and for that one day, he allowed in the pain. If anyone had told him a year ago that Chip and Elise would be getting married and he wouldn't be there . . .

As time went by, word got out that a nationally renowned pediatric oncologist was now practicing in Concord. Before he knew it, he was treating six children with cancer from various corners of northern New England, in consultation with his former colleagues at Children's. Ted was satisfied to able to keep a hand in his former specialty and to save their parents the extra travel time.

When he wasn't working, he ran—usually twice a day—and worked on the old house outside of town he had bought on a whim. He kept his distance from the people in town, especially the women who eyed the new doctor with interest.

He'd called Caroline only once, to give her his new cell phone number and address and to discuss a few financial matters pertaining to the condo in Boston. He'd been in Concord for six weeks when he finally worked up the fortitude to ease the wedding band off his left hand and put it on his dresser.

His parents and grandfather came up for a weekend visit, but Ted refused to discuss Caroline, his friends, his career, or any of the painful memories he had worked so hard to put behind him.

A few days before Christmas, he went into town for dinner at an Irish pub he had heard good things about. He was sick of his own cooking and his own company after a Saturday spent sanding floors. A live band entertained the crowd of locals. Ted recognized a few of them from his practice and nodded to say hello but didn't encourage anyone to approach him as he took a seat at the bar. He had ordered the roast beef special and was nursing a beer when the band took a break and switched on some canned music. The Lifehouse song "You and Me" filled the pub, transporting Ted back to their wedding night at the Ritz. The pain of losing Caroline shot through him like a bullet, leaving him breathless with longing. He got up, tossed a twenty on the bar, and left the pub.

Because he couldn't bear another stiff-upper-lip holiday in Weston, he volunteered to cover Christmas Day at the hospital so the other doctors could be with their families. The day after Christmas, he received an invitation in the mail.

John & Marjorie Smith
request the honor of your presence
at a dinner to celebrate their marriage
Saturday, January 9
7:30 p.m.
21 Club
21 West 52nd Street
New York, New York

ACROSS THE BOTTOM, in his familiar scrawl, Smitty had written, "I expect you to come. It's the least you can do."

CHAPTER 39

On the ninth, Ted caught an early-morning train to Boston where he met his parents and grandfather at South Station. Tish and Steven had been invited to the party but had chosen to stay home with baby Lilly.

The foursome boarded a second train to New York's Penn Station. During the long ride through Connecticut, his mother tried to engage Ted in conversation, but he preferred to stare out the window. He couldn't imagine what Smitty was up to and wasn't sure if he should be relieved or nervous about the night to come. Either way, he couldn't wait to see his friends again, even if they ignored him.

His father had sprung for adjoining rooms at The Plaza, and his grandfather joked about being Ted's roommate. The old man seemed to be holding up pretty well without his wife, and Ted was happy to be the butt of his jokes if it kept his grandfather smiling.

Mitzi took off to do some shopping, and Ted went for a long run in the frigid cold through Central Park. He allowed his mind to wander to all the weekends he had spent in the city since Chip and Smitty had moved there after graduate school. They'd had so many good times in so many different places that it was hard to be anywhere and not think of one or all of them. And it was impossible to be back in New York City without thinking about his middle-of-the-night sprint to get to Caroline and their first two magical days together.

That night, Ted dressed in a dark suit and tie and checked his appearance in the mirror at least three times before he went into his parents' room for a shot of the whiskey his father had brought.

At seven fifteen, they took a cab to the 21 Club and were the first to arrive in the private room Smitty had reserved. Ted realized this was going to be no ordinary evening when he saw the place card next to his on the large square table that read, "Mrs. Caroline Duffy." His heart was suddenly in his throat. It hadn't occurred to him that she would be there, but with hindsight, he should've expected it since Smitty had unfinished business with her as well.

A waiter came around to take drink orders, and Ted asked for a beer even though he wanted more whiskey.

The door opened, and Parker came in with Gina and two young boys in dark suits and ties. He greeted Ted's parents and grandfather with warm hugs and introduced them to Gina and the boys. Ted noticed a huge diamond on Gina's left hand and was thrilled to know his friend now had everything he'd ever wanted.

Parker shook hands with Ted and introduced him to Gina's sons, Anthony and Dominic. They politely shook hands with Ted even as the younger one tugged at his tie and fidgeted in his stiff suit. Parker put a hand on Anthony's shoulder and whispered something in his ear. The boy looked up at him, smiled, and nodded.

Every time the door opened, Ted's heart hammered as he waited for Caroline. Parker's father, James King, was the next to arrive with a buxom blond on his arm, followed by Chip and Elise.

Elise launched herself into Ted's arms. "So good to see you, Duff," she whispered. "I've missed you so much."

"Me, too." He kissed her cheek and hugged her again. "How was the wedding?"

"Almost perfect. We missed you and Smitty terribly."

"I'm sorry, Elise. I really wanted to go, but . . ."

"I know. Where's Caroline?"

He shook his head and held up his left hand where his ring used to be.

Her face fell. "No." She looked at him with disbelief. "No. Not after everything you sacrificed, not after everything we *all* sacrificed . . ."

With a grim expression, Ted shrugged. "Doomed from the start."

"Duff . . ."

Chip came up to her and put his arm around her. Like Parker, Chip shook Ted's hand but had nothing much to say to him.

The next time the door opened, Caroline came in wearing a black dress that offset her pale beauty. Her hair was swept up, her green eyes were big with nerves, and to Ted she had never been more lovely. He was surprised when his mother went over to Caroline like she had been expecting her and embraced her warmly. *What the hell?* Mitzi took her daughter-in-law's hand and led her into the room.

Before Ted had time to contemplate the obvious change in his mother's relationship with Caroline, Smitty came in holding hands with two women, one who looked young enough to be his daughter and the other, well, she looked just like him.

"Hello, everyone," he said in that big booming voice that was all Smitty. "I want to thank you for coming tonight and introduce you to my wife, Marjorie. Her friends call her Margo, and I know she'd be thrilled if you were to call her that."

Marjorie gave him an adoring look and nodded.

"I'll bring her around to meet each of you shortly. And this," he said with a glance at the other woman he had brought, "is my mother, Sarah Beth Smith."

The room fell completely silent.

Smitty helped both women into chairs at the head of the table. "I know you have a lot of questions," he said with a gracious smile. "And I'm going to answer them all. But for now, please take your seats, and let's have dinner."

Ted stood behind his chair and waited as Caroline crossed the room to him. When she lifted her eyes to meet his, his heart staggered in his chest.

He kissed her cheek. "Hi, honey."

"Hi, Ted. You look well."

He held her chair for her. "You look beautiful."

"Thank you."

"Happy birthday."

"You remembered," she said with a sigh.

"Yes."

Ted and Caroline whispered about Smitty's mother and made polite small talk as they were presented with a staggering array of appetizers and numerous entrée choices. He wanted to reach for her hand under the table to help calm the nerves he felt coming from her. But he didn't.

"You're not wearing your ring anymore," she said sadly.

"No, but you are."

She shrugged. "Foolish hope, I guess."

"Caroline . . ."

She put her hand over his on the table. "Let's just get through this because we owe it to Smitty."

THEY WERE between courses when Smitty brought Marjorie around to meet their guests. He introduced her to each of his friends as if nothing had ever happened between them.

Ted found her accent charming and her obvious love for Smitty a big relief. As Ted talked to her, he realized she was much older than she looked, which was also a relief.

"So after John came back to Sydney to finish the review of my father's company," she was saying, "he said to me one night, 'Marjorie, I think I could do something great with this place. What would you think of taking it off the market and giving me a year?'"

"Were your partners mad?" Ted asked.

Smitty shrugged. "I found another Australian company that

was a good fit for them, so we parted on good terms. I decided I have all the money I need. I want to build on what Marjorie's father started. It's a lot more satisfying than playing the market every day."

"Sounds like it," Ted said.

"I'm still taking care of James, though," Smitty said with a smile as he shook hands with Parker's father. "He wouldn't take no for an answer."

Smitty and Marjorie moved on to talk to James and his date before dinner was served.

The waiters had finished serving dessert and more champagne when Smitty stood up. "I'd like to propose a toast to my wife, Marjorie. The day I landed in Sydney was the luckiest day of my life, and I'll be forever grateful to her for seeing the real me, the real John. She's the only person in the world who really knows me, and she loves me anyway. To you, sweetheart."

Ted was touched by Smitty's toast, but confused, too. The only person who really knew him? What's that supposed to mean? He exchanged glances with Caroline, who shrugged.

"To you, John." Marjorie looked up at him. "My sweet, gentle giant, the most generous man I've ever known. I love you."

Smitty touched his glass to hers and leaned down to kiss her as his guests applauded.

Ted watched his mother wipe tears from her face before she accepted his father's handkerchief.

"Next I want to propose a toast to my best friend, Ted Duffy, and his beautiful wife, Caroline."

Ted felt his stomach drop. *Oh, please. Please don't let him ruin this for his wife by being an asshole.* In an unconscious gesture, Ted reached for Caroline's hand under the table.

She held on for dear life.

"Duff, Caroline, we've had a tough year." Smitty used his eyes to include Parker, Chip, and Elise. "In fact, this has been the best and the worst year of my life during which I lost something I thought would last forever and found something I'd given up on ever finding. I don't know about you guys, but I'm having a hell of a time enjoying one without the other."

Ted felt his throat close and tears sting his eyes. He looked down in a desperate effort to control them.

"There's an old saying that everything happens for a reason," Smitty continued in a low, soft voice filled with emotion. "I've come to see I owe the two of you a debt of gratitude."

Ted and Caroline looked up at him with surprise.

"I had no plans to go to Sydney." He paused to let that settle. "If things hadn't happened the way they did, I would've sent someone else. I'd never have met Marjorie and maybe never have found true love and with it, the courage to face all my demons head on."

Smitty walked around the table as he spoke. "Lillian called me home to ask me to forgive you, Duff. She said if I didn't, I'd never find room in my heart for love because the bitterness would be taking up all the space."

By then, all the women and most of the men were frantically dealing with tears.

"Turns out she was right. After her funeral, after that terrible day when I had the chance to say what I needed to say to both of you, I let it go. I forgave you. I didn't realize it at the time, but I figured it out when I got back to Sydney and Marjorie was waiting for me. I knew I'd forgiven you when I was so filled with love for her that there was no room left for bitterness."

He turned to Parker. "I was unfair to you, and I apologize."

Parker nodded and wiped discreetly at the corner of his eye.

Gina put her arm around him. Her boys were busy coloring, oblivious to the drama playing out around them.

To Chip, Smitty said, "I was *horribly* unfair to you, and I apologize for that and for missing your wedding. My wife begged me to go. That I didn't go will surely go down as one of the great regrets of my life."

Chip did nothing to try to hide his tears as he nodded.

Elise reached out to both Chip and Smitty.

"I want my friends back," Smitty said in a whisper as the emotion of the moment finally got to him and he broke down. He swiped a big hand over his face. "Nothing's the same without you guys."

Ted was the first one out of his chair.

Smitty lifted him off his feet into a bear hug.

Parker was next, followed by Chip.

Smitty put his hands on the shoulders of Parker and Chip. "If I can forgive him," he said with a nod to Ted, "so can you. If he has with Caroline even half of what I have with Marjorie then he's a lucky man, and we all need to be happy for him."

Parker and Chip hugged Ted, who had given up on trying to hold it together.

Smitty turned next to Mitzi. "I also owe you an apology."

Perplexed, she shook her head and mouthed the word "no."

"For the last twenty years, you've been my mother, Mitz. You know that. But for all that time, I had a mother. I was dishonest with all of you about her and about my childhood."

"John." Sarah Beth held out her hand to her son. "Let me."

"You don't have to, Mom," he said, returning to his seat and taking her hand.

"Yes, I do."

Smitty sat down next to her.

She stood up and twisted her hands with nerves. "I'm so very grateful to know my John has had such exceptional people in his life for all these years. He's a wonderful man, a self-made man in every way."

Overwhelmed, Smitty hung his head, and Marjorie reached out to him.

"I'm ashamed to say he raised himself because I was so addicted to drugs I was unable to care for him." She took a deep breath before she added softly, "I was unable to even give him the name of his father."

This time, Caroline reached for Ted.

"His childhood, in what can only be called a ghetto, was a horror, and I'm entirely to blame for that. He left for college, and I never saw him again until he and Marjorie showed up at my house last week. I've been clean for twelve years, and I've hoped and prayed every day of those twelve years that he would find his way back to me." Her voice broke, and there wasn't a dry eye in the room. "I'm so very proud of what you've made of yourself,

John, the people you've surrounded yourself with, the life you've created with no help from me." To Marjorie, she said, "Thank you for convincing my boy to find his way home and for showing him that the truth will always set us free."

With one hand, Ted dealt with his tears while Caroline clung to his other hand.

Smitty stood up to hug his mother. "Mom's agreed to come home to Sydney with us so she can be with her grandchild when he or she arrives later this year."

The group erupted into applause and congratulations.

"Wow," Ted whispered to Caroline. "I just never had any idea. You think you know someone. Really know them."

"It explains a lot."

Ted nodded and with a deep breath he released her hand and stood up. "I'd like to propose a toast of my own. First, I'd like to welcome Marjorie, and while I'm at it—Gina and her boys—to our temporarily dysfunctional little family."

The others chuckled.

Still addressing Marjorie, Ted continued. "I know this may sound presumptuous, but if everything had been normal, I might've been the best man at your wedding."

Smitty nodded in agreement as new tears filled his eyes.

"That everything *wasn't* normal is entirely my fault. I owe you, Smitty, as well as Parker, Chip, and Elise, an apology for being cavalier with something far too valuable to ever be taken for granted. It was only when I didn't have it anymore that I could fully appreciate what I'd lost, and what I'd caused all of you to lose as well." He paused when emotion threatened to derail him. "My friendship with you guys has been among the most important things in my life. I promise I'll never be cavalier with it again. Congratulations Smitty and Marjorie. I love you, and I wish you well."

The others applauded.

Ted sat down and glanced over at Caroline.

Her eyes bright with tears, she nodded her approval.

~

As the party began to break up around midnight, Ted watched Caroline hug his parents, his grandfather, Smitty, Marjorie, and the others. When she finally returned to him, she kissed his cheek. "I'm so glad for you that you've worked things out with the guys."

"I'm glad for all of us."

She nodded. "Well, it was good to see you, Ted. Take care of yourself."

"That's it?" He took hold of her arm. "See you later? Have a nice life?"

Her eyes narrowed, and she tugged her arm free. "What do you want me to say? I'm not the one who left."

"Caroline . . ."

"Are you ready to come home, Ted?"

"Maybe."

"You know where I am when you're ready." With one last kiss to his cheek she was gone.

Ted stood frozen, watching her go, his heart aching with regret and remorse. And then all at once he realized he would never again be whole without her by his side. No matter what, he had to find a way to win her back. Elise was right—they'd all sacrificed too much to settle for anything less than happily ever after.

He dashed through the halls of the restaurant, down the stairs to the front door. "Caroline! *Caroline!* Wait!"

CHAPTER 40

He reached the curb in time to watch her taxi pull away. Running into traffic, he gave chase, but couldn't catch the car. With his arm in the air and shivering from the cold, he tried to hail another cab as hers got further away. When he realized he wouldn't be able to catch up to her, he jogged back to the restaurant, dropped his hands to his knees, and tried to regroup.

That's where his parents and grandfather found him a few minutes later. His father handed him his coat.

"Ted, darling, what's wrong?" Mitzi asked.

"Nothing." For the first time in months, he meant it. "Nothing's wrong." Everything had clicked into focus with such startling clarity it had left him breathless. He put up his hand again to signal for a taxi. "Do you know where Caroline's staying, Mom?"

"No, I don't," Mitzi said with genuine regret.

"Will you be all right in that hotel room by yourself tonight, Grampa?"

"I think I'll get by," Theo said with a smile. "Your Grandy would've been proud of you tonight, Third. Smitty, too. Now, go get your wife."

Ted kissed them all and hailed a second cab for them before jumping into his. "JFK, please," he said to the driver.

He got to the airport to learn the last commuter flight to Boston was long gone. So he rented a car and reversed his middle-of-the night odyssey from the summer before, arriving at the condo in Boston just after four in the morning. This time, though, Caroline wasn't waiting for him with open arms.

Because his keys were in his hotel room in New York, he was relieved to find the house key still under the flowerpot on the front porch. He let himself in, deactivated the alarm, and flipped on the light to find that not much had changed in the two months since he'd last been there.

No, that wasn't true. Everything had changed. He wasn't sure exactly when it had happened, but this wasn't his place anymore. It was *their* place.

She wasn't home, though, so nothing was where it belonged. On the fridge he found the list they'd made on their wedding night. She'd checked off number five, he had a new job. And number six—her book was finished. Ted felt as if he might burst with pride. She'd really done it. And number seven. . . Oh God, she'd checked off number seven: have a baby.

"Caroline," he whispered, running a hand over the creamy vellum.

As the emotion of the evening finally caught up to him, he leaned his head against the list and let the tears roll down his cheeks. What a fool he had been. What would he ever do if she couldn't forgive him? When he was all cried out, he sat down to wait.

He slept on the sofa and woke up hungry. Shedding his suit coat and tugging his tie all the way off, he got up to make coffee and toast. After he ate, he went upstairs to take a shower and changed into clothes that still hung just where he'd left them in the closet. Even his toothbrush was unmoved. He might have walked out the door two hours ago rather than two months ago.

Dressed in jeans and a sweater, he went back downstairs and

wandered into what used to be his office. Here he found her. She had made this space her own. Ted was perplexed to discover, mixed in with the papers on the desk, brochures for Children's Hospital Boston, the Dana-Farber Cancer Institute, and the Jimmy Fund Clinic. Each was adorned with sticky notes containing her handwriting. Also on the desk was a neat stack of paper. Her book. As he rested a loving hand on the book, a framed photo caught his eye. Their second wedding. They had been captured in an unguarded moment when he had swept her into his arms. He picked up the frame and studied the image.

"Come home, Caroline," he whispered. "Please come home."

He could call her. He knew that. But he was too afraid she wouldn't come if she knew he was there. Maybe he had waited too long to realize what he'd had and walked away from. Maybe he had pushed her too far away. Maybe he had taken too much for granted. It wouldn't be the first time.

No, he would wait. And until she came home, he would read.

HE FINISHED the book at five o'clock that afternoon and sat back with amazement. The story was captivating, the characters compelling, her descriptions vivid. He had even found himself rooting for Cameron to triumph in the highly satisfying ending.

"Damn, Caroline! You're good, baby." He checked his watch. "But where are you?"

Gathering up the papers that had scattered during his reading frenzy, Ted returned the pile to the desk. He fixed himself a sandwich and was reaching for the remote to turn on the TV when he heard her key in the door.

She came in, dropped her bag on the floor, and was taking off her coat when she let out a startled gasp. "Ted? What are you doing here?"

"I've been here since about four o'clock this morning."

Her eyes softened as she studied his tired face. "Have you been speeding again?"

He nodded and held out his arms to her.

She took a step toward him but then stopped herself. "I can't. If you aren't back to stay, I can't go near you. It was hard enough to sit next to you last night and pretend we're still together."

He extended his hand. "There's so much I need to say to you. Please?"

With what seemed to be great reluctance, she took his hand and let him lead her to the sofa.

"Were you going to tell me?"

"Tell you what?"

"Number seven."

"Oh. You saw that, huh?"

He nodded.

"I was trying to figure out how to tell you. I knew you'd come home because of it, and as much as I wanted you home, I didn't want it to be for that reason."

He ran his hand over her smooth blond hair. "How far along are you?"

"About twelve weeks."

"Have you seen a doctor?"

"Yes, Dr. Duffy." She laughed through her tears. "Yes, I've seen a doctor."

"I've spent all night trying to figure out when, how . . ."

"Since you're the doctor, I would think you'd know how, and I'd say you sealed your fate when you chucked my birth control pills into the trash."

He grinned. "One of my finer moments, if I do say so myself." Brushing away her tears, he said, "I love you so much, Caroline. Right after you walked away from me last night I realized I couldn't live another minute without you. I'm so sorry I left when things got hard. I took the coward's way out, and I'll always regret that."

"You did what you needed to do."

"What I need is you. After everything we've been through, do you still love me?"

"I never stopped loving you. Have you forgiven yourself, Ted?"

He folded her into his arms. "I decided to forgive myself somewhere between unsuccessfully chasing your cab down West 52nd Street and Greenwich, Connecticut, where I think the same state trooper stopped me for speeding. Again."

She laughed and cried at the same time.

"I want my wife back."

"Ted," she sighed, closing her eyes against the tears that spilled down her cheeks. "I want the magic back. Without the magic, we were just two people living together."

"I know, baby." He kissed her softly at first and then with more passion as her arms tightened around him. "It's important to me that you know . . ."

With her hand on his face, she asked, "What?"

He took a moment to get a handle on his emotions. "Even if I'd known I was in for a spectacular fall from grace the night I met you, I wouldn't have changed a thing. You were always worth it, Caroline. Every bit of it. All the craziness led us right here."

"It also led Smitty to Marjorie," she reminded him.

He rested his hand on her belly. "And it brought us this little person."

"Edward Theodore Duffy, the fourth."

"A boy?" he asked, wide eyed.

She nodded.

"No way." He shook his head. "No way am I giving my son a Roman numeral."

"But I promised Mitzi."

He groaned. "What's *with* you and my mother anyway?"

"We've . . ." She scratched her chin as she pretended to search for the right word. "*Bonded* in your absence."

"Oh *God*. Has she got him registered for Harvard Medical School yet?"

Caroline cracked up. "The application is in the mail."

"So would she have anything to do with how you ended up with brochures from the hospital all over your desk?"

"Maybe," she said with a coy smile.

"They'll miss you when you move to New Hampshire."

"Am I moving to New Hampshire?"

"Well, you'll probably want to come straight back here when you see the house I bought up there. Calling it a fixer-upper would be charitable."

"Will you be there?"

He smiled. "Yeah."

She shrugged. "Then Edward the fourth and I will adapt."

"I read your book," he confessed.

"Did you?"

"It's unbelievable, Caroline." He kissed her. "Truly. I couldn't put it down. I'm so proud of you."

"You're the first one to read it."

His eyes widened with surprise. "Really?"

She nodded. "Cameron and I talked about it, and we decided we wanted you to be first."

"I've had just about enough of him."

"I'm thinking about a sequel," she teased.

He groaned with dismay as he lifted her into his arms and took the stairs two at a time on his way to their bedroom. "No sequels. We need to write a whole new story. You were right about one thing, though."

"What's that?"

He lay down with her on the bed and was overwhelmed with wonder when he ran his hand over the small but unmistakable bump in her once-flat belly. "It's one hell of a romance."

"Yes," she said with a contented sigh. "Yes, it is."

"I want some number nine." He kissed his way from her lips to her neck. "I've had two long, lonely months to discover that nine's my favorite number."

She smiled as she ran her fingers through his hair. "Before you get any nine, I need you to promise me we're going to get to ten."

"I promise you, Caroline." He slid his lips over hers. "I promise that you, me, and Fourth will live happily ever after."

"You are *not* going to call him that!"

He chuckled against her lips.

"Ted?"

"What, honey?"

"The magic's back."

HAVE you read Marie's Wild Widows Series yet? If not, turn the page for a sneak peek at book 1, *Someone Like You*...

SOMEONE LIKE YOU

CHAPTER ONE

Roni

Five and a half months ago today, I married Patrick Connolly, the love of my life. During the spring semester of my junior year at the University of Virginia, where he was attending grad school, Patrick stopped by my dorm room with my roommate Sarah's boyfriend and never left. We were a couple from the moment we met. Sarah told me later she'd never witnessed such an immediate connection between two people. After Patrick was shot and killed on October 10, just over two months ago, she told me she's still never known any couple more "meant to be" than we are.

Or I guess I should say than we *were* because we're over now. He's gone at thirty-one, and I'm left to face the rest of my life without him. I'm a widow at twenty-nine, and it's my fault Patrick was killed. I wasn't the one who fired the stray bullet that hit him in the chest and killed him instantly. But I was too lazy to go to the grocery store the night before, which meant we had nothing for him to take for lunch. He left his office on 12th Street to go grab a sandwich and was on his way back when an argument across the street escalated into the shooting that left my husband dead.

Of course, Patrick could've gone to the store, too, but that was something I did for both of us, along with the laundry and the dry-cleaning pickups. As an up-and-coming Drug Enforcement Agency IT agent, Patrick worked a lot more hours than I do as an obituary writer for the *Washington Star*. I can bring work home with me, but due to the sensitive nature of his cases, he couldn't do that. So I took care of the things I could for both of us, including the grocery shopping. For the rest of my life, I'll have to wonder, if I'd gone to the store that night, would Patrick still be alive?

I've shared my guilt about that only once—at a grief group for victims of violent crime that my new friend Sam Holland invited me to attend. She's the lead Homicide detective for the Metro DC police department—and the nation's new first lady. For some reason, she's decided we need to be friends, which is funny because I've had a huge lady crush on her for the longest time. She's a badass cop who happens to be married to our new president, but she doesn't let that stop her from chasing murderers. The day Patrick was killed, she was the one who had to tell me the horrific news.

I'll never forget that day, or how I went from being happily married to my one true love to being widowed in the span of ten unbearable seconds. I can't even think about that day, or I'll put myself right back to the beginning of a lifetime without Patrick. At first, I was surrounded around the clock by people who care, especially my parents, sisters, brother, extended family and close friends. They saw me through the dreadful first week and the beautiful funeral at the National Cathedral. They took care of the massive influx of food, flowers, gifts and sympathy.

One by one, they had no choice but to return to their lives, leaving me alone to pick up the pieces of my shattered existence. My mom held out the longest. She was with me for three weeks and even slept with me many a night, holding me as I cried myself to sleep. Once, she found me on the floor of the bathroom at two in the morning. I have no idea how I got there or how long I was there before she found me shivering violently.

I shook for hours in bed afterward, unable to get warm.

Sometimes I wonder if I'll ever be warm again.

Our bed, which once bore the scent of Patrick on the pillows next to mine, now smells like my mother. I'm left to live alone in the Capitol Hill apartment we chose together and furnished with loving care over countless weekends spent at flea markets and antique sales. We wanted something different, funky and special, not just another living room or bedroom plucked from the floor of a furniture showroom. We wanted our place to reflect us—a little artsy (me), a little nerdy (him), with an emphasis on music (both of us) and cooking (both of us, but mostly me). We also wanted to be able to entertain our friends and family in a warm, comfortable space. Our apartment is gorgeous. Everyone says so. But now, like everywhere else that meant something to us, it's just a place where Patrick will never be again.

For something to do, I've been taking long walks through the neighborhood, getting lost on side streets for hours. Anything to keep me away from the apartment where I see my late husband everywhere I look, and not just in the framed wedding photos in the living room and on the bedside table. I see him on the sofa watching football, hockey and baseball. I see him lounging on the bed, completely naked and erect, a smile on his handsome face as he reaches for me and drags me into bed with him, making me laugh and sigh and then scream from the way he made me feel every time he made love to me.

I miss his hugs, his kisses and the way he had to be touching me if he was anywhere near me. Whether on the sofa, in bed or in the car, he was always touching me. I crave his touch, his scent, his smile, the way he lit up with delight anytime I walked into a room. I fear no one will ever again look at me like that or love me the way Patrick did.

Our life together was perfection, from Ella Fitzgerald Sundays to Moody Blues Mondays to Santana Taco Tuesdays to Bocelli Italian on Wednesdays. Every week, seven different themes chosen by my music aficionado husband from the fifteen hundred records he was collecting since he was fourteen, when his grandfather introduced him to the magic of vinyl.

The first minutes of every new day are the worst, when I

wake up, reach for him and have to remember all over again that he's gone forever. He was the most important person in my life. How can he be *gone*? It makes no sense. He was thirty-one years old, with his whole life ahead of him, a dream career, a new wife and more friends than most people make in a lifetime.

One random second of being in the exact wrong place at the wrong time, and it's all over. That's what I think about as I walk for miles through the District, finding myself in places I've never been before even after living here for more than five years. I came to DC right out of college and lived in Patrick's nasty apartment in Shaw for a couple of years before we moved to our dream place on Capitol Hill after Patrick received a huge promotion—and a raise.

Fortunately, he also had awesome life insurance through work, which means I won't have to move. Not right away, anyway. Eventually, I'll probably want to live somewhere else, where the memories of the life I had with him aren't present in every corner of the home we shared.

In addition to the emotional trauma, no one tells you how much *work* death is. The endless forms to be completed, not to mention the number of times you need to produce a death certificate to close an account or change something simple. Every piece of mail comes with someone who needs to be told the news—a credit card company, an alumni association, an insurance agent. It's endless and exhausting and results in a slew of fresh wounds every time someone expresses shock at the news of Patrick's sudden death.

And then there's the criminal element, which is marching forward with hearings that must be attended by the loved ones of the murder victim. That includes the special joy of dealing with the anguished family members of the shooter, who made a tragic mistake and ruined multiple lives in the span of seconds. I feel for his heartbroken mother, sister and girlfriend. I really do, but he took Patrick from me, so my empathy for them goes only so far.

It's all so screwed up, and every day I'm left to wonder how my perfect, beautiful life has evolved into this never-ending nightmare. Thank God for my parents, sisters, brother and a few of my closest friends, who've been so relentlessly there for me. I say *a few* of my closest friends, because some have all but disappeared off the face of the earth since Patrick died.

Sarah, the college roommate who was part of us from the beginning, told a mutual friend who *has* been there for me that she just can't bear it. I know this because I pleaded with the mutual friend to tell me what the hell was going on with Sarah, and she reluctantly told me what Sarah had said. How sad for Sarah that she can't bear the loss of *my* husband. The minute I heard that, a close friend of ten years was dead to me. If she can't put her own needs aside to tend to mine in my darkest hour, then I guess we were never friends to begin with. I'm tempted to cut her out of the wedding party photos.

On top of this already huge mountain of crap, I feel like absolute shit most of the time. I can't eat without wanting to puke. I can't sleep for more than an hour or two at a time. My head hurts, my eyes are probably infected from all the tears, and even my boobs are aching as if they're mourning the loss of Patrick, too. I've lost fifteen pounds I really didn't have to lose, as I'm one of those women you love to hate—the one who struggles to keep weight on while everyone else is trying to lose it.

It's okay to hate me for that. I'm used to it. But losing fifteen pounds is not a good thing for me, and it has my family freaking out and insisting I see a doctor immediately. I have that to look forward to tomorrow.

In the meantime, I walk. It's barely seven in the morning, and I've already been out for an hour when I circle back to Capitol Hill to head home. I'm walking along Seventh Street near Eastern Market when I see a man on the other side of the street. He's moving in the same direction I am, so I can't see his face. He's built like Patrick, with the same lanky frame, and has the fast-paced stride that used to annoy the hell out of me when I tried to keep up with him. We fell into the habit of holding hands whenever we walked somewhere together so I wouldn't get left behind.

I pick up my pace, curious to see where the man is going. I'm not sure why I feel compelled to follow him, but hey, it's something to do. I went back to work two weeks after Patrick died and decided I just wasn't ready to be writing about death, so the *Star* management insisted I take paid bereavement leave for a few more weeks. That's super generous of them, but it leaves me with way too much time with nothing much to do. Following a man who looks like my husband from behind seems like a good use of fifteen or twenty minutes.

When he ducks into one of my favorite coffee shops, I go inside, standing behind him in line. He's wearing gray pants and a black wool coat that I stare at while we wait to order. He also smells good. Really good. What the hell am I doing here? I don't even drink coffee. I hate the taste and smell of it, and Patrick tended to his morning addiction after he left the house most days so I wouldn't have to smell it.

I glance at the menu and see they have hot chocolate and decide to order that and a cinnamon bun because I need the calories, and the pastry looks good to me. I can't recall the last time food of any kind tempted me. My mom bought me those Ensure drinks they give to old people in nursing homes because she's so alarmed by the weight I've lost since Patrick died.

I lean in a little closer so I can listen to the man in front of me order a tall skinny latte and an everything bagel with cream cheese to go.

That's all it takes to send me reeling. Patrick *loved* everything bagels loaded with cream cheese. I used to complain about the garlic breath they gave him after he ate one.

I turn and leave the shop before I can embarrass myself by bursting into tears in a crowd of strangers who just want their coffee before work. They don't need me or my overwhelming grief in the midst of their morning routine. Tears spill down my cheeks as I hustle toward home, feeling sick again. I'm almost there when the need to puke has me leaning over a bush a block from home. Because I've barely eaten anything, it's basically another round of the dry heaves that've been plaguing my days and nights for weeks.

"Gross," a man behind me says. "That's my bush you're puking in."

I can't bring myself to look at him. "I'm sorry. I tried to make it home."

"Have you been drinking?"

"Nope."

"Sure, you haven't. Move along, will you?"

I want to whirl around and tell him my husband was recently *murdered*, and he needs to be kinder to people because you never know what they're dealing with, but I don't waste the breath on someone who probably isn't worth the bother. Instead, I do as he asks and move along, half jogging the remaining block to my building and rushing up the stairs to my third-floor apartment full of memories of my late husband.

There's nowhere to hide from a loss of this magnitude. And now I'm doing weird shit like following men who remind me of Patrick. I'm glad I never saw the guy's face. For now, I can hold on to the illusion that it could've been Patrick, even if I know that's not possible. Maybe me seeing someone who resembled him from behind was a message from him. Sometimes I feel like he's close by, but those moments are fleeting.

For the most part, I feel dreadfully alone even in a room full of people who love me. Bless them for trying to help, but there's nothing they can say or do to soothe the brutal ache that Patrick's death has left me with. I've read that the ache dulls over time, but part of me doesn't want it to. As long as I feel the loss so deeply, it's like he's still here with me in some weird way.

I'm aware that I probably need therapy and professional support of some kind, like what I got from Sam's group for victims of violent crime. It was helpful to know there're others like me whose lives were forever altered by a single second, but again, that support doesn't really change much of anything for me. Patrick is still gone.

Thinking of Sam reminds me I owe her a call to find out if she meant it when she asked me to be her communications director and spokesperson at the White House. A few months ago, a call from the first lady asking me to join her team would've been the biggest thing to ever happen to me. Now I have to remind myself to call or text her or something, but that'll take more energy than I can muster right now.

I remove my coat, hat and gloves, toss them over a chair and head for the sofa where I've all but lived since Patrick died. As I stretch out and pull a blanket over myself, I feel sleepy for the first time in a few days. I hope Sam won't mind if I call her tomorrow. Or maybe the next day. She said she'd hold the job for me until I'm ready. What if I'm never ready? What would being ready for something like that even look like in the context of my tragic loss?

I'm so confused and lost and trying to figure out who I am without Patrick. That's not going to happen overnight. It'll probably take the rest of my life to figure that out.

My eyes close out of sheer exhaustion, and I'm shocked to wake up sometime later to realize I slept for a couple of hours, waking when my mom uses her key to let herself into my apartment.

"Oh, thank goodness you're all right." My mom, Justine, is tall and whip thin, with short gray hair and glasses. "I was worried when you didn't pick up."

While she gets busy in my kitchen making me food I won't eat, I check my phone to see I missed four calls from her. My family is worried I might take my own life, even though I've promised them I wouldn't do that to them. Not that the temptation isn't tantalizing, because it is, but I love life too much to ever consider ending mine prematurely, even if it would mean I could be back with my love sooner rather than decades from now.

Decades—five, six, seven of them. That's how long I'm probably going to have to live without Patrick. The thought of that is so overwhelming, I can't dwell too much on it, or I won't be able to go on.

I never gave much thought to the concept of time when I thought there was plenty of it. Now I know that's not necessarily the case. Why would we think about such a thing when we're in our late twenties or early thirties and just starting our lives? It's not until disaster strikes that we understand that time is the most precious thing we have, and we don't know it until it's too late.

Time used to stretch out before me in an endless ribbon of possibility. Now it's a vast wasteland of nothingness that'll need to be filled with something until I run out of it.

I have no idea what that "something" will be.

Someone Like You is available in print from *Amazon.com* and other online retailers, or you can purchase a signed copy from Marie's store at *shop.marieforce.com*.

ALSO BY MARIE FORCE

Contemporary Romances Available from Marie Force

The Gansett Island Series

Book 1: Maid for Love *(Mac & Maddie)*

Book 2: Fool for Love *(Joe & Janey)*

Book 3: Ready for Love *(Luke & Sydney)*

Book 4: Falling for Love *(Grant & Stephanie)*

Book 5: Hoping for Love *(Evan & Grace)*

Book 6: Season for Love *(Owen & Laura)*

Book 7: Longing for Love *(Blaine & Tiffany)*

Book 8: Waiting for Love *(Adam & Abby)*

Book 9: Time for Love *(David & Daisy)*

Book 10: Meant for Love *(Jenny & Alex)*

Book 10.5: Chance for Love, *A Gansett Island Novella (Jared & Lizzie)*

Book 11: Gansett After Dark *(Owen & Laura)*

Book 12: Kisses After Dark *(Shane & Katie)*

Book 13: Love After Dark *(Paul & Hope)*

Book 14: Celebration After Dark *(Big Mac & Linda)*

Book 15: Desire After Dark *(Slim & Erin)*

Book 16: Light After Dark *(Mallory & Quinn)*

Book 17: Victoria & Shannon (Episode 1)

Book 18: Kevin & Chelsea (Episode 2)

A Gansett Island Christmas Novella *(Appears in Mine After Dark)*

Book 19: Mine After Dark *(Riley & Nikki)*

Book 20: Yours After Dark *(Finn & Chloe)*

Book 21: Trouble After Dark *(Deacon & Julia)*

Book 22: Rescue After Dark *(Mason & Jordan)*

Book 23: Blackout After Dark *(Full Cast)*

Book 24: Temptation After Dark *(Gigi & Cooper)*

Book 25: Resilience After Dark *(Jace & Cindy)*

Book 26: Hurricane After Dark *(Full Cast)*

Book 27: Renewal After Dark *(Coming 2024)*

The Green Mountain Series

Book 1: All You Need Is Love *(Will & Cameron)*

Book 2: I Want to Hold Your Hand *(Nolan & Hannah)*

Book 3: I Saw Her Standing There *(Colton & Lucy)*

Book 4: And I Love Her *(Hunter & Megan)*

Novella: You'll Be Mine *(Will & Cam's Wedding)*

Book 5: It's Only Love *(Gavin & Ella)*

Book 6: Ain't She Sweet *(Tyler & Charlotte)*

The Butler, Vermont Series

(Continuation of Green Mountain)

Book 1: Every Little Thing *(Grayson & Emma)*

Book 2: Can't Buy Me Love *(Mary & Patrick)*

Book 3: Here Comes the Sun (*Wade & Mia)*

Book 4: Till There Was You *(Lucas & Dani)*

Book 5: All My Loving *(Landon & Amanda)*

Book 6: Let It Be *(Lincoln & Molly)*

Book 7: Come Together *(Noah & Brianna)*

Book 8: Here, There & Everywhere *(Izzy & Cabot)*

Book 9: The Long and Winding Road *(Max & Lexi)*

The Wild Widows Series—a Fatal Series Spin-Off

Book 1: Someone Like You

Book 2: Someone to Hold

Book 3: Someone to Love

The Miami Nights Series

Book 1: How Much I Feel *(Carmen & Jason)*

Book 2: How Much I Care *(Maria & Austin)*

Book 3: How Much I Love *(Dee's story)*

Nochebuena, A Miami Nights Novella

Book 4: How Much I Want *(Nico & Sofia)*

Book 5: How Much I Need *(Milo and Gianna)*

The Quantum Series

Book 1: Virtuous *(Flynn & Natalie)*

Book 2: Valorous *(Flynn & Natalie)*

Book 3: Victorious *(Flynn & Natalie)*

Book 4: Rapturous *(Addie & Hayden)*

Book 5: Ravenous *(Jasper & Ellie)*

Book 6: Delirious *(Kristian & Aileen)*

Book 7: Outrageous *(Emmett & Leah)*

Book 8: Famous *(Marlowe & Sebastian)*

The Treading Water Series

Book 1: Treading Water

Book 2: Marking Time

Book 3: Starting Over

Book 4: Coming Home

Book 5: Finding Forever

Romantic Suspense Novels Available from Marie Force

The Fatal Series

One Night With You, *A Fatal Series Prequel Novella*

Book 1: Fatal Affair

Book 2: Fatal Justice

Book 3: Fatal Consequences

Book 3.5: Fatal Destiny, *the Wedding Novella*

Book 4: Fatal Flaw

Book 5: Fatal Deception

Book 6: Fatal Mistake

Book 7: Fatal Jeopardy

Book 8: Fatal Scandal

Book 9: Fatal Frenzy

Book 10: Fatal Identity

Book 11: Fatal Threat

Book 12: Fatal Chaos

Book 13: Fatal Invasion

Book 14: Fatal Reckoning

Book 15: Fatal Accusation

Book 16: Fatal Fraud

Sam and Nick's story continues...

Book 1: State of Affairs

Book 2: State of Grace

Book 3: State of the Union

Book 4: State of Shock

Book 5: State of Denial

Book 6: State of Bliss (Dec. 2023)

Book 7: State of Suspense (Coming 2024)

Single Titles

Five Years Gone

One Year Home

Sex Machine

Sex God

Georgia on My Mind

True North

The Fall

The Wreck

Love at First Flight

Everyone Loves a Hero

Line of Scrimmage

Historical Romance Available from Marie Force

The Gilded Series

Book 1: Duchess by Deception

Book 2: Deceived by Desire

ABOUT THE AUTHOR

Marie Force is the #1 *Wall Street Journal* bestselling author of more than 100 contemporary romance, romantic suspense and erotic romance novels. Her series include Fatal, First Family, Gansett Island, Butler Vermont, Quantum, Treading Water, Miami Nights and Wild Widows.

Her books have sold more than 13 million copies worldwide, have been translated into more than a dozen languages and have appeared on the *New York Times* bestseller list more than 30 times. She is also a *USA Today* bestseller, as well as a Spiegel bestseller in Germany.

Her goals in life are simple—to spend as much time as she can with her "kids" who are now adults, to keep writing books for as long as she possibly can and to never be on a flight that makes the news.

Join Marie's mailing list on her website at *marieforce.com* for news about new books and upcoming appearances in your area. Follow her on Facebook at *www.Facebook.com/MarieForceAuthor,* Instagram at *www.instagram.com/marieforceauthor/* and TikTok at *https://www.tiktok.com/@marieforceauthor?*. Contact Marie at *marie@marieforce.com.*

Printed in Great Britain
by Amazon